To my girls – Miranda and Rose

Chapter 1

'Fold, fold, roll.'

It was a mantra; a three-word instruction representing a sequence of finger movements. I had been doing it daily since I was thirteen.

Capital FM's breakfast show hummed in the background from the radio on the window ledge as I mumbled the words under my breath.

Picking up another vine leaf from the blanched stack on the plate, I scooped up a measure of the mixture of rice and herbs and repeated the action. A plate of finished *dolmádes* – ready to be cooked – sat beside me on the kitchen table, a mug of coffee slowly losing heat next to it. My fingers were already prune-like beneath the latex food gloves.

I wiped sweat from my forehead with my arm and shifted on the chair. The kitchen lacked ventilation with only a small window above the sink – our neighbours' side brick wall the only view – but today was extra sticky. An unexpected June heat wave had hit the West Midlands and the flat was unbearably hot and would be stifling by mid-afternoon once the vents from our deli downstairs began pumping out fumes that always filtered through to the rooms above.

The clock on the wall ticked closer to six, reminding me that I needed to pick up a bit of speed. Usually, I had plenty of time between the hours of five and eight to make sure the one hundred *dolmádes* were ready for the deli's opening and for dropping off another one hundred at the office of our one and only corporate customer.

But today I needed to carve out an extra half hour for my day job at the Birmingham Museum & Art Gallery. In fact, it was crucial I got to the lab before my boss got in. I was *so* close to making that discovery, I could feel the expectation of resolving the puzzle tingling in my bones. The grooves in the pieces had to match. I knew they did. I had dreamed of them lining up for days. And if they did, this could be it; my chance to prove myself and to stand out as the best contender for promotion to curator. My interview was on Monday. While I didn't have the experience of some of the other candidates, the lining up of two tiny metal plates to complete a Roman brooch found at the HS2 site near Solihull would definitely raise my status.

As I placed the final stuffed leaves into the casserole dish on the stove, I heard the shuffle of slippers along the hallway.

'*Ángelé mou*,' Dad sang out, stepping into the kitchen in his striped pyjamas. Even though I was twenty-eight, he still loved to call me his angel. My full name's Angelina but it had been shortened to Lina as soon as I started primary school and was teased for sharing my name with an animated ballerina mouse.

'Morning, Baba.' I yawned, bending my neck backwards to relieve the locked-up tension from leaning forward for so long.

'Why so early today?' He took out a mug from the cupboard and filled it with coffee from the pot that was on the warming plate. It was the first thing I had made as soon as I woke up after swallowing a couple of tablets. The cramps this morning had been especially bad, but I was trying not to think of what that meant.

'I need to get to the museum before eight. I have a lot of work to do.'

'You will still be there at closing time?'

'Of course,' I said reassuringly, pulling off the food gloves. Dad never liked to close the deli on his own. It had always been like that, ever since the robbery seven years ago when a couple of youths had smashed up the place, one holding a knife to his throat, threatening to 'do him in' if he didn't acquiesce and hand over the month's takings. Since that day I had sworn I would never let him close alone.

I filled the casserole dish with a seasoned brew I had whipped up in a measuring jug – a secret recipe Mum had penned long ago.

'Tonight is the reunion, yes?' He nodded; his thick dark eyebrows raised.

Drops of boiling liquid splashed my hand and I winced before carefully placing the lid on the pot and turning on the gas.

I sucked my fingers hard before running them under the cold tap. 'I am not sure I will go,' I said, my teeth clenched – the pain throbbing at the tip of my middle finger.

'I thought Nik will pick you up for it.'

'I think I'm going to pass. I fancy an early night tonight.' I let the cold water numb the digit for a couple of minutes.

The truth was Stockland Academy was the last place I wanted to go back to. It was our ten-year reunion. Ten years since Mr Collingwood – the head – wished us well for the future in his closing speech, handed out our yearbooks with various 'most likely to ...' awards filling the pages and sent us on our way into the big wide world; most of us directionless and scared of what the future held once we left the confines of secondary school.

Angelina Georgiades. *Most likely to ... be travelling the world.* That was what my award had been. I had laughed hollowly when I opened the email invite I received last week with a PDF file of the yearbook attached. Apparently at eighteen I was confident that it would be easy to take a gap year after finishing my archaeology degree at Birmingham University instead of getting a job. I had come close to fulfilling that wish, but my life had taken an unexpected turn at twenty-one. Ten years had now passed since the school gates shut behind me and not once had I stepped foot on a plane.

I kissed Dad on the cheek. 'I've set the timer, Baba. The *dolmádes* will be ready in an hour. I've already made the order for Mr Markos. You'll be OK to take the rest downstairs today?'

'Of course, I'll be fine.' He patted his chest, like he always did when I asked him if he was OK. It was a reassuring gesture and one I knew he did to appease me and stop my fussing.

'See you at six.' He smiled and blew me a kiss.

On my way out later, I noticed the lights of the deli were still off but knew Dad would be down any minute to set up for the breakfast run – our usual gaggle of regulars keen to pick up their polystyrene containers filled with a mezze of Greek Cypriot delights and a black coffee. My museum lanyard hung around my neck and my backpack was weighed down with two large boxes of *dolmádes* ready to be dropped at Markos Insurance – a mile from the museum.

My daily fifteen-minute walk along Slade Road to Gravelly Hill station always took me past my old school – the 1970s concrete building set on an acre of grounds housing over twelve hundred students. But today I found myself turning the corner before I crossed at the lights even though I knew I would have to rush once I got to Birmingham Central to deliver the food and get to work in good time.

Thoughts of the reunion had made me think of him. Ash.

I stood outside his house – the side gate that was always unlocked now replaced by a ten-foot black door with a padlock; the sand-coloured pebble-dash render replaced with smooth grey stucco.

Ash's semi-detached house – my refuge growing up. But he no longer lived there, nor did his family.

Would he be at the reunion? I shook my head and walked on by. Of course he wouldn't. He lived in Mumbai now and swore he would never return to Birmingham. And who would blame him? I was the last person he would ever want to see again.

Chapter 2

My fingers twisted the dial to zoom in further. One more time. It had to be this piece.

Please, please. Line up.

Two solid hours I had been hunched over the microscope, left eye scrunched up, peering into the lens with my other.

'Nope.' I sighed and carefully lifted the bronze specimen from the glass dish with a pair of tweezers, placing it back into the plastic bag.

'Oh, Lina,' Greer said, her American accent elongating the 'ee' sound in my name. 'Here, try this one.' She handed me the sample labelled 364. Her box braids framed her face that was full of hope, her nose ring catching the glare of the fluorescent lamp next to the microscope.

I checked the number against the list on my laptop. 'Already have. It's no use. We're not going to find the right grooves.'

Greer laid a reassuring hand on my shoulder. 'Here, drink this.' She passed over a tall paper cup with the museum's logo branded on it.

I peeled off my blue plastic gloves, wiped my sweaty hands on my apron and let the heat of the beverage unfurl my tense fingers. I brought the coffee to my lips and blew steam away. It was a dark roast with two sugars. I might as well have an intravenous drip pumping it through my bloodstream – this was already my third cup this morning.

My shoulders dropped. 'It's no use, Greer. I have tried *every* single piece three times. And I've got a stack load of documenting to do today. I won't get another chance before the interview on Monday.'

She gave me a nudge and theatrically pulled out another pair of plastic gloves. I slipped off the stool and let her take over.

'I gotta hunch,' she said, unearthing specimen 276 from the collection and placing it on the lens. You had to love her for her unfailing sense of optimism.

'Well?' I asked eagerly, before noticing her shoulders drop as well.

'It was worth a shot.' Her bottom lip protruded, and she disposed of the gloves.

I sank onto the stool next to her and stared at my laptop showing a 3D design of what the Roman brooch might look like.

'Don't worry, Lina. I still think you're the best candidate. No one knows the museum better than you. You're one of the longest-serving members of the team.'

'With no real experience out on the field.'

'That's not your fault. You put in enough hours here. And the school tours love you. Your ratings are sky high.'

'Thanks to you.'

'Ugh, Lina. Drop this self-deprecating British bullshit. You're great at the assistant job. You'll be a shoo-in for the next level.' She bumped my shoulder with hers. '*And* you smell better than Mr McCrusty who should've retired centuries ago.'

A message pinged in my inbox. A cursory glance showed it was an email reminding me about the reunion tonight. Greer grabbed her screen glasses and leaned in. She never gave me any personal space. It had taken a while to get used to that. 'American brashness' she had once called it when I saw her reading my texts over my shoulder. It was the same brashness that had got her the six-month placement at the museum. She was in her penultimate year at UCLA and would soon be heading back to California to complete her studies. She had beaten a list of over a hundred undergraduates to get this coveted placement. I was getting too used to having her around, though. She brought a lightness to my life that had been missing for years. Or maybe it was that I had missed female company. I dreaded her leaving and wondered when I would see her again once she left.

'A reunion, huh? You going?'

I shook my head and scrolled through my other emails.

'Why not?' She pressed her finger on my touchscreen, opening up the attachment. 'Is this your class?'

'Yup.'

'Ooh, fun. Shove over.' She scraped her stool across the linoleum floor and brought it flush next to mine, taking control of the mouse. 'Let's see if I can find you.' She zoomed in on the picture and dragged it left and right. 'Jeez, it's like *Where's Waldo?* You all look the same in those dark colours.'

Although Stockland Academy was a state school, it modelled itself on being like some of the private ones in the area and encouraged its sixth formers to come smartly dressed each morning and wear only black, grey or the mottled green colour of the younger kids' uniform. Some girls tried to flout the rules, as evidenced by the splashes of hot pink and lime green on the photograph.

'Found you!' she said triumphantly. 'Those are major bangs you got. So ... who did you hook up with from this lot?'

'Greer!' I put my finger to my closed lips. We weren't the only ones in the lab room today and our boss – Mr McCrumb, or McCrusty as Greer called him – could come in at any moment. Awkward coughs and shuffling of seats filled the room from the rest of the archaeology team and I cowered. 'Keep your voice down,' I whispered.

'I don't care. I'm outta here in a few weeks and I can't wait. God, I miss the ocean. Birmingham is so land-locked.'

I couldn't be more jealous of Greer though I knew it was silly to be. I had a good life here, my expenses were low, and I was saving for ... well I had no idea at this point what for, but everything would be different once I got the promotion from assistant curator to curator. My boss had an exciting career, moving from museum to museum, all round the country, sometimes even abroad. The only thing I hadn't figured out was how to tell Dad that there might be times I wouldn't be around to help. Maybe with an uplift in pay we could afford to hire a part-time worker for the deli on the odd occasion I was away. But I would reassure him that I would never move out; that it would always be me and him. Forever.

'OK, so who did you …' She put her hand by her mouth to whisper '… fool around with?'

'No one.' A flush crept into my neck and my skin would soon be all blotchy – an affliction I had had since I was a teenager whenever I was nervous or had told a fib.

'Your eyes are all shifty. You definitely got down and dirty with someone. Let me guess.'

I did my best to keep a poker face. 'I didn't have sex with anyone from my year,' I said, holding my hand over my throat to hide the blemishes.

'You're such a spoilsport. How about that guy, the one you spend every weekend with? The one who knows how good-looking he is, whose shirts are tighter than an eighteenth-century corset.'

'You mean Nik?' I said, pointing at the guy sitting in the front row. Nikolas Markos. *Most likely to … be driving a Lamborghini, living in a mansion and modelling for Hugo Boss.*

'Yeah, the one you have a "relationship" with.' She did quotation marks with her fingers. 'Or wait, your "friend with benefits", isn't that what you call him?'

The truth was I didn't know what to call me and Nik.

'Woah, he's a cutey.' I sat up with interest to see where she had zoomed in on. 'Who's that?'

That was Ash Patel. My best friend. Correction. He *was* my best friend. 'Yeah, he and I were good mates once. But he won't be there. After he went to study maths at Cambridge, he went to work at a bank in London before relocating to Mumbai.'

'Hmm. Smart and loaded. You missed out there.'

'You're so shallow, you know that, right?'

My phone vibrated on the counter and Nik's name flashed up. Before I could reach for it, Greer had grabbed it and answered.

'Hey, Nik,' she drawled. 'Nah, she's right here. I am trying to persuade her she has to go to the reunion.' She nodded. 'I know, right? That's what I told her. Ah huh. Yeah.'

I shot her a 'can I have the phone now' look but she dismissed my request with a flick of her hand.

'OK, great,' she said with a broad smile. 'I'll tell her.' She hung up and put the mobile back on the counter before zoning in on my screen and inspecting the faces of my classmates some more.

'Well?'

'Well, what?' she said with a coquettish smirk.

'What did Nik say and why didn't he want to speak to me?'

'He said he'll pick you up at your flat at seven.'

'Let me call him back. I'm not going,' I said, reaching for my phone. She swatted my hand away. 'Ow.' I scowled. She really was being difficult, acting more like a toddler than someone only six years my junior.

'Why on earth don't you want to go?' she said.

I rubbed my hand. 'Because ... oh you wouldn't understand.'

She twisted on the stool to face me. 'I might.'

'Because ...'

It wasn't just any old reunion. It was a dance. And I made a promise to myself years ago that I was never *ever* going to dance again.

Chapter 3

'Where am I?' I said, slowly opening my eyes.

A sunset hovered on the horizon – the sky polluted and murky. My feet scrunched the wet sand between my toes. Thick, humid air invaded my nostrils, seeped with the smell of incense and cardamom. Lurid green trousers billowed around my legs and a scarlet cropped top decorated with gold brocade peeked from beneath a silk maroon sash that hung from one shoulder and draped over my chest. My black hair fell in ringlets over my shoulder to one side.

Two arms wrapped around my waist, and I leaned back into him – his heartbeat reverberating through me at a steady pace, calming my racing thoughts.

'Are you ready?' he said by my ear.

I turned to face him and wanted to get lost in those dark chocolate eyes. A white shirt hung loose on his body. I trailed my hand down his naked chest, dipping in and out of his muscles, and he sighed contentedly.

He leaned down and placed his lips on mine. A chaste kiss at first, but when I pushed myself up to him, the kiss intensified. My hands reached up to his face, fingers brushing against his light stubble, not wanting to let him go, ever. His hands grasped mine as if he didn't want to let me go either.

Pulling back from the embrace, I stared up at his face – those eyes, deep and intense. I noticed my hands against his chest – olive skin against brown.

'You don't have to do this, Lina,' he said.

He stroked my cheek and I melted beneath his fingertips.

'I want to do this; I want the pain to go away. And I need to do this. For me. For Mum. For your sister.'

He pressed his lips together, trying to keep his emotions in check. 'I want to do this too.'

The music drifted over the water.

'Has the movie begun?' I asked him.

He nodded. 'Don't be scared. It's not our part yet. You can look.'

Turning in his embrace, he tightened his arms around me. There in the distance across the sand sat a man with a guitar. The tune was soft and melodic. His fingers strummed, the twang increasing in intensity as he moved his hand up and down. More musicians appeared and joined him on the sand – a drummer, an electric guitar and a piper.

From stage right a chorus of women in elaborate saris came into view. An explosion of colour against the pale yellow sand. Their movements were fluid and in sync – hand gestures indicating this was a time for celebration.

A band of men in more modern clothing followed next, weaving in and out of the women. I let the music wash over me and I could feel it: the rhythm pulsating through my veins. It began with a foot tap, a twitch of the knee, a flick of the hip.

He grasped my waist tighter, and his voice began a sweet tune against my ear. Before I knew it, I was singing back to him.

Wait … since when did I speak Hindi?

And … cut.

Chapter 4

I studied my reflection in the mirror on my cupboard door. Nope. Too formal. I peeled off my third choice of outfit and threw it onto the floor beside my wet towel and a couple of pairs of shoes and tried on a pale blue sundress.

My nap had disorientated me. The mindfulness technique I had learned at the pain clinic wasn't intended to make me fall asleep but a combination of the medication I had been given at the last visit and a long day at work must have pushed me over into dreamland. Thankfully the cramps that had plagued me on the journey home from the museum had lessened but, with these tablets in my system, I knew alcohol was a bad idea tonight.

It had felt so real; the Bollywood movie with me and Ash as its stars. Looking over that school photo must have catapulted him to the forefront of my mind.

I rubbed my temples to banish the images and took in the sight of me in this dress. What did this look say about me? Twenty-eight-year-old Lina Georgiades totally in control of her life, knows exactly what she wants and where she's going. My body sagged. This look said nothing of the sort. More like

I nabbed it from the Primark sale last summer with what little cash I had to splurge on a frivolous dress I knew I would only have limited opportunities to wear.

Why did I let Greer and Nik talk me into this?

Nik had promised to be by my side the whole night. He knew why I didn't want to dance and never challenged me on it which I appreciated. I had called him back after fobbing Greer off with the excuse that I had nothing to wear, but before I could get a word in, Nik had persuaded me. He wanted me there by his side so he could face up to those that had tormented him during his years at Stockland.

'*Matia mou*,' Dad said, appearing at the doorway. 'You look beautiful. Just like your mother.' His smile turned sad with that last word.

I glanced back at my reflection. I had Mum's dark hair and eyebrows. That much was obvious from all the photos Dad had of her around the flat. Before I could reply, the doorbell sounded. Dad shuffled out and I heard his enthusiastic greeting all the way to my room – the words of endearment in Greek, the playful slap of the back and the sound of cheek kissing.

My heart skipped a beat when Nik strode in, a roguish grin plastered over his face. He was decked out in a sharp dark suit with a thick knotted grey tie. His smile could easily melt a piece of granite.

'For you.' He revealed a big bunch of white roses from behind his back.

'You didn't have to do that.'

'For my best girl? Yes, I did.' He leaned in and kissed me on both cheeks. His aftershave pricked my nose and I inhaled. A memory from long ago stirred in my mind.

'You promise to have my daughter back by midnight?' Dad said from the threshold of my bedroom.

'Baba!' I giggled. 'I'm twenty-eight. I don't have curfew any more.' I gave Nik a once-over and whistled. 'Check you out. New suit?'

He held the lapels of his jacket and spun around. 'Yup.' Straightening his tie, he glanced at the mirror and stroked his shaved face. 'And I've got the Lexus for the night.'

This was all part of the plan; Nik's way of showing everyone at school that he had made it. Never mind that the car was his dad's and he never had to go up for promotion at the insurance company he worked at because it was run by his father, Nik had scores to settle and was clearly going all out tonight.

'And –' he turned back to me with a serious expression before taking my hand and kissing it '– I will also have the most beautiful girl on my arm.' His thumb caressed the bracelet he had given me for my eighteenth and he smiled as he stroked the jewel nestled in the middle of it.

I lightly punched him on the chest. 'Show-off.'

'Come on, we'd better go,' he said. 'Mr Georgiades, I promise I will take good care of your daughter.' He gave me a cheeky wink to which I rolled my eyes.

I threaded my arm into Nik's as we approached the school hall and gripped it unnecessarily hard.

'Hey, it's fine,' Nik said, putting a hand over mine. 'I'm here. I'll be by your side. Always.'

I nodded and we carried on walking down the corridor. The smell of cabbage permeated off the walls from the canteen at the far end; the cabinets lining our way proudly displaying the school's prized alumni.

I stopped still at one photograph and Nik scoffed.

'Thank God Patel won't be here,' he said.

Ash's cheesy grin beamed through the glass. It was a picture of him receiving the Maths Challenge gold award in Year Eleven. He was also immortalised in another photo from our sixth-form days for being the first from our school to ever go to Cambridge.

'I never understood why you two weren't friends,' I said. 'Remember when we were at Stockland Primary? We were inseparable – the Three Musketeers.'

'We grew up and I soon realised what a tool he was.'

'You weren't exactly ever nice to him, or me for that matter.'

He stopped and retracted his arm. 'When was I ever not nice to you in primary school?'

'Have you forgotten? End of Year Three?'

He shook his head.

'You told me and Ash a meteorite would hit the Earth in twenty years.'

He snorted. 'No, I didn't.'

'Yes, you did. You absolutely freaked us out. We were doing that assignment with Ms Bell where we had to write a story about what we would be doing in twenty years. We even had to do a sketch of what we would look like. You told me and Ash in the playground that it was pointless because we would be dead.'

He dipped his head and gazed at his shiny new shoes. 'You have an impressive memory, Lina, because I don't remember any of that. You and Patel were always so serious, though – not surprised you fell for it if I did say it.'

I hugged myself tightly, thinking back to how Ash and I had responded to Nik's teasing. Twenty years had passed since that time. We had made a promise to each other to always be friends and now we weren't.

I linked my arm in Nik's again. 'It doesn't matter anyway, we're still alive.'

'Do you remember what you wrote?'

I stilled. Did he know about the secret box? How could he? It had been mine and Ash's secret. 'What I wrote for what?'

'For the assignment. This mysterious piece of homework set by a Ms Bell who I have no recollection of.'

My heart rate steadied. 'Oh, that. No, haven't got a clue.' My parents never kept my work – not enough room in the flat, they always said. And who would remember something they wrote twenty years ago?

'Are you doing what you always dreamed of doing?' Nik said, looking at me a little more seriously now.

'An assistant curator at Birmingham Museum? I doubt I wrote that. What about you, Mr Regional Assistant Manager of Markos and Son insurance company?'

'Oh yeah, insurance was always my dream, baby.' He grinned, a wicked grin, and I nestled into him – his bicep flexing at my touch. 'Come on.' He flicked his head in the direction of the hall. 'Let's do this.'

As we opened the door, we were hit by a cacophony of strobe lighting, music and laughter. At the desk by the entrance, we picked up our badges and made our way further towards the crowd of our old classmates, stopping at the bar to pick up a couple of drinks. A few people that Nik and I had known in the loosest sense came over and we exchanged pleasantries. It was all so fake. The 'God, I've missed you' and 'we should keep in touch' statement after we had chatted about their lives but not told them much about ours. Who were we kidding? We all knew after tonight we would probably never make the effort to see each other again.

'God, this is lame,' Nik whispered at my ear.

I took a few sips of my orange juice. 'Look over there.' I tipped my chin. A guy who I vaguely remembered as being the head of the football team had a captive audience around him, his stance wide and arrogant. I knew he had been one of Nik's tormentors when we were about fourteen, fifteen, but when Nik had joined the First XI at the beginning of sixth form, things had changed for him, and he had been part of that crowd.

'Shit, he's coming over.' Nik cleared his throat and straightened his tie.

'Nikolas Markos.' He slapped Nik on the shoulder. Toby. *That* was his name as I clocked his badge. 'How the hell are you? And ...' Toby made an obvious glance down towards my chest where my badge was probably a little too close to my neckline, but his eyes lingered at my cleavage and I kicked myself for choosing this dress over the other two outfits.

'Lina,' I said as he continued to look at my boobs.

I could tell from the wrinkles in his forehead that he didn't have a clue who I was. He drained his beer and swayed a bit. Another song came on the sound system, the opening chords to 'Demons' by Fatboy Slim from the soundtrack to our last year of school.

'Are you both ...' He did a gesture with his hands, mimicking putting a ring on his finger.

'No, we're not married,' I said.

He staggered forward and I could smell the alcohol on his breath as he leaned in. 'Then you're fair game?'

He grabbed me by the elbow and pulled me towards the dance floor and my heartbeat escalated. I tried to wrestle from his hold. 'I don't want to dance.'

'Hey,' Nik said, stepping between us. 'Let her go.'

'Don't be such a wanker, Markos, you can spare your bird for one dance.'

'I *don't* want to dance,' I said, loud enough that it caused a few heads to turn.

The next few seconds seemed to happen in slow motion. Toby increased his grip and Nik took another step forward and shoved Toby hard in the shoulder. He turned, relinquishing his grasp of me almost immediately before holding both his hands up and shoving Nik so hard in the chest that he stumbled backwards. The commotion caused a group of five lads who I also recalled had played in the team to be instantly by Toby's side as if we had all been transported back to our schooldays and weren't getting close to our thirties.

Toby strode forward and jabbed his finger into Nik's chest. 'You and me. Outside.'

Nik stroked his suit, as if Toby's touch had left a stain on it. 'I'm not going to fight you, Toby.'

'Pussy,' Toby spat, rolling up his sleeves. One of the other guys held onto his shoulder trying to calm him down, but the slur that came from another in the huddle caused Nik to still.

At first, I wasn't sure if Nik had heard it, but when I noticed the expression on his face, I knew he had – I could see the tension radiate from him like steam from hot tar being spilled onto a road. It was the same hurtful moniker he had heard many times before.

Another track from our graduating year bellowed from the sound system but I couldn't focus on the words or even register the name of it because my full attention was on Nik. I knew what I had to do. I clasped his arm and pulled him towards me, reaching on tiptoes to his eyeline. I held his head in my hands and kissed him.

Flashbacks popped in my mind – the thrill and excitement of locking lips with him for the first time, the sexual desire flooding my veins as his tongue met mine. But this was different – so much time had passed. There wasn't the same eighteen-year-old lust coursing through me or the anticipation of my first sexual encounter on the immediate horizon.

It was only when I pulled away and settled back on the balls of my feet that I noticed it wasn't only the whole hall which was the audience for my public display of affection but that someone was standing in the doorway; the one person in the world I had never expected to walk in at that moment. Ash Patel.

Chapter 5

Nik stirred in bed next to me, his arm draped across my hip, pinning me to the mattress. My room still had my single bed from my childhood and wasn't big enough for a double so there was no room to move away.

'Nik, wake up. You've got to go and sleep on the sofa.' He groaned and rolled onto his other side. I poked him. 'Get up, Nik. If Dad catches you in my bed, he'll freak.'

'Why?' he mumbled. 'You stay at mine every Saturday night.'

'Yes, but I tell him I sleep in the spare room.' I prodded him again.

The sheet slipped down his back as he dragged himself up. His Achilles tattoo that snaked up his arm was visible in all its glory – the ink illuminated in the early-morning sun peeking through the curtains. He looked back over his shoulder and that's when I saw the full extent of last night's drama plastered over the right side of his face.

'What? Is it bad?' He winced when he touched the skin around his eye.

'I knew we should've kept that ice pack on longer.'

'What will your dad say when he sees me? Maybe I should go home now. I'm awake already. I can return the car before my dad notices it's gone from the office car park.' He picked up my digital clock. 'I can't believe you wake at five on a Saturday and then put in a full day's work downstairs.'

'Dad needs at least one day off. He can't run the deli on his own all week.'

Nik shuffled out of bed and rearranged himself inside his boxers before dropping to the floor for a few press-ups.

'You still coming round tonight?' he said, his breathing a little ragged as he held his body in a plank position.

'Of course,' I said, opening my chest of drawers. 'Maybe we'll have a quiet one, though. Don't think I'm up for the pub tonight. But you can go to the Fox without me if you want.'

The Fox was our favourite Saturday-night venue – the atmosphere welcoming and the vibe laid-back – and a handy fifteen-minute walk from Nik's Birmingham city-centre flat.

He yawned. 'Nah. I don't feel up for it,' he said, holding his temple. 'I'll order takeout, my treat. It's the least I can do after last night.'

'It wasn't your fault. And I appreciate you were defending my honour, but it wasn't necessary to get into a punch-up with Toby the Tank.'

He chuckled. 'Forgot that's what everyone called him.'

'I didn't even remember his name but then it all came back to me.'

'Did I imagine it, or was Patel there too?'

I steadied myself on the dresser. 'I think you imagined it.'

A lie. It was definitely him. He had stood glowing in the doorway but that's when Toby had thrown his punch. The next few minutes were a blur, and by the time they were prised apart, Ash was gone. What on earth was he doing in Birmingham?

Nik rubbed his hand over his non-bruised eye, yawning. 'Could've sworn it was him.' He shrugged and got changed while I threw on my Saturday deli work clothes of white T-shirt and three-quarter-length jeans. 'Glad he was a mirage, then. He's the last person I want to see.'

I decided to let that comment slide because I knew it was a conversation that wouldn't end well if I said anything different.

As I said goodbye to Nik at the side entrance to the flat, he slapped his forehead.

'Shit, I forgot. Mum and Dad are coming for brunch on Sunday. You'll stay, won't you?'

I rubbed my hand up and down my arm. 'I really need to prepare for my interview on Monday.'

He stroked my cheek. 'You don't need to prepare. You're going to knock it out of the park. They'll be fools not to give you the job.' He clasped my hands and dipped his chin, looking back up at me with those puppy-dog green eyes – those eyes I had fallen for years ago. 'Please, stay. I'll order in all your favourites from that Italian place. You know Mum and Dad will be expecting you.'

Brunch with his parents had become a monthly obligation and I knew Nik hated the interrogation he had to endure about his life and valued my support.

'OK,' I acquiesced.

He planted a huge soppy kiss on my cheek which I quickly wiped away and I shoved him out of the door. 'Will you go already. I've got food to make.'

He walked off, half turning to blow me a kiss and pose as if he was on an ad shoot: jacket slung over his shoulder, white shirt unbuttoned more than halfway down, his pecs dancing beneath the fabric. I giggled and waved him away.

I closed the door and went back upstairs and set to work on making the *dolmádes*.

'Fold, fold, roll.' My three-word instruction flowed from my mouth as I tried to process the events of last night. Eventful was an understatement. Nik and Toby were now barred from the school indefinitely.

But why had I lied to Nik about seeing Ash?

A sharp cramp interrupted that thought. I dropped the vine leaf and pushed the skin at my hip inwards, willing the pain to abate. I stumbled to the bathroom, ripping my food gloves off, and pulled out my prescribed medication from the cupboard above the basin. I swallowed a couple of tablets with several scoops of water from the tap.

Day Six. I scrunched my eyes tight and breathed through clenched teeth. The monthly pattern seemed to be changing. Maybe it was the spicy kebab Nik and I had shared late last night once we got booted out of the dance. The last GP I had seen had told me to record any flare-ups after eating certain foods to see if there was a pattern.

I sank onto the bathroom floor and let my mind wander to the Bollywood movie I had imagined yesterday: colours, music, dancing. Always dancing. Me and Ash together, like time had been suspended. I floated on the ridge of the pain as the minutes passed, allowing myself to believe in the fantasy of a happier time.

As the pain eventually eased, I returned to my tasks for the deli and made a mental note – avoid spicy kebabs in future.

Creeping down the stairs to the deli a couple of hours later, I slipped on my apron and switched on the lights. I made several salads in the small kitchen at the back and brought out some prepared meals from the fridges that Dad had cooked last night.

When I pulled up the blinds my heart lurched as I saw who was waiting outside, leaning on the window. Ash. Decked out in a navy-blue polo shirt and jeans, he had his arms folded over his chest as if he were nervously waiting for something.

When he saw me, a smile flooded his face – the creases by his eyes intensifying. I flipped over the Open sign and unbolted the door.

'Hey.' His voice was soft, almost apologetic.

I took in the sight of him for a second – the glimpse last night had been too fleeting. His face was as I remembered, but his shoulders and chest were broader, a day-old stubble caressing his jaw, hair a little wet as if he had just had a shower.

'What are you doing here?' I asked.

He pointed to the sign in the window. 'You sell coffee, right?'

28

I laughed. 'Yes, of course we sell coffee. Come in. I'll make you one.' I ushered him inside.

'Thanks.' He brushed past me, a hint of shower gel confirming what I had suspected.

I placed some beans in the percolator and pulled down the handle until it poured out into the portafilter. Out of the corner of my eye, I saw Ash drag out a chair and sit at one of the three tables we had tucked away in the deli. I guessed that meant he was staying.

Bringing him his coffee, I turned to go back to behind the counter when I felt a touch on my hand. Ash held it lightly – the tingle from his touch fizzing up my arm, igniting a warmth inside me that I hadn't felt in years.

'Do you have time to talk?' he asked.

The ding of the bell above the door caused Ash to pull his hand away.

'I'd love to, but I've got to work,' I said, with a nod to acknowledge the customers.

His face fell. 'Maybe later? What time do you close?'

'Five thirty.'

'I'll be back then. It's been what ... six years?'

'Seven,' I said without hesitation.

He twisted his cup. 'That's a long time. We have a lot to catch up on. I wasn't even sure you'd still be here.'

I tightened the belt of my apron. 'I'm still here,' I said with a note of resignation, spreading my hands out to take in the sweep of the room.

I went to the group that had just come in and didn't even notice Ash leaving. My mind whirred. What did he want to talk about? I didn't want to go back to the last time we had seen each other – it was too painful.

I swept the broom around the last remaining diners, hoping they would get the message that I was closing. Dad had helped with the lunchtime crowd as usual but now he would be happily playing cards and backgammon with his friends at the Hellenic Greek centre – a hall in a neighbourhood a few miles away from ours, where a large group of men in their fifties and sixties liked to congregate to talk about the old days and drink ouzo.

I checked my watch. Quarter to six. There was no sign of Ash. I guessed something must have come up. Oh well, there was no point in dwelling on what he had wanted to talk about.

I still had a couple of hours free before I was due at Nik's. My feet throbbed and I was looking forward to reclining on the sofa upstairs and having a cup of tea. It would also give me time to run through some practice interview questions.

As I went to turn off the light, a tap on the window made me turn. Ash stood outside looking contrite. I unbolted the door.

He held his hands flat against each other as though he was praying. 'I am so sorry. It was a struggle to get away. Family.' It was a one-word excuse, but I understood without any need for an explanation.

'That's fine. I wasn't waiting long.'

He comically swiped his hand across his forehead. 'Phew. I thought I might have missed you.'

'I actually have plans this evening but—'

'Of course.' He nodded. 'You're busy, I understand. But ... do you have time for one drink?' His eyebrows raised. 'We could go to the Village Green, for old times' sake.'

I took in his pleading look. 'Sure. Let me lock up and freshen up a bit. I smell of grease and oil. I'll meet you round the side in a few minutes.'

His shy smile warmed my insides. I battled to suppress the feelings that his presence was stirring in me. If I closed my eyes, I would be in that meadow again, with him – our hands entwined, grass in our hair, sun on our faces.

After a change into a vest top and skirt, I grabbed my bag and headed down to meet him. The sun was still warm enough for no jacket.

As we walked down the road towards the pub, we didn't look at each other. So much time had passed, I guessed he didn't know where to begin and neither did I.

I turned and caught him looking at me, but he pursed his lips and shoved his hands into his pockets.

'I guess the obvious first question is, why are you here? I mean, back in Birmingham. I thought you live permanently in Mumbai.'

'I do.' He rubbed his chin, his face looking sombre. 'I'm back for a few days.'

'Surely you didn't come all the way from India for the reunion?'

He laughed. 'Definitely not. I came back because ... well ...' He clenched his hands. 'There's no easy way to say it. My dad is dying.'

I stopped suddenly and turned towards him. 'Oh, Ash. I'm so sorry.'

He shrugged and carried on walking. 'That's what he believes, anyway. I still have hope. It's leukaemia. He's being stubborn. Refusing treatment. My mum is beside herself. She begged me to come to try and talk some sense into him.' He held his palms upwards. 'He is convinced his life is in the hands of the gods and we can't disrupt their plans. My parents usually come to see me in summer. I have not been back here since ... well since I left after university. But how could I not come now? I got the reminder about the reunion and thought that maybe, well, I wondered what it would be like to go back.'

'But you didn't stay long.'

He didn't elaborate and I sensed the awkwardness between us. Had he seen me kissing Nik? He must have.

'Do you work at the deli every day?'

'Only Saturdays but I help prepare the food in the morning like always and I do lock-ups too. I've worked as an assistant curator at the museum for a few years now.'

He nodded enthusiastically. 'I'd love to hear about it.'

I filled him in on my day-to-day life – the documenting of findings, school tours, hours spent staring into a microscope. The more I talked about my role, the more I realised I had stagnated there – this promotion was essential for progression.

Before long, we reached the pub and Ash held the door open for me.

'Shall we sit in the beer garden?' he said. 'It's quite stuffy in here.' He tugged at the neckline of his polo shirt.

'OK.'

'What can I get you?'

'Something refreshing.'

'The usual?'

I smiled, surprised that he remembered after all this time. 'Yes, but without the vodka.'

Out at the back of the pub, the atmosphere was convivial – large beer barrels were spaced out on the grass with punters sitting in front of them swigging drinks from plastic cups. Outdoor lights lined the perimeter of the fence and were also strung in criss-cross patterns across the garden – ready to be switched on once day turned to dusk. I settled at a barrel close to the back, far enough from the chatter of families enjoying the balmy summer's evening – their kids' raucous cries filling the air as they ran around in the children's area at the far side.

Ash came out a few minutes later with a beer for him and a glass of cranberry and grapefruit juice for me. It was a mixture that always raised eyebrows from the barman, but had been my favourite drink since Ash and I had come up with the combination one day after my first A-level exam and I had needed to offload.

'I had forgotten how much a pint of beer costs here,' he said.

'You've been gone from England too long.'

He nodded. 'I have.'

I took a sip of my drink through the straw – the tartness of the grapefruit juice catching on the roof of my mouth. Stirring it, the ice cubes clinked against the sides. It was a measured movement because I had no clue what to say. Apologise straight off the bat?

I stroked the glass, my finger growing wet as it wiped off the condensation. 'The last time I saw you, Ash—'

'It doesn't matter. I put you in a very awkward position and I am sorry.'

'You have no reason to be sorry.' I shook my head. 'It's me that should be apologising to you.'

'Perhaps we can call a truce. There's no need to hash out what was said back then. Too much time has passed now. Too many things have happened.' He clutched his glass, a faraway look in his eyes.

And too much pain.

I wasn't sure I could ever forget what had happened that night in Cambridge – the last time we had been together. But my absence after that time in the coming weeks when he had so desperately needed a friend had haunted me for years – too long a time to offer any credible excuse.

'I tried to get in touch … but I understand why you've kept your distance. I've missed you, though.' I whispered the words, not daring to look back up at him.

'I've missed you too,' he said, his voice deep and measured, ignoring my first statement.

He moved his clenched fist across the barrel and let his little finger stretch out. It was then I clocked the absence of the plaited bracelet he had once worn around his wrist – a friendship bracelet I had made him during a sewing class in Year Eight. It had been frayed at the edges when I had last seen him wear it in Cambridge.

Slowly but surely, I moved my hand across to meet his in the middle of the table and let my little finger clasp his. Our eyes met as the lights around the garden flickered on and his smile sent butterflies skittering through my stomach.

'Forever?' I said hesitantly.

'For always,' he murmured. After a moment, he pulled his hand back and cradled his beer before taking a swig and looking around the pub garden. 'Do you remember when we came here after your exams? The relief you felt.'

'Yeah. Me in floods of tears because I thought I had messed them all up. You helping me drown my sorrows even though you were still in the middle of yours. You know what else I remember?'

'No, what?'

'The time we hid that box – the one we thought would survive the apocalypse.'

'Oh my.' He laughed. 'Yes, I remember. Surely it's been twenty years by now.' He flicked his fingers one by one, counting under his breath. 'We should be dead.'

I reached out and pinched him on the arm.

'Ouch.' He rubbed his skin. 'What was that for?'

'I'm just checking you're real; that a meteorite didn't hit the Earth and we are all robots.'

'Well, I felt that, so yes I am very real.' He shook his head. 'I can't believe we fell for what he said.'

'You mean Nik?'

His face darkened. 'I saw you with him last night. I had no idea that you were ... together.'

I didn't want to go into details about our relationship. 'He was the one who persuaded me to come. I wasn't keen. You know how I feel about dances.'

'I do,' he said sadly, sweeping a few crisp crumbs off the barrel.

'I wonder if it's still there. The box. Wasn't that our plan: to open it after twenty years?'

'I think it was.'

We held each other's gaze and his warm smile tickled my insides.

'Shall we go and see if it is still there?' I asked.

'Go to Stockland Park with a shovel and dig it up?'

'Good point. We don't want to draw attention to ourselves. It is still quite light.'

He bit his bottom lip, lost in thought.

Those lips. Kissing them had been a mistake. I only wished we could roll back time and I had not ruined everything by kissing those lips. That kiss changed everything.

Love changed everything.

'How about later tonight?' Ash said, breaking my thoughts. 'You said you have plans, but maybe you could meet me afterwards, say eleven? I'm going back to Mumbai tomorrow. My family duty is complete for now. Dad is visiting the local hospital next week for his first round of chemo. This would be my only chance to do it with you.'

I hesitated. Saturday nights were my nights with Nik. There was no way I could tell him I was not staying after dinner because I had plans with Ash. I knew how he felt about him, and I had learned long ago never to get involved with whatever had caused them to become sworn enemies. Perhaps I could come up with something important I had to do back home. Staying over had become routine but it wasn't fixed.

The idea of sneaking around to go to the park under a veil of darkness brought that night twenty years ago into sharp focus. No one knew what we had done. It was always our secret. And I was good at keeping secrets.

'OK, let's do it,' I said.

Chapter 6

When we were eight

'I'm going to sneeze,' Ash said.

'Pinch your nose,' Lina whispered.

'I can't. Then I'll get dust in my throat, and I'll start coughing.'

The dust mites under Lina's parents' bed were tickling her nose too and scratching at the back of her throat but she knew they had to keep as quiet as church mice. Why it was only church mice that were expected to be quiet often baffled Lina. It was a phrase her mum always used when she dragged Lina and her big brother Alex to the Greek Orthodox church on a Sunday. The incense the high priest waved continuously made her sneeze, so she had learned to hold her nose.

'Do we have to stay under the bed?' Ash asked, his nose twitching.

'Sssh,' Lina said a lot more loudly than Ash had uttered those words. Footsteps from outside the room got nearer and a door creaked.

'Lina, are you in here?' The tone in her dad's voice made Lina fear she was in trouble. Ash laid a hand on hers and squeezed it but when she turned to look at him, she realised he had clutched it for his own benefit. There was fear etched on his face and he was biting his bottom lip. Lina wondered if Ash had *ever* done anything naughty.

The door closed, and the footsteps faded.

'We're going to get in trouble,' Ash said, his voice trembling.

'Wait,' Lina said, shuffling away.

Ash grabbed the sleeve of her jumper. 'Where are you going?'

'I want to show you something and I need to go get it.'

'But what if they find me?'

'They won't as long as you don't sneeze, or cough.'

Lina slithered out from under the bed like she was getting herself out of a rope net on an army assault course. She scampered around, opening the drawers from the chest in the corner of the room and the bedside table. No luck. There was only one other place it could be: the wardrobe. She opened the door and got inside, pulling it back as far as it would go. It never closed because it was broken.

In the darkness she rummaged, deep behind her mum's collection of sweaters and shoes. She often snuck in here when she was scared. The smell of her mum's perfume was always comforting and the soft wool she enveloped herself in was what she thought sinking into a giant marshmallow would be like. Not that she was often scared, she wanted to add. Nothing made her scared.

There it was. In the deepest right corner of the wardrobe. The wooden box. Her mum had once brought it to her bedroom to show her the contents. Jewels and rings and necklaces filled the velvet-lined interior. The letters 'ES' had been engraved on top and she had asked her mum what they stood for, but she couldn't remember the explanation she had been given because her pounding heart was drowning out her thoughts.

She knew she would be in big trouble if she or Ash were caught in this room. It was never locked but her parents reminded her and her brother that it was out of bounds. That made Lina want to explore it even more.

Lina was relieved to find Ash still under the bed when she lifted the valance sheet, but his eyes and mouth were scrunched closed. He was clearly following Lina's advice to hold his breath. She poked him and he let out a sound that resembled a squeal. His eyes popped open. Wide and fearful.

'Come on,' she urged. 'Let's go to my room.'

He shook his head – cheeks still firmly puffed out.

Lina rolled her eyes skyward. Ash was going to have to toughen up, especially if he wanted to survive Year Three at their primary school, as he was the new kid. The boys had been pushing him around in the playground during his first week. She had noticed. Not Nik, though. He had tried to be his friend – even once stood in front of Toby Morgan when he had shoved Ash in the shoulder during PE and called him a dog poo. Ash had cried and had to leave the lesson to go to the nurse. Nik had told Toby he was a bully but ended up getting shoved too and crying off to their form teacher. In fact, if both those boys didn't toughen up, they would have a rough time until they left school.

Not to worry, she thought. Ash had *her* now and she knew she was tough. Like Lara Croft. *Shh*, she told her thoughts. No one knew she had crept out of her room last night after she was meant to have gone to bed to see what her brother and Dad had been watching. Her mum was already asleep, and the lights were off in the living room. There was a spot between the sofa and the armchair that she could sneak into without being seen. She had sat and watched *Tomb Raider* and knew that's who she wanted to be. Lara Croft. The actress who had played her even had the same name as her she noticed as the credits began to roll.

Lara Croft was brave and fearless *and* beautiful. That's who Lina wanted to be.

Ash made a choking noise that cut through her thoughts.

'You can breathe now. But you have to come out quickly, before someone comes in.' She held out her hand and helped him from underneath the low bed. They waited until the coast was clear before scuttling along the hallway to her room. She didn't relinquish her grip until they were on the other side of her bed and back on the floor – out of view if anyone from her family were to suddenly enter.

'I got it,' she whispered.

Ash stared in wonder as she opened the box. Inside lay a treasure trove of necklaces and earrings plus two jewels. Lina held the stones in her hands and raised them up to the light. Ash followed her gaze as they caught the sunlight flickering through the branches of the tree outside the window. Lina thought they looked like planets with stars trapped inside.

'This is what I wanted to put in our box. If we survive, we can sell them and have money to buy food and clothes.'

'Won't your mum notice they're gone?' Ash said, always the cautious one, the non-risk taker. She had noticed that about him. In fact, this whole homework date had needed a lot of careful planning because Ash's mother hadn't been too keen on him coming over. She didn't know why. Lina's mum had reassured Ash's mum that they would be supervised if they needed to use glue or scissors for their Hadrian's Wall history project. Lina knew this was a lie because her mum worked in the deli all day and would only be popping up periodically to check on them. It was obvious that Ash was like his mum – cautious.

'She won't notice. There are so many jewels in here. I'm sure she won't miss these.'

When her mum had shown her these precious objects on a rainy day back in the Christmas holidays, she had told Lina about how she had discovered them in Cyprus. That was where her mum had lived before she came to England with her dad. The jewels were in the ground apparently which seemed like a stupid place to leave them, but Lina's mum had found them and brought them here. She had told Lina they were thousands of years old, or had she said millions? She couldn't remember. But she knew from her history lessons that anything found a long time ago could be worth a lot of money.

But what if Nik was right?

'Are you scared we might not open this box in twenty years?' she asked Ash.

'How come?'

'You know. We might explode in the apocalypse, like Nik said.'

Ash pinned his arms back. 'No, I'm not scared,' he said. 'Because when we die, we are reborn.'

Lina rolled her shoulders. 'What does that mean?'

'When we die, we are reborn into another being. If we have been good, it could be a person but if we have been bad then maybe into an animal.'

This was brand-new information and it confused Lina. 'But how can that happen if there is no one left after the apocalypse?' Lina shook her head vigorously. 'No. That can't be true.'

'But you believe in karma, yes?'

'I don't know what that is.'

'Whatever you do in this life will be noticed by a higher being. They will always watch. And if you are bad, then you might come back as an ant or a fly.'

Now Lina was beginning to feel less like Lara Croft. There was someone watching her. Had they seen her glued to *Tomb Raider* in the darkness hidden behind the sofa? Did they know about her stealing her mum's jewels? Her bottom lip began to wobble. She squeezed her eyes shut and reassured herself that she wasn't stealing the stones – only borrowing them. There was no way she was coming back to be a bug.

A knock at the door made Lina jump up and the jewels fell from her hand and rolled under her bed.

The door creaked open, and Lina's mum peered behind. 'There you both are,' she said, exasperated. 'It's lunchtime. Come downstairs please. You haven't got long before Ash's mum will be here. Hope you've finished your project.'

Lina nodded dutifully and prayed to the high priest at her Greek Orthodox church that her mum didn't open the door any wider and notice that Hadrian's Wall was more of a crumbling fence than a battlement.

When the door closed, Lina felt her tense shoulders instantly drop. She crawled under her bed, moving aside boxes of old toys and empty crisp packets from midnight feasts with Nik and found the jewels. They had rolled to a tin box – an old biscuit container that Nik's mum had given Lina to commemorate the Queen's golden jubilee last year. Nik's mum was fancy, and Lina thought she must have got the tin from the Queen herself. She had forgotten it was under here.

She wiped her hand over the lid to clear the dust. It had a picture of the Queen in the middle with a map of the world in gold surrounding Her Majesty's face. Lina was good at geography. She knew where all the countries were because she had a world map on her bedroom wall. She had little stickers on some of the countries: Greece, where her dad and Nik's parents were from; Cyprus, where her mum was from; and last week, when she found out she had been paired with Ash for this history project – India, where Ash's grandparents lived.

'That's where your family's from, right?' Lina pointed at the upside-down triangle poking out beneath the Queen's head. 'My mum is from this island.' She held the tin up close so Ash could see the small dot. 'It's called Cyprus and it's really tiny.'

Ash nodded but was looking nervously at the door. 'Shouldn't we go downstairs?'

Lina was right. He did always follow the rules. How on earth was she going to convince him to go out at night to bury the box?

She placed both of her hands on Ash's shoulders and gave him a slight shake. 'Look here, Ash Patel. You have to be tough if you want to survive life. But it's OK, because you've got me. And I will get it all sorted. I'll fill the box with all the things we might need. And in twenty years, we will know the apocalypse is coming and we can build a special tunnel into some rocks – you know, like the ones in the park. We can have a secret cave and crawl inside. Then we can dig up our box and we will be OK. Right?'

'Right,' Ash repeated.

An idea suddenly popped into Lina's mind. 'Hey, I know, wouldn't it be fun to write a letter to you and me for when we're grown up. Like what we did for Ms Bell. Can you imagine opening it up in the future?' She giggled. 'Do you know what you want to be when you're that old?'

Ash shook his head. 'No. I'm not sure.'

'Come on, there has to be something you want to do when you're a grown-up. What do you like to do now?'

Ash sat back onto the floor and clasped his hands together. 'Cook,' he said, almost in a whisper.

'Really? So, you want to be a chef?' Lina crossed her legs, her knees bobbing up and down – never one to sit still for even a minute.

Ash shrugged his shoulders and twisted his hands before looking back up at her. 'Can I tell you a secret?'

Lina bounced, waving her hands. 'Tell me!' She loved secrets. Shuffling closer to Ash, she waited expectantly for him to speak. But he didn't say anything. Instead, he reached into the back pocket of his beige trousers and pulled out a letter and handed it over to Lina. She put her finger beneath each word and read it out slowly.

'"We are happy to inform you that you have been accepted onto *Junior MasterChef*."' She glared at him, her mouth wide. 'Oh my God, that's so exciting.' She noticed that Ash didn't look as excited as she sounded.

'I can't do it,' he said, sinking further into the floor.

'Why not?'

'When my parents find out I applied without asking them, they will be so angry with me.'

'But why? You're going to be on TV. You'll be a star. I can talk to your parents. They'll listen to me. I will tell them they have to let you do it. And then I can say my best friend is on the telly.'

Ash smiled – the first time Lina had seen his face light up. She noticed the gap in his two front teeth even more. 'I'm your best friend?' he said.

Lina nodded. 'Sure. You and me. Together. Forever.' Lina held out her little finger and smiled encouragingly, willing Ash to grasp it. He did and she noticed how his brown skin was a few shades darker than her own skin. She knew they were different from most of the other kids in school. Nik was different too, but she was cross with him right now. She didn't know if she wanted to be his BFF any more. As Lina shook Ash's little finger, another two words popped into her head. 'And always,' she said with a confident tone in her voice.

'Forever, and always,' Ash repeated.

'This is going to be *so* fun,' Lina said, slapping her hands on her knees. 'Write a letter to your future you. Then I will

come to your house at eleven tomorrow night. My parents
will be asleep by then. We can take the box with the jewels
and the letters and hide it in the park.'

'I am not sure if I can go out of the house in the dark.'

'Sure, you can. I'm going to fill my bed with cushions, so it
looks like I am asleep. I'll bring my beach spade too so we can
dig a hole.'

'Umm …' Ash swallowed hard, the corner of his mouth
twitching. 'OK, I'll do it.' He smiled broadly.

Lina did a little fist pump. She knew Ash would eventually
come round. Lina liked to get her way. She was resourceful,
like Lara Croft.

'This will be *our* secret. We can't tell anyone we're going to
do this. Promise?'

'I promise,' Ash said.

The plan was cemented. All Lina had to do now was figure
out what to write.

Chapter 7

The tears came slowly at first before falling relentlessly. Lina swiped at her face, her hand clutching the pen tightly as she struggled with her words. The few sentences she had written were now smudged and she crumpled up the paper and threw it over her shoulder.

Her door creaked and her mum popped her head around.

'*Ángelé mou*,' she said soothingly. 'What is the matter?' She knelt down beside Lina's chair and stroked her hair, placing a section behind her ear.

'I don't want to die,' Lina said as she choked back a sob.

'My sweetheart.' Lina's mum pulled out a tissue from the box on Lina's desk and gently wiped away the tears. 'Why are you thinking these thoughts?'

'Nik said we are all going to die in twenty years.' She slumped onto her desk, her shoulders shaking as the tears flowed free and fast. Her mum's hand caressed her back. She mumbled some words in Greek – too fast for Lina to understand.

Every Saturday morning, Lina went to the Ayia Triada Greek School to attend classes. She hated them and prayed every Friday night that she wouldn't have to go and that she could attend ballet classes like Emily Walters – the most beautiful and popular girl in her year.

A squeeze on her shoulder made her turn her face. She sniffed and grabbed another tissue from the box, blowing her nose noisily.

Lina's mum grabbed her hand and pulled her onto the bed – their weight making an indent into the soft mattress. 'You must not listen to that Nikolas Markos boy. He doesn't know what he is talking about.'

'But he said there would be an apocalypse and we would all die.'

'And what evidence does he have for this fantastical tale?' Lina's mum raised her eyebrows. They were thick and dark like Lina's – the most notable feature on their face alongside their matching moles on top of their upper lip.

Lina shrugged.

'You see, my angel. You must always have evidence before you believe such a tale.'

'Ash said we will be reborn. But I don't want to become a bug.'

Lina's mum sighed and rubbed the back of her neck as if she was trying to unblock some tension after a long day at the deli. 'It is because of Ash's religion that he thinks that. We are Greek Orthodox, remember? He is Hindu. His family believes in different things.'

'So ... I won't become a bug?' Lina looked up at her mum hopefully.

'No, you will not become a bug.' Her mother stroked her hair again. She noticed the balled-up paper on the floor. 'What were you writing?'

'Ash and I are creating a time capsule, and we have to do letters for it.'

'How exciting.'

'Do you want to see the box?'

'Of course.'

Lina rummaged under her bed and found the biscuit tin. She opened it and remembered to take out the jewels before presenting it to her. Lina's mum peered inside. There were some coins, an old wrapper from a KitKat bar and a selection of photographs. Lina's mum took in each one and smiled. 'Where did you get these?'

'I found them in one of our photo albums. Sorry, I know I should've asked.'

'It's OK. These are lovely. You were such a beautiful baby. That shock of black hair, eyes the colour of the Aegean.' She pinched her cheek. 'And still so beautiful.'

'But I'm stuck. I don't know what to write, to future me.'

'How old will you be?'

'Well … twenty plus eight is twenty-eight of course.'

'Very good maths.'

'I hate maths.'

'OK, so maybe you won't be a mathematician or an accountant.'

Lina pulled a face. She knew Nik's dad did something with maths, but his job sounded boring. And Ash's dad also did something with numbers. Maybe men did jobs with maths. But no, that couldn't be true because her dad was a cook and that's what Ash wanted to do.

Her mum stared out of the window. 'Maybe you will be an explorer, travel the world.'

Lina gave this idea some thought and focused on the map stuck to her wall, wondering where she would go. India, perhaps, with Ash and to Cyprus to see where her mum was born. Lina's mum never liked to talk about her life growing up, but Lina didn't know why. She had found a chapter on Cyprus in a book in the school library and saw it was an island surrounded by beaches and the most beautiful greeny-blue sea. She also wanted to go to Disneyland in California to meet Minnie Mouse.

'Whatever you want to be, my girl, you will achieve it. The world is yours to do with whatever you want. You are strong and brave.'

'Like Lara Croft.'

Lina's mum shuffled back on the bed. 'How do you know about Lara Croft?'

'Oh … um … Alex has that poster on his wall. She looks strong and brave.'

'She is an archaeologist,' her mum said, her mind drifting off again.

'An archaeologist,' Lina repeated. It sounded cool.

Lina's mum shut the lid on the box and shook her head a little. 'When and where are you going to bury the time capsule?'

Lina twisted her hands in her lap. 'Ash said I could go to his house after school tomorrow and maybe we will bury it in his back garden. Can I?'

'Of course, if his parents don't mind.'

Lina nodded her head rapidly. 'They said it was OK.' She held her fingers crossed behind her back and hoped that Ash's gods would understand the gesture too – that it negated the lie. She really didn't want to be a bug.

'When you finish your letter to your future self, make sure you put it in a plastic bag and seal it. It is the best way to preserve it. And make sure you talk about your life now. It would be like looking at a diary from the past. Write down your thoughts and your feelings. Say what are your favourite things.'

'Hmm,' Lina mused.

'Who are your best friends?'

'Ash and Nik.'

'There are no girls who are your best friends?'

Lina screwed up her face and shook her head. 'The girls are mean in my class. I prefer boys.'

'I thought you said you liked Emily.'

Lina shook her head again. 'She doesn't want to be my friend. She only wants to be friends with the girls in her ballet class.'

'Oh,' her mother said, placing the box on the desk. 'Anyway, hurry up with your letter, I want lights out in ten minutes.'

She turned to go but Lina clutched her mother's hand tightly. 'You won't die, will you?'

Lina's mum placed her other hand on her daughter's fingers. 'I am not going to die. And when I see Nikolas's dad, I will tell him his son needs to stop going around spreading such horrible rumours. There will be no apocalypse. I promise. When you open the time capsule in twenty years, you will see. We will *all* be alive.'

Lina shivered beneath her hooded jacket. She pulled out a torch from its inside pocket and flipped it on, shining it towards a window at the back of Ash's house. It was the smallest opening. She flicked the ON/OFF button back and forth. Once. Twice. Three times. She waited. No movement. She tried again and this time the curtains twitched. The windowpane lifted and Ash popped his head out.

'I'm coming,' Ash said in a hushed voice.

Lina did a little jig on the spot. Project 'make Ashok Patel tough' was working. He was becoming more fearless by the day. She shone the torch on him and illuminated the path he needed to take to get onto the ledge beneath his window. From there it would be an easy shuffle to the end and then a short jump to the next ledge and onto the bench below.

Lina and Ash had carefully planned out the mission during lunch break. Nik had come over and asked what they were whispering about but Lina had told him they wouldn't tell because it was a secret. This had made Nik mad. He had pinched Lina's arm and Ash had immediately leapt up and stood between them and told him not to be mean. Nik had said sorry but continued to badger Lina to tell him what the secret was. She had stood firm in her resolve not to tell him of their plan. Nik had huffed and puffed, folding his arms before stropping away. But Lina knew he still wanted her to be his friend. He needed her. He needed her to protect him from Toby the Tank.

So far, the plan had worked. Ash had persuaded his mum to let Lina come round after school to do some maths homework. This was apparently 'acceptable', Ash had said, and Lina's mum had said yes on condition she call her when she was leaving so she could be waiting outside the deli for her. Lina had told her mum they would be burying the tin in Ash's back garden. She made her mum swear not to tell anyone about their time capsule because they didn't want anyone else to know.

Lina had left the tin box on her desk all yesterday and put it in her rucksack before school that morning. It was only once it got to ten to eleven in the evening that she unearthed the two jewels from under her bed and placed them inside the box before laying it in her favourite *Toy Story* rucksack that her mum had picked up from one of the local charity shops.

Although she wanted to believe that her mother was right about the apocalypse, when she had told Nik his tale was stupid, he had insisted that she was wrong. She wavered and thought it best to leave the jewels in the box just in case they would need them once they had escaped into their cave.

'Catch.'

Lina was shaken from her thoughts by Ash who was dangling his backpack from the ledge. She put the torch on the ground and held out her hands to grab it. Ash turned around and slowly climbed down before jumping off the bench. He crouched like a ninja before springing up.

Lina handed him his bag and he slipped his arms into the straps.

'Do you have the box?' Ash said.

Lina nodded.

'And the spade?'

She stuck her thumb up.

'Then let's go.'

Lina held out her hand and Ash took it. He might be brave enough to climb down from his bedroom window, but Lina doubted he was brave enough to wander the streets in the dark.

Stockland Park was only fifty yards from Ash's home. They had counted the steps and Ash had done some calculations in his head that had baffled Lina, but he reassured her he knew the sums were right. She couldn't understand why he needed to know this, but she went along with it and pretended to understand the maths.

As they got closer to the park gate, Lina heard a loud noise. She flinched before flinging herself at Ash and wrapping her arms around his waist.

'I'm scared,' she whispered. 'I think I heard someone.'

Ash pulled her down beside the iron railings. She buried her head inside his hold and began to shake.

'It's OK,' he said reassuringly. 'There's no one around.'

'Are you sure?' Lina mumbled into his jacket.

He stroked her arm. 'Yes, it's fine, you can open your eyes.'

Lina suddenly remembered that she wasn't a scaredy-cat and pushed back from his embrace before clambering to her feet. 'Oh, I thought I heard somebody following us. I wasn't frightened or anything. I promise.'

'I know,' Ash said, nodding his head. 'It was probably a fox.'

Lina opened the gate and ran towards the playground, forgetting her earlier show of worry. Ash followed behind and soon they came to the section of trees to the left of the swings.

'How about here?' Lina asked, pointing to one of the largest trees in the middle of the clearing.

'Sure,' Ash said.

Lina unzipped her bag and handed Ash the tin box. He took out his letter, which he had also placed in a plastic bag along with some photos and a small strange-looking statue.

'What's that?'

Ash held the figurine up towards Lina and it became more visible in the moonlight. It had many arms and was made of bronze. 'This is Vishna. He is the preserver and the protector of the universe. He will look after us if we survive the apocalypse and will keep us safe when we begin our new life.'

'Oh,' Lina said, nodding even though she really didn't have a clue what Ash was talking about. She hoped he wouldn't start blathering on about karma again as she was struggling to see how any of what they were doing was going to bring them good fortune – stealing, lying, sneaking out after hours. The list of misdemeanours was growing by the hour.

Ash put his precious objects, letter and photos inside and took out a larger box which had a small padlock attached to it. 'This way we can protect everything from thieves. There are two keys – one for you and one for me.'

'Good idea.' Lina beamed at Ash – he really was smart. 'You watch out while I dig,' she said in an authoritative manner.

It took several minutes for Lina to make a deep enough hole. She laid the box inside and covered it up with earth and arranged a few bits of twig and bark over the top. She noticed that Ash wasn't keeping watch at all. He was scribbling on a piece of paper.

'What are you doing?' Lina asked.

'I'm making a map of where we are burying it, otherwise we might never find it again.'

'Oh.' Lina was a little disappointed that she hadn't thought of that. 'Let me see,' she said, snatching it from his hands. She knew from her science lessons at school that this piece of paper was missing some key facts. 'Hmm. Do you have any coloured pens?'

Ash nodded and took out his pencil case. Lina noticed there was a calculator and a tape measure inside. He handed her a red and a green pen.

She took the red one and wrote in capitals at the top.

LINA AND ASH'S SPESHAL MAP.

She underlined it as neatly as she could just as Ash handed her a ruler. She took it and made another, deeper line beneath, but the pen pushed through the paper leaving a hole. She took the green pen next and in smaller letters wrote:

This is the tresure map where we have buried the time capsool.

A loud noise made both of them stop dead.

'I heard someone,' Ash said, his voice quivering.

From deep within the recesses of her bravery chest, Lina took charge. She grabbed the spade and shoved it into her rucksack and hurled the pens and paper into Ash's before grasping his hand and running back towards the gate. It swung back behind them before they increased their pace. Lina didn't relinquish her grip until they had reached Ash's house, slipped down the narrow alleyway to the side of it and shut the garden gate behind them. They were both panting and puffing, and Lina had never felt so alive.

She was Lara Croft – brave and fearless.

She flung her arms around Ash and hugged him as tightly as she could before pulling back.

'That was *so* exciting. Did you think it followed us?' Lina said, the lack of gender reinforcing the fact she believed it was most likely a headless monster.

Ash was still trying to catch his breath – his chest rising and falling rapidly. 'I hope not. My dad will be so angry with me if he finds out what I did.'

'Hey.' Lina gave his shoulder a comforting squeeze. 'He won't find out. Look,' she said, pointing up to his house. 'There are no lights on. You'll be able to sneak back inside. Our plan worked.'

'But what about you? How will you get home? What if it's still out there?'

Lina swallowed away her fear and put her hood over her head. 'I'll use my super invisible powers to get back home.' She smiled broadly and Ash instantly relaxed. A sudden thought popped into Lina's mind. 'This will always be our secret, right?'

Ash nodded. 'When will we dig it up?'

'In twenty years of course, silly.'

'But what if we no longer live here?'

'Of course we will still live here, where else would we be?'

'I don't know. Will we still be friends?' Ash asked hesitantly.

Lina put out her little finger emphatically and Ash grabbed it. 'Best friends forever.'

'And always,' Ash added.

Chapter 8

Now we are twenty-eight

'I'm so glad you came,' Ash said.

'Did you think I would leave you here on your own – looking rather suspicious, if I might add?' I nodded at his rucksack that appeared to have the handle of a shovel sticking out of it.

'How else were you planning on digging the box up?'

I laughed. 'My God, I actually didn't think any of this through.'

I had taken the train home from Nik's and gone to the flat to change into more suitable clothes for our mission. Jeans and a hoodie were also practical for the cooler evening. There had been no inquisition as to why I wasn't staying over at Nik's. He accepted my reasoning – that I wanted to do some interview prep and needed my books which were at the flat. The lie had sat uncomfortably in my stomach or maybe it was the curry sauce from the takeout. I had chewed a couple of Gaviscon in case it was something more serious and taken my medication. The last thing I wanted was to be doubled over in pain in the middle of the park.

Ash opened the gate and we slipped inside, making our way across to the playground – the only illumination from lamps spaced evenly down towards the lake.

'Do you even remember where we buried it?' I said.

'It's a good thing I'm the brains behind this partnership.'

'Hey.' I nudged him.

'What? We all know you're the brawn.'

I flexed my arm, squeezing my eyes from the effort, but it was no use. I spent my life at either the museum or the deli with little time for any sport or going to the gym. 'I don't think so.' I reached out and touched his chest. 'You're still packing at least a four-pack in there somewhere.'

It felt like the most normal thing in the world – to tug his polo shirt as if we were still back at school, making fun of each other.

He playfully slapped my hand away. 'OK, OK. Enough with the teasing. What I meant to say is . . . look what I found.'

He unzipped his rucksack and handed me a piece of paper. I unfolded it and my mouth dropped open. 'You kept this?'

I smoothed my fingers over the childish scrawl of two eight-year-olds, my misspellings which Ash had corrected in another-coloured pen.

'When did you do this?' I said, pointing to the words 'treasure', 'special' and 'capsule'.

'Probably when I got home that night. I don't really remember. But it's the sort of pretentious thing I would've done – ever the perfectionist.'

'Where did you find the map?'

'My parents packed up all my stuff when they moved and left everything in the new loft, and I hunted around this evening and found a box filled with some keepsakes, mementos, special maps for finding buried treasure, that kind of thing.' He smirked. 'And I also have this to open it,' he said, producing a small silver key from the inside pocket of the bag.

'Now when it says "four paces from the gate", do you think we have to do our eight-year-old paces or ...'

'Check out the key at the bottom.'

I laughed at where Ash had measured out the paces in inches. 'You really did think of everything back then.'

He rubbed his hands together and gestured for me to lead the way. 'Shall we?'

We carefully followed the map to the nth degree, veering off the path, the darkness closing in on us. Ash's phone's torch guided the way until we eventually came to a spot by a giant tree. A man out walking his dog in the distance stopped and turned in our direction before moving on. We must have looked like a couple of youths up to no good.

'OK, I think the coast is clear,' Ash said, shifting his gaze around. He reached into his backpack and took out the mini shovel and handed it to me. 'Want to do the honours?'

I nodded, pulling up the sleeves of my hoodie. 'Sure.'

We kneeled on the soil, and I began to dig while Ash pushed the earth to one side.

But the search proved fruitless. Our initial excitement turned to disappointment as it became abundantly clear it wasn't there.

Having dug at least six inches deep in a rectangular shape, I wiped my brow and flopped onto the grass.

'Want me to take over?' Ash asked.

I handed him the shovel. 'Be my guest.'

Ash widened the search area but to no avail.

'Are you sure we have the right spot? It's very dark out here.'

Ash fished out his phone again, the torch illuminating the bark of the tree. After a minute or so he settled upon one patch. 'Look.'

I leaned in to where he was pointing. Etched into the tree trunk were the following characters: A + L 4 EVA.

My heart lurched. 'Did you do this?'

Ash nodded. 'I came back to the park the next day and measured out the paces and marked the spot more accurately. Remember we heard that sound and got freaked out?'

'Honestly, Ash. I don't really remember that much at all.'

'I remember you were really brave.'

'I doubt it.'

'You were. That sound we heard was *so* loud. I was paralysed to the spot. But you grabbed my hand and didn't let go until we got back to my house.'

'That doesn't sound much like me and, honestly, it's been twenty years, I'm amazed you recall precise details.'

He shook his head. 'I confess. I found a diary I had written from around that time. Dad always insisted I write a few sentences every night to improve my writing skills. The entries were mostly about how much I hated the kids in school and how you had taken me under your wing. That night I wrote that it had been the most exciting thing to have ever happened to me and that I wouldn't have been able to get through it if you hadn't dragged me back home before the boogeyman got us.'

'The boogeyman?' I laughed.

'Apparently that's what I thought had followed us.'

'Did you mention in your diary what you wrote in your letter?'

'You mean about our dreams?' he said.

I nodded.

He sat back down beside me, hugging his knees. 'I said you would be a dancer. You were always pirouetting in the corridors at school. I found an earlier entry where I mentioned it.'

I shivered and zipped up my hoodie all the way to my chin then back down again. 'What about you? What did you want to be?' I said, wanting to move on from that declaration.

'I thought I would be the next Gordon Ramsay.' He laughed. 'That was around the time I got that letter about the cooking competition I entered. You came round one day after that night and confronted Dad. I remember the anger my father displayed when you had gone home; the smack he gave me when he read the letter from *Junior MasterChef*.'

I reached out to squeeze his hand. 'I'm sorry, Ash. It's sad how we sometimes remember painful memories and not enough of the happier times.'

A flashback suddenly popped into my mind – a poster, on my brother's wall. A smile slowly crept along my face.

'What?' Ash said. 'You've remembered something?' He leaned his elbow on his propped-up knees.

'Yeah, I think I have. Lara Croft. I think I said I wanted to be Lara Croft.'

'Of the computer-game fame?'

'No, from the movie. Angelina Jolie. My brother was obsessed with her, and he had a poster of her on his wall – it's still there,' I said wistfully. 'The sequel had just come out on DVD, and it was set in Greece. I think Dad and Alex had it on one night and I crept in and watched it with them.' I shook myself from the reverie remembering that I no longer thought of my brother with warm nostalgia.

'I wonder what you thought I would be doing?' Ash said after a beat.

I looked at him – at that face that had been such a big part of my life, a face that I had missed these last few years – and shrugged. 'I'm sorry, I don't remember. Maybe I put chef because of that TV show. And I know you're an excellent cook.'

'Not any more. I haven't even made so much as an omelette in years.'

'You order takeouts all the time?'

'No. I have a housekeeper now. She does all the cooking and the cleaning.'

'Oh, how the other half live,' I said with a teasing tone.

He nudged me. 'I am not "the other half"'. It's normal to have a housekeeper in India. And besides, my working hours are ridiculous. If I didn't have her then I probably wouldn't eat at all.'

'That's a shame.'

'What? Not eating?' he said, deadpan.

'No. That you no longer have time to cook. I remember that incredible meal you made me for my eighteenth.'

'You do?'

I nodded. 'It was that mouth-watering picnic: the samosas and onion bhajis, the mint raita dip. Mmm,' I moaned, remembering how I savoured every morsel. 'You definitely should pick it up again. Cooking, that is.'

'Maybe.' He pulled out a few blades of grass and flicked them away, looking pensive. 'It would've been fun to find the box and read the letters, but I guess it wasn't meant to be.'

He stood suddenly. 'It's getting a little chilly,' he said, rubbing his bare arms, the movement breaking the spell of our reminiscing.

I got up and wiped the earth from my knees and shoved my hands into the back pockets of my jeans.

'So … you're going back to Mumbai tomorrow, huh?'

'Yes. There's nothing else to keep me here.'

'You'll be back again soon?'

'I doubt it. Hopefully Dad's treatment will go well, and my parents will come and visit.' Ash packed the shovel in his backpack and zipped it up.

'And if the treatment doesn't go well?'

He left the question unanswered, and an unwelcome awkwardness descended over us. We walked out of the gate and made our way slowly back to the deli.

'Ash,' I said, holding him by the elbow, not wanting to say goodbye without clearing the air. 'I really am sorry for what happened in Cambridge.'

'It's OK. Old news. I was wrong to take advantage like that and ruin our friendship.'

'No, you didn't. I was the one who ruined it. When I didn't hear from you again, I knew I had hurt you.'

'Our friendship could never be like it was after that night. That night changed everything.'

It had. I thought back to that day and how it ended – the lie that I had told that had sat heavy in my heart for so long. We carried on walking in silence until we reached the deli.

'Why do you still work here?' he said, tapping his fingers on the glass. 'What happened to your dreams of travelling?'

'Things changed. Dad needed me so I had to stay.'

'And he still needs you? You're going to spend your whole life here in Birmingham, running a café and matching grooves in ancient artefacts?'

'And what's wrong with that?' I said, my tone now defensive.

Ash kicked a stone with his foot. 'Isn't everything wrong with it?'

The hairs on my arms stood on end beneath my hoodie. His words shocked me. *So* blunt. Sensing my unease, he changed tack.

'I mean, I understand you feel obliged to stay with your dad—'

'Obliged?' I spat out. 'It has nothing to do with obligation. Dad almost had a heart attack when the deli was robbed seven years ago. This is more than duty. But anyway, you know nothing about obligation. If you did, you wouldn't be running off back to Mumbai when your dad is dying.'

I could tell from Ash's reaction that I had also hit a nerve. 'I'm sorry, that came out wrong.'

'Maybe you're right, but at least I've done something with my life. If I'd stayed here and—'

'And what, started up your own restaurant, you wouldn't have been happy?'

'I didn't mean all those things I said that afternoon in Cambridge. It would've been a big mistake to have not taken up that internship and stay in Birmingham.'

'So, you think I'm the one to have made the mistake? You think I should have left my dad the same way you left your family when they were hurting?'

Ash's look hardened. Another nerve I had hit. But this wound was more raw, judging by his expression. And a wash of regret flooded my face as soon as I had said it.

'Me leaving that internship would've hurt them more. And I did come back for a bit before leaving. Anyway, they're proud of what I do. I make close to a quarter of a million a year, more with bonuses. I earned enough to pay for them to move out of that crumbling home of theirs, I own my own apartment. Couldn't have done any of that if I ran a restaurant.'

He said 'restaurant' with so much disdain. This wasn't the Ash I knew – this was some new version that seemed at odds with the values he used to hold dear.

'OK, I get it. You followed your "dream", and I don't doubt that your fortune makes you and your family very happy. But accept I'm happy here. I'm with the only family I have left. I have a secure and stable job. In fact, I'm even up for promotion on Monday and my chances are good. I might not be Lara Croft, but I'm happy with the choices I have made.'

'And Nik?'

'What about Nik?'

'You and he are … happy?'

I hesitated. 'Yes, we are.'

Ash nodded and absent-mindedly tapped his watch. 'Well … it's been fun reminiscing, but I really should be heading back. My flight is early, and I need some sleep.' He chewed his bottom lip, looking lost. 'Goodbye, Angelina,' he said, not even meeting my gaze.

'Goodbye, Ashok.'

It was childish. The only time we had ever used our full names was when we had been mad at each other, when we were kids – or rather were pretending to be mad. Ash and I had hardly ever fought, and our little-finger promise always ensured we were best friends again a moment later.

Ash headed away, shifting the strap of his rucksack on his shoulder. I watched him go and an emptiness settled deep and low in my chest. Before I went round the back of the deli to the front door of the flat, Ash turned. My heart leapt. Maybe this was the apology; the chance to make up, a promise to stay in touch because I had missed this – the two of us – together, even though we were having a spat.

'Good luck for Monday,' he said. 'I am sure you will get the job you have always dreamed of.'

It was like I had received another punch to the gut. The expression on his face was hard. Did he really want to end it like this?

But there was nothing to end. It had been over for years.

'Ash – wait,' I said, causing him to stop and look over his shoulder.

This was *my* chance, my last chance to tell him why I acted the way I did that night in Cambridge, but the words were lodged somewhere deep in the back of my throat, guarded. It was something I couldn't even put into words myself.

'Have a safe flight,' I said.

And with that sentence uttered, he left.

Chapter 9

'Sweet, sweet, Angelina,' Nik's dad said.

George Markos pulled me into an awkward hug. I say awkward, because I had the boxes of *dolmádes* balancing precariously in my hold as he flung his arms around me and kissed my cheeks.

Each morning when I brought the food order to his insurance firm, he greeted me like a long-lost daughter. And this morning was no exception even though I had only seen him yesterday for brunch at Nik's.

'When will my son make an honest woman out of you?' He clapped his hands together as if he was praying.

And each morning, that very same sentence would spill from his mouth.

He wagged his finger at me. 'You play hard to get, no?'

I smiled sweetly, conscious of the time. I had exactly twenty-five minutes to make it to the museum for my interview. There was no way I could rely on the bus. Usually, Mr Markos liked to chat but this morning I didn't have a minute to spare. I yawned. My evening with Ash had rattled me and it had taken me ages to fall asleep but I needed to park our 'reunion' for now. He was no doubt already in the

air, on his way back to his 'high life' in Mumbai. But his
words had left a sour taste in my mouth.

'We're still very young, Mr Markos,' I said, trying to avoid
getting into a deep discussion.

'No, no. You must call me *petherós*.'

Did I have to? Nik and I weren't married, not even engaged,
so calling him 'father-in-law' didn't seem appropriate.

Nik's dad was always exquisitely turned out: a Pierre
Cardin watch peeking from the sleeve of his Yves Saint
Laurent blue suit. His shoes were no doubt designer too,
always polished. His full head of black hair was sleeked back
with a ton of gel and belied his mid-fifties age. He struck an
imposing figure.

'My Nikki is running late,' he said. 'The traffic is heavy
this morning. Why he doesn't walk, I have no idea. Or
maybe, if he listened to his baba then he would still be living
with us, and he could save his money instead of wasting it
on such a lavish place in the centre of the city. Maybe he
listen to you, Angelina. Tell him. His mother misses him.
We have to book an appointment with him always at the
weekend. I know I see him every day, but it is always
fleeting.'

I knew full well that the last thing Nik would ever want to
do was move back home but I was painfully aware that he
had overextended himself with his mortgage on the flat.
He had called it a necessity whereas I was tempted to agree
with his dad.

Mr Markos peered into one of the boxes and lifted a *dolmá*
out and put it into his mouth. He moaned before licking his

fingers. 'Oh, Angelina. This is as delicious as your mother used to make.'

My smile fell instantly, and a pain thumped in my heart – a jarring throb.

'She was a very special woman.' He cleared his throat and grabbed a tissue from his desk to wipe his fingers.

'Yes, she was,' I said in a whisper.

'Ah, Angelina. I am sorry. I bring you sad thoughts. Please forgive me.' He placed a reassuring hand on my shoulder. 'You know you can always count on me and Maria as a support for you. Please, sit. Let me get you a tea. I am sure Nikki will be here soon and happy to see you.'

He caught the attention of his secretary.

'Please don't think me rude,' I said. 'But I have a very important meeting at work. I don't have time for tea.'

'Yes, yes, of course,' he said, waving his secretary away. 'I understand. You are very driven, I like that. You are good for my son. I fear he drifts in and out.' He wriggled his hand like a fish swimming against the tide. 'I know you are a positive influence. Please be patient with him. His head is in the clouds, but he cares for you a lot.'

The note of affection filled me with warmth. 'I know. He's one of the good guys and I love him very much.'

This response seemed to please Mr Markos and he retreated to his desk. 'Don't worry, I will get my secretary to take the food to the kitchen. You go. And remember, if you ever need to talk, you know me and Maria are here for you.'

I placed the food down and left, relieved that I had avoided any further interrogation about my relationship with Nik.

No one would understand. It suited us and that was all that mattered.

Two hours later, I was stood on the steps to the museum, my arms buckling under the strain of holding a box full of stationery, books and other crap that I had emptied from my locker. Seven years of my working life boxed up. Seven years.

'Lina.' Greer's voice from behind made me turn. She ran up to me, took one look at my face and grabbed the box before it slipped from my grasp. She put it down on the ground and held onto my hands, rubbing feeling into them.

'What the hell happened in there? I was just finishing off a tour, came back to our desk and someone had licked it clean.'

I was focused on the road in the distance: fumes belching from a passing truck, the horn of an impatient car, a swarm of children crossing – their excited chatter unable to be silenced by the harassed-looking chaperones; Greer's school group, no doubt, filled with excitement at what they had seen and heard from her lecture. A school tour. Something I would never conduct again.

'Earth to Lina,' Greer said. 'Hey.' She shook my arms a little and I broke out of my fog. Her face was filled with concern, lips pinched tight.

'They … let me go,' I said in almost a whisper, searching her eyes.

'What? Why?'

My legs felt wobbly, and I reached out and grabbed Greer's arm for support. She pulled me down, so we were sitting on the steps.

'I got there on time. I was ready; prepared to answer any question they had. But it wasn't even Brian doing the interviewing. They sent some guy up from London. I had no clue who he was. But he sat there looking through some papers, said this was no longer an interview and had I not got the memo on Saturday. I had no clue what he was talking about. He kept apologising and talking about budget cuts, restraints, hands tied … I, I wasn't really listening because he began by saying straight off that they were making me redundant.'

'Whaaaat? They can't do that. Can they?'

I nodded. 'They already have. Seven weeks' full pay. One week for every year of service.'

'But you're the best on the team.'

'Not according to them I'm not. They've got someone coming over from Germany – someone with a masters in conservation. "Lucky to have found him," he said. He has a vision, apparently. I didn't even know I needed one of those. But what I do know now is they don't have a budget to hire him and keep me on, so they went with him. They didn't even give me a chance to argue my case as to why they should promote me.'

'Shit. I don't know what to say. What are you going to do?'

I shrugged. 'No idea.'

The distant chime of the church clock rang out around us. Eleven o'clock. I should be working, not sitting on the steps with my museum pass rescinded.

'Listen,' Greer said. 'I have to get back, but …' she flung her arms around me, her Afro tickling my face '… you're gonna figure things out. Maybe this is for the best. This could be the start of something big in your life. There are other museums out there.'

But there's only one in Birmingham that I'm qualified to work at ... or so I thought.

She leaned in and kissed me on the cheek. 'Today will drag majorly without you.'

'Do me a favour, Greer.'

'Sure, anything.'

'Find that piece and make it line up before this guy comes over from Germany and figures it out.'

She nodded. 'I'll do my best. And then I will give all the credit to you, and they'll have to rehire you. You're gonna be fine.' She gave me a reassuring pat on the arm.

In return, I gave her a brief 'I'll be OK' smile which crumbled as soon as she left.

As the bus pulled away from Aston station, winding its way towards Stockland Green, I leaned the side of my head on the glass and scrolled through the job alerts for museum positions. As I suspected, most of them were for roles outside the West Midlands. And there was no way I could move to London. I could never leave Dad. I had made a promise to stay close after the robbery and it was a promise I planned to keep.

A Closed sign was on the front door when I arrived at the deli and the lights were off. How strange, I thought. I placed the box of my work possessions on the pavement and peered through the window, cupping my hands against the glass.

Dad was slumped in a chair with his back to me. I twisted the handle, and it was locked. Dad didn't move. A wash of panic flooded my body. I banged my fist on the glass and thankfully the noise roused him, and I let out the breath I had held in my throat.

He muttered to himself as he came over to unlock the door.

'Baba, what's happened?' I asked, shoving my box inside the entrance.

He turned and raised his hands to the ceiling. 'Tax, tax, tax.'

'What about tax?'

He put his hand to his forehead and paced the floor, muttering again, in Greek. My knowledge was of a reasonable standard, though without much opportunity to practise it, I often struggled to comprehend what Dad was saying, especially when he spoke fast and under his breath.

Beads of sweat began to coat his forehead and he reached into the pocket of his apron and took out his handkerchief and mopped his brow.

'Baba, come and sit down,' I said, coaxing him back to his chair. 'I'll get you some water and you can tell me what has happened.'

I ran the cold tap and filled a glass, noticing the chopping board had been abandoned mid slice of cucumber.

I pulled out the chair beside him and handed him the drink. He clutched it tightly, shaking his head.

'Take your time, Baba.'

He took a few tentative sips and laid the glass gently back on the table. 'A man came here this morning. He said he was from the tax office. He says he try and reach me by the internet and then the phone. I explain that the computer is not working now and that often I am busy in the deli, and the answer machine upstairs ...' He swallowed hard.

I knew what he couldn't say. The message box was full. Neither of us could bring ourselves to wipe it clean so new messages could be stored. There was one message fifteen years old that we could *never* erase. I knew Dad still listened to it.

I reached over and patted his hand. 'Go on, Baba,' I encouraged him.

'There was a tax hole, and we didn't fill it. It has been accumulating for several years. I thought everything was fine with the accounts. I check them myself, but now they want the deficit cleared. They say they already give us plenty of warning. Apparently, there were even letters, but I don't know what I did with them. Usually when I receive mail from them, I file the correspondence away ready to read them in the new year. I don't know what happened, Angelina. I thought I understood but I don't. And now ... now they close us until we pay.'

'Close,' I repeated as if I hadn't fully understood what he was saying.

'Yes. The deli is closed now. We owe the tax people ten thousand.'

'Ten thousand!' I screeched, causing Dad to sit upright. 'I'm sorry. I didn't mean to say that so loudly.'

'No, no. You are right to be shocked. It is a large sum of money. Money we do not have.'

'What are we going to do?'

'I have been sitting here for two hours, thinking. Thinking hard. My dear child. My sweet, sweet Angelina.' He released his grip on the glass and held my hands. 'You have been by my side for many, many years. You haven't taken a break in so long. Every morning you rise before the dawn to help me. Maybe this is a good thing, maybe it is time for us to stop.'

I pulled my hands away. 'Stop running the deli? But we can't,' I said, a little more harshly than I intended. 'I mean, we have to fight, we can't let them take the business from us. You have been running it for over thirty years. How will we live?'

'But you have your job, your future ahead of you, you will be fine.'

I slipped down further into my chair. 'Not any more.'

'*Paidí mou*. My dear. What happened? You didn't get the job?'

I shook my head. 'They gave it to someone else and, even worse, they said they couldn't afford to keep me on.'

He shuffled his chair closer and placed his arm around my shoulder. I sank into his embrace and choked back a sob. Stroking my arm, he repeated the phrase '*óla tha páne kalá*'. But would it all be OK?

'I made a decision,' he said.

I sniffed and sat up looking at his face – his kind face that appeared more weathered in the gloom of the deli.

'I spoke to our Alexi,' he said.

'You did what?'

He placed the palm of his hand out towards me, silencing my protest. 'Angelina, please. Hear me first. He cares a lot for you and for me.'

I let out a sound resembling a snort.

'He wants me to go and see him, to take a break. Maybe he can help us.'

'We don't need his help.'

'Why you always have to be so hard with him? He has said sorry, why you not forgive him?'

'I don't need to hear his pathetic apologies. And we don't need his help.'

'Please. I am tired. I think a break would be good for me. And I have never been to LA. I haven't seen my son in so many years.'

'And whose fault is that?'

'He has tried to get us to fly to be with him, but always we haven't been able to go. Come with me. Alexi said he would pay for both our tickets. Imagine it, the family back together. It is not anyone's fault that we have been apart for so long. Please, *ángelé mou*. I have found it in my heart to forgive what happened. I should have handled the situation better. It is my fault he left and now I have a chance to make amends. I leave on Wednesday.'

'Wednesday?' I said, my mouth dropping open.

'Yes. Alexi has already booked my ticket. Just say the word and he will book for you too. He paints such a lovely picture of this Malibu life. The ocean, the sand. I think I need the break.'

I picked at the ridges in my fingers – where the skin was peeling from making the *dolmádes*. It was puckered like I had sat in a bath too long.

A thought hit me. My morning routine.

'I can't go. I have to make the order for Mr Markos.'

Dad shook his head. 'We can't. We have to cease trading. This is what the man said.'

'But what if we can't pay?'

'Then we close permanently.'

'Can we not pay in instalments? I have saved some cash. Surely there is a way to do a payment plan. And I have my redundancy package. That could pay a part of it.'

'I missed that opportunity because of my stupidity.'

Dad's face reddened and he clenched his fist. I noticed for the first time that the wrinkles etched into his skin appeared deeper, his eyes sadder.

'No, Baba. You were not stupid. I should have been around more. Helped you.'

He waved away my words. 'You do enough already. Such a kind girl, so good to her baba. But no, I cannot take your money. That is for you to figure out your next steps.'

'My next steps are here, fighting for our livelihood.'

'Please, Angelina.' He grasped my fingers. 'I have wanted to go to LA for a while now. I miss my son. I believe things happen for a reason. Come with me, we can sort this out as a family.'

Family. My only family was sat right in front of me. And the reason why it was like this was because of me. It was my fault it was only the two of us.

The circles under Dad's eyes appeared darker, his hands in mine more weathered. I had tried to protect him for so long, but I hadn't been able to this time.

'I think you're right,' I said finally. 'You need a break. Go to LA. But I need to stay here. I have to look for a new job and

I can study the accounts, all the paperwork, and maybe talk to the tax office, see if there is a way to pay back in instalments. We can't let them take the deli away from us. I promise this will all be sorted by the time you return.'

He patted my hand, a hesitant smile creeping over his face. 'I don't expect you to fix everything, Angelina. Remember that.'

No. That's not what I wanted him to say. I wanted him to stay. With Dad away, it would be my first-time home alone, no job, no deli, no purpose. Those thoughts crowded my mind and left me cold. I had been running away from the silence for too long and I wasn't ready to face it.

Chapter 10

I sipped my black coffee as I headed back upstairs to the flat – the local newspaper nestled in my arm.

I had taken Dad to Birmingham Airport this morning, helped him manage his luggage and stayed with him up until the departures gate. Tears had streamed down his face and mine as we hugged goodbye. As soon as I had returned to the flat it hit me – the silence. It was deafening.

I laid the newspaper on the kitchen table and flicked to the local job ads. Accountant. Chef. Nope, nope. Housekeeper? Hmm. I had spent the last fifteen years keeping house – I didn't really want to do that for someone else.

What did I want to do, then? Aside from my archaeology degree from Birmingham University and seven years employment at the Museum & Art Gallery, I had no other work experience, no other qualifications. Maybe instead of rushing headlong into something else, I could use the redundancy money to take my time and figure everything out.

Closing the pages of the newspaper, I headed to the living room. The wooden cabinet sat in the corner, where Dad said he kept all the paperwork relating to the deli. I suppose now was as good a time as any to try and make sense of the tax issue.

Nik had offered to pay the fee. He had wrapped his arms around me, cocooned me in his strong hold and told me everything would be OK. But I couldn't accept such a large handout from him. He was in enough debt as it was. His dad would no doubt offer to step in once he heard the deli had closed and I was unemployed. I had lost count of the times he had told me he would always be there to support me. It was almost as though he felt he had to – like he owed me something. But I didn't want to be put in that position. Dad and I would sort it out. There had to be a way.

Dad had told me he kept the key to the cabinet in the kitchen drawer. A lift, twist and pull motion made it fly open and I fell backwards onto the floor as a cascade of papers poured out on top of me.

'Oh, Dad,' I exclaimed into the silence as envelope after envelope containing official letters scattered around me, some with 'final reminder' plastered over them. 'Why didn't you let me help you?' I whispered into the empty room.

Numbers, spreadsheets, tax jargon. It would take me ages to make sense of all this. Maybe I should call Nik, and we could go through it together. But no. He was at work. The only other person I knew who was good with anything business-related was Ash. I sank back onto my knees. Ash would know instantly what to do with this mess, how to help. He had always been there for me until I screwed everything up. It was all my fault, no matter what he had said the other day when we met.

An hour later I had several piles of paper in year and date order. I clipped each one and stacked them on top of each other and slipped them into a large envelope. Maybe I could drop them at Nik's office and see if he could make sense of it. The only other option was to pay for an advisor. Maybe that would be a better use of my redundancy money.

As I went to lock up the chest, curiosity got the better of me and I opened one of the little drawers at the back. A pungent smell of flowers and musk filled the space around me. Inside lay a collection of perfume samples. Mum's perfume samples. Dad had kept them, all of them. She occasionally bought fashion magazines for the deli customers to read. But she loved to keep hold of the samples of perfume that came inside some of the advertising spreads. Now, I wondered why she kept them. She never got dressed up and went out – she had dedicated her whole life to working at the deli.

I brought one to my nose and closed my eyes. Nothing. No nostalgic feelings wrapped me in warmth. This wasn't her scent. It evoked nothing in me. I went to put the samples inside the drawer and noticed something wedged into the back of it. It was a notebook; leather-bound with the initials ES in the corner in gold leaf. The edges were bent, and it was wrapped with an elastic strap. I opened it and began to read.

Why did this writing look familiar?

A thought popped into my head. I went over to the fridge. One precious piece of paper was stuck on the white surface with the recipe for the *dolmádes'* cooking broth. My heart pounded in my ears, drowning out the silence. It was Mum's writing. I turned my attention back to the notebook. The year stamp on the first page placed Mum in her mid-twenties. In fact, this would have been the year when she and Dad decided to move to England, to start a new, more prosperous life. Only it hadn't turned out that way. Dad never talked much about their life before they came here; he always said it was too painful and I had never pushed for a reason. And it had never occurred to me to ask Mum because I was only young when she died.

I had no clue how long I sat there reading, absorbing the words, struggling to make sense of it all. Pins and needles fizzed in my feet. I changed position several times, not daring to move away from the spot I was in.

As I turned the last page, my mouth dropped open wide. There was only one place I had to go. I stood and wobbled, grabbing hold of the side of the sofa to steady myself until blood flowed back into my limbs.

The door to my parents' bedroom creaked as I peered in. It felt wrong to be here. Dad always kept the door closed. Inside, it was like she had never died. Neither of us had gone through Mum's things. Her creams and hairbrush still sat on the dressing table; her clothes still hung in the closet.

And that's where I went. The large oak wardrobe – a key nestled in the hole. It had to be locked otherwise the doors wouldn't stay shut. Dad had bought the piece of furniture at a flea market for less than twenty quid because it had this defect. He always moaned at the extravagance of rich people who would choose to get rid of something so beautiful only because you needed to lock it.

A swift turn allowed the doors to spill open. There were Mum's clothes taking up two thirds of the wardrobe with Dad's trousers and shirts hung in the rest. I had camped out in here many times in that first year after she died, thinking I could stay close to her.

I didn't really know what I was looking for, but the journal talked about some jewels that belonged to a necklace. I vaguely remembered a box Mum used to keep all her jewellery in and I could have sworn it was in here.

Pulling out folded tops and jumpers revealed nothing. Where was it? Had I imagined it? I closed the wardrobe and checked the chest of drawers. No box. The bedside tables contained only books and medicines. There was only one other place in this room it could be – under the bed.

I lifted the valance and coughed as dust balls flew out. There were countless boxes – each one containing Mum's old shoes: her slippers that she put on when she came up to the flat after a long day at the deli, her comfortable sandals and sensible heels with only half-an-inch wedge. I was no longer able to crawl underneath like Dad said I always did, but my arm was long enough to stretch. My fingers grazed over something wooden, and I repositioned myself so I could get a finger to it; then two, before my whole hand was in reach of it.

I wiped the layer of dust off and saw those same initials as the ones on the journal – ES. Holding a breath in my chest, I opened it. I rummaged through earrings and necklaces but there were no jewels. Where could she have kept them?

The story of how these treasures had come to light had my head in a spin. Mum had been on an archaeological dig and found them, but no one believed her discovery: three precious stones purported to be from a Phoenician necklace.

It didn't make any sense. Why wouldn't they believe her? The diary entries had relayed in some detail the painstaking lengths she had gone to in order to unearth them. But what had happened after she made the discovery? I returned to the notebook to see if there were any more clues.

The last words she had written were 'I'm going to confront Elias.'

I sat down on the sofa. Who was Elias? Perhaps he was on the dig with her. It was then that I noticed something. I closed the notebook and held it up to inspect it. Yes. There were missing pages. Had Mum torn them out or had someone else done it?

Goose pimples rippled up my arms. Unearthing my phone, I typed the words 'Cyprus archaeological dig Phoenician necklace' into my search bar. The first result that popped up was an article from a French journal. I copied and pasted it into Google Translate and slowly read the English version. There had been a significant discovery of a tomb thirty-two years ago. Many artefacts had been found. It listed each object in detail: five solid-gold lunate-shaped earrings, several signet rings – and there! A necklace. Fourteen beads had been unearthed. There had been some speculation as to whether there were some missing, but these claims had been dismissed.

At the bottom of the article was a picture of a man – his hair dark, peppered with grey, thick creases lining his eyes as he grinned broadly holding up one of the artefacts. Under his picture was the name Elias Demetriades.

I reread the article and the countless references listed at the bottom of the journal entry. No mention of Mum. Other members of the team were highlighted and thanked. It was as if she hadn't even been there. At the top of the page was the date it was penned: the year after Mum's diary had been written.

I typed in the name of the site and found some more information. It was open with a small museum next to it as well as a new excavation site established, but it was now in financial difficulty. I scrolled down and sat bolt upright as I read the final sentence.

Volunteers needed to continue this valuable work before its forced closure.

A loud noise startled me. It was only the bins being collected by the refuse truck. They always wheeled the large communal bins from the back of the deli and the noise made the windows of the flat shake.

My mind whirred. Mum was an archaeologist. Her name not immortalised. It all seemed so unfair. What could I do? I had to share this with someone, but who? Dad was away and I knew he never liked talking about the past.

I scrolled to Nik's name.

'Hey, what's up?' he said after a few rings. I heard a rustle of papers.

'Sorry, I know you're working.'

'Not a problem. Shoot.'

I filled him in on what I had unearthed: the notebook, the dig, the discovery.

'Woah, your mum had this secret past life. How cool is that?'

'Yes, but why keep it all hush-hush? Why no credit for her findings? Seems so unfair. I really wish I could go and find out what happened.'

'Go to Cyprus and play detective?' He gave a half laugh.

'Yeah, stupid, huh? I mean it's not like I've got the money to be splurging on a frivolous trip abroad with the deli in so much debt.'

'But your dad said he wouldn't accept your redundancy money. I say go for it.'

'Really?'

'Could be fun. Don't worry about the tax stuff. It'll all come good.'

I sighed. I wished I had half of Nik's optimistic outlook and devil-may-care attitude to money. Archaeology jobs in Birmingham also didn't drop from the sky and the weight of unemployment would sit heavy on my shoulders until I had resolved that issue. But ... would this always haunt me if I didn't at least try and find out what happened to Mum all those years ago?

'Would you come with me?' I asked hesitantly. 'For ... moral support.'

'I'd love to. It'd be a blast. When were you thinking of going?'

I took in the sweep of the flat. There was a stillness, an unnerving silence. I hated being on my own. 'Tomorrow,' I said boldly.

'What?' Nik screeched. 'Lina, some of us have jobs.'

His words stung.

'Sorry, I didn't mean to be so blunt, but I can't go with such little notice. I've also got that three-day insurance seminar starting Monday that Dad's roped me into. He'd kill me if I bailed.'

'I understand. It was a stupid idea anyway.'

'Look, Lina. I gotta go. I have a meeting about to start. My advice? Nothing's stopping you from going. I'll miss you like crazy, but you won't be gone long, right?'

'Probably a week.'

'So, I'll only miss my girl for one weekend. Text me. Keep me posted.'

He hung up and there it was again. Silence.

Barely moments later, my mobile buzzed in my hand, and I stilled when I saw his name. Ash. He had given me his new number that night in the pub in case I wasn't able to meet at Stockland Park. The message was brief.

Sorry. What more can I say? Call me if you want. I'll understand if not.

My finger hovered over the receiver symbol.

'Lina?' His voice had traces of surprise and bewilderment and I sank into the sofa as it washed over me.

'Hey,' I mustered.

'It's so good to hear from you. I was such a jerk to say those things to you. I'm sorry.'

I tucked my feet under me. 'You have nothing to be sorry about. I said things I regretted too.'

'It certainly wasn't the reunion I had dreamed of,' he said.

A lump formed in my throat. He had been dreaming of it.

'Hey, how did the interview go? I'm sorry I said all that crap about it not being what you wanted to do with your life.

I had no right to pass any judgement when I don't really have a clue about your life these last seven years. I just got so caught up in the emotion of looking back to when we were little.'

'It's fine, Ash.'

'So ... you're a curator now?'

'No. I didn't get it.'

'Oh, no. I'm sorry.'

'And what's worse, I got made redundant.'

'Can they do that?'

'They already did. I got seven weeks' paid leave and came home to find the deli closed down because Dad hadn't stayed on top of the accounts, and we owe ten thousand.'

I heard him take a sharp intake of breath. 'That sucks. What are you going to do?'

I stared at the ceiling – water stains in one corner and peeling wallpaper in another – and wondered the very same thing.

'I don't know. Dad left for LA today to see Alex. I couldn't quite believe it. He's never travelled abroad since he moved to England and then in a moment he was gone, no second thoughts.'

'And you're alone now? In the flat, I mean.'

'Yes, I am.' I shivered and went back into my bedroom to grab a cardigan before sitting down on my bed. 'I thought I'd make a start on organising Dad's accounts. Nik said he would take a look at them.'

'Oh.' His tone was measured.

'Only I stumbled across something. It's probably nothing, but ... it reminded me a little of what we talked about the other day.'

'Sounds intriguing. What was it?'

I leaned back onto my headboard. 'A journal. It was my mum's. I found it buried in that locked cabinet in the living room that I never knew how to open. It was shut in a drawer.'

'Did you read it?'

'I did. I can't believe it, Ash. My mum was an archaeologist. She made this incredible discovery – a Phoenician tomb filled with ancient artefacts – but there's no record of her involvement anywhere online. It looks like some pages have been torn from the journal too. None of it adds up. I wish you were here to read it.'

'Me too. Perhaps you could screen-shot some pages and send them to me. I'll have time tonight to look over them if you want?'

'Hmm.' A thought was scratching at the back of my mind, desperate to break free. Jewels. Ash and me and the time capsule. And that's when it hit me.

'The box!' I cried, sitting up.

'What box?'

'The one we hid in the park. It had two jewels in it.' Her diary had mentioned three stones so where was the third one? 'How could I have been so stupid to put them inside the box?'

I slapped my hand on my forehead, cursing myself. Why hadn't I asked Mum? There would have been a straight, direct answer. No.

'Don't beat yourself up, Lina. You weren't to know. We were only eight. I'm not surprised you'd forgotten. I only remembered details of that night because of what I wrote in my journal and finding that map. Can't believe your mum was an archaeologist. Do you think that's why you wrote you wanted to be Lara Croft?'

'Maybe. But I don't recall her ever telling me that's what she was. Since we went down to the park on Friday, I've been having these flashbacks to that time. They're like parts of a puzzle but there are still so many missing pieces. And I just wish we had found it now. What if I had written something about her in my letter? As the years have gone by, she's slipped further from my memory, and I thought that maybe the box could have brought me closer to her.'

I could hear Ash breathing deeply down the line. If I closed my eyes, it would feel like he was there, beside me. And suddenly I wished to God he was.

'What are you going to do now?' he asked. 'Are you going to talk to your dad?'

'I don't want him to know that I've been snooping around his private things.'

'He might be able to fill you in on what happened around the time before they left Cyprus.'

'Dad will never want to talk about it. Every time I bring up Mum's name, he folds in on himself. I can't do that to him – bring him more pain.'

My eyes wandered across my room. I had slept here my entire life. Aside from spending a few holidays camping on the Welsh coast and one night a week at Nik's since my early twenties, this was the only room I knew. I had changed the decor as I had grown older, but one poster remained from my childhood – the map of the world. I stood up and went to stand in front of it. The tabs over countries that I had never visited were curled at the edges. I focused on one particular country.

'I want to go,' I said with more certainty.

'Where?'

'To Cyprus. I want to find out what happened all those years ago. When I was researching the site, it said they were looking for volunteers to help maintain the dig before it was closed down.'

'Maybe this is your chance to be Lara Croft.'

'Maybe it is. Would you come with me?' I let the words tumble out of my mouth before I had a second to change my mind. 'I'm not sure I'm brave enough to do this by myself.'

'Sure, you are. You're the bravest person I know.'

'Not any more. Perhaps I was once.'

But everything changed fifteen years ago.

Chapter 11

When we were thirteen

I stared at my reflection in the mirror and wrinkled my nose. My fringe was at the annoying stage of being long enough that it dragged across my eyes, all scratchy and in the way, but not long enough to be tucked behind my ears. It would take a ton of hairspray to ensure it stayed slicked back for the big event on Friday.

Wriggling out of my dungarees, I slid on the pink sequined dress that Mum had found in Oxfam and adjusted. The sparkly jewels caught the light from my bedside-table lamp, and I twirled round and round, each time striking a pose as I faced the mirror on the front of my wardrobe.

'Lina,' Mum's voice called from outside my room as she knocked gently. 'Nik is here.'

'Coming,' I hollered back. I stretched down to pick up a CD from the floor and heard a ripping sound. Reaching to my side, I felt my skin through a massive hole. *No, no, no.*

'Mum!' I screamed.

She opened the door. 'You don't need to shout; I'm right here. Oh, *ángelé mou*. You look beautiful.'

'But I got a hole in it.' My bottom lip pouted. 'I promise I didn't mean for it to happen. I am so sorry.'

Mum leaned in and tugged at the fabric, tutting. 'I wish you would take more care. I'll stitch it up later.' Her tone was measured but I knew she was mad.

'I wanted to practise our routine wearing it. Can't you fix it now?'

'Angelina Georgiades, the world does not revolve around you. I have much preparation to do for the Markos party tonight.' Mum came into my room and picked up some clothes off the floor. She huffed as she did so, mumbling under her breath in Greek. These events always stressed Mum out, but she had to do them because they brought in extra cash.

The Markos family was always hosting parties. It didn't matter, though, because I loved going there and sneaking to Nik's room to watch movies all evening. His parents never checked on us and Mum was always too busy catering to notice what we were doing. Sometimes, I even crashed overnight which meant Nik and I could stay up as late as we wanted.

'Please learn to tidy your room, Lina. It's a mess. You can't have Nik in here.'

'Sorry, Mum.' I eased out of my costume and handed it to her before rummaging in my chest of drawers for a pair of black leggings and a sweatshirt.

I pirouetted out of my bedroom, checking my posture in the mirror as I left, chanting 'one, two, three'. Nik was hovering in the corner of the living room, wearing his Nike tracksuit. There were mud stains on it.

'Eww,' I said in disgust. 'Didn't you go home and shower before coming here?'

Nik nudged his glasses. 'I didn't have time. You said four sharp. My game only finished half an hour ago.' He shifted uncomfortably.

'Did you win?' I asked, not really caring for the answer.

Nik's shoulders slumped and he shook his head. He had only just joined Stockland's football team as part of the B-squad. Mr Barnes – our PE teacher – had seen him dribbling a ball in the playground and asked him to try out. But the other guys on the team had been giving him a hard time. Still, I didn't care for the football team. I only had one goal in my mind: winning the Stockland Come Dancing competition. When one of our other PE teachers announced the event, I had been desperate to enter. It was based on a show on the BBC called *Strictly Come Dancing*. Each week, a handful of celebrities danced with professionals and competed against each other, hoping to win the favour of the public to go on to the next round. Every Saturday night, I stared transfixed at the TV – my face almost pressed up against the screen. All the dresses, the glamour, the movement, the golden glitter balls lighting the stage. There was nothing else in the world that I wanted to do but be crowned champion of our school's version of the show.

There was stiff competition for the prize. Emily Walters. Year Eight's most popular girl. She was not only beautiful, with sweetcorn-coloured hair and light blue eyes, but she had been taking dance classes outside school since she was six. But I had been watching the episodes of the show on repeat since it finished airing last month. I knew the ten steps of the cha-cha, the slow, quick quick sequence of the foxtrot, and knew Nik and I could win it with sharp movements of the tango as well as my splits at the end of the dance.

'I suppose it doesn't matter if you're dirty,' I said, giving Nik another once-over. 'Mum needs to fix my dress anyway, so I'll have to practise in this.' I pinched my 'Dream Big' jumper before nudging the sofa to one side. 'Can you give me a hand?' I said, my voice strained.

Nik helped me push back all of the furniture to increase our practice space. It would have been so much easier to rehearse at Nik's, but he said his parents didn't want us under their feet while they were preparing for their big party this evening. Mum said I couldn't go with her tonight but hadn't given me a reason, so we would only have this afternoon and tomorrow to make sure all our moves were perfectly in sync as Nik was busy in the week.

I pulled out the CD for our dances and slipped it into our sound system. Grabbing Nik's hand, I put my other one on his waist and began counting out loud. Feet shoulder width apart, knees slightly bent, our arms locked in a perfect circle. The first time, he stepped on my foot; the second take, his right arm was limp.

Letting out an audible huff, I went to turn off the CD player. 'What's the matter with you?' I said with my hands on my hips. 'You're not concentrating.'

'I'm tired, Lina. Been running around a pitch for an hour and a half. Surely, we can just wing it on the night. I promise I'll raise my game for the real thing.' He flicked his hair out from his eyes – their green colour enlarged by the frames of his glasses.

'We can't afford to "wing it", Nik. Emily and Will have been meeting after school every day in an actual dance studio and there's a rumour that they're getting private lessons too.' I pouted. 'So unfair.' Pulling up my sleeves, I shook out my limbs. 'Come on,' I said, my chin lifted high. 'We can do this. We can beat them fair and square without professional help.'

I pressed Play again and this time Nik focused harder. We glided around the room, and I felt my heart soar.

A muffled laugh made me miss a step. My brother was in the doorway smirking as he watched us. I immediately dropped Nik's hand.

'Go away, Alex.'

'Nah, I'm having too much fun watching you lame weirdos thinking you can dance. You look so gay, Nik. Can't believe my sister roped you into this.'

'Agh,' I said, moving over to where he was standing and putting my hands on his chest; trying but failing to push him out of the room. 'You're so annoying. Go!' But it was no use. His six-foot-two frame was too big to shove. Mum said he was still growing as he wasn't yet eighteen, but not far off.

'I'm not going anywhere,' he said, his arms folded. 'I need the living room.'

'Why?'

'I gotta run through my lines.'

'Can't you do that in your bedroom?'

'Nope. I need to do the movements as well as the speech. Dad said I could have the run of the flat, so beat it.'

'That's so unfair.'

'Get used to it, squirt.'

'Dad!' I hollered.

'He's down at the deli, you loser. He can't hear you.'

'Mum!'

'She's there with him, getting ready for the party.'

'Then I'm going downstairs to tell them.' I tried to sidestep him, but he moved to block me.

'You're such a squealer and anyway I know what they'll say. My play is ten times more important than your pissy little dance competition. There's going to be scouts at my opening night. You'll see. Once I'm discovered, I'm outta this hellhole.'

Acting was Alex's life. He had been taking drama lessons every Saturday morning for three years ever since he landed the lead role in the school's production of *Grease*. Alex's Danny Zuko was the talk of the school for months – his face proudly displayed outside the drama department. Once his A levels were over this summer, he was planning on going to acting college.

Alex's lessons were the reason why I couldn't dance outside school. Mum and Dad had been saving hard to get him those classes. My dancing obsession was only a passing phase, they said. I wanted to prove them wrong. I wanted them to see that I had talent too, and that dancing lessons might mean I could become a professional one day.

I squared up to Alex the best I could, but he was intimidating – his large frame looming down over me.

'Lina, it's OK,' Nik said, grabbing my hand and pulling me back. 'I gotta go anyway. Mum and Dad wanted me to help out tonight and I should go home and change.'

'But we gotta practise.'

Alex repeated my words, imitating my hand gestures and putting on a high-pitched voice.

'Argh,' I squealed, slapping him hard on his chest. 'Stop being so mean.'

Alex held my wrist in a vice-like grip to stop me from hitting him again. 'God, you're so annoying. Go, will ya. Your boyfriend wants to get the hell out of here, so why don't you be a good little girl and listen to him.'

My cheeks flushed and I pulled my hair behind my ears, hoping Nik hadn't seen the effect Alex's words had on me. I pushed past him with renewed strength, taking the steps down to the deli two at a time. I burst into the kitchen to see Mum and Dad shouting at each other. I cowered behind the doorframe and tried to listen to what they were saying. The words 'debt' and 'obligation' came from Mum's lips while Dad talked about 'distrust'.

A customer came in – their heated discussion over in a heartbeat. Warm smiles replaced the frowns on their faces, arms flung open in their typical Greek Cypriot welcome.

I had no clue what their argument was about, but it didn't look like the right time to add to their worries. Maybe the deli was in trouble. Maybe there wouldn't be any money for dance lessons even if we did win. It was all so unfair. I had never wanted anything so much in all my life, but it was always Alex that came first. I hated him. Hated him with all my guts.

The next afternoon, I rang the buzzer to Nik's house on Dover Street. It was the biggest one, with an electric gate and a large forecourt, and had the perfect view of Stockland Park. From Nik's bedroom in the roof, he could see all the way to the pond. He sometimes let me use his binoculars when I came round so we could spy on people.

The Markoses' housekeeper answered the door and spoke to me in Greek. I only wished I could understand what she said. The Saturday lessons were so hard, and I spent most of them wishing I was at the dance studio – the same one Emily went to.

Agatha always spoke fast too. I found if I smiled with both rows of teeth on show, I could get away with saying nothing and letting her pinch my cheeks instead. Nik's Greek was as bad as mine though he had taught me every rude word there was. That test I could ace.

But this time Agatha didn't greet me with her usual sunny smile and embrace. The lines on her forehead were deep and she was clutching her Saint Michael the Archangel charm on her necklace before bringing it to her lips.

'What's the matter?' I said.

'It is Nikolas. Come, come.'

I wiped my feet on the mat, trailing my dance bag as I went inside. Through the open double doors, I could see his parents crowding around the sofa. As I came nearer, Nik was lying down wrapped in blankets, his arm in a sling. My mouth dropped open.

'Hey,' Nik said a little sheepishly when he saw me cowering behind his folks.

His mother was stroking his hair. 'Angelina, my dear. See my poor Nikki.'

'What happened?' I came a little closer as Nik's dad stepped to one side.

'These boys,' Nik's dad bellowed, and I took a tentative step backwards. His face was plum-coloured. *Tsantisménos*, Nik would say. Pissed off.

I caught Nik's eyes and raised my eyebrows, waiting for an explanation.

'It was just a bad tackle. I sprained my wrist. We just got back from the hospital.'

His mum continued to stroke his hair. 'Why you play this violent sport, my son?'

'Because he needs to toughen up, Maria,' Nik's dad said, flinging his arms in the air before slapping them by his side. 'And now he will be out of action for at least three months.' He muttered under his breath in Greek as he went off to his study and I knew more swear words were uttered.

'I will leave you both for a minute,' Nik's mum said, fluffing the cushions behind his head. 'But Nikolas needs to rest.' Her expression I read as 'don't outstay your welcome'.

I watched her leave the room. She always reminded me of Mary Poppins – prim and perfect-looking, almost angel-like. Once she was out of sight, I leaned in and whacked Nik on the leg with my dance bag.

'Ow,' he grumbled. 'What was that for?'

'I can't believe you sprained your wrist, you doofus. What about the dance competition? You didn't even play a real game today; it was only a practice.'

'I'm sorry,' he said, looking contrite.

'Let me see it.'

'No!' Nik pulled his hand away before I could inspect it. 'You can't.'

'Why not?'

'Cos it really hurts.'

Something smelled rotten with the scene in front of me. Why was Nik lying flat on the couch if he only had a sprained wrist? Before I had the chance to interrogate him further, his mum had bustled in with a tray laden with hot chocolate, marshmallows and a plate of biscuits.

'*Antio sou*, Angelina,' she said, with a nod to the door.

Those words were a little more direct. She wanted me to go.

I sighed and patted Nik gently on his leg this time. 'Get better soon,' I said but my tone lacked warmth. I honestly didn't mean to be such a cow, but I remembered spraining my ankle last year and I still got dragged to church. And no one ever brought *me* hot chocolate and cookies.

As I trudged down his road towards the corner, my dance bag scraping along the pavement, I stopped and looked back down the street – or Millionaires' Row as we liked to call it. I sometimes wondered why Nik didn't go to private school, but he said all their money was tied up in property and the family business.

'Agh,' I wailed into the freezing-cold air, jumping on the spot in frustration. Now I would have to pull out of *Strictly*.

Once I reached the corner of Nik's road, a thought flashed across my mind. I remembered the day we were partnered up for the competition. Not everyone in class had wanted to dance. There had been one person who had his hand up but had been left partnerless because we all knew he had two left feet. I had felt really bad for him. It was worth asking if he was interested in stepping in, wasn't it?

I slung my bag over my shoulder, crossed the street and began to run, careful not to slip on the icy patches on the pavement. Five minutes later, I was stood outside his house. As I knocked on his front door, I held my hand behind my back with my fingers crossed.

The distant sound of voices behind the frosted glass grew louder and a shadowy figure came closer. As the door opened, I was immediately engulfed in the aroma of spices. Ash was stood in the doorway in a blue-and-white-striped apron, holding a wooden spoon. He beamed when he saw me.

'Hi,' he said. 'What's up?'

I breathed in and out deeply. 'Ashok Patel. Will you dance with me?'

Chapter 12

I knew this was a mistake.

'Ow,' I said through gritted teeth, my hand reaching to rub my sore toe.

'Oh, no. I am so sorry.' Ash ruffled his hair with a big puff of breath. 'I told you I'm no good.'

'It's OK. You're doing really well,' I lied. 'You've pretty much nailed all the steps of the cha-cha.'

'But we still have the tango and our signature dance to learn.'

In fairness to Ash, it was almost impossible to complete the tango in his bedroom without treading on each other's toes.

Hail lashed against the window – winter still gripping February with a stranglehold – any hope of us dancing in the park out of the question. Not that we would be allowed to. Since starting secondary school, Ash was expected to do two hours of homework a night, even when we didn't have that much given by the teachers. And his list of chores was endless. I couldn't help but notice he always seemed happiest at the stove with his auntie and grandmother who lived with him, his older sister Divya, and his parents.

'Just count in your head,' I said patiently. 'Let me show you again.'

I grasped his shoulder and hand as he put his other lightly on my waist. 'When the music goes "dah, da da", that's when we turn.' I swung him round a little too forcefully and our arms knocked a stack of books onto the floor, making a loud 'thud' noise. Moments later, there was a knock on the door.

We resumed our positions in a second as we had rehearsed so we wouldn't get caught – my head in a book that I grabbed from Ash's bed and him at his desk, pen poised in the air.

Ash's sister came in without even being asked. 'What's going on in here?'

'Nothing,' we both said in unison.

'Liars.' She walked over to me and snatched from my hold the book which I then realised was upside down. 'Tell me or I'll rag to Dad.'

'Div, please, no. We'll tell you.'

'God, you're such an easy target, Ash.' She laughed as she flopped onto his bed. Her lips were painted scarlet red, and as well as a nose ring, I noticed both her ears had three piercings.

Divya was one of the coolest girls at school. She was three years older than us and taking her GCSEs this summer – with dreams of becoming a DJ or a record producer, Ash had told me. He had also said there was no way his parents would ever agree to that career path, but it didn't stop her from dreaming it. She had long, curly black hair and wore a cropped T-shirt with Metallica splashed across it and floaty trousers. At school her singy-songy Brummie accent was thick, but I noticed it disappear as soon as she was around her family at home, and I often wondered who the real Divya was. Ash talked more like his parents but with a Brummie inflection which his dad constantly corrected.

'We're dancing,' Ash said hesitantly. 'In the *Strictly Stockland* competition.'

Divya looked wide-eyed from him to me and back to her brother again.

'Get outta town. You're not.' She tossed her hair over her shoulder before twirling a section in her fingers.

Ash nodded.

She nudged me in the arm. 'How the hell did you end up with this loser, Lina?'

I stood up abruptly, feeling the need to defend my best friend. 'Ash is not that bad,' I said, my voice a little squeaky. 'We're just having trouble with the tango, and we need to learn one more dance.'

'Show me.' She folded her arms.

'It's a bit rusty,' I said. She shot me a glare and I knew there was no point in protesting, and Ash was hopeless at standing up to his sister but her teasing always came with good humour unlike my brother who was just plain mean.

We resumed our position and began to dance. Barely ten seconds in and Divya began to snigger. My cheeks flushed and I dropped my hands from Ash's.

'I'm sorry. I just never thought I'd see my little Bashy dance.' I knew Ash hated this nickname but never felt the need to challenge his big sister to call him anything else.

She sprang up from the bed and held Ash in a brace lock and ruffled his hair as he squirmed beneath her hold. When she finally let him go, she clapped her hands.

'Right, you two, you need my help, desperately. I'm doing the sound and production for the event, and there is no way I am allowing my little brother to embarrass me. It's bad enough that you do maths and science Olympiads.' She wrinkled her nose. 'And you'll need my help coming up with an excuse to get you out of the house on Saturday night too, Bashy.'

'Really? You'd help us?' A warm smile spread across my face.

'Yeah. And I think we have a secret weapon.'

'We do?' I asked.

'My li'l brother might have two left feet,' Divya said. 'But there is one kind of dancing he is bostin at.' She paused for dramatic effect and wiggled her hips from side to side. 'Bollywood.'

A still of a movie I had seen recently with Ash's gran came to mind: the movement, colour and vibrancy of the closing number. My bones tingled at the prospect of learning to dance like that. I clenched my fists close to my chest and bopped up and down. This was the best news ever.

The next few afternoons were a whirl of fun and laughter. Each day after school, I headed to Ash's house. Divya would plug her CD player to the outside wall socket and, wrapped in warm coats, Ash and I used the paved back garden to practise. He was doing his best to learn the steps of the tango, but he kept counting out loud every time we moved, and I could see the tension in his shoulders when he held me.

It was the day before the competition, and I was in Divya's room standing with my back to her long mirror. She had lent me one of her old *lehenga choli* outfits that she had worn to a family event. It had been sent over from India by one of her relatives. The magenta fabric embroidered with gold brocade needed taking in and she had been pinning me for the last ten minutes.

I was glad to be out of the flat this afternoon. Alex had been insufferable this morning, making everyone at breakfast know he was stressed about the opening night of his play. We were all going, and I knew I had to get home soon as he would throw a fit if I was late. He would then blame me if it turned out that he wasn't in fact this megastar he always thought he was but an absolute loser who had made a complete fool of himself up on stage.

A door slammed and Divya dropped a pin.

'Dad's home,' she said, tugging the fabric a little too tightly.

'He's early, isn't he?' I grimaced until she loosened her hold. So far, we had managed to do all of our rehearsals without the watchful gaze of Ash's parents who were both at work – his mum at the local post office and dad at an accountancy firm in town. Their grandmother and auntie were always too busy watching Indian TV or cooking to notice what we were up to.

Divya stuck a couple more pins at my waist.

'Ow,' I shrieked as one grazed my skin.

'Sorry, I'm almost done.' She wrapped the luminous green shawl over my shoulder and around my hips, tucking it in to the sash belt. 'There, you can turn around now.'

I took in my image in her mirror, my eyes marvelling at the colourful sight.

'You look gorgeous,' she said. 'And your hair is super-cute with those French braids.'

Footsteps thundered on the stairs and a loud gruff voice bellowed.

'Ashok!'

Divya and I froze and heard a door open.

'Yes, Papa.'

'What is the meaning of this?' There was a rustle of paper. 'Ninety-two per cent.'

Divya rolled her eyes and slumped on her bed. 'Dad goes through Ash's school bag every day. He must've left it in there, stupid boy.'

'What happened to the other eight per cent?' his dad asked.

Ash mumbled something indecipherable. The rest of Mr Patel's words were in Hindi, sentences growing in volume. And then there was one word I recognised. My name.

'Shit,' Divya hissed as she swung her legs over her bed. 'We've gotta get you out of here.' She picked up my jeans and jumper and flung them at me.

'Why?'

'Well, if Dad sees you dressed like that, he'll start questioning why you're here and there's no way he'll buy any bullshit that we were "hanging out", because you're a loser Year Eight kid. No offence. And Ash isn't allowed anyone around during the week. In fact, come to think of it, I don't think anyone comes around at the weekend either. Are you like his only friend or something?'

I gave this question some thought. I mostly hung out with Nik and a few other girls from my tutor group who were more into wearing make-up and flouting the rules than I was. Ash was always in the library during breaktimes, and I never saw him until the end of the day when we walked home from school together, so I didn't really know who else he hung out with. But it was becoming increasingly awkward doing that with him – my friends were beginning to nudge me during break saying he had a crush on me. I knew they were stirring. But if it deflected the attention from who I had a crush on, then that was OK. It hadn't helped that they had seen me give Ash the friendship bracelet I had made in textiles class which he hadn't taken off since.

Divya's door suddenly swung open without even a knock as she shoved me behind the wardrobe.

'*Jaan,*' her dad said.

'Yes, Papa.' She tugged her cropped top downwards, I noticed as I peered through the gap in the wardrobe door.

'You are studying hard?'

'Of course.' She smiled sweetly, picking up one of her biology books.

'That's my girl,' her dad said.

The door closed and I heard her breathe out deeply.

'He'll be in the sitting room in about ten minutes cos it's almost time for the news,' she said, closing the wardrobe door. 'We can sneak you out then.'

'Is it always like this when he's home?'

She nodded. 'Pretty much. He even comes and feels the back of the TV to see if it's hot to check if we've been watching it. Gran and Auntie have a set in their room, so he knows it would be me or Ash – not that Ash would ever do that anyway; he's always swotting up for some test.'

'So ... it's my fault that Ash only got ninety-two per cent?'

She clutched my shoulder and squeezed. 'Don't beat yourself up. This is the single coolest thing Ash has ever done, and I have never seen him as happy as he has been this week. You know he's not the most sociable kid in school and you're gonna put him on the radar.'

'But how are you going to make sure he gets there tomorrow?'

She patted her chest knowingly. 'Don't worry about that. I got Dad wrapped around my little finger.'

Chapter 13

'Why can't Dad drive me there?' my brother wailed. 'I don't want to walk, it's freezing.'

'My sweet boy, I need the car if I am to make it to see you perform,' Mum said in that way that made me imagine she was stroking his hair as she spoke.

I rolled my eyes before looking back to the bathroom mirror, smearing the pink eyeshadow across my lids. I held a tissue underneath and blinked rapidly to let the excess powder fall. I had seen a double-page spread about how to do perfect dance make-up in this month's *Seventeen* magazine. One of the girls in my tutor group had left it in our form room. She'd swiped it from her older sister, and I had managed to sneak a peek. I bet Emily Walters didn't have to go through all this. In fact, I bet Emily Walters had her own make-up artist to do *her* make-up.

'And anyway,' Mum continued, 'it's too cold for your sister to be outside in her dance outfit, even with her coat.'

'God, why does she have to do this on *my* big night?'

The rest of the conversation switched to Greek. They always did that, knowing full well I would only be able to get a very general understanding of what they were saying. But they were both right, it was freezing. A winter storm had hit England last night, throwing a blanket of snow across the whole of the West Midlands. Rain had melted it in the day, but the temperature had dropped by another ten degrees since the morning. Black-ice warnings sounded from the radio in the kitchen.

'No one cares about my big night,' Alex said, switching back to English, in a voice that made him sound eight years old, not almost eighteen.

'Alexi, of course we care,' Mum said.

A pain suddenly stabbed in my lower stomach, and I clutched the spot tightly and gritted my teeth. That was the second spasm I had felt there in the last ten minutes. God, was this stage fright? An explosion of butterflies? I breathed in and out deeply and applied my lipstick with a shaky hand. But the pain continued. Maybe I needed to pee.

A loud knock on the door startled me.

'Hurry up in there, you doofus,' Alex called from the other side. 'I gotta get ready.'

'Give me five minutes, loser.'

As I pulled off my pink sequined dress that Mum had fixed and wriggled down my pants, I slapped my hand over my mouth when I looked at the lining of my knickers. Red stains. Huge ones. There was also a noticeable blemish on my dress.

'Oh no, no, no,' I said, my cheeks burning.

With my foot I nudged open the cupboard under the basin but couldn't see Mum's sanitary towels. The pad she forced me to carry in my school bag I had given to my friend Alessa when she had been caught short during class and was too embarrassed to go and ask the nurse for one because she didn't have twenty pence for the vending machine.

Why was this happening to me now? My first period. Why now?

Another knock. 'I'm serious, man. Get out of there. I've got to do my hair.'

'Agh. Do your hair in your bedroom.'

'I got my gels in there, idiot.' He banged the door with increasing volume.

I rolled toilet paper round my hand several times, shoved it in my pants and pulled them up. Running the tap, I scrubbed at the stain on my dress which thankfully washed away.

When I opened the door to the bathroom, I avoided all eye contact with Alex and ran to my room. A quick change of knickers before burying my bloodstained pants in my laundry basket, I vowed to wash them later so Mum wouldn't notice. We had never had a chance to chat about any of that girlie stuff. She was always so busy with the deli and catering for the Markos family.

The rush to get out of the door made my skin prickle with anxiety. Alex moaned several times that it was the injustice of the century that he had to walk the mile and a half to the theatre for his play. I knew he was stalling in the hope that time would run out and Mum and I would have no choice but to walk to school. What did it matter if *I* was late? he said.

Alex shrugged away Mum's kiss and hug and sulked out the door. Heated words were exchanged between Mum and

Dad in Greek before Mum called my name to get me to follow her. Sheesh. Why was everyone making this into such a big deal? Alex had already had his opening night. Why couldn't tonight be about me? For once.

As soon as Mum dropped me at the side entrance to the school, I ran down the long corridor, past the science department, straight to the girls' toilets. I fished out a coin and slotted it into the sanitary-pad machine. The relief was instant. I crouched in the stall clutching my stomach. I wished I had a best girlfriend I could confide in because I had so many questions. Was this pain normal? Was it true tampons gave you toxic shock syndrome?

The bathroom door opened and several girls from my year floated in in a haze of hairspray and perfume. They eyed me suspiciously and resumed their chatter in front of the mirrors. I gave my reflection a cursory glance and left in the hope of finding Divya, keeping my fingers and toes crossed that she had somehow managed to get Ash out of the house.

'Lina.' A voice from behind made me stop and turn.

Divya appeared in one of the classroom doorways, headphones on. Bangles rattled down her arm as she took them off.

'Ash is getting ready in the boys' toilets. He'll be out soon.'

I bounced from foot to foot. 'Thank God. I want to win so badly, you know.'

She studied my face. 'Did you do this?' She waved a finger in front of me.

I touched my cheek. 'Yes. Why, is it awful?'

She gave me a warm, sympathetic smile. 'Come with me. I'll sort it.' Grabbing her bag, she led me to the area backstage where several other dance couples were chatting excitedly.

Students dressed in black were checking the set, and the distant sound of an audience beyond the curtain brought butterflies to my stomach – their wings flapping frantically. The pain in my pelvis had moved to a dull ache.

'Are you nervous?' Divya said as I closed my eyes.

'Don't tell Ash but yeah, I am.' A soft brush tickled my upper lids before I felt a finger smudge the corners of my eyes.

'I gave this same pep talk to my little brother. Enjoy it. Relax. Look at each other like you were both born to do this. And if you see Ash staring at you a little adoringly, I told him a trick I learned whenever I get nervous standing in front of an audience.'

'What's that?'

'I told him to look at you like you were the most precious person in the whole world and that nothing ever mattered when you danced – imagine no one was watching, that it was just you and him. It should help him strengthen his frame and stop counting those steps under his breath. And I *so* want him to show the whole school that he is a shit-hot Bollywood dancer.'

'That's the dance I am worried about. I mean, I am not Indian. I'll look stupid.'

'No, you won't. And besides, everyone will probably be so focused on Ash that they won't pay much attention to whether you forget a couple of moves. I think what the two of you have achieved these last few days is incredible. Enjoy it. It's your time to shine. Right, now open ...'

My eyes took a moment to adjust to the bright stage lights but when they landed on Divya's beaming smile, the tension in my chest eased. I thanked her and she resumed her efficient producer mode, barking orders and issuing instructions.

My Indian outfit was hanging up ready for the costume change during the interval and I marvelled at the way the sequins of my pink dress were sparkling in the overhead spotlights. Our PE teacher came over to do a roll call and run through the order of performers. A surge of adrenaline shot through me. I felt delirious and when I saw Ash coming towards me with his hair sleeked back my grin widened.

'Oh my, Mr Ashok Patel. You look wicked.'

He smoothed the lapels of his jacket. 'Really?'

'Yeah. And Divya is the best – she gave me a great pep talk. You're so lucky to have her.' I pointed to the order sheet pinned to the board. 'We're third on for the tango and cha-cha and then last for the final routine.'

A chorus of shushes filtered along the ranks as we all huddled together. The curtains separating backstage from the main hall opened a fraction and in the aisle of the third row I could see Mum. But she wasn't facing the stage like all the other parents. She was looking at her watch, peering behind her to the exit.

Why couldn't she just be present for once? I wished I had told her to drop me off. I could have got a lift home from someone. If Alex's performance was so damn important to her, why didn't she go? I pushed these thoughts to the back of my mind and turned to Ash who gave me a broad smile – his metal braces on full display.

On the other side of the stage, Divya stood behind the control panel and pressed some buttons and pulled up some levers. The familiar *Strictly Come Dancing* theme tune came out through the sound system and our headmaster shuffled onto the stage for his welcome.

The first two dances went by in a blur. Ash had stepped on my foot only once and we had turned early halfway through the tango, but I prayed that no one would mark us down too harshly for those errors.

Emily Walters and Will Baker's routines were flawless. I couldn't help but envy her hair which was pulled into a tight ponytail with flowing blonde ringlets cascading down her back. I self-consciously touched my black bun. Her dress was layers and layers of orange silk organza which floated around her just like the celebrities wore on the BBC show. She had so much poise and elegance, I was enthralled by her every move. Her showstopper dance had been cowboy-themed and I was secretly relieved that Nik had broken – sorry, *sprained* – his wrist and couldn't be here tonight otherwise it would have seemed like we had copied them. Emily's rhinestone-encrusted hat shimmered in the overhead lights, and she showed that she could not only waltz and samba but also do the do-si-do with a superior level of talent.

A tap on my shoulder brought me to the present. Ash and I were next for the finale. The crowd appeared restless. Parents twitched in their seats and Mum seemed increasingly anxious. I turned away to the other side of the stage where Divya was giving me a massive double thumbs-up and I nodded; a wash of determination and confidence pulsing in time to my heartbeat. I straightened my sash and lifted my chin.

A bhangra drum struck a rhythm and Ash sauntered onto the stage, in blue jeans and a yellow shirt.

And then. Bam. His body popped and he delivered a flawless sequence of moves that made the audience whoop and cheer. I grinned from ear to ear as I sashayed towards him. We danced and danced and lost ourselves to the rhythm of the drum and the singer crooning in Hindi. Ash grabbed my hands and gazed at me in a way I had never seen before – a look of love?

No way. I reminded myself that that was what his sister had taught him to do. Besides, we were best friends. My heart belonged elsewhere. Yes, I knew I was only thirteen but whenever I came near him, it would beat thunderously. Nikolas Markos. It was a crush of epic proportions. It was why I couldn't be any madder at him for letting me down. This feeling, being with Ash, was different.

I ran up to him for the final move, jumped high for the lift and thankfully he caught me and spun me without my sash falling out of place. The audience erupted as the music came to a climax. Ash put me down gently – our chests rising and falling in the same pattern as we attempted to regain our breath before turning to the audience. By now the entire room were on their feet cheering. We bowed three times, as rehearsed, before exiting the stage. We were immediately greeted by other classmates who hugged us and said we were brilliant.

My cheeks glowed with pride, and I felt Ash's hand in mine, clutching it tightly. He seemed as unused to the attention as I was. But then I noticed Mum hovering by the exit, coat already on, and wrestled myself from the crowd of well-wishers.

'Did you see me?' I said, still trying to calm my escalated breath. 'What did you think?'

'You were wonderful, Lina, but the show ran over by thirty minutes. We have to go.'

'But I can't go. They haven't done the results yet.'

'What does it matter about the results? It was the taking part that counts. Come, please hurry and get dressed.'

'No!' My voice was louder than I had expected, and Mum drew her head back.

'Angelina, please. We have to go now otherwise we will miss the start of the play.'

'But we have already seen the play. Why do we have to go now?'

'We have been through this already. Tonight is very important for Alexi and I have to be there.'

'Tonight was important for me too.'

She sighed. 'Put it into perspective. This is just a school dance competition. Your brother is being watched by talent scouts and it is important the whole family is there to support him. So please, go and get dressed and I will meet you by the car.'

I opened my mouth to say more but Mum had already left.

A tap on the shoulder made me turn. There in front of me, clutching her rhinestone cap, was Emily Walters.

'Hey, Lina.' She smiled with two rows of perfect white teeth. 'You were really good out there.'

'Thanks,' I replied tentatively. Emily Walters had never even uttered my name let alone paid me a compliment. The only classes we shared were PE and art and I doubted she would even have noticed me during any of them.

'Um. You were amazing too,' I replied, suddenly realising that I had accepted her compliment without returning the favour.

'Our dance troupe could use some new talent,' she said. 'Do you do any classes?'

I shook my head.

'Wow, raw talent. Come find me next week and I will give you the details of where I dance. We have regional tournaments and stuff like that, and we like to put out a strong team.'

'Is it free to join?'

She threw back her head and laughed. 'Course they're not free. But they're not that expensive, I don't think. Maybe a hundred for the annual membership which lets you compete and then fifty a month. But don't worry, you get to do as many dance classes as you want during that time.'

I nodded, wondering how on earth I would get Mum and Dad to agree to something like that. But if Emily Walters thought I had talent, then what did I have to lose in asking them? Surely, they wouldn't have to keep paying for Alex's acting classes once he was talent-spotted.

'Anyway.' She touched my hand. 'Good luck.'

She slipped back through the crowds to the front as we were called for the results. I chewed my bottom lip. How could I leave now when they expected us to be on the stage? Surely Mum could wait five more minutes. Ash was beckoning me over and I knew where I wanted to be.

My heartbeat thundered in my ears as they read out the scores for the first two dances. Three 9.8s and one 10 had us neck and neck with Emily Walters and her partner. My hands grew sweaty, and I reached out to hold Ash's and he held it tightly. As the final scores for Emily's dance were announced, I knew it would take a straight row of 10s for us to win but runner-up was still good, right?

It happened so fast I didn't even register it. Our scores were read out and then the bellowing voice of our headmaster came across the microphone.

'And the winners are Angelina Georgiades and Ashok Patel.'

The screams were deafening, and I couldn't be sure where they came from initially but when I turned to my right, I saw Divya jumping up and down. I then felt nudges in my back as others propelled us forward to the front of the crowd. The spotlight fell on me and Ash and it was blinding. But what did it matter that I couldn't look out into the crowd – there was no one there for me.

Confetti spilled down on us as we collected our trophy and held it aloft. I hugged Ash so hard he might have broken in two if it hadn't been for Divya prising us apart, grabbing our hands and holding them aloft.

'I am so, so proud of you guys,' she said over the *Strictly* theme tune. 'But you need to go and get ready for the encore.'

'What encore?' I asked.

'The winners have to do their last dance once more.'

'But I have to go. My mum is waiting for me in the car park.'

She tutted. 'Come on. Five more minutes won't matter. I'd better go and get the track on. You got this.'

I hesitated. But what did it matter if we missed the first few minutes of the play? This was *my* big moment.

But it wasn't a few minutes. After the dance, there were celebratory drinks and snacks, and everyone wanted to come and wish us congratulations. By the time I reached the car, Mum was fuming. I knew I was in trouble when she barked, 'Get in!' She then walked round to her side of the car and slammed the door shut.

A pain so overwhelming speared my lower abdomen and I felt the flow of blood. It stained the *khameez* trousers. *No.* I should have gone back to the toilets and got another sanitary towel. I remembered my friend Alessa saying her first period wasn't that heavy, so I hadn't thought I needed another one.

As Mum pulled away sharply from the car park, I twitched uncomfortably in the back seat.

'I need the toilet. Can we go home first . . . *please*?' I whined.

'You should've gone before you left school.'

'Please, Mum. I'm begging you. I really need to go home.' The pain was beginning to be unbearable, and I pushed my hand deep into my pelvis in the hope it would lessen the discomfort.

'Honestly, Angelina. Can you for once in your life think about others. You knew we were in a rush, yet you chose to stay after I asked you to come straight to the car. When we get to the venue, then you can go to the toilet.'

'But I want to go to *our* toilet, and I need to change my clothes.'

She rubbed her temple and her eyes met mine in the rear-view mirror – my face contorted in pain. 'I am sorry, my sweet. I don't mean to be so harsh, but I promised your brother we would be there and now we are late.'

I sank further into my seat and let the belt tighten its grip, so it sat flush against my pelvis, numbing the pain a little. The next words I uttered were borne from agony and frustration but fell on deaf ears.

Mum picked up speed and I felt the need to hold onto the handrail. Her mobile rang on the passenger seat, and she mumbled something in Greek – with Dad's name nestled in the middle of her increasingly annoyed-sounding words – until it rang off.

Streetlights whizzed by in a blur as I stared outside the window. I clutched my trophy tighter to my chest, wishing I could be back there – in that room where I felt on top of the world.

The mobile rang again. Mum turned to pick it up but before she could, she reached back suddenly to the steering wheel which had begun to move. As she grabbed it, she pumped the brakes hard and that's when the car began to spin.

I was freefalling, my body trapped tightly by my belt. There was a whipping sound, a screech and then a juddering stop as my head smashed against the window. There was nothing after that except darkness.

Chapter 14

Now we are twenty-eight

I threw open the shutters and a fragrant smell drifted in with the breeze. Drilling from a renovation across the road drowned out the peaceful ambience the Airbnb had promised. The Larnaca accommodation didn't quite match the images I had seen on my mobile either, but it had been a late-night decision and it was cheap. Stupidly, I hadn't read the description closely enough when I had input two adults into the filter. This apartment only had one double. The sofa bed didn't look too bad, I thought as I pushed my hand into the fabric and it sprang back, and I didn't mind the idea of crashing on it seeing as it was my mistake.

Switching on the overhead fan, I went to the bedroom and opened the doors to the balcony. What greeted me was what had initially drawn me to this place – the distant view of the ocean: waves crashing against the shore, umbrellas spaced evenly along the sand.

I couldn't believe it. I had done it – got on a plane for the first time.

The buzzer made me jump. As I opened the door, my heart did a little leap for joy. Ash was standing in the doorway, a suitcase at his feet, dressed in a similar-looking suit to the one I had seen him wear at the reunion.

'You made it.'

'You were very persuasive on the phone,' he said.

I stepped aside and let him in.

He loosened his tie and tugged at his collar. 'It's hot,' he said.

'Surely not hotter than Mumbai?'

'I don't really experience it. My life moves from the office to my car, then to my apartment.'

'Well, I am sure you will cool down after a shower and a change. Please tell me you brought something other than your suit.'

'I have a couple of investors living in Cyprus, so thought I would touch base with them while I was here.'

I studied his 'far from relaxed' demeanour. 'Do you ever switch off, Ash?'

He let my question hang in the musty air and that same uncomfortable feeling circulated us – like when we had said goodbye in Birmingham. Could we ever get back to being friends again?

I grabbed the remote for the fan and jabbed at the buttons. 'Surely this thing has other settings.' My shoulders dropped. 'I'm sorry, Ash. I've lured you here and all I have to offer you is this.' I swept my arms around the living space – a small but functional kitchenette, 'cosy' couch and two-seater dining table.

'Lina, it's fine. I don't mind slumming it for a few days.' He smirked.

'It's not *that* bad.' I playfully batted him on his arm. 'It's roomier than home, *and* it's got a better view. In fact, I haven't yet been on the roof terrace, but I could do with a freshen-up first, then maybe we could head out and explore, get our bearings.'

'Sounds like a plan. Shall we toss a coin?'

'For what?'

'Who gets the shower first?'

I folded my arms in mock offence.

'Only kidding. Ladies first.'

There it was. A hint. A hint of the playfulness we used to have. I relaxed into the moment and grabbed my suitcase and hoped that this light mood would continue once I told him what I had planned for his time here.

After a wash and change into a green T-shirt and black shorts, I slipped on my sandals and headed to the kitchen while Ash took over the bathroom. Opening up the fridge, I was stunned to see it full of the basics plus some local produce and Cypriot wine. I prepared a tray of snacks and laid two glasses on it before nestling the bottle in the crook of my arm.

Climbing up the spiral staircase at the back of the kitchen, I nudged open the door to the roof terrace and stilled as I took it all in. It was like an oasis of calm. Pot plants lined the perimeter, with a large overhanging umbrella creating a shady spot above a small glass table with two chairs. In the other corner was an egg-shaped swing chair. Placing the tray and bottle on the table, I walked to the edge of the terrace and leaned on the railing – the Mediterranean Sea in the distance. The sun was dipping low in the sky – a cascade of orange spilling into the water. It was breathtaking.

Why on earth would my parents want to leave this behind? I had never thought to ask Dad. He had always remained tight-lipped when I enquired about their lives here, but I hoped these next few days would provide some answers.

Perspiration coated my neck from the humid evening, and I slipped off a tie from my wrist, scooped up my hair and fanned my face.

'What a sight.'

I peered over my shoulder to see Ash standing there in a white polo shirt – the collar popped – teamed with beige cargo shorts.

'It's lovely, isn't it?' I said.

He came to lean on the railing beside me.

I breathed in the air – a mixture of wild herbs and jasmine.

'What's all this?' Ash said, clocking the tray I had brought up.

'The owner left us a welcome basket. Thought we could have a light aperitif before heading out.'

Ash broke the seal of the bottle and poured out a measure of wine into the two glasses and handed me one before putting an olive in his mouth. 'Mmm,' he moaned. 'Delicious.'

I popped one into mine and nodded in agreement.

'It's all in the olive oil, I reckon,' he said.

'Do you now?' I raised an eyebrow.

'Do you not agree?'

'I don't know the first thing about olive oils, but I know Dad likes to use a special brand for the deli.' I savoured a few more plus some cubes of feta before looking back out at the view. 'This all feels so familiar, even though I have never been here, and I haven't got the faintest idea why.'

'Didn't your dad tell you anything about the time he lived here?'

'It's all a mystery. I know he grew up in Greece, but I don't know when he moved here or how he met Mum. I don't even know if I have any relatives living here either.' I took a sip of wine. It was sweet with an acidic aftertaste that was sharp and lemony.

I looked to Ash who appeared tense – his shoulders locked beneath his shirt.

'When was the last time you took a holiday?' I asked.

'I don't have time for holidays,' he said, very matter of fact.

'What?' My tone came across accusatory, and I was hardly one to talk. I hadn't taken a proper holiday in years. My days off from the museum were spent helping Dad at the deli. 'I mean, surely your company is legally obliged to let you have time off?'

'I book the days, so it's official, but I'm expected to be accessible; even went to Goa a couple of times but made sure to stay in conference hotels so I could host clients.'

There was a sadness behind his words – the expectation that I knew he had lived with all his life; it hadn't gone away like he had once wished it would.

'So this will be your first real holiday in years, then?' I asked.

He twisted the stem of the wine glass in his fingers before taking a sip. 'Like I said downstairs, I have meetings planned for this week.'

'But you'll be done by late afternoon, right?'

He narrowed his eyes at me. 'Why do I get the feeling you have lured me here under false pretences?'

I stroked my neck, aware that it was probably becoming blotchy, and steeled myself to confess.

'I thought long and hard about what we talked through the other night – you know, when we were hoping to dig up that box.'

'What are you referring to?' he said in a way that made me think that night hadn't left an impression.

I pinched my lips. 'You wanted to be a chef. That's what you wrote in your letter.'

He laughed. 'Childlike naivety.'

'No, it wasn't.'

'Lina, that dream died the day my dad ripped up the acceptance letter to the *Junior MasterChef* competition.'

'It didn't stop you from cooking, though.'

'I was just being a dutiful grandson and nephew, that's all. Gran could barely hold the wooden spoon with her arthritis and Auntie wasn't the best in the kitchen – continually adding too much salt to everything. I always thought she had impaired taste – probably all that tobacco she kept chewing.'

'But the last time I saw you, in Cambridge, one of your friends told me that you used to hold the best Indian parties on your staircase.'

'I made the odd curry, nothing more.'

I could sense Ash's unease, his reluctance to go back to the past, but I wanted to break down the barrier.

'Twenty years ago, when we wrote what we wanted to be at this age, we had been convinced that the world would be ending, only it's not.'

'I never believed it would be.'

'Yes, you did. Nik put the fear of God into both of us.'

'Perhaps. Where is this leading, Lina?' He took a step back, creating distance between us. 'I thought you wanted me here for a bit of moral support, which of course you have – you know that, right?'

I nodded. 'Of course, and I am really grateful you came. Nik was busy with work and—' I noticed a tightening of his jaw at the mention of Nik and I felt bad he now knew I hadn't asked him first to come on this trip. 'I really am grateful you dropped everything to be here and support me. But … after our call, I got to thinking. What if our "ending" was only the beginning?'

'You've lost me.'

'I've booked you on a cookery course.' The words spilled from my mouth, and I turned and focused out to sea, not wanting to see his reaction.

'You what?'

Placing my wine on the table, I reached into my back pocket and unearthed a folded sheet of paper and handed it to him. He took it tentatively and unfolded it, scanning the words.

'I figured, if I was going to live out my eight-year-old dream then so should you.' I crossed my arms defiantly, or perhaps a little childlike.

Ash opened his mouth to speak but closed it again, rubbing his hand across the back of his neck.

'It won't interfere with your work, I promise.' I reached out to point at one particular paragraph. 'It's only six until eight every night. And you even get to bring home whatever you make. I thought it would be nice. After a day on the dig, we could dine up here, relax, have some wine.'

'What's wrong with the countless restaurants I saw lined up along the shore on the way from the airport?'

'Ash, please. I think it would be fun. And it's only five days. Surely you can manage that in between whatever work you've brought with you.'

I could see his demeanour soften. 'It's very thoughtful of you, Lina ...' He trailed off, lost in his thoughts. 'As long as you have no expectations of me pursuing this afterwards.' Lines creased on his forehead.

'Of course not. I can see how much you love your life in Mumbai, your work, your lifestyle. The same way this week is just a break from the norm for me, it can be for you. Although ...' I pulled out a chair and slumped down into it '... I don't actually have any work to return to.'

Ash sat in the chair opposite and laid the paper on the table, reaching out to squeeze my hand. 'I'm really sorry about you losing your job and the deli closing.'

I shrugged. 'It is what it is. I just hope something else comes up in the area and that we can figure out how to find the money to pay the tax on the deli.'

'I am sure everything will work out.' He rubbed his thumb over my knuckles before pulling back suddenly, breaking what felt like a moment passing between us.

I took another sip of my wine, sensing Ash's unease. 'Anyway, I have more important things to do now, like figure out how on earth I am going to find out what happened on that dig all those years ago.'

'Did you get in touch with the site?'

'Only to sign on as a volunteer. When I told them I was coming all the way from the UK, they were quick to say that they couldn't provide any expenses.'

'Did you ask about that guy mentioned in your mum's diary?'

'Not yet; didn't want to arouse any suspicion.'

'Good thinking. Best to ask in person anyway.'

'All the correspondence was in Greek and my level of competence is mediocre at best, so I was hoping it would be easier to converse face to face or pray that someone's level of English is good enough for me to ask.'

Ash averted his gaze back to the sheet of paper and I could see the briefest of smiles twitch in the corner of his mouth.

'Admit it, Ash. You're excited.' I popped another cube of feta into my mouth.

He folded his arms. 'Maybe. Just a little. Don't get any ideas,' he said, trying but failing to pull a serious face, pointing his finger at me.

I held my hands up in defence. 'No expectations, I promise.'

I grabbed my glass and raised it high. 'Let's toast this adventure.'

Reluctantly, Ash lifted his up towards mine.

'To endings,' I said, with a nod to Nik's tale of the apocalypse. 'And new beginnings.'

Chapter 15

A drop of sweat trickled down my face and onto the earth. I swiped my arm across my forehead and sat back on my heels. My muscles ached from crouching in the same position for three straight hours. Around me, a group of other volunteers seemed uninterested and only there to clock college credits.

I had arrived at the Kition archaeological site this morning and was greeted by a foreman whose English was limited. He had handed me some basic tools, told me which area to dig and left me to it. So much for having a superior teach me what to do and how to do it with skill. Luckily, I could draw on previous experience even though the last time I was on a dig was during my degree course at Birmingham. The climate had been in stark contrast to the scorching sun here and all the students had been hard-working and motivated. Teamwork was crucial – I knew that, so it was no wonder that this site was going to close.

'Looks like you know what you're doing,' a voice with a deep Southern American twang said.

I turned around. It was one of the other volunteers – Marie, who I had been buddied up with when I arrived but who had disappeared the second the supervisor left the site.

'I know a little,' I said as I planted my trowel in the ground and dug around.

'You're British, right?'

'Yes, I am. And you?'

'I'm from North Carolina.'

Marie shifted and pulled up the padded mat she was kneeling on, shook off some earth and laid it back down so she could sit. She peeled off her gloves and picked up her Diet Coke bottle and took a large sip. She wiped the rim with her fingers and offered it up to me. 'Want some?'

I smiled. 'I'm good, thanks. I'll take my break later.'

'You're *so* serious. It's totally OK if you don't find anything, you know?'

Her honesty took me by surprise. 'I'm holding out some hope that I will,' I said with a weak smile.

'Whatevs.' She took another swig of her drink. 'Anyway, the rest of us are going to one of the local tavernas for lunch. You're welcome to join us if you want.' She pulled out her phone and checked the time. 'We're leaving soon.'

'But it's not even midday.'

She threw her head back with a snort. 'You've got a lot to learn. The supervisor always checks in at eleven and then not until four. There's no obligation to stay, you know. It's not like they're paying us or anything.'

'I appreciate the invite, but I brought some lunch with me.'

She gave a slight shrug. 'Up to you. Just don't go showing us up or anything.' She gave a short laugh, but her smile was tight, and her look almost threatening. I didn't care. I wasn't here to make friends. I was here to find out what happened to Mum.

Marie drained her drink and went over to one of the other volunteers – a guy with low-slung shorts and a cap with 'Duke' on it. She laughed at something he said before sitting down beside him and stabbing at the ground without even looking at what she was doing.

I shifted my weight onto my other knee and carried on digging. About a half hour later, the supervisor came and did a circuit of the site before lighting up a cigarette and leaving just like Marie said he would. As I resumed digging, my trowel hit upon something hard. I used my small pickaxe to loosen the compacted soil to reveal an object triangular in shape, dark red in colour. I grabbed my brush and swept around the area to gauge the size of the piece. It was no more than two inches by one inch but as I carefully lifted it, there appeared to be a marking of some kind on the back – perhaps a Roman numeral? I placed it in a plastic bag and made some notes regarding the location in my notebook.

My eyes squinted in the bright sun. No one was around. I shook out the pins and needles from my legs and carried my bucket of earth and plastic bag to the bench in the sheltered area. Picking up my cooler bag, I unearthed the bottle of water I had put in the freezer last night so it would slowly defrost during the day. It felt good against my pulse points.

Opening up my phone, I texted Greer to see if she was free for a chat. She typed back instantaneously that she just needed to step out into the corridor, and before I had time to take another sip of my drink, my phone was flashing with a WhatsApp video call from her.

She squealed once we were connected. 'Oh my God, I can't believe you did it. You're in Cyprus. What's it like, tell me everything.'

'It's ... interesting.'

'Flip your screen, show me.' I turned the focus on my phone and did a panorama of the place before switching it back to my face.

'I didn't see anything.'

'There's kinda nothing to see. It's just dried earth with various markings in the soil. And all the other volunteers have headed off for a four-hour lunch break. It's no wonder the site is going to close. No one seems to care about it at all.'

'But you're not there to save the site, you're there to figure out what happened to your mum, and you've only got a few days, right?'

'I thought of waiting until the end of the day, see if I can corner the supervisor and ask him some questions. Anyway, how are things at the museum?'

Greer stuck her tongue out and pointed her finger in her mouth like she was gagging.

'That bad, huh?'

'It's the pits, Lina. This German dude has zero sense of humour and is *so* serious. He's shaking up everything and I've been told I got only two twenty-minute breaks in the whole day to improve on efficiency. I'm literally counting the days until I'm outta here.'

'Poor you. Sorry your last couple of weeks will suck.' I puffed out my cheeks and shook the bucket of earth I had collected for sieving. 'Anyway, I'd better get back to it,' I said.

'Wait, aren't you going to do some digging around?'

'I already am.' I flicked the screen to show her my bucket of earth.

Greer groaned. 'That's the worst archaeology joke I have ever heard.'

'It's about all I got.' I yawned. 'I didn't get enough sleep last night.'

'Oh yeah. Why's that? Ash keeping you up?' She winked. Not just a little wink; an obvious zoom-into-the-camera full-on slow wink.

'What are you implying?' I said.

'Nothing.' She pinched her lips shut and mimicked zipping them. 'I know you and Nik … are, you know, but … while the cat's away and all that.'

'It's nothing like that. Ash and I had a lot of catching up to do and dinner dragged kinda late and the sofa bed was really uncomfortable.'

'Why on earth are you sleeping on a sofa bed?'

'Long story. I'll fill you in when I get back. I gotta go. Lots of sieving to do.'

'Ooh. Exciting,' she said, deadpan. 'Laters.' She waved and disconnected the call.

It suddenly dawned on me that I was all alone. Maybe I could do my sieving once I had had a look around.

I went over to the Portakabin where the supervisor had greeted me this morning. Peering in through the window, all I could see was his desk and an ashtray filled with cigarette butts on the windowsill. There was no one inside. I gave a quick glance over my shoulder before turning the handle.

Locked. I peered in again and noticed there was a window on the other side.

A path took me round to the back, but it was overhung with bushes and the width between the Portakabin and the fence was barely half a foot. I crawled underneath the plants, wincing every time a thorn scraped my legs. As I made it through, I noticed the window had an opening right in the top corner that was slightly ajar with a latch keeping it in place. I reached my hand up and stretched it as far as I could. But it was no use. I couldn't get a finger to it. The only way would be to hitch myself up on something or someone, but confiding in one of the other volunteers wasn't an option.

A noise made me fall back onto the ground and I clenched my teeth in agony as my arm scraped against the stone wall beneath the windowpane. Blood trickled down my elbow. I reached into my shorts pocket and fished out a tissue to stem the flow before slowly peering back up through the glass. It was the supervisor. I thought Marie said he didn't return until late afternoon. Through the window on the other side, I could see him pick up my bucket that I had stupidly left on the decking. He examined it, threw it on the ground somewhere and picked up a bag and filled it up again.

What the heck? All those hours of work gone. What would I find if I sifted through that? Nothing, probably. I prayed he hadn't noticed the plastic bag I had left next to it with the possible finding.

He wiped his hands down his jeans and unlocked the door to the office, lighting up another cigarette as he made his way to his desk.

This was my chance. I needed to talk to him. I crept down low and back along the path and slipped away without being seen, casually retrieving the piece of porcelain in the bag on my way to the door.

I knocked and he ushered me in with his hand, the other clutching his mobile to his ear. He took another drag of his cigarette before finishing off his conversation in Greek.

'Can I help you?' he said gruffly, not looking up from his laptop.

'Umm.' I thrust forward what I had unearthed. 'I think I found something.'

He raised his brows suspiciously. 'Give me.' His tone was wary, and I tentatively held it out to him. He turned it over in his hands before flinging it back. 'This is junk. Throw it away.' Picking up his mobile again, he tapped on it, ash dropping down from the cigarette hanging between his lips.

His analysis stunned me. Back at the museum, we would have labelled it and then given it more serious thought; at least use the microscope to see if there were any other recognisable features and compare it to other finds.

I stood resolutely in front of him before clearing my throat. 'I thought that maybe—'

'You can go back now.' He stubbed out his cigarette and it fizzed in the ashtray.

'I just wanted to ask if it is possible to go into the museum. Do I need a ticket?'

'It is free. You can go anytime you like from morning until five.'

'Thanks.'

What a charming guy, I thought as I left the office and retrieved my bucket. It was no wonder no one had found anything to ignite interest in the site and encourage visitors from abroad. Why did they even bother hiring volunteers? It was inefficiently run and there was obviously something untoward going on.

Where did the staff go for hours on end? Why had my mother felt the need to confront this Elias and then flee to the UK not long afterwards? These questions and others spun around my mind as I returned to my digging patch. I was determined to find out.

Chapter 16

I rocked back and forth in the egg chair on the roof of the apartment. A glass of wine was half drunk on the table beside me. My skin tingled from a thick application of aloe vera aftersun that I had rubbed into my lightly tanned skin once I had stepped out of my cold shower. My body ached, especially my calves. But now that I was in this position of contented bliss, I couldn't move.

The door to the roof pushed open.

'Leftovers,' Ash announced as he stepped outside.

I gave him a very obvious once-over. 'You went to the cookery class in your suit?'

'My meetings overran, *and* I had to sprint several blocks to get to the place because my taxi got tied up in traffic.'

'Why don't you go and shower and get changed, then?'

He shook his head, loosening his tie. 'I'm starving. Two hours of cooking with only mini tasters has left me ravenous.'

'You seem very confident about how good it's going to be.' I swung my legs over the side of the chair.

'Good point. Hope you've got some backup food just in case.'

I nodded at the table. 'I picked up some more olives, cheese and bread from the deli round the corner.'

'Oh, you of very little faith.' He let out a brief laugh.

I uncorked the wine and poured a glass for Ash before topping up mine. He took off his suit jacket and laid it on the back of his chair. Unbuttoning his sleeves, he rolled them up a little.

'How were your meetings?' I asked.

'Productive.'

I waited for him to elaborate but he didn't. Instead, he clicked open the plastic containers and handed me a fork before tucking into his portion.

'Aren't you going to tell me what it is first?'

Ash grabbed a napkin and held it over his mouth. 'God, sorry. I'm so used to eating on my own or in front of a screen, I forgot my manners.' He swallowed, his Adam's apple bobbing up and down, before wiping his mouth.

'On tonight's menu, I bring you a starter of *féta me méli*,' he said, pointing at the container that he hadn't yet opened, 'and a main of vegetable moussaka with a tangy tomato and béchamel sauce.'

I unclipped the starter and used a knife to dissect the dish in half before cutting off a piece and slipping it in my mouth. I bit into the crispy filo and groaned as the feta fizzed on my tongue before honey oozed out and replaced the tartness with sweetness.

Ash raised his eyebrows. 'It's good?'

'Good? It's amazing,' I said as I took another bite and licked my lips and fingers. 'I'm not sure I want to share it.' I pulled the container away.

'It's all yours,' he said, before tucking into the main again. He scoffed down several more forkfuls before sipping his wine. 'You didn't warn me the classes would be in Greek.'

'Oh no, were they? I'm sorry. I didn't really check the fine print when I booked it. How did you manage to follow what the chef was saying?'

'It's weird. I understood a lot. Remember how I used to help you study for your Saturday classes?'

I slumped in my chair, thinking back to that time. Those lessons lasted until I was fifteen. I hated them and Dad finally relented and let me stop going when I was knee-deep studying for my GCSEs. On the many occasions I went round to Ash's to study, he would test me on vocab and help me write sentences. With hindsight, I wished I had continued. Maybe I could have understood what the supervisor was saying on the phone this afternoon.

'Yeah, I remember those classes,' I said.

'I guess I must have picked up some knowledge along the way. But also ...' he shrugged '... the chef was understanding and made sure to repeat some of the key steps in English for my benefit which was a little embarrassing.'

I reached over to cut up a piece of moussaka. It was as tasty as Dad's and that was a massive compliment. 'This is good too,' I murmured, my mouth full of tender aubergines and nutty cheese sauce.

'Just good?' His face fell but there was a trace of humour in his downturned mouth.

I narrowed my eyes at him. 'Stop fishing for compliments.'

We sat for a while and ate, Ash asking me about my day at the site in between tasty bites.

'So, the museum had no trace of your mum?' he said.

I wiped my mouth and put my scrunched-up serviette in one of the containers that had been scraped clean. 'No. It was pretty basic. A few glass displays showing some of the finds, with photos of the dig back in the nineties. I scoured every single photo but couldn't see her. The information was all in Greek, and I think I would need some time to go in and read each one in detail. A guy came to turf me out at exactly five to lock up. I asked him why the tomb was roped off with a "No Entry" sign in Greek on it, but he shrugged as if he didn't understand me.'

I puffed out my cheeks and marvelled at the night sky. A blanket of stars lay above us, and I was suddenly caught breathless at the sight of it. Growing up and living in such a bustling big city meant you could count the stars on two hands on any given clear night. The closest to this view had been on a sixth-form trip to Snowdonia where we stayed on a campsite and toasted marshmallows by a fire. 'Family' holidays were never with both my parents, as someone always needed to be there to look after the deli, and were spent on the Welsh coast – but I never remember taking the time to look at the night sky. And after Mum died, there were no more family holidays.

'Earth to Lina,' Ash said.

I met his gaze. 'Hmm?'

'I asked you what your plan was next, but you completely checked out.'

'Haven't thought it through yet.'

A spasm of pain suddenly pulsed in my lower stomach, and I held my hand close to my hip.

'You OK?' Ash's voice was full of concern.

'I'm fine. Probably ate a bit too fast.'

'Is my food that bad that I've given you indigestion already?'

'No, it was delicious. Maybe it's a day of crouching down for hours on end catching up with me,' I said, desperate not to have to think about what the pain really meant. It wasn't the right time of the month to experience it. And it was of the same depth and sharpness as the night of the reunion. 'I might go and lie down on the sofa for a bit.'

'I feel awful that you're sleeping there.'

'It's your fault for being too tall,' I said with a smile, but it was getting increasingly hard to grin through the pain.

Ash settled back in his chair. 'This is nice.'

'What?' I asked, thinking that there was nothing nice about what I was feeling.

'This.' He swept his arm around the table, the roof terrace, the view. 'I can't remember a time when I felt this ... chilled.'

'Mr Ashok "I work twenty-four hours a day" Patel who considers even sleeping a waste of time. Did you just admit you're relaxed?'

'When did I ever say sleeping was a waste of time?'

'Mmm.' I put my finger on my chin as I thought back to our schooldays. 'Pretty much every day of Year Thirteen.'

'I was under pressure.'

'I know you were. It was relentless, wasn't it?'

He nodded and lost himself in his thoughts. 'Sometimes...' He swallowed hard. 'Sometimes, I wish I had enjoyed it all more.'

'What? School?' I made a snorting kind of sound. 'School was awful to you, and Nik.'

I noticed Ash flinch. My mobile buzzed on the table, and I clocked a message from Nik on it. Christ, did he have a sixth sense? I swiped left to clear his name, but I knew Ash had seen it.

He poured himself another glass of wine. 'So, Nik and you see each other a lot?'

'Yeah, we do. He's been there for me over the years.' I saw hurt in his eyes. Ash had been the sole occupier of that role long before Nik. Was he thinking back to the night I lost the right to his friendship? 'What Nik and I have is ... special. It's hard to explain.'

'He's a lucky guy.'

I opened my mouth to tell him the relationship was nothing like he thought it was, but that would mean telling him things Nik and I had promised to never share with anyone.

Ash suddenly pushed back his chair. 'I think I'm going to take a walk.' He stacked up the containers before heading inside.

The mood had been soured with talk of school and Nik. And the truth was I still hadn't fully processed what had happened when we were all eighteen – when the friendship between me and Nik shifted. But the memory of that time was blighted by another spasm. I was glad that Ash had left.

I didn't want him to see me like this. The list of triggers was increasing by the day. When was it going to stop?

I had reconciled myself to being one of the unlucky ones whose life was marred with pain on a monthly basis, but one night I realised that the agony I had to endure went deeper than that.

Chapter 17

When we were eighteen

I unscrewed the wand from the tube. 'I think tonight's the night,' I said casually as I stretched out my upper lid and swept my eyeliner across it.

Emily grabbed my arm and dragged me away from the mirror, pulling me down onto my bed. 'Umm. What?' She stared at me all glassy-eyed.

I bit my bottom lip and grimaced. 'Or maybe not. Agh.' I flopped back onto my pillow. 'Why is this so hard?'

'Losing your virginity? It's a pretty big fucking deal.' She flicked a bit of the nail polish that she had applied out from the crevice of her finger.

'How would you know? You haven't done it yet.'

This fact I would never get over. Emily Walters. The most beautiful girl in school. Still. Her teenage years had been kind to her – her one-a-month spot neatly hidden in her hairline, her locks never greasy and eyebrows never needing endless plucking like the rogue caterpillars I had been born with.

Emily Walters. *My* best friend. I still had to pinch myself every time she linked arms with me at the school gates at eight twenty-five every morning and we would stroll in together. We became close the day I left the hospital after the car accident. She had brought round a week's worth of meals to help with my recuperation. But our blossoming friendship had forced all other acquaintances to one side once they tired of Emily monopolising my time. Secretly I loved that she did. She made me feel good about myself and had been the one I turned to when I needed to buy my first bra, and she vouched for me on the days when PE coincided with that time of the month, when I couldn't face going to school and being forced to run ten laps of the tennis court. Painful periods were something I had grown used to ever since my first one.

'I might not have done *it*,' Emily said, as she fiddled with a cushion on the trundle under my bed that I always pulled out when she stayed over, 'but I know others who have, and they all said it hurt like hell.'

'But I think he'll be gentle, don't you?'

'What, sex god Nikolas Markos? I bet he likes it rough.' She giggled.

I nudged her. 'Em, don't say that. I'm already freaking out as it is.'

'But you haven't even kissed him yet. What makes you think tonight's the night?'

A giddy smile spread across my face, and I reached beneath my pillow to grab a small velvet box. 'This.'

Em's eyes sparkled as she opened it and fished out the bracelet – a gold band with an oval-shaped red stone nestled in the centre which I was convinced was a ruby.

'He got me this for my birthday,' I said proudly.

Em squealed. 'This is huge. Why didn't you tell me?'

'Just a small matter of you doing your final A-level exam. I wanted to wait until tonight so we could pore over what it means.'

'God, we have so much to catch up on. When did all this happen?'

'On Wednesday. You know I always take the Markos order from the deli to his dad's office every morning?'

'Ah huh. Though I still don't get why you have to wake at five to do that six days a week.'

'I just gotta do it. Please don't keep asking me why. Anyway, he was there.'

'Who?'

'Nik, of course. He was doing some work experience because I think that's what he's going to do after uni – work with his dad. And when he saw me, his face lit up and he asked if I wanted to go for lunch. He knew it was my birthday and everything. Anyway, he took me to the Ivy.' I pushed my hair behind my ears and grinned inanely.

'Seriously? God, that's dead posh.'

'I know. He was saying all this stuff about how much my friendship means to him, how he feels he can tell me anything. And then he pulled out this box and said he'd got me something for my birthday – something special, that he hoped I would like.'

Em admired it once more. 'It must have cost him a fortune.'

'I know. And, my God, when he hugged me goodbye, he smelled soooo good.' I flopped dramatically back on my bed again, and Em followed me down, so we were both looking at my mottled ceiling. 'I could feel how ripped he was underneath his shirt. It was the first time I had held him.'

Em tickled my arm. 'You're such a smitten kitten.'

I giggled and batted her away. 'I never thought he'd really look at me like that. I mean, we talk a fair bit. Every time I go and waitress at one of his mum and dad's parties, he's always finding reasons to come and talk to me.'

'So, you're going to make your move tonight? At the leavers' party at his house?'

I propped myself up on my elbows. 'It's crazy, right? I know I've heard the rumours about him preferring older girls but even a snog would be a start.' Sitting up, I held a cushion to my chest. 'There's a part of me that wants to get *it* out of the way. And what's better than with someone you've had a crush on since you were thirteen?'

'Come on, then.' She dragged me off the bed and sat me down in front of my dressing table, grabbing her make-up bag. '*I* am going to take over and make you completely irresistible. And I think I know just the dress to make his eyes bulge. And maybe that's not the only thing that will bulge.' She snickered; her hand held over her mouth.

I elbowed her. 'You're so naughty.'

'Ooh,' she shrieked and catapulted herself across my tiny bedroom to her overnight bag. 'You can have this.' She unzipped her bag and held her push-up strapless bra aloft. 'I think your need is greater than mine.'

I blushed furiously. What was I even doing? But this was my last chance, and I wouldn't have to suffer any embarrassment at school if he rebutted my advances because school was almost finished. It was our big leavers' party and I wanted it to be a night to remember.

Em and I had spent many sleepovers poring over copies of *Cosmo*, reading up about what to do, what bits go where, lubing up, the best positions. I had my protection tucked into my clutch bag and hoped that once I had a couple of drinks inside me, I would have the Dutch courage to make my move. What could possibly go wrong?

The marquee pulsed with a thumping techno beat that could be heard half a mile down the road. The Markos family knew how to throw a party. It was a joint celebration: the end of exams but also Nik's eighteenth birthday, which was yesterday.

Em held my hand as we walked round the side of the house. She struck an imposing figure in a blue velvet dress that had a slit all the way from her ankle up her leg, but I felt a little exposed in the black strappy number she had insisted I wear. Even with the push-up bra, I didn't have enough boob to fill the dress and the straps kept slipping down. But Em said I looked sensational.

The first group to see us was the football team. They were knocking back beers in plastic cups, looking uncomfortable in their black-tie suits. The gold-embossed invites had insisted on that dress code.

When Toby the Tank saw Em, he wolf-whistled and headed over.

'Oh God,' I heard her mumble under her breath, and felt her squeeze my hand tighter.

'You look fucking hot, Emily.'

'Thanks,' she said nervously.

'Save a dance for me later, will ya?'

'No, thanks,' she said, as she tugged me forward so we could get past him.

But he grabbed her arm. 'Where you rushing off to, gorgeous?' He loosened his grip but leaned in and stroked her cheek. 'You're such a prick tease, aren't ya?' His hand moved down her back and he grabbed her bottom, pulling her flush against him, causing his beer to spill and soak the front of her dress.

Em took a sharp intake of breath and her cheeks flushed.

With no thought to the fact that Toby the Tank was six foot three and built like a . . . well, a tank, I shoved myself between him and Em, grabbing her by the shoulder and saying quite dramatically, 'Get off her.'

I dragged her away, pushing past the rest of the football gang who were making inappropriate comments about how Toby had failed to pull. But we hadn't got far enough away before we heard him shout back.

'You fucking pair of dykes.'

We quickened our pace until we had reached the bar at the back of the marquee. Em's face was all red, tears falling down her cheeks.

'Are you mad we didn't correct him?' I said.

'Mad?' She choked a laugh through her sobs, fishing out a tissue from her clutch bag and dabbing at the stain on her dress. 'Toby has been cornering me at school, making lewd gestures and trying to put his tongue down my throat at every single Year Thirteen party we've been to. If he now thinks I'm a lesbian and leaves me be, I can handle the fallout from that. Besides, in a couple of days, this will all be behind us. But for your sake, let's hope Nik doesn't find out.'

I wrinkled my nose. 'I'll just tell him I swing both ways.'

Em grabbed both my hands and held them tightly. 'I'm gonna miss you *so* much next year.' Her tone had turned serious. 'Birmingham to Manchester isn't that far, and you'll be coming back to see your folks, right?'

She nodded hesitantly. 'Sure. Let's get some drinks down us, shall we? And your cherry popped.' She wiped her tears with the back of her hand and leaned over the bar to attract the attention of the waiter.

An hour later my head was spinning. I had downed three cups of punch in rapid succession while watching Em boogie. She knew why I never liked to dance and never hassled me to get over my fear – the association I had with the last time I had done it. The disco-ball lights were blinding and still visible even when I closed my eyes; the music deafening. When Em finally took a break, I had to shout in her ear to tell her I was going to look for Nik.

'Good luck,' she mouthed.

I stood on tiptoes to peer over the heads of other revellers happily bopping away to Fatboy Slim's 'Demons' track but couldn't see Nik. I left the marquee and shivered a bit in the summer-evening breeze and wrapped my arms around myself, inadvertently raising my modest cleavage further up and out of the push-up bra.

The sliding doors to the back of the house were open and other partygoers were laughing and talking over a different track belting out of the living-room's sound system.

And then I saw him. He was sat on the leather couch, dressed head to toe in black, looking unbelievably hot and sexy. He was talking animatedly to a guy on his left. It took me a second to place him. It was our Spanish exchange student who had spent the last term at our school, soaking up the 'culture' that Stockland Academy had to offer.

I took another swig of my drink for courage and placed it on the nearest table before walking over – my dress riding up with every step. When Nik saw me, his jaw dropped and I bit my bottom lip as I adjusted the thin straps of my dress, nervously tugging at the hem. I prayed my knickers weren't on display at the back.

Nik turned to the Spanish guy and whispered something in his ear before giving him a fist bump. The Spanish guy left, and Nik stood up. My heart lurched from my chest into my throat where it pounded deeply. I was glad for the dimmed lights so my no doubt blotchy neck wouldn't be too visible. Even in the heels I had borrowed from Em, Nik towered several inches above me. The spicy scent of his aftershave tickled my nose as I breathed him in. His black shirt had the top three buttons popped to reveal the thin gold chain that dipped in and around the muscles in his neck with a pendant of Agios Nikolas hanging from it – his name-day saint.

Even in the low lights of the living room you could see a hint of his tan on his smooth chest. I often wondered whether he used a sunbed because there hadn't been any tropical weather in the Midlands since last summer.

Nik kissed me on both cheeks and drew me in, his eyes sparkling and causing my heart to beat even faster.

'Happy birthday to you,' I said huskily in what was my best impression of Marilyn Monroe.

'Thanks,' he said, his lips twitching.

He grabbed my wrist and his touch sent shockwaves through every part of me. There was a tingle in between my legs, a feeling I hadn't felt before. I pushed my thighs together.

'You like it?' He stroked the bracelet.

I grinned like a loon. 'Like? I love it. Thank you *so* much.' I flung my other arm around his neck, pushing my chest up against his. He reciprocated the hug, and his hand lightly touched my bare back and sent more pulses round my body. I leaned back a little – his face so close to mine.

'You look amazing,' he said, and my lips parted in anticipation.

There was a commotion behind me, and Nik dropped his arm and stepped back. Some of the guys from our year were being vocal. Nik kept looking over my shoulder and his expression hardened. I tried to drown them out and focus on Nik's lips which I was sure had been about to kiss mine.

'I got you something,' I said, suddenly remembering what was in my clutch bag.

He beamed. 'You did?'

'Yeah, of course. You think I'd turn up to a party without a gift?' I playfully tapped him on the arm.

He tutted. 'Everyone else has.'

'Oh, well . . .' I fiddled with the clutch of my bag and pulled out a small box and held it up to him. 'Happy eighteenth.'

'That's so thoughtful.' He took the present and ripped off the wrapping paper before opening the box inside. I studied his face for a reaction as he picked up the chain bracelet which had his initials engraved on the thin plaque on the top.

He swallowed hard and shook his head a little. 'I don't know what to say, Lina. This must've cost you a fortune.'

'No more than you must've spent on mine,' I said as I held my hand over my wrist. The truth was I had spent all of my savings from my Sunday job at a local café. That was my only day free what with all my commitments at home and the deli.

I helped him fasten the clasp and he pulled the sleeves of his shirt up his forearms, revealing even more of his lush, tanned skin.

His appreciative smile reached the corners of those intense green eyes of his. God, if he didn't lean in and kiss me now, I was going to combust into a fiery ball of lust. He glanced over my shoulder again and his jaw tightened. I turned to see some of Toby's gang watching us, whispering and making crude hand gestures.

And then it happened. I felt a tug on my wrist as Nik brought me close again, and before I could register what was happening, his lips were on mine. My mouth opened and I let his tongue explore. The wolf-whistles ringing out around me added to the cacophony of trumpets bursting into song in my head. Five years. I had wanted this for five years.

He drew back, breathing heavily against my lips, our foreheads touching.

'I'm sorry,' he whispered.

'Why?' I said, struggling to keep my heart from bursting through the thin satin material of my dress.

'I didn't mean to—'

'I've wanted to do that for so long,' I blurted out. This time I placed my lips on his and the kiss was more tender. Instinctively, I pressed my body into his, my hands on his shoulders, moving him backwards until he collapsed onto the couch, as I sat astride him. With no thought to who was watching, my hands twisted in his hair, while our tongues danced together and teeth occasionally clashed. I was so caught up in the moment. But it soon became impossible to drown out the wolf-whistles behind us. Self-consciousness poured through my veins.

I broke free from the kiss. 'Can we go to your room?'

His cheeks were flushed, and I hadn't realised that my hands had moved from his hair to his shirt, where a fourth button was popped. He didn't say anything. Oh God, was this all a big mistake? Was he about to let me down gently and say, 'I'm flattered, Lina, but you're not really my type'? In fact, his nervousness and the way he kept looking over my shoulder made me think that I had completely misjudged whatever *this* was. I hopped off his lap and tugged at my dress.

But then he grabbed my hand before giving me a cheeky wink. He dragged me through the crowd, calls of 'get in there' from behind growing quieter. I glanced over my shoulder briefly as we climbed the stairs, in time to see Em at the front door. She gave me a massive thumbs-up and mouthed, 'I'm going home.'

Her encouragement spurred me on, so that when we went into Nik's room, I immediately planted my lips on his and began unbuttoning his shirt again. I wanted to have the confidence of all the older girls he'd slept with before, even though my fingers were trembling and it must have been obvious that I didn't know what I was doing. An article from *Cosmo* sprang to my mind and I moved my hand to his crotch.

'Woah, slow down,' he said, and my cheeks flamed with embarrassment.

'Sorry.' It's my first time and I haven't got a clue what I'm doing, I thought but couldn't say it out loud.

He moved to his bed and pushed some coats to one side and sat down. He clasped his hands in his lap and I wondered whether he expected me to make a move.

I could feel the mood shift and knew I needed to do something to show him I was still interested. I thought back to all the late-night conversations with Em where we had rehearsed exactly what we would do and what guys would like us to do. Slipping the straps of my dress down, I wriggled my hips, so the fabric fell to the floor revealing the strapless push-up bra Em had lent me and my sexiest pair of black cotton knickers.

He swallowed deeply as he drank me in before switching off his bedside light – the only illumination from the lamp outside on the pavement. The semi-darkness was a relief. As I came closer, he edged himself up the bed so I could sit astride his legs. I began to unbutton his jeans and my hand brushed over his boxers. Tentatively, I slipped my fingers inside and grasped him in my hand. He groaned. For a second, I thought I had hurt him, but when I looked up his head was tipped backwards, eyes firmly closed, soft moans emitting from his mouth. He liked it. I wasn't sure if I was tugging him too hard or too softly, but his increased moaning gave me the impetus to keep going. After a while, it grew harder and harder.

The next bit happened fast. He pushed his jeans and Calvins off, and I wriggled out of my knickers. Nik fished inside his bedside table and pulled out a pack of condoms. He rolled one on while I lay back on his bed suddenly wishing we had talked more. The next sensation I felt was something I had heard about, but it was so strong that I couldn't breathe for a moment.

Pain. Excruciating pain. After the first few thrusts, I prayed it would lessen but it didn't. It was sharp and reverberated deep inside me. The only other time I had felt such pain in that region was during my period.

Nik continued to move inside me, not once looking me in the eyes. The grunt that emanated from my mouth every time he thrust must have sounded like I was enjoying it, but I wasn't.

The next thing I knew, Nik had rolled off me and was holding his arm over his eyes. Oh God. Had I been that bad? Before I could say anything, the bedroom door-handle shook, followed by a knock. Nik yanked the condom off and hurled it in his bin before scrambling for his clothes. I struggled to put my dress back on as the pain continued to pulse inside me.

'You OK?' Nik said as he buttoned up his shirt, giving me the briefest of looks.

'Um, yeah, I'm fine.'

'I need to get back to the party, be a good host and all that.'

'Yes, of course.'

'See ya.'

And with those words he unlocked the door. A girl from one of my history classes huffed as she swayed in, looking for her coat among the ones Nik had tossed aside. Once she left, I sat on Nik's bed and mentally scanned my body. I felt different and still in pain.

Em had warned me it could hurt but I never realised it could hurt that much. I pulled out my phone from my clutch bag and sent her a text. She probably wouldn't even be home yet. Maybe she could come back and stay over at mine for one more night. I was desperate to talk it all through. Why had I told her not to stay?

A few minutes later – no reply. As I left Nik's room, I got a few stares, the odd whisper. Did they know? Was it obvious? Angelina Georgiades – virgin no more.

I suddenly felt sober and naked – the thinness of the dress barely covering me. Cheap and used. There had been no kiss goodbye from Nik. No hug. It was all over so quickly. In fact, we hadn't even kissed while we were doing it.

There was something in my knickers, a dampness. I knew what it was. How stupid not to have brought a sanitary towel with me.

I quickened my footsteps as I walked down the dimly lit road, hugging myself tightly, wishing I had brought a jacket to the party.

Why did it still hurt?

My pace increased to a run as I felt a wave of emotion choking me. As I quietly closed the door to the flat, I breathed out the air I had held in my chest since leaving Nik's house.

Dad would kill me if he knew I had walked home alone. If he asked me in the morning, I would tell him someone had been with me, and that Em had had a change of heart and wanted to go home. Em and I had made deliberately vague plans because we knew it depended on what happened with Nik. Only I hadn't expected that – to feel so used.

Still no reply from Em, I noticed as I headed to the bathroom. I was desperate for a shower, to wash away the pain and these confused feelings, but I didn't want anyone to wake up and the pipes always rattled when someone ran the tap.

I changed into a pair of tracksuit bottoms and a sweatshirt I found buried in the laundry basket and slipped a sanitary towel into my knickers.

A noise made me stop still. Was someone still up?

I creaked open the bathroom door to the sound of laughter coming from Alex's room. But the laughter turned to something that resembled groaning. I held my hand over my mouth. Alex had a girl over and they were having sex.

Curiosity got the better of me and I crept along the hallway to outside his room. Much like my encounter with Nik, it was over in minutes, but when I heard them talking my heart beat wildly in my chest and, without thinking, I opened his door.

'What the hell?' Alex hissed when he saw me standing in the doorway – the hall light instantly illuminating his face.

But my horrified expression wasn't directed to him. It was on my best friend – Emily Walters – clutching the bedsheet up to her chin, a look of abject panic on her face.

It was hard to breathe. I closed the door behind me, scrabbled around for my phone and trainers, and left the flat, the midnight air hitting my face as tears welled in my eyes again.

There was only one person I wanted to turn to, the only other friend I could confide in; and, knowing him, he was still probably awake studying. He was the only one from our year who hadn't finished exams and couldn't come to the party because tomorrow was his Cambridge STEP paper.

No. I couldn't distract him – his future depended on that one exam.

But I had no one else to turn to.

When I reached his house, I slipped open the side gate and went to the back garden. I could see him bent over his desk – the lamp on it throwing a glow around him. I texted him to say I was outside and seconds later his head bobbed up and he lifted his window, peering into the darkness. I held my breath. If he told me he was busy, I would go.

'Lina?' he whispered.

I hopped onto the bench and shimmied myself up the side of his house, planting my feet on the nails we had secretly hammered in for this very purpose until I reached the ledge where I could tiptoe along to his window.

Ash hauled me in through the opening and I clattered to the floor in a heap. Then I crumbled. Big ugly sobs choked me as I curled up in a ball.

'Lina, what's wrong? What happened?'

'Everything's a mess. My life is a mess.'

Ash pulled me up into his arms and I buried my face into his T-shirt where my tears soaked through. He held me and rocked me back and forth and, when I could find the words, I told him everything. Everything. Sleeping with Nik, how much it had hurt and seeing my best friend in bed with my brother. I had no clue whether anything I said made sense, but he held me for ages until sleep washed over me.

Chapter 18

Now we are twenty-eight

The next couple of days of our Cypriot adventure fell into a similar pattern. Ash would be up at the crack of dawn to run along the coast, and I would have left for the dig by the time he returned. The only opportunity to see each other was in the evening when he brought home leftovers and we would talk about our day. But the initial excitement of being here together had faded. And worst of all, I was no closer to solving the mystery surrounding Mum's discovery.

At the end of my fourth day of digging and having my findings dismissed by the supervisor, I figured I had nothing to lose but to come straight out and ask him about what had brought me here.

I knocked on the Portakabin's door and the supervisor beckoned me inside.

'What did you find now?' he said, not looking up from his phone.

His tone couldn't have been more impatient, and it irritated me. What if I had found something of value? Would he just shrug and throw it away again?

'I wanted to find out how I could speak to Elias Demetriades – the man who *unearthed* this site.'

He stopped typing on his mobile. There was distrust in his eyes. 'He's busy, so no.'

'But I really need to speak to him. I have some important things I want to discuss.'

He pushed himself up from his seat, cracking his knuckles on the table. 'What do you have that is so important?'

I stood straight. 'I think my mother worked with him, about thirty-three years ago. I think she was the one who discovered the jewels from the tomb, only no one believed her at the time. Anyway, I think she was here with Elias and that's why I want to talk to him.'

He came to stand in front of me, too close, observing me through narrowed eyes, his hands rubbing against his stubbled chin. Before he could respond a commotion outside caught his attention. There was shouting and calls for first-aid assistance.

One of the other men that worked on the site tapped on the door. The supervisor grunted for him to come in and a brief conversation passed between them. I understood enough words to deduce that Marie had fallen down a pothole and couldn't walk on one foot.

The supervisor swore under his breath and pounded his fist on the desk. Before leaving, he turned to me and said, 'I'll be back soon. Sit.'

His last word came more as an order, and I took heed and slid down into the nearest chair. But as soon as he was out of sight, I saw an opportunity to nose around. The door at the back was locked and a quick rummage in the desk drawers revealed no key. I scanned the room. There was a cabinet in the corner which wasn't locked.

With a peek over my shoulder in case he was coming back, I opened it. There were folders inside marked with various Greek words. A quick flick through a couple unearthed some bills and receipts. I noticed a folder at the back labelled 'USA' that piqued my interest. Inside was correspondence with a museum in California. One sheet had a picture of a stone on it. The year at the top of the letter was the same year Mum and Dad moved to England. Could this be the third jewel that Mum's diary mentioned? I fished out my phone and took some photos.

Something else caught my eye as I went to put the file back in the cabinet – a bunch of keys tucked away in the corner.

Another glance over my shoulder and I could see the supervisor making his way back. I slammed the cabinet shut and quickly returned to my seat.

He huffed as he entered the office, coming to stand inches from me, his physique intimidating. 'These crazy Americans. They will probably sue us. And you.' He jabbed his finger at me. 'You think we lie about this site, my father's discovery?'

'Your father? Elias Demetriades is your dad?'

He nodded. 'And these accusations you make are incorrect. If you know what is good for you, you will drop them.'

'Can I not at least talk to him? Perhaps he can explain these jewels that my mother found.'

He reached out to grab my arm and lifted me up. 'Please. Leave.' His grip tightened and my heart rate picked up speed.

'I … I'm sorry. I was probably mistaken. I'm sure my mother was wrong.'

His mouth turned up in one corner and his hold on me loosened. 'I think your time here is done. You are released from your volunteer duties. Thank you for your ... assistance.'

And with those words he returned to his desk and pulled out his phone. With a flick of his hand, I was dismissed.

'You were *fired*?' Ash said to me as we sat in an outdoor taverna by the beach, two ice-cold Peronis at our fingertips.

I had persuaded him to meet me here and not back at the apartment. Our evenings there were becoming too stifling, and I didn't know why. It seemed like Ash couldn't wait to finish up whatever leftovers he had brought, end our strained conversation and head out for his evening walk alone.

'Yup. Let go. Twice ... in two weeks. Yay me.' I lifted my beer in mock-cheer and took a swig.

'How do you fire a volunteer, though?'

'I don't know, but they did.'

'You think that means they're hiding something?'

'Of course I think that, but now I have lost my chance to look around and ask more questions. Unless ...' I picked at the label on the beer bottle.

Ash loosened his tie a fraction. 'Unless what?'

'Well, the other day I was looking around and found that there's a way to unhook one of the windows and get inside the office, and I noticed a bunch of keys that might give me access to whatever it is they're hiding behind that door at the back. When I was snooping round the Portakabin the first time, it seemed to connect to something – maybe a hidden passage to the tomb Mum discovered.'

'What are you going to do, then?'

I leaned in so I could whisper. 'Break in. And you're going to help me.'

'Me?'

'I need a leg-up. Just like we used to do getting in and out of your house.'

He mirrored my posture. 'And when were you planning on breaking and entering?'

'Tonight. After midnight.'

'Aren't there cameras all around the place?'

'I clocked three, two of which are broken, and I think I can find a way for us not to be seen by the third.'

Leaning back in his chair, he folded his arms across his chest.

'I have to do this, Ash. I've come this far. I need to know what happened to Mum all those years ago and why my parents had to leave soon after.'

Ash picked up his beer and looked away from me, out towards the sea: the waves lapping against the shore in a steady rhythm; the playful laughter from a couple darting in and out of the water drifting over.

I noticed his jaw tighten as he stared off into the distance.

'You don't want to be here, do you?' I said finally.

He turned. 'Why would you say that?'

I studied him intently – jacket on despite the warm evening, back rigid. 'I don't think I have seen you out of a suit all week. And every time I ask you about the cooking class, you say it was fine without elaborating and then it seems you can't wait to finish the leftovers and get the hell away from me. I even feel like I had to beg you to come out tonight.'

Ash rubbed his thumbs up and down the beer bottle. 'Why did you ask me to come, Lina? Not here, tonight. To Cyprus.'

'Because ...' I shrugged. 'I don't know. Seeing you at the reunion and the day after brought up so many emotions from the past. All that talk about our dreams ... I thought you would be a good person to have here with me.'

'No other reason?'

I shook my head. 'You were always my best friend, Ash. And I miss it. I miss what we had.'

'Whenever you needed me, I was there,' he mumbled as the bottle hovered by his lips.

'You say it like I was a burden on you.'

He drained his drink and placed it back on the table. 'Look, I'm pretty tired. I think I'll head back to the apartment.'

There was a hard expression on his face.

'What about going to the site?'

'Lina. Let it go.'

'What do you mean?'

'I think you're chasing a ghost. And no amount of digging up the past is going to bring your mum back. Move on with your life. I appreciate you trying to fulfil what we said in our notes when we were eight, but they were childish dreams. That's all they were. Dreams. Tomorrow night, I'll be on that plane back to Mumbai, back to my "real" life, and we can put this week behind us.'

What could I say to that? There was so much anger behind his words. I should have known it was a mistake to try and erase the memory of the last time we had seen each other seven years ago. Our friendship was destroyed that night in Cambridge, and it was clear that I was not only chasing the ghost of my mother but the ghost of a time when I thought it possible for Ash and me to be together.

Chapter 19

When we were twenty-one

The pain in my lower abdomen had returned to its usual dull ache. Like it always did by Day Seven of my cycle. I breathed deeply and felt peaceful as the train pulled into its final destination: Cambridge.

Three years Ash had studied here, and I hadn't been able to visit even once. Our brief reunions at Christmas and Easter had been back in Birmingham; brief because Ash would always return here to get ahead with his studies, ready to take on mid-year or year-end exams. The last two summers he had spent in London doing internships at merchant banks.

The train juddered to a halt and hissed as the automatic doors opened. I hauled my overnight bag onto my shoulder and left with the crowds of students who all seemed to have their noses buried in a book or a phone – headphones tuning out the world around them.

I inhaled a smell that was unfamiliar. Fresh air.

I strode out of the exit with purpose, pretending that I belonged here when I knew I didn't. I had scraped the A-level grades needed for my archaeology degree at Birmingham while Ash had met his triple A* offer plus a 1 in his Cambridge STEP paper.

When I saw his face through the crowds, his smile mirrored mine. I ran towards him, threw my bag on the ground and flung my arms around his neck.

A feeling of comfort and belonging filled my body. I had missed him. This. Our friendship. It was the dearest thing to me in the whole world.

'Woah, woah, woah – what is all this, Mr Ashok Patel?' I said, sliding my hands up and down his arms before pulling back. 'Are these muscles?'

He jabbed me playfully in the shoulder. 'Hey. They've always been there.'

'Methinks there is a girl you are maybe trying to impress.' I wiggled my eyebrows up and down.

'I don't have time to be dating.'

I put my hands on his chest beneath his North Face zip-up top and rubbed my fingers over his white T-shirt. 'And a six-pack too?' I giggled.

'Lina, cut it out. There's no one I'm trying to impress. You know I'm part of St John's First VIII this year, so the training has stepped up a gear and we've got a few races coming up after finals. I've just been working out a lot, that's all.'

He grabbed my bag and slung it over his shoulder.

'Mmm-hmm,' I nodded, not buying this line of defence. Ash's transformation from gangly eighteen-year-old schoolkid to this hunk had been noticeable the first time he came home in his first year and we went out for a drink at our local. I had teased him about it then. He had brushed aside the compliment and said it was down to his new rowing obsession – the desire to be up at the crack of dawn and out on the river; the stillness, the ability to clear his head before putting in the ten hours of daily study to stay on top. And he was always on top. A double first for part one of his degree had cemented that status and he was on course for a repeat in that result for his finals.

'So where are we going first?' I asked, sensing his unease at my teasing.

'I am going to give you a grand tour of Cambridge as we walk to my college,' he said, with a dramatic sweep of his hand as we made our way from the station along the road heading into town.

The first half of the walk was past a busy shopping street teeming with restaurants and cafés. Ash pointed out some of his favourite places to grab a coffee and have brunch on a Sunday. It all sounded idyllic.

As we turned onto Trumpington Street and the first college – Peterhouse – came into view, my jaw dropped.

'This is the oldest and one of the smallest colleges, with its rival Pembroke across the road.'

I turned my head to see the other college. 'They're both beautiful.' I snuck a peek through the iron railings of Peterhouse. A chapel was in the distance surrounded by a sparkling green lawn with sprinklers creating rainbows in the sunlight.

As we walked down past more colleges, they became bigger, grander. Ash pointed out the Senate House, where he was due to graduate in a few weeks, and his favourite sandwich shop. Tourists abounded – their selfie sticks held aloft. Ash explained that because exams were still going on, most places were not open to visitors, but he had got me a special pass into where he studied.

If the previous colleges were impressive, St John's was in a league of its own. The entrance was like a castle, complete with turrets and arched windows. We passed under an opening in a large wooden gate, through a porters' lodge and came out into the serenity of Chapel Court, a large expanse of lawn surrounded by centuries-old buildings. The din of tourists was immediately extinguished once the door closed behind us, replaced with the casual chatter from students milling around and birds chirping in stone recesses.

'This is ...' I had no words to describe what this was. 'I can't believe you get to study here.'

'Yeah, I'm going to miss it.'

I fanned my face with my hand, hot from the emergence of the sun through the clouds. 'So where do you live?'

'My rooms are over there,' he said, pointing to another archway. 'You must be tired after all this travelling. I thought you might like to freshen up and then I am going to take you punting.'

'Sounds fun. But haven't you got to work? I feel awful coming in the middle of your exams.'

'Hey, it's fine,' he said, putting his arm round my shoulder and giving it a gentle squeeze. 'I only have two left and they're not until Friday. I think I can manage one day off for you.'

When the events of the previous night had unravelled there had been only one person I wanted to turn to. Through my tears, Ash hadn't hesitated in telling me to get on a train out of Birmingham, that he would cheer me up.

As we walked up several staircases to the third floor of another ancient building, a couple of guys greeted Ash with slaps on the back. When he introduced me as 'an old friend from home', they gave him a knowing look and elbowed him in the side. A girl stepped out of her room wearing a cropped T-shirt and low-slung shorts and made some reference to something Ash had cooked last night before blowing him a kiss and eyeing me suspiciously.

'Here we are,' Ash said finally as we reached his door.

'You're very popular,' I said, stepping inside.

'You get to know people on your staircase very well and we do a lot of things together.'

I didn't think my eyes could get any wider, but I certainly wasn't expecting his room to look like this. It was a large space with oak panelling, lattice windows and a wooden desk sitting under the windowsill. A three-seater sofa sat on one side of the room with an overflowing bookcase covering the opposite wall. Through a doorway was a separate bedroom and bathroom.

'This is like a hotel suite,' I marvelled. 'Are all the rooms like this?'

'This is the largest because it's a scholar's room.' He nodded to the bedroom. 'You can go and freshen up and that's your room for the night. The sofa becomes a bed.' He unzipped his jacket and slung it over his chair. 'Would you like a cuppa before we go out?'

'Yeah, that'd be great.'

'Then maybe you'd like to tell me what happened?'

A fog drifted through my mind. It had been easier to suppress last night's events than have to face them. And I knew I would do what I always did – give edited highlights. The reality was too painful and embarrassing to share. Ash was a great friend, but he wasn't a 'girl' friend.

A few minutes later, we were sat on Ash's sofa, a couple of Cambridge rowing mugs on a small wooden table with a pack of digestives open between them. I held a biscuit in my fingers and passed it between my hands.

'He said he wasn't into me any more.' I couldn't say out loud what he had actually uttered.

'Just like that, after six months? No explanation?'

'He said we were too young to be tied down.'

'And he didn't think to say this before you booked your round-the-world tickets?'

'It was stupid to have booked them in the first place.' I blew ripples across my tea before taking a sip. 'They're refundable.'

'You're not going?'

'On my own?' I shook my head. 'Anyway,' I tapped him on the knee, 'can we not talk about him any more. I came here to escape my life in Birmingham for one night.'

'If that's what you want.' Ash chewed his lip, and I knew he was desperate to get something off his chest.

'What? Come on, you're dying to make a comment.'

'He sounds like a loser.'

'You don't know him.'

'I don't want to know him. You can do better than him, Lina.'

'Can I?' I pulled my legs onto the couch and tucked them to the side.

'You deserve someone that will treat you right,' Ash said. 'Someone that knows he's the luckiest guy in the world to have you in his life.' He turned to me with those dark brown eyes that always looked at me with kindness, words spoken with that mouth that never had a bad word to say. Ever.

I dropped my shoulder into his and gently nudged him. 'You're such a lovely guy, Ash. Can't believe no one has snapped you up here.'

'I don't have time for relationships.' He slumped forward, cradling his mug in his hands before draining it and placing it on the table. 'Right.' He clapped and stood up. 'I promised you the best day of your life to forget about this guy whose name shall not be named, and that is what I will do. But first, I need to get out of this sweaty gear. I came straight to the station from training. I won't be long.'

He went off to the bedroom while I scanned his room. The shower came on as I picked up some of the books on his desk – *Calculus for the Ambitious* and *Symmetry and the Beautiful Universe*. There were papers filled with complex equations and his exam timetable. A pang of guilt filled me when I saw the two major exams he still had left to take. But he had promised me on the phone he could spare the time.

I glanced over my shoulder and a breath caught at the back of my throat as I saw Ash through the crack in his bedroom door. He had stepped out of the shower in only a towel, the muscles in his arms flexing as he bent down to pull out a T-shirt from a drawer and a pair of boxers. Droplets cascaded down his back into the crevices of the two dimples at the base of his spine. He unwound the towel and stood naked in his room, his back to me, drying himself. I couldn't look away.

My pulse beat loudly through my body. He began to turn around and I stood frozen to the spot. But he moved out of sight before I got a flash of his front, returning with his jeans on, naked chest visible. I was right. There was indeed a six-pack. I bit my bottom lip before shaking myself out of my trance and moved back to his desk. But even when I closed my eyes to centre myself, I could see him in my mind. Lush, naked, wet skin. It was a crime to look that good.

No. I couldn't be having feelings for Ash. He was my best friend. The only true friend I had. I had made some girlfriends on my course but there was no one that knew me like Ash did. There was no one else who had been there during my darkest times.

I heard the door creak and grabbed a book from his desk.

'I didn't know you were into differential equations,' he said with a laugh.

I turned. He was wearing a St John's rowing polo shirt and his hair was ruffled as if he had quickly towel-dried it. 'Sorry, what?' I said, still completely thrown by his naked display.

'The book.' He nodded to what I was holding.

I clocked the title on the cover. 'Oh, differential equations. They're my favourite.' I giggled like a silly schoolgirl whose high-school crush had spoken to her for the first time, but thankfully Ash didn't seem to notice.

His warm smile broadened. 'Come on. Let's get out of here and see some sights.' His arm stretched out again to squeeze my shoulder but this time something different happened.

His touch sent sparks through me – speared me, made my legs feel jelly-like. And his scent. Oh boy. What was it? Shower gel? Deodorant? Eau de Ash? It was clean and crisp and … I sighed. Heavenly.

We walked out of his college and Ash told me where we were headed but I couldn't focus on his words.

Agh. No. This couldn't be. I cared for Ash too much to cross that boundary from friendship into anything more. And besides, even if he ever felt the same way, I could never tell him why I was incapable of having a proper relationship. It was far better to remain just friends. Whatever 'that' was back in his bedroom was a blip. A mere appreciation of the fact that he was no longer a boy, but a man, albeit a very hot hunk of a man. Inappropriate thoughts crowded my mind again and I attempted to stamp them out. *No, no, no.*

Friends.

Nothing more.

I lay back and let the warm sun heat my skin. My hand was clutching a plastic glass of champagne and the other a half-eaten strawberry. I moaned as I took another bite.

'Feeling relaxed?'

I squinted up at Ash who was practically glowing with the sun behind him – his hands expertly planting the punt pole in the water and pulling it up rapidly as we glided along the River Cam. The Sainsbury's bag of goodies sat at my feet.

'I could get used to this,' I said, sliding further down onto my cushion – the red velvet soft against my bare arms.

'Legend has it,' Ash said, resuming his serious guide voice, 'that Mathematical Bridge was built by Sir Isaac Newton as an exemplary example of physics and that it was held up entirely by its own design and didn't need any nails or screws.'

I nodded with interest as I popped another strawberry into my mouth, dropping the stem back in the punnet as we drifted under the unusually designed bridge. Ash flattened the pole so it wouldn't get caught in the wooden structure.

'The story goes,' he said, 'that a bunch of students took the bridge apart to prove the theory and failed to put it back together.'

'So, who did?'

Ash shrugged. 'I don't think it actually happened. From memory, it was designed by someone else entirely – and I've checked and there are certainly screws holding it up.'

A few other punts passed by in the opposite direction, spilling over with students downing beers and glasses of wine, raucous laughter bouncing off the colleges' buildings on either side of the river.

'A lot of exams have finished,' Ash said. 'I'm sorry, I thought this would be a lot more relaxing for you.'

'It's fine, I'm enjoying it.'

'I have an idea, though,' Ash said, his voice laced with intrigue.

I breathed in and out deeply. This felt amazing. Getting out of Birmingham was something I hardly did. And Cambridge had this magical feel to it, like I had stepped back to another century. I couldn't wait to see what else Ash had planned for the rest of the day.

Only trouble was it was getting increasingly hard to focus on his words as my eyes couldn't stop roaming over his body: the curve of his muscles every time he pulled the pole out of the water; the veins that snaked their way up his forearms. Was it obvious to him that I was staring at his lips when he spoke? I shook my head. No. These were rebound feelings. I was drawn into Ash's thoughtfulness, how he was making me feel special and cared for. No guy had ever made me feel that way without wanting more from me.

As we moored the punt, Ash held out his hand to help me onto the bank by the Mill pub. There it was again. That rush of heat as his hand clasped mine. I wobbled precariously as I stepped out and ended up crashing into him. He laughed as he stumbled backwards but managed to keep us upright. Ash told me to wait while he went to organise our next adventure.

I was surrounded by students drinking beer, the rush of water as it churned by the bridge where a multitude of punts rested, ready to be filled with more tourists or drunk students. In the distance, blankets were laid out with picnic baskets. It was almost impossible to see a patch of grass that wasn't occupied.

'Cycling?' I said when I saw Ash wheeling two bikes down the pavement.

'Yeah, I borrowed them from a couple of friends who go to a college near here.' He leaned one towards me. 'Let's see if this is a good size for you.'

After a few minutes spent lowering the saddle and adjusting the handlebars, we set off over the bridge and weaved our way through passers-by and roaming cows. But once we were out of the city centre and on a quieter stretch of cycle path, we were able to ride side by side.

'It's beautiful out here,' I said, breathing deeply and inhaling a heady mixture of cut grass and fragrant flowers. I did a scan of my body, and I could honestly say I had never felt this relaxed.

No pain. No dark thoughts crowded my mind. I smiled and angled my head back, taking in the blue sky and the trio of birds passing over.

Ash told me how his life was always spent at St John's or on the river and that this was an escape for him too. He slowed as we came to an opening where deckchairs were laid, some filled with people sipping from china cups.

'Where are we?' I said as I came to a stop beside him.

'Grantchester, and that,' he pointed to the café in the distance, 'is the famous Orchard Tea Rooms where the likes of Rupert Brooke and Virginia Woolf used to come. I'll go and get us some tea and cake. Why don't you find a spot to sit? We can do chairs or grass. I'm easy.'

We chained the bikes in the designated cycle park, and I noticed a sign which welcomed visitors to 'a corner of England where time stands still as the outside rushes by'.

I wandered away from other diners, through apple trees, stroking the bark as I passed by until I came to a quiet area. From this vantage, the meadow seemed to go on forever, as if the world ended up ahead. The long grass tickled my legs as I walked further away, the tips of my fingers touching the blades as I leaned down. I closed my eyes and let my other senses reignite: the distant chatter of tea lovers, my face hot then cool as the sun played chase with the clouds.

I took off my cardigan, laid it down on the ground and sat hugging my knees. A quick glance over my shoulder and I could see Ash coming towards me holding a tray.

It was undeniable now. The rhythm of my heart was picking up speed as he drew close, and I eyed his muscles gently flexing at the rim of his shirt as he held the tray tightly. Whatever rowing regime he was on had transformed him. It felt like I was objectifying him, thinking of his body beneath his clothes. Heat rose into my cheeks again.

'Couldn't find you for a moment,' he said. 'Should have known you'd be hiding out here.'

He put the tray down and I shuffled over on my cardigan.

'Want me to go and get a blanket?' Ash said hesitantly.

'No, it's fine. There's space,' I said, patting beside me. 'Wow, look at those scones.'

'Wasn't sure what you wanted but thought I couldn't go wrong with a traditional cream tea.'

I sat cross-legged, my knee resting on Ash's – the heat emanating from his skin soothing, comforting, so I didn't pull away. My thoughts weren't being typed out on a ticker tape – they were safely ensconced in my brain. A good thing too, as all I could think about was how his nearness was making me feel: hotter than the sun beating down on us.

I sipped my tea in between mouthfuls of scone with lashings of cream and jam and tried not to look him in the eye, instead gazing straight out across the meadow.

'Thanks for all this, Ash. I really appreciate you letting me come and see you. I feel ... more like myself now.'

'There's never any need to thank me.'

'I know, but it was a bit dramatic, wasn't it? Me ringing you so late last night. I just had to get out. Life has become so stifling recently. I get up every day at five to make that order for Nik's dad and then straight to uni. But I was OK with it because I thought everything was going to change, that I had an out.'

I finally looked at him. It was a brief glance, but it was enough to make my insides do somersaults and backflips as I took in his kind eyes, his lips and a hint of stubble. Staring back down at the piece of scone in my hand, I let the jam drip off it onto the plate before swiping it with my finger and licking.

He nudged me gently in the shoulder. 'You do have an out. You can still travel.'

I shook my head. 'I haven't told Dad about my plans. I'm not sure how to. And there's no way he'll say yes to me going alone.'

'Do you really need his permission? You're twenty-one.'

'It's the way it's always been. And I'm all he's got. He relies on me.'

'But you're not planning on staying in Birmingham forever, are you?'

'I applied for all these museum jobs, but only the one in Birmingham has come through with a firm yes. It's only on a volunteer basis to start with, but it's a chance to get my foot in the door. That'll mean I have to stay living at home – keep my expenses low, try not to make that student debt any bigger.'

'All the more reason why you have to travel this summer, see the world.'

I finished my tea and laid it on the tray, not knowing how to respond. My world map came to mind – the one on my bedroom wall with all the places I dreamed of going to.

'I'll come with you,' Ash said suddenly.

I sat back. 'What?'

'I'll buy the other ticket from you. We'll go together.'

'But you can't. You've got that internship this summer. You told me all about it. A thousand candidates and three spots. And one is yours.'

He pushed the tray away and leaned back on his arms, stretching out his legs. 'I don't really want to do it. In fact, I'm not sure I want any of this.' He nodded to the open meadow.

'You're about to graduate, so you won't be here in Cambridge much longer.'

'I don't mean that, Lina. I mean the pressure. The expectations. It never ends. The interviews I had to do for this investment bank were brutal. I felt like I was on some survival-of-the-fittest show, proving my worth, my ability. But once I'm there, I'll be spending the whole summer trying to prove that I am worthy of the golden prize – the one place to join the firm as a permanent employee. I thought it would all stop once I got to Cambridge, but it didn't. I had to be number one in my subject in my college, then the whole university, applying for this scholarship and that scholarship.'

He flopped onto the ground, his weight pushing the tall grass beneath him, gazing up to the sky.

'I want to be free, Lina. I don't want this life any more.'

'Have you told anyone this?'

He sat up, resting on his hands. The look he gave me made my heartbeat escalate again.

A small shake of his head. 'Only you,' he whispered. 'You're the only one I've ever confided in, the only one I feel I can ever be myself around, and not some stereotype of a good Indian boy – maths genius, Cambridge scholar.'

I hugged myself, stroking my arms.

'When I am with you,' he continued, 'I feel I can be who *I* want to be.'

'I don't know what to say.'

He shrugged. 'You don't have to say anything. Just consider it. We could travel anywhere we want to. India, China, Japan. Imagine it.'

A breeze tickled my bare skin and I shivered. Without any need to say anything, Ash had picked up my cardigan which we were no longer sitting on, shaken it out and handed it to me. Something passed between us. A moment, the softest of touches when our fingers brushed together. Had he felt it too?

I casually flicked a blade of grass from the lapel, not daring to admit how his nearness was making me feel as I put it on.

'But you'd be giving up so much for me, Ash. I don't think I could let you do that.'

'You're not asking me to do it. It's my decision.'

'But what about after we come back from travelling? What then?'

'I don't know. I'm tired of having everything always mapped out. I want what Divya has ... freedom.'

'But it came at a price, Ash. She cut herself off from your whole family.'

He hugged his knees, mirroring my posture. 'She didn't have a choice. Mum and Dad made it clear that there would be consequences for her actions. All she wanted was to follow her dream of being a music producer. And after all she had suffered when she was a baby, why couldn't they let her do it?'

Born with a congenital heart defect, Divya had been having hospital check-ups since she was a baby. Ash's parents had wanted her to go to a local college after she finished school, but she had been 'discovered' DJing at a club in Birmingham and the lure of California had proved too great.

'I guess they wanted to protect her?' I said.

He tutted. 'And who's protecting her now when she's so far away from all of us?'

'Hard to believe she and my brother are both in LA.'

'Have you spoken to him?'

I lay back on the grass, staring up at the pale blue sky like Ash had a moment ago. 'No.' I crossed my arms. 'Nor do I want to.' Nor would I ever say *her* name out loud again. The one who lied to me, the one who was now my sister-in-law.

Love, they called it. The 'relationship' between them had been going on for six months behind my back. And when Alex announced an agent had approached him from California, keen to sign him for an action movie, they announced they were going there together – her university education put on hold indefinitely in the hope she would get discovered as a dancer.

Dad had been furious when he found Alex and Emily together in bed that night after hearing me slam the flat's door. He had a massive row with Alex and banned him from going but that added fuel to the fire and made him want to leave even more. Emily's parents had been horrified and tried all they could to stop her from joining him. I couldn't care less for either of them. But the pain of that time was still there, even after three years.

I put aside those memories and contemplated getting out of here with Ash. Alex had left us without a second thought; surely Dad would be OK with me gone for the summer.

'Yes,' I said finally.

'Yes what?'

I sat up. 'Let's go travelling, see the world together.' The sun was behind his head, pure bliss etched on his face.

He reached his hand out to me, casually pulling a blade of grass from my hair. The action made my pulse quicken again.

'You mean it?' he said.

'I've spent the last eight years serving everyone in my family. Maybe it's time I thought of myself. And you too. Why start a career that's only going to make you miserable?'

Ash twisted the friendship bracelet round his wrist. It was adorable that he still wore it. It was frayed, as if it might disintegrate at any moment. But then I noticed a shift in his expression. Concern? Was he already having second thoughts about leaving everything he had worked for behind? Could I really be responsible for encouraging him?

'Hey.' I reached for his hand. 'You OK?'

He nodded. 'Yeah.' He swept his thumb over my fingers, and I tightened my hold.

There it was again. A shift. A moment. Heat surging through me. I studied his thumb and the measured movement, before slowly daring to look up. Our eyes met and my lips parted.

Ash suddenly pulled back. 'We should probably be heading off. There are some papers I need to pick up from my tutor before this evening's entertainment.'

I tried to ignore the change of his tone and let my mind wander. A whole month of travelling with my best friend. These new feelings I was having towards Ash weren't real, I reassured myself. It was the champagne and the longing to be cared for. Nothing more.

Chapter 20

Candlelight flickered along the table as the Master of St John's uttered a grace in Latin. Students and Fellows responded with 'Amen' before everyone sat down. This was Formal Hall – dinner in the Samuel Butler Room. Ash had purchased a 'wine' ticket for me as a treat.

Students chatted animatedly, seemingly oblivious to their incredible surroundings – stained-glass windows soaring up into the roof, gold-framed portraits of distinguished-looking men lining the walls. Everyone was wearing a black gown, including Ash. I tugged at my T-shirt, conscious that my bra strap had been on display and that I felt horrendously out of place.

A three-course meal was served by waitresses with a glass of wine for each course and the whole experience couldn't have been further from my student days.

At the college bar later, a couple of girls made a beeline for us and demanded that Ash buy them a drink, so he excused himself. My head was beginning to buzz after the champagne on the punt and the wine at dinner.

'So, you're Ash's Birmingham school *friend*,' one of the girls said to me as I stood nervously in the corner of the room.

She said the word 'friend' with great emphasis, and I wasn't sure what she was implying.

'Yeah, we grew up together. His family lives round the corner from me.'

She nodded. 'How cute. Childhood sweethearts.'

'Oh no, we're not together.' I shook my head.

'Oh, really? Sorry, my mistake. I knew Ash was crazy in love with someone from back home. I guess I must have mixed you up with someone else. Still, I can't believe you got him to come out to the bar in the middle of finals,' she said. 'We haven't seen Ash here in weeks.'

I had no reply. What girl could Ash have been in love with from back home?

They giggled and reminisced about an event in their first year, where they had held Ash hostage one night when he had come out to their communal kitchen to make some tea and two guys had dragged him to the bar for a drink. But I wasn't really following their story.

'I'm sorry,' I interrupted, 'but are you sure that this girl – the one Ash is in love with – that she's from Birmingham? Could she not be from another college, or maybe from his course?'

The blonde snorted. 'Have you seen those maths geeks?' She tossed her head backwards. 'Ash is far too hot to be dating one of those girls.'

'Can you believe no one has won the bet on when he's going to have his cherry popped?' the brown-haired girl said. 'Maybe he's still pining for that Greek girl.'

I could feel blood rushing to my face. Greek. I turned suddenly and inadvertently knocked into someone holding three very full drinks. Ash. His T-shirt became soaked through. My cheeks flushed even more than they already were. 'God, I'm so sorry.'

'It's OK,' he said. 'I'll pop back to the bar and get another one for you.' He handed over the drinks to the two girls and placed my now half-empty rum and Coke on the table.

I picked it up. 'No, this is fine, honestly. I've already had enough wine over dinner, and champagne for that matter.'

'Well then, I won't be a sec.' He flapped his T-shirt away from his chest. 'This is pretty sticky, so I'll go up and change.'

I panicked at the thought of being left with these two girls any longer. Sucking the entire drink through the straw until there was a slurping sound, I shook the glass and let the ice cubes rattle.

'Finished!' I said, swallowing a burp which I hoped the present company hadn't heard. 'I'll come with you.'

'No need,' Ash said. 'It won't take me more than a few minutes.'

I turned so my back was to the two girls. 'I'm pretty tired,' I whispered. 'I think I'd like to go to bed. Leave you to do some more study.'

'Are you sure? I thought I was meant to be showing you the best of Cambridge.'

'You did, it was great. But I have an early train tomorrow.'

'Oh, I thought you'd stay the whole day. Sunday is your free day from the deli, isn't it?'

'You have to study, Ashok Patel. I am not letting you jeopardise your degree to show me around Cambridge any more.'

He acquiesced and we headed up after a round of goodbyes.

Back in Ash's room, my mind reeled. I noticed a box of decaf tea and set about making us both a cup, trying not to look through the doorway to his bedroom as he changed out of his shirt.

Ash was in love with me? How long had he been feeling this way?

'It's a bit early to be going to bed, isn't it?' Ash said as he took one of the mugs. His arm brushed up against mine and there it was again. That charge. That feeling I could no longer ignore.

'I might read for a bit,' I said casually as I scanned his bookcase.

He sat down at his desk and picked up some papers. I pulled down the only book that didn't have something mathematical in the title and sat on his sofa. But after a few minutes I realised I had reread the first page three times and the words hadn't registered in my mind at all.

Ash turned and caught me staring. 'Everything OK?'

I nodded and a half-hearted 'hmm-hmm' sound came from my pressed lips.

Ash narrowed his eyes and closed his book. He leaned on his elbow, pen playing on his lips. Those lips. Why had I never noticed how full they were? I couldn't help but notice the curves of his arms again; his smooth, dark skin.

'You don't sound very convincing. Are you still thinking about the break-up?'

I blinked. 'What? No, I'm not. It's just ... never mind.'

He pushed his notes to one side and came over to sit next to me. His nearness made my heart beat a little faster. I held my hand over my neck, aware of the heat beginning to coat my skin and dared not meet his gaze.

'Lina. Why can't you look at me?'

I twisted my fingers in my lap. 'Are you in love with me?' I said boldly.

Ash's mouth dropped open wide. 'Um, what?' He let out a laugh, but it was tinged with embarrassment. 'What made you say that?'

'Those girls. The ones at the bar. They said you were in love with someone from back home and that she was Greek.'

He held my eyes for several beats. The room seemed to close in.

A pop. A crackle of electricity. The light bulb on Ash's desk had burned out. But neither of us moved. The only illumination in the room now was from the lamps on the quad outside the window.

Then … a simple nod. A nervous look on Ash's face. 'Yeah. I am,' he whispered. 'Sorry.'

'Why are you sorry?'

'I don't know. Because … well …' His lips twitched and I stared at them, long and hard. His tongue popped out and licked them ever so slightly, and now they glistened in the semi-darkness.

I didn't know whether it was because I was feeling vulnerable or whether the rush of feelings that had been mounting all day spurred me on, but I leaned in and kissed him. It was only a brush of lips. But the fizz that sparked on mine made me crave more. I leaned in a little closer. He held his hand on my cheek, the pad of his thumb stroking my face, a look of bewilderment on his.

I closed my eyes and felt his body shift, his lips on mine again. I opened my mouth and let the kiss deepen. I didn't want to break away. As we kissed, I laid a hand on his chest, his heart thundering under my fingers. His arms were encircling me now, his hands moving over my back. He had hugged me so many times over the years: when I was upset because I had suddenly been overwhelmed by grief again, celebrating an achievement or just because …

He was Ash, and I was Lina. Best friends forever. And always.

But now? Now I was sitting astride him, his hands running gently up and down my spine, fingers resting on my skin where my T-shirt ended, and skirt began. My hands were in his hair, and it was as soft as I had idly imagined when we were punting.

I finally pulled back to catch my breath, lips tingling. 'I think you'd better get back to work,' I said with a smile, trying to break the intensity of what had happened.

He focused on my mouth. 'I doubt I'll be able to concentrate on work now.'

I swallowed away a sinking feeling. A feeling that I knew couldn't be squashed; that the kiss was a mistake. I got up off his lap and stood awkwardly in the middle of the room, tugging at the hem of my skirt.

What had I done? That line. That imaginary line had been crossed.

'I'll see you ... later.' I turned and went to his bedroom, shutting the door, hoping my tone of voice hadn't been suggestive. But Ash wasn't like that. He wasn't that kind of guy. That kiss had been special though, and I knew it would inevitably lead to more.

Would it really be Ash's first time? Surely those girls had been mistaken. My pulse quickened and memories stirred of that night three years ago, my first time, and every time since. The pain. The inevitable pain. The car accident had left an internal scar. I saw it as a punishment for what had happened.

I lay in Ash's bed in the darkness, my mind churning, holding my hand over my lower stomach and rubbing the area by my left hip. When I heard Ash's chair scrape across the floor, I rolled onto my side and didn't move. There was a creak of the door and a rustle of movement as he made his way to the bathroom. When he came out again, I heard him whisper my name. It was so soft and tender. It took all of my strength not to stir, not to open my eyes and invite him into his bed and into my arms, where I wanted him to be, where I knew I could never let him be.

I didn't drift off at all. I waited; waited until I hoped he was asleep, then, using the torch on my phone, I got up and found a pen and paper. I wrote him a letter. A coward's way to let him down, to tell him I didn't love him and not the truth, that I could never love him, not in the way he deserved, not in the way he needed. He was a bloke, after all. And sex would inevitably be a part of any relationship with him.

I waited until just before dawn to leave, asking the porter at the gate to let me out of the college. There was a look of concern on his face as he jangled his keys and asked if I was OK. The tears that were streaming down my face can't have convinced him when I said I was fine and would be walking to the station, as he insisted on ordering me a taxi and handing over a five-pound note. An act of kindness from a complete stranger.

I looked out from the window of the cab as it sped away. *Goodbye, Ash. Goodbye, my friend. I'll miss you.*

Chapter 21

Now we are twenty-eight

The only light that guided me was from the moon. I zipped up my jacket to my chin and pulled the hood over my head, tugging the drawstrings tight.

I didn't need anyone's help. As soon as I had arrived at the Kition archaeological site after midnight, I noticed one of the buckets that I had used to collect earth had been left out. I stood on the base, shifting my weight from side to side to check it was steady. Stretching my arms, it was easy to open the window and reach for the latch to open it wider. A push on the balls of my feet propelled me and I swung my leg up so I could climb inside. It was a short drop down onto the cabinet below and then a jump to the floor.

I stood in the room, my breathing rapid, trying to swallow away the fear.

After the heated discussion with Ash at the beach bar, he had walked off and I hadn't followed. I wasn't chasing a ghost. I was trying to right a wrong.

I pressed the torch button on my phone and flicked it over the cabinet. Opening the drawer revealed the stack of keys I had seen before. I tried each one in the back door's lock. Lucky number seven turned in the hole. I flashed the torch into the darkness. It was an empty room. My heart sank. Moving my phone, illuminating each wall, it finally highlighted something. A safe? There was another lock. An opening for a smaller key this time. I checked the hoop and tried a few until it unlocked. Inside lay some documents – receipts similar to the ones I had seen in the filing cabinet and underneath them was a logbook.

As I flipped to the last page of entries, my hands began to tremble. My mother's writing was staring back at me. There it was. The date and time of her discovery. This was it. This proved she had been the one to discover the tomb.

A sound startled me, and I dropped my phone; the light extinguished.

'Lina?'

It was Ash. What was he doing here?

'Lina, are you in there?'

'Yes,' I said, reaching for the door. But it didn't open when I turned the handle.

'Lina, I heard a car pull up. You'd better get out of there.'

Shit. I wrenched the handle again and again and felt underneath it only to discover there was no hole. 'Can you open it from the outside?'

The handle shifted but the door remained shut. I reached to the floor, but there was no gap, no possible way to slip the key under.

'I'm going to have to break it down,' Ash said. 'Stand as far back as you can, OK? I'll count to three.'

'OK,' I said, reaching back to the floor to find my phone, still clutching the logbook. As my fingers grazed the screen, I could feel ridges in the glass, and it didn't come to life when I pressed the side switch.

I took a large step backwards but what was behind me wasn't solid, and I didn't have time to correct my footing as Ash began his countdown. The wall came crashing down with my full weight. The backs of my knees hit something sharp, and a pain shot straight through me. Then I was rolling, scraping the skin on my elbows and shins until I came to a stop. I choked on the air that was thick with a smell reminiscent of the basement room at the Birmingham Museum.

My hands felt the floor until they found something made of stone, round in shape. I grabbed it to try and pull myself up. Then ...

Chapter 22

When we were thirteen

A hand against mine, squeezing my fingers tight. A machine beeping. And a voice whispering ... mathematical equations?

I forced my eyelids open.

That smile. It dulled the pain; the fear that was gripping my throat.

'I knew it,' Ash said brightly. 'I knew maths would wake you up.'

I smiled broadly but it made the pain in my pelvis deepen and I grimaced.

'It's OK, you're going to be OK,' Ash said, leaning in.

I took in my surroundings. White sheets and a blanket tucked under my arms, one of which had a drip that was pumping some clear liquid into me. Ash's chair was up close against the bed which had a clipboard hanging off the end and a pull-out bed was under the windowsill with ruffled sheets on it. And there on the bedside cabinet – a small figurine.

Ash caught me staring and picked it up. 'Dhanvantari,' he announced, showing it to me more closely. There were multiple arms adorning the figure and loads of bright colours. 'The god of healing and medicine.'

I nodded, not really appreciating the significance. 'What happened?' I asked.

A look of horror crossed Ash's face. 'You don't remember?'

I shook my head ever so slightly from side to side. The memories were fragments. And I was too mortified to say out loud to Ash that I had my period. Didn't I? I lifted my sheet but pulled it back down immediately when I saw a tube there. Oh God, what the hell was that?

Where's Mum? I needed to say sorry. I was shouting before everything went black. I told her I hated her. She must be so mad at me for missing Alex's play. It must be over by now. Was that her bed under the window?

A squeeze on my fingers again pulled me back into the room.

'Did we win, Ash, or was it a dream? Did we win *Strictly*?'

A nod. 'We did, Lina. We did.'

'I remember now. Emily wants me to join her dance club. Only Mum said I couldn't. It's like when your dad said you weren't allowed to do *MasterChef*. Remember when he shouted at me, told me not to interfere. I was only trying to help. I was only sticking up for you. I thought we could convince him that you could do both: you know, the show and keep up with all your schoolwork. Maybe you could help me convince Mum. You know how much I hate Greek school on a Saturday. I would do anything to dance instead.'

A single tear trickled down Ash's cheek. It was then that I knew something was horribly wrong.

'Ow!' I screamed as a pain so forceful pierced my lower stomach. It was impossible to pinpoint the actual location.

Ash released his grip on my hand and fled out of the room, returning moments later with a nurse.

'There, love,' she said, checking the tube inserted into my arm and noticing a kink in the plastic. 'You were leaning on the medication, and it wasn't getting into your system.'

'It hurts,' I whimpered.

'I know it does. But you're getting the best care here and you'll be on your feet in no time at all.'

She bustled out of the room and back in again with a tray of instruments – a needle and some other objects in sterile bags. She told me to look away and within minutes I felt woozy. She stroked my hair and told me to rest. I closed my eyes momentarily, only to open them to see Ash sitting back down beside me.

'If it's OK with you,' he said, 'I'm just going to sit here reading my book out loud until your dad comes back. He only left to get a coffee. You can go to sleep again. We'll be here when you wake up.'

I smiled as I drifted over the tide of pain, over to the other side where it didn't hurt as much. The figurine on the table appeared to come to life, its arms moving up and down, holding its healing hands out towards me. A picture came to mind of me and Ash dancing, then holding our trophy aloft. My sweet friend Ash. Always there. Best friends forever. Always. Forever. Always.

Chapter 23

Now we are twenty-eight

A hand over mine. Reassuring. Comforting.

I opened my eyes. White sheets and a blanket lay on me. The view out of the window was different to what I thought I had seen. But then it hit me that it had been only a dream.

'She's dead, isn't she?' I turned my head to see Ash staring back at me. 'Mum's dead.'

Ash's eyebrows knotted together. 'You're OK, Lina. Everything's going to be OK.'

'What happened? Where am I?'

'I tried breaking the door down, but I couldn't. There was this rumbling sound, almost like an earthquake. Then you screamed. Somehow, I got the door open right as these men burst into the office. We found you half buried under these huge boulders.'

His jaw pulsed as he took my hand in both of his, his eyes misting.

'Why, Lina? Why didn't you listen to me?' He bowed his head. 'I thought I'd lost you again.'

'The logbook!' I cried.

Ash sat up. 'What?'

'The logbook. I found it in that room. It was proof that my mum had been the one to find those jewels. Where is it?' I tried to pull myself up but winced.

Ash gently held a hand to my shoulder, and I lay back down. 'It was a pile of rubble around you. Those men pushed me around and I couldn't get to you. I'm sorry, Lina. It was a race against time to get you out of there before the whole thing collapsed. You're lucky to be alive.' He choked back those last words and the muscles in his jaw tensed again.

'Why were you there?' I asked.

'I felt so bad about what I said to you. I went back to the apartment and waited for you, thought maybe my words might have convinced you to change your mind, but then I realised how important this was to you. I felt awful for letting you down. I should've been there; I shouldn't have left you to do this on your own.'

I stared deeply into his eyes. 'You didn't let me down. You were right in a way. I am chasing a ghost. I keep thinking if only I could clear her name, then maybe she could forgive me for what happened that night.'

'Lina, the accident wasn't your fault. There was ice on the road.'

'But if I hadn't wanted to wait to get our trophy, she wouldn't have been speeding.'

'They don't know if she was speeding or not.'

'But the things I said to her ...' A tear trickled down my cheek and Ash brushed it away with his finger. His touch – soothing.

I grimaced again.

'The doctor said she'd come in when you woke up. Let me go and get her.'

I reached for his hand and held him back. 'Not yet. Please, Ash. Stay a little longer. I'm scared.'

'Hey,' he stroked my hair. 'I'm not going anywhere.' He sat back down, clutching my hand in both of his now. 'And there's nothing to be scared of. The doctor said as much. But as a precaution, I've extended my stay. Our stay. Rebooked both our tickets.'

'You have?'

'When I spoke to the doctor earlier, she advised against travelling until you're back on your feet and you weren't lucid for a long time, so I went ahead and got us a place to stay for you to recuperate. It's ...' he shrugged '... a bit of an upgrade. If I'm going to work out here for a while, I need better Wi-Fi.' He smiled, that familiar smile.

I searched his eyes. 'I've missed you.'

'I've missed you too.' He squeezed my hand.

The door opened, and a woman with dark hair held tightly in a bun, silvery strands threaded through it, came in wearing a doctor's coat. 'How is the patient?' she said with a warm smile.

'She's in pain, doctor,' Ash said, his voice full of concern.

She lifted the clipboard off the foot of the bed, flipped through the pages and came to stand beside Ash. 'You're a lucky lady, Lina. If one of those boulders had fallen somewhere else ...' She trailed off before flicking over another page.

My throat tightened as I thought of Dad. 'My mobile,' I said frantically.

'It's OK,' Ash said. 'I was waiting for you to wake up before going and getting you a new one. Yours was smashed up but I'm hoping I can get the SIM card transferred. Are you OK if I leave you with the doctor?'

I nodded and he held my hand to his lips, briefly brushing his mouth against my skin before leaving.

When the door closed, the doctor's face turned serious. She checked my pulse and ran some checks before peeling off the sheets and lifting my hospital gown. There were bandages covering my pelvis. It was like a flashback to when I was thirteen.

'I'm going to very gently take these off and see how the wound is.'

Every time her fingers touched my skin, my face contorted in pain.

'It hurts all over?' she asked.

'Yes.'

'Lina, when you were in surgery, we did a procedure to see the extent of the trauma and found some scarring of the tissue around your pelvis. Have you experienced a previous trauma there?'

I nodded, choking back the emotion as the flash of that time came to mind. 'I was in a car accident when I was thirteen. I was carrying a trophy and when the car crashed it speared into me pretty much in the same place as these bandages.'

'Did it heal normally, or did you have any more discomfort there?'

This was like déjà vu. The same conversation I had had with several doctors. *The pain you feel every month is normal, but let's try another pill, maybe therapy will heal you. The pain should lessen etc., etc.* Only it never had.

'During my menstrual cycle it hurts … a lot. I've seen several doctors and tried various contraceptive pills. Some have lessened the pain. But they all have said it's normal to experience that kind of discomfort.'

She shook her head. 'Not necessarily. If the pain is acute, debilitating, affects your ability to carry on normally with your life, then no, it's not normal. How about when you're intimate with someone? When you have sex.'

I pressed my lips tightly. Flashbacks to every single time. My first experience with Nik. The shooting pain at every other sexual encounter – trying to numb it with alcohol, a bit of Ecstasy once with a one-night stand in my early twenties. 'Frigid bitch', the words my university boyfriend called me that night I said I didn't fancy having sex; that night he broke up with me. That was the night that had made me want to run – to Cambridge, to Ash. But it had been the reason why I had then run from *him*.

'It really hurts when I have sex. It's like a searing pain. Like someone has shot a lit sparkler up my vagina,' I said with a laugh tinged with embarrassment. It always seemed easier to downplay the agony than to confront how bad it was.

'Have you spoken to your partner about this?'

'I don't have a partner.'

'The young man that was in here?'

'Ash? No, he's just a friend.'

She nodded knowingly. 'Well, he's a very good friend, then. He hasn't left your side since you came out of the operating theatre. Listen, Lina.' She stood a little closer to the bed. 'I don't think this pain is normal at all. Sounds to me like you've been fobbed off in the past. If we have your consent, I would like to undertake a laparoscopy. It's a non-invasive surgery. You'll be under general anaesthetic for the procedure. I have an idea what might be causing your problems. Yes.' She gave a measured nod. 'It could be linked to the accident but that might not be the whole story. Have you ever had a coil fitted?'

'Once. But it hurt so much when the nurse tried to place it inside that we didn't go ahead with it. I ended up getting that one you get injected into your arm. But that was removed after the pain became worse.'

'You've really been through it, haven't you? I promise, Lina, that you won't leave here until we get to the bottom of everything.' She smiled again, the lines by her eyes intensifying. 'I don't mean to alarm you but there were some men here earlier wanting to ask you questions about what you were doing at that site.'

A chill of fear coated my skin.

'Your friend sent them away. We can ask Security to inform us if they reappear. Are you an archaeologist or something like that?'

'Not really. My mum was. That was the site she worked at back when she lived here.'

The doctor gripped the sides of her face and sat down on the edge of my bed. 'You're Elina Sallas's daughter?'

Before I could answer and say no, a thought popped into my head. *Elina Sallas. ES.* The initials on the notebook and on the wooden chest. 'My mum was called Alara, and her maiden name was Phyrillas. But recently I found a diary of hers and there were the initials "ES" on it.'

Her eyes misted over. 'I gave her that notebook. And a jewellery box, for her birthday. I can't believe it. I haven't seen her in over thirty years. She was my best friend.'

I smiled broadly. 'She was?'

She nodded. 'The last time I saw her, she said she was leaving Cyprus. She couldn't tell me why, nor did she leave me any details. I never heard from her again. How is she?'

I didn't need to say the words out loud. She could read my face instantly. She clasped my hand in hers, squeezing it tightly. 'Oh, you poor girl. My poor Elina.' She stroked my cheek and swallowed deeply. 'You look so much like her.'

I couldn't believe it. She knew Mum. Maybe this was my chance to find out more about what happened before she left Cyprus.

'I can see the similarities in your eyes, the shape of your face. Tell me everything about you.'

We talked for a while, me filling her in on my life, recalling what few memories I had of Mum from my childhood. The instant connection between us soothed the increasing pain in my pelvis. But it wasn't long before we reached the present day and what I had read in Mum's journal.

'I was at medical school at the time,' she said. 'My hours were horrendous; well, they still are but I had been on several night shifts, and I hadn't seen Elina in days. I knew she was in trouble, yet I couldn't help her. I waited, waited so long for her to get in touch. They put posters of her up. Some men came to my door; they hassled me, accusing me of knowing where she was. I never said she had gone to England, and I was sure they had my phone tapped. When a year became two, I resigned myself that she had moved on with her life, that I needed to let her go.'

'I think the place I fell into was the entrance to the tomb Mum found. They dug from a different direction – the one they have on display in the museum. They covered up the fact that Mum had made the discovery. I found a logbook when I broke in and it proved that the entry of her find predated the information displayed in the museum. The only problem is my friend said the logbook wasn't nearby when they found me. And I have no idea why they would keep the evidence, albeit secretly.'

'You took a big risk going there. Those men that came round. They are connected to a rather wealthy family in this town. They're Elias Demetriades's nephews, I believe.'

'He's the one Mum worked with on the dig. I have to—' I sat up but gritted my teeth in pain.

She laid a reassuring hand on my arm. 'You don't need to do anything. We need to get you better first. Doctor's orders. Elina was my closest, dearest friend, and I will make it my priority to help you in any way I can.'

Chapter 24

'En-do-me-tri-o-sis,' I said out loud.

Ash's hands tightened around the steering wheel as I said each syllable with great emphasis.

I sank into the leather front passenger seat. It was a hire car. Ash had rented it as he said the place he had booked was a little remote and he didn't want to keep taking cabs every time he needed to get somewhere. All I knew was that it was still close to the sea, and I would have my own bed.

My head was spinning from the diagnosis. It had been reassuring to learn that I had not imagined the seriousness of the pain. It was very real and apparently it was unfortunate that it hadn't been discovered before now.

'And this is the first time you've known you have this condition?' he said.

'Yes. The procedure they did was simple and didn't have any complications.'

'But ... you've been living with all this pain, and you never said anything to anyone?' He gave me a brief sideways look before concentrating back on the road ahead.

'Nik knows.'

Ash's jaw did that crunching thing again and his knuckles whitened as he gripped the wheel tighter.

But Nik didn't know everything. He didn't know about the pain he had caused me that first time we slept together, nor about why my track record with guys was so awful. He had always assumed I had gone out with jerks, not that I had pushed guys away repeatedly.

'And he didn't suggest you see someone?'

'Of course he did. I've seen several doctors, but I think I was fobbed off with various explanations; no real answers.'

'And now?'

'Doctor Lamos said the operation was a success; they scraped away some cysts, removed all of the endometriosis. Now I have to rest for a few days, limited movement, and then I should hopefully see an easing of pain during my ... periods.' I blushed furiously. 'If not, she gave me all sorts of things I could try.'

Ash's brow wrinkled and I could see he was doing his best to process what I had said.

We pulled into a driveway, and he lowered his window to punch some keys into a security system. The gates opened and I gasped. A whitewashed single-storey house was in the distance surrounded by lush green bushes, lemon trees and a manicured garden with sprinklers scattering droplets around the lawn.

'Ash, what on earth have you booked?'

He left my question unanswered and opened his door, coming round to my side. I got out gingerly, grateful for Ash's arm to lean on as he helped me to the house. Inside was even more grand, with marble surfaces and cream walls at every turn. But when we walked through the entrance hall, a breath caught at the back of my throat as I saw the view out to the sea. The water was so close I could reach out my hand and almost touch it. There was a hammock and a double recliner on one side of the deck, with a table and chairs on the other. A lap pool glistened at the far end of another lawn before it appeared to spill into the ocean.

It was mesmerising. The colour of the sea was azure, taupe. Plain old blue seemed to diminish its beauty. Ash opened the glass doors at the back and let the breeze in. A heady scent of flowers and saltwater filtered through, and I took in the deepest breath.

'This is too much, Ash. How can I ever repay—'

'Please, Lina.' He smacked the car keys down on the counter in the kitchen, his jaw still visibly tight. 'Let me do this for you.' His face wasn't angry, only full of concern. 'The doctor said you needed someone to look after you. And I think you've been looking after others most of your life. It's time you let someone do it for *you*.'

I nodded and wrapped my arms around myself. 'You could've cared for me at the old place.' I grinned with both rows of teeth on full display, hoping to diffuse the tension.

'I've told you already, terrible Wi-Fi,' he said, letting a brief smile touch his lips. 'And every other place I found had steps or was high up. If you're going to convalesce for a few days, I thought what better way than to do it by the sea, where you don't need to move far to dip your feet in the water. Now, no more arguments. This is where we're staying. I'm going to fix us some lunch. Relax. I got you some books and magazines as well.' He nodded to the coffee table. 'I also bought an iPad and loaded it up with some movies.'

I clocked the mountain of reading matter and the technical device. 'Ash, you've really gone overboard.'

'Well, I didn't want you to be bored while I work. You can call your friends on that too,' he said, pointing to the rose-gold Apple box on the top.

I took halting steps over to the sofa and sat down, a sudden rush of dizziness making me feel light-headed, but I didn't want to say anything to Ash.

Forced bed rest. Doctor's orders. It felt wrong. I had been active my whole life – well, as far back as I could remember. After the car accident, I took on the role as carer for Dad and surrogate mum for Alex. They both worked hard, and it seemed easy at the time to fit the cooking and cleaning around school, then university, then my job. But now, I had nothing.

I watched as Ash bustled around the sleek kitchen, shuffling through cupboards, rattling plates. As he opened the fridge, I couldn't believe how well stocked it was. I picked up a magazine, but my eyelids were heavy.

Sometime later, Ash called me out to the deck, and I woke with a start, not realising I had drifted off. Outside, there was a table set with cutlery for one – a silver dish in between the knife and fork.

'Madam,' Ash said with a cheeky grin and an over-exaggerated sweep of his hand.

I giggled as he pulled my chair out and I sat down. He lifted the lid to reveal an omelette oozing with cheese and pancetta – a side-salad garnish beside it drizzled with balsamic dressing. My stomach growled on cue. 'This looks heavenly.' I laid my napkin on my lap. 'You're not joining me?'

'I have a Zoom call I have to log into. Sorry. I might be able to join you later for dinner, though. Oh, and wait, I forgot.' He dashed back inside the house and returned holding a small box. 'The mobile guy dropped this off a few minutes ago while you were napping. He was able to transfer everything from your SIM card. Hope no one has been worrying about you.'

As he passed it over, I reached for his other hand. 'Ash, I don't really know what to say. I'm sorry if I seemed ungrateful earlier on. My mind is a mess. Think I am still woozy from the anaesthetic, maybe.'

'Hey, you don't need to apologise. I'm just happy to be here for you.' He stroked my hand. A rush of comfort rippled up my arm and I pulled away, remembering a moment from the past – that day in Cambridge.

Ash left and I poured myself a glass of orange juice from the carafe. I switched on my mobile and as it came to life, it buzzed continuously. The messages from Dad were brief. Merely asking how I was, telling me how wonderful it was being with Alex, how much they all wished I was there. He also asked about the job hunt. My fingers trembled as I typed a reply, apologising for the delay. No truth about where I was or what had happened. The lies sat heavy in my stomach and that all-too-familiar flush coated my neck.

I took some bites of my omelette and closed my eyes to savour it.

Could I tell Dad the truth? I had thought this trip would be short. But it had turned into more than I could ever have imagined. If he got even a whiff of the accident and the subsequent operation, he would probably be on the first flight out of LA straight to me. I completed the message by saying I was fine and that there hadn't been any leads on the job front.

Looking again at my inbox, I saw a message from Greer, who was now back in LA and missing me. She had been asked to end her internship earlier than planned. More cost-cutting, no doubt. A text from Nik made me pause for thought. He said he was looking forward to seeing me tomorrow. I swallowed my mouthful and took in the cloudless sky. What should I say? I took a sip of juice before typing out the following words:

Change of plan. I've extended my stay. Made some interesting discoveries and need to explore further. Will let you know my return plans soon.

Thankfully, he didn't call me back. He would probably know instantly I was lying if he heard my voice. The connection between us was too strong.

My eyes widened as I took in the capital letters of a text from an unknown number. Two words: GO HOME.

I dropped my fork on the plate, flicking my head left and right as if I was being watched. Could this have come from those men that had visited the hospital? But how did they have my number? Of course they had my number. When I signed up as a volunteer, I had to give my contact details. Maybe they had already gone round to our first Airbnb apartment. Suddenly I was relieved Ash had booked us this place. It was so remote I was hoping no one would find us. Across the low hedges of the garden, the nearest house was at least half a mile away – far enough for complete seclusion.

After hoovering the rest of the food, I retrieved the iPad from the living room. Ash's raised voice could be heard from the end of the corridor. I hadn't yet explored the place and had no clue how many bedrooms it had.

Back out on the deck, I downloaded WhatsApp and called Greer.

After several rings, the call connected and when I saw her bleary face fill the whole of the screen, I grimaced. 'Shit, sorry. I forgot how early it is out there.'

'Lina!' She yawned. 'It's so good to hear from you. Where you at?'

'I'm staying in Cyprus a bit longer.'

'How come, babe?'

'It's quite a tale. I can tell you another time, I'll let you get back to sleep.'

'Nah. It's all good. I'm *so* jet-lagged. I have no clue whether it's day or night.' She chuckled. 'Let me get to the kitchen and make some coffee first. Show me where you are. Full panorama.'

I swept the iPad around, giving her a 360-degree view. She whistled. 'Woah. That's some beautiful place you're staying at. I thought you told me it was barely big enough to swing a cat in and I didn't realise it was on the beach.'

I filled her in on everything that had happened over the last few days. She munched away at a bowl of granola; periodically nodding, listening to my every word. It made me realise how much I had missed this. The connection. *Female* connection. There had been no one in my life since … Emily. No one I ever felt I could fully open up to.

When I had finished my tale, she pinched her lips, nose wrinkling. I had walked to the edge of the pool, marvelling at the fact that the Wi-Fi was still strong. I sat down, dipping my feet in the water. The temperature was perfect.

'I can't believe you never told me about the pain, Lina,' Greer said. 'I knew you had some seriously bad periods, but I didn't realise they were *that* bad. My cousin has endo. Had that same operation you had. It didn't completely wipe out the discomfort, but she's made some adjustments to her life – you know, she does all that meditation, yoga shit. I have to ask …' She walked out of her kitchen and back into her room, shutting the door before sitting on her bed, screen closer to her face. 'Is sex painful too?'

I dipped my head, twirling my feet in the pool and nodded. 'Really painful. So much so I haven't had any in a long time. The few guys I have slept with since my university boyfriend have all been one-night stands. What's the point in having a relationship with someone if I can't do the one thing you're meant to do together … be intimate? How do I explain that I use alcohol not only to relax but also as a pain suppressor?' I paused, thinking she would tell me I was being ridiculous.

But there was nothing but understanding in her expression. 'Did you talk to the doctor about this?'

'It's one of the first things she asked me before I had the operation. But this might not have fixed "that" issue.' I shrugged. 'I guess I won't know until I try.'

'How does Nik feel about it all?'

I lowered my eyes. 'Nik and I … we're not intimate with each other.' Our unusual relationship suddenly weighed heavy on my shoulders. I screwed up my face. 'Shit, this is so hard to talk about.'

'Babe, it's fine, I get it. You said many times it was complicated and it's difficult to explain. I'm not going to push you for details. If whatever you guys have going on suits you, that's cool, but now … it sounds like things have changed for you. Think about yourself, your needs. Going forward, this shouldn't be a problem. *Sex* shouldn't be a problem.'

'God, even hearing the word makes my shoulders tense.'

'Tantra,' she said defiantly.

'Excuse me?'

'You need to try tantric sex. You need to get that connection first with someone. Even if it doesn't lead to actual penetrative sex. You've probably got years of hang-ups associated with sleeping with someone. Maybe doing something different where performing, climaxing, isn't the actual goal would help. It's all about the flow of energy. One of my previous girlfriends was massively into it. And let me tell you, I was sold until she took her energy onto someone else.' She cocked her head back and laughed. 'But guys … well let's just say they see it as more like hard work to get something that they could get a lot quicker with regular plain old vanilla sex. You just haven't met the right guy, Lina.' She tutted. 'And neither have I.'

I thought about what Greer had said. I *had* met the right guy, but I had ruined all hope of being with him.

'What are your plans now?' she asked. 'Just R&R? Kinky tantric with Ash?'

'Greer!' I shrieked and peeked over my shoulder, hoping Ash hadn't made a sudden appearance.

'What? I saw that picture you sent me on your first night in Cyprus. He's a hottie. And from what you have told me about him and how he is treating you like a princess in some amazing beach palace, he sounds like your perfect guy. Come. On. Lina. You've got to stop being so scared of intimacy. And … Nik's not around.' She winked and let her eyebrows dance. 'Anyway, enough about guys, what about solving the mystery of your mum's finding?'

'Actually, there is something I wanted you to help me with,' I said, relieved that the conversation had moved on.

She moved closer to the screen. 'Ooh, tell me. I am so bored out here. I miss going to the pub with you and downing a pint. Everyone is so uptight in LA. All kale this, pea protein that. I miss the grease of Pete's fish and chip shop, the cider and the red buses belching out fumes.'

'You know you're welcome back to Birmingham anytime.'

'I wish. Got my final year to get through before I can travel again. But come on, tell me. How can I help?'

I filled Greer in on the receipts I had found in the cabinet the first time I had snooped around the office of Elias's son. I sent her the pictures I had taken, and she said she would investigate.

After we hung up, I took the iPad to the hammock. My finger hovered over the search bar before typing the word 'tantra'.

Time slipped by; my mind absorbing all this new information, a sense of hope filling me the more I discovered – the idea of being able to move from pain to pleasure.

My phone buzzing on the table made me flinch. It was only a message from Nik. He was happy about my archaeological discoveries but thankfully didn't have time for a chat. A relief. The truth was, I didn't know how to tell him everything that had happened the last few days and that I had lied about coming to Cyprus with Ash, and I didn't know why.

Actually, I did.

Any mention of Ash always set him off and vice versa. Ash would never understand the relationship I had with Nik. Nik and I had grown close over the last few years. We shared all our secrets. But there was one secret between us that would bind us together forever. And I swore to Nik that no one would ever know.

Chapter 25

When we were eighteen

The last day of secondary school had been uneventful. Emily hadn't turned up. But I knew she had been here briefly because when I opened my locker, there was an envelope inside. I recognised her curly script. Initially, I had crumpled it up. I didn't want to know what she had to say but by the time everyone had said their goodbyes, I had an overwhelming desire to be on my own and read it. Luckily, Ash had rushed home to help his grandma prepare for a family celebration and Nik had been doing his best to avoid me since the night of his party, so I had no clue where he was. And the truth was, I was avoiding him too. How could I look him in the face after what had happened? I shuddered as I remembered the pain.

I found a spot out beyond the sports field – a place where I couldn't be seen. I sat down on the grass beside the massive oak tree surrounded by bushes, close to the changing rooms. Smoothing out the envelope, I ripped it open.

Dear Lina

I'm sorry. I've tried calling so many times, but I understand why you wouldn't want to talk to me, and I can't come round because your dad said I am banned.

Please forgive me. I didn't know how to tell you. But please try and understand this. I love him and I want to be with him. I hope one day you'll be happy for me.

Love Em

Tears welled and I crumpled up the pink sheet of paper and hurled it into the grass. What the hell was I meant to do with that? I clutched my stomach tightly. It wasn't fair. Why did Alex have to take away the one person I cared for more than anyone else? Why? Selfish dick.

But maybe Emily had never wanted to be my friend. We only became *really* close at the start of sixth form. Maybe she was only my friend so she could be close to Alex. I didn't even know how long they had been together. And she hadn't mentioned loving or caring for me in the letter. It was about her and him.

A gust of wind blew the paper away and I shot up to grab it and shoved it in my school bag.

Distant voices startled me. I gulped back my tears and wiped my sleeve over my eyes. I hid behind the nearest tree and peered out slowly. The voices were coming from behind the changing rooms – in the gap between the back wall and the wooden fence that ran the perimeter of the school. It was known as Shag Alley, if you believed the rumours. But it was broad daylight. Surely no one would be so reckless as to be doing anything there now.

I shifted position to get a better look. Someone was obviously taking an opportunity for one last hook-up before school was over. I trained my ear to see if I could hear anything.

'I'm going to miss you,' a deep voice said.

'Me too,' came the reply.

Then silence.

I peered through some low-lying branches and my heart plummeted. His back was to me, but I knew it was him. Shirtsleeves rolled up, showcasing his tanned, muscular arms. A hint of his saint's-name necklace peeking out from the collar of his shirt. His head was tilted, and when the other person came into view, it was obvious what they were doing. Kissing.

As their bodies turned, I had a side-on view of them together. I was transfixed. It was voyeuristic but I couldn't help it. They rested their foreheads together and appeared lost in the very essence of each other. Then their lips were touching again. It was mesmerising watching them. It hadn't been like that when we kissed. This had more emotion, more depth. It was slow and sensual. Tongues not afraid to explore. I knew I should look away now. Or at the very least feel hurt? Angry?

Their hands roamed freely over each other's bodies. There was a tenderness mixed with a sense of urgency, as if they were trying to squeeze in a lifetime of lust into these precious moments.

The button of Nik's jeans was popped open, a zip pulled down, a hand slipped inside. A groan, a wanton guttural sound, exploded from his mouth before their lips locked again. A tongue on his neck – his head thrown back as if he had wanted this all his life.

The release came and Nik's hands hit the wall – teeth biting down on his bottom lip.

'You have no idea how much I am going to miss you.' Nik grinned broadly.

He laid a chaste kiss on the other person's lips.

His lips. Mateo's lips. The Spanish exchange student.

'Now it's your turn,' Nik said, his voice laced with a teasing tone.

A twig snapped beneath my foot, and they turned their heads. I hadn't realised I had moved away from the tree and was standing in full view.

'Lina,' Nik said, pulling up the zip of his jeans and wiping his hand across his lips. 'It's not what you think.'

Mateo smirked. He knew all too well it was exactly what it looked like. He grabbed his school bag and blew a kiss to Nik. '*Hasta luego,*' he said and walked back in the direction of school.

Nik stood straight in front of me and tried to grab both of my hands, but I shook his hold away and folded my arms.

'Listen,' he said, clutching his hands together as if he was praying, 'please, I beg you. Don't tell anyone.' His face contorted in agony. 'I'm sorry, really I am. It's just ...' His cheeks flushed and he ran a hand through his hair. 'I'm confused, really confused. But no one can know. I didn't mean to hurt you. The other night was ... great. I mean, I'm not sure if it was for you but ... the truth is, I like you, a lot, only I'm not sure I like you in *that* way. I know it was wrong of me. I shouldn't have let things get that far with you. Only ... I've been having these ... other ... feelings for a while. And ...'

He bit his bottom lip again. Hard. Those lips I had fantasised about kissing for so long. My first crush. My first everything. This conversation felt surreal. I didn't know what to think, what to feel.

'I kept telling myself it was wrong,' he continued. 'It couldn't be – I couldn't be like *that*. But I can't lead you on, I know that. I was going to tell you, I promise.'

What could I say? Had he led me on or was it me that had thrown myself at him? Had *I* taken advantage?

'*Ta gámisa,*' he mumbled under his breath, and I couldn't help but let out a laugh. He was being unbelievably hard on himself. He hadn't fucked up. He didn't know who he was or how to be who he wanted to be. And I couldn't even imagine how hard that must be – having to hide who you really are.

'It's fine,' I said finally, taking hold of his hands, forcing him to look me in the eyes. 'Honestly it is. Your secret is safe with me.'

Chapter 26

Now we are twenty-eight

I lay in a pool of perspiration, the thin cotton sheet clinging to me. The humidity had hovered in the nineties all night and early-morning light was now spilling through the gap in the blinds.

The air-conditioning unit had come to a spluttering stop in the night. I had fiddled with the remote, but to no avail. Had I put it on a timer by accident? I hadn't wanted to wake Ash to ask him to fix it. He needed his sleep. His whole schedule was completely out of sync with mine. He blamed the Asian markets which he had to be up for. But it seemed he needed to be awake for all global markets. I couldn't shake this feeling that he was avoiding me again like the first week here in Cyprus. He had made me breakfast, lunch and dinner and hadn't sat with me for any meals all week.

My wound was healing, and I was feeling twitchy. I wanted to do something. Anything. Go sightseeing, see more of the island. But a part of me was afraid. I hadn't received any more texts from the unknown number, nor had I told Ash about the 'GO HOME' message.

What did it matter now anyway? Ash had booked me on a flight back to Birmingham tomorrow with his flight to

Mumbai leaving later on. That was it. Our time was coming to an end. A longing sat heavy in my chest, a need to say something to him before we said goodbye; but the words hadn't formed clearly in my mind, nor had I had any opportunity to catch him when he wasn't working.

I lowered my shorts and peeled back the edge of my plaster. I clenched my teeth and ripped it off, wincing at the pain. But the discomfort was only momentary. I had been told to keep the wound covered and dry for a few days and that time had passed. So now? Now I was aching to go in the water. It had been tempting me all week. I had lain in the hammock reading and watching movies and letting the sun cover my skin with warmth, but I longed to dive into the sea.

Stepping outside my room, I stretched my arms into the air, my vest top riding up my body. It was certainly cooler out in the living room. Why hadn't I come and slept on the sofa last night?

The clock on the wall signalled it was almost six. I yawned. I needed coffee but the view outside was breathtaking. A burst of orange was creeping over the horizon.

I pulled open the doors and slipped onto the deck, heading straight for the sand. The morning breeze tickled my bare arms and legs. I hugged myself tightly. I didn't want to leave this. But what was this? This wasn't my life. It was a fantasy, being here, being cared for by Ash. Besides, I didn't need looking after. What I needed was something I had never had before.

I turned to see Ash far in the distance running along the beach. My hair whipped my cheeks and I struggled to pull it back from my face.

He came to a halt, breathing heavily, his naked chest glistening with sweat. 'What are you doing up?' he panted, his hands on his hips, bent forward as he struggled to regain his breath.

'I couldn't sleep. The air-con unit broke in the middle of the night.'

He stood up. 'You should've woken me.'

'I didn't want to disturb you. You probably get ... what? ... five hours' sleep at most. Do you always run in the morning?'

He nodded. 'Yup. Best way to start the day.' He swiped his hand across his forehead as the sweat continued to pour off his face.

'I'd rather swim,' I said.

'I don't think that's a good idea.'

I cheekily pulled down my shorts to reveal my scar. 'I took the plaster off. So technically it is a great idea.' I took a couple of steps backwards before breaking into a run.

'You shouldn't be running, Lina,' he called after me.

'I'm fine,' I screamed as I made my way to the waves, turning back to see that same concerned look on his face, the one he had worn every moment I moved the last few days.

'Come and catch me if you're so worried.' I giggled and tripped as my feet made contact with the sea, sending me tumbling towards the water. Wet sand coated my legs. I lay back and let the waves wash over me. It felt amazing.

Ash stood over me, his eyebrows knotted. 'Are you OK?'

'I'm fine, Ash. I'm not made of porcelain.' I pulled myself up, kicking the water at him, soaking his shorts and realising that my top had become completely see-through.

'OK, now you're asking for it.' He had a twinkle in his eye as he lunged towards me, sweeping me up in his arms. I wriggled in his hold, but he was much too strong for me to break free.

He walked into the waves until the water was waist high and counted to three before throwing me into the air.

I resurfaced, spitting out what felt like a gallon of water. 'That's it! You are in serious trouble now.'

He laughed and dived in. I waited for him to pop his head up, but when he did, he was far away. I had to wade in further and further to try and reach him.

We treaded water, smiling, giggling. It was the first time I had seen him look so happy since ... since that day in Cambridge when he told me he would travel the world with me and then again when we had kissed.

I opened my mouth to say how wonderful this break had been, how much I appreciated everything he had done, but a sudden sharp pain caused me to yelp instead, and I sank under the water as I clutched my side.

It happened in a flash. Two strong arms wrapped around me, dragging me to the surface, a reassuring hold pulling me through the water.

'Don't move,' Ash said, his voice low and desperate-sounding.

Before I knew it, I was in his arms again, being lifted. He carried me to the deck, laying me on the sunlounger. 'I'm calling the doctor,' he said as droplets poured down him.

'It's fine, Ash,' I said, trying to hide the discomfort through gritted teeth.

'We can't be sure.'

He had already left through the doors before I had any time to protest further.

An hour later, I was lying down in my bed, Doctor Lamos by my side. Her soft hands pressed my pelvis, checking where it hurt most. My hair was still damp, but my body was dry. Goose pimples covered my skin as Ash had got the air con restarted but it was turned up too high.

'I think swimming in the sea was probably a little premature, Lina. I know there's probably still a lot of internal bruising. You need to take it easy still.'

'I'm sorry Ash called you. I would've been fine going back to the hospital for a check-up. Did he wake you?'

She arched an eyebrow. 'He was pretty insistent. But I was already up, getting some paperwork done before going in for my shift. I was hoping to see you again. I've thought only of you and your mother since you left the hospital.'

'Then do you have time to stay, for breakfast maybe? This is my last day. I would love to hear more about her.'

'I'd love that too.' She smiled warmly. 'Let me call the hospital and tell them I won't be in for a little while.'

Before I could put out a bowl of cereal and make something to drink, Ash had insisted on whipping up some scrambled eggs with smoked salmon, a fresh fruit salad, two rounds of toast and a cafetière of coffee. Yet again he hadn't stayed to eat but this time I was glad. I had so many questions to ask Marika, as Doctor Lamos now insisted I call her.

'Well, he's a keeper,' Marika whispered behind her hand as Ash left to go back to his office.

I blushed. 'I told you in the hospital. Ash is a friend. Though ...' I pushed a piece of strawberry around my plate with my fork '... he's what you might call "the one that got away".'

'Sounds intriguing.'

'Just friends,' I repeated, as if to convince myself. I thought we were friends, but I hadn't even had the chance to talk about how we were meant to remain as such when we lived so far from each other.

She tucked into her eggs, before moaning and rolling her eyes skywards. 'A friend who also happens to be a great cook.'

I took a mouthful and nodded in agreement. 'I tell you, it's been five-star treatment the whole week.' I tugged at the waistband of my shorts. 'None of my clothes are going to fit me any more.' But I couldn't care less. This trip had been restorative, a break from the hard grind of life.

We sat and ate while I filled Marika in on how the first week on the island had been, with Ash reluctantly attending the cookery course and how strange an experience working on the dig had been. When we finished our breakfast, we took our coffees over to the outdoor sofa and put them on the low glass table.

'What was she like?' I asked tentatively. 'My mum.'

Marika turned her head out to sea. 'She was the bravest woman I ever knew. Stubborn.' She plumped the cushion next to her and rested it behind her. 'Tenacious. All the guys were crazy about her in college, but she was so dedicated to her studies. We shared a room in our final year, and she loved to cook for me when I had done a long training shift at the hospital. She was so warm and caring, a softer side that I think she kept hidden.'

'Did you ever meet my father?'

'A couple of times. He was older, I remember, and she thought he was handsome and had big aspirations – something about wanting to run his own restaurant, in England. I begged her not to follow him if he ever went.'

'What happened? Why did she have to go if she was happy here? I really want to get some more information on why no one believed her about what she found – that tomb. Do you remember the last time you saw her? Was she scared?'

Marika held the coffee cup to her lips, cradling it before taking a few sips. She looked lost. Lost in a tidal wave of memories. Then she placed the drink on the table, causing it to rattle on its saucer. 'Wait. I remember now. She said something to me before she left. It was the strangest thing. She said, "My favourite book will always be your collection of Shakespeare."'

'Was it?'

She shrugged. 'I honestly don't know. It was a book I was given when I was at school by my mum and dad. Elina was close to them too. They were like surrogate parents. She never got on with hers, and when she left her hometown in the west, she was rarely in contact with them. But I don't ever recall her reading Shakespeare. Archaeology was her passion. She spent hours at that site. Sifting, digging. I always remember complaining whenever I met her for lunch on the rare occasions we were both free. She would be covered in dirt – it was always deep under her nails. She never cared for her appearance. But something changed when your dad turned up on the scene. She started to style her hair, put make-up on. Then she became obsessive again about the site and she cancelled on me many times in the run-up to her leaving.'

We sat silently with our thoughts, me imagining what must have been going through Mum's head at the time, why she felt she had to leave Cyprus so suddenly. Had Dad forced her to go to the UK?

'I got a text,' I said finally. 'From an unknown number. It said, "Go home".'

Her forehead wrinkled with concern. 'Was it from those men, do you think; the ones who came to the hospital?'

'I'm not sure.'

'Maybe you should talk to the police.'

'A police officer came to my room before I was discharged and said Elias wouldn't be pressing charges if I didn't mention what happened to me ever again. It made me think that what you said about him in the hospital was true – that even if I did have evidence to prove that my mother had been wronged, no one would believe me anyway.'

Marika shook her head slowly. 'None of this seems right, Lina.'

'It doesn't matter. I don't want to cause any more trouble for myself. I need to go back to my father. He is all I have got.'

'Do you not have any siblings?'

I leaned my arm on the back of the sofa, picking at a strand of wicker that was poking out. 'I have a brother. But we don't get on.'

'That is a great shame. I think your mother would be sad about that. She always said she wished she'd had a brother or a sister. There was always so much pressure from her parents to succeed. But she hated the … conformity. She was a free spirit. She wished there had been a brother or sister who wanted to stay close to home and work in the family business.'

Marika filled me in on what she remembered about my grandparents' olive-oil company, and I wondered how I might try and find out if I had any relatives alive.

When she had finished regaling me with tales of her and Mum's time together, she turned serious. 'Life is short, Lina. Precious. Don't regret not having a good relationship with your brother.'

I sat back on the sofa and hugged my knees close to my chest. 'He left us. Me and Dad. He wanted to be a famous actor.' I gave a laugh thinking back to his Danny Zuko days. 'Mum would've loved that. She always thought of him as a star. A shining star. I was just a disappointment.'

She tutted. 'No. I knew Elina far too well to know that she would never think that of a child of her own flesh and blood.'

'I was difficult, self-centred. And horribly jealous of my brother. Everything always seemed to revolve around him.'

She readjusted the cushion behind her back. 'Ah yes, that is the Greek way. The cherished son. Is he older or younger than you?'

'Older. Four years.'

She paused, lost in thought again, and then pressed her lips tightly. 'Oh my. I think Elina must have been pregnant when she said goodbye to me. She must have been scared. I don't think children were part of her life plan, at least not at that point.'

Ash suddenly popped his head out of the glass doors. 'Sorry for the interruption. Can I get you ladies anything else?' He came over and picked up our empty cups.

'I'm fine, thank you, Ash,' Marika said. 'It was delicious.'

He looked down shyly before peering back up at me, his eyebrows raised.

'Best breakfast ever.' I patted my stomach. 'Couldn't eat another thing.'

He smiled and left us, closing the door with his shoulder.

I caught Marika staring at me with eyes narrowed. 'Hmm.'

'What?'

'Tell me more about what is going on here?' She pointed at me and back towards the glass doors.

Heat crept up into my neck. 'Nothing's going on here.'

She tucked her legs underneath herself. 'You said something about him being the one that got away?'

'It's complicated.'

'And you also said that before. Maybe if you told me about it, it would become less complicated.'

I relaxed my knees and adopted a similar sitting position to Marika. 'Ash and I have been friends since we were eight years old. He was my stable. My rock. I depended on him more than I realised. But when we were twenty-one something happened and I'm not sure how to recapture any of what we had – the friendship or if there is still more there.'

A lightness filled me as I opened up to Marika. She listened. Nodded occasionally, a sympathetic smile here and there, gentle probing questions when I came to tell her why I walked out on Ash that night in Cambridge. My deep-seated fear of intimacy and rejection. Once I had said everything that I wanted to say, she let me sit in the space I had created for myself.

A breeze tickled my skin, and I stroked my arm rhythmically. 'Is this what it would have felt like? If Mum had lived. I hardly know you, yet I have told you things I have never told anyone.'

Her eyes misted and I found myself crumbling. The wall I had built around me was beginning to tremble, its foundations shaking. My arms encircled her and I cried: for the loss of Mum, for never knowing her, really knowing her; for all I had lost with Ash.

After a while, my breathing steadied, and I pulled back, reaching for a tissue from the box on the table.

'I know I will never replace your mother, Lina. But I promise you this. I will always be there for you. She would be so happy to know that I was looking out for her daughter. Anytime you want me, call me. I'll give you my mobile number, my pager. Anything. Even anything medical. You can always ask. You have been through so much, and I know you still have a lot to process with the endometriosis. But you don't have to live a life of pain any more – physical or mental. I am no therapist, but I do wonder whether some of the pain you suffer ... sexually ... could be psychological. The operation will help heal some of the discomfort you experience, but I believe you might have created a barrier to letting anyone get close to you. Only time will tell. But you need a partner you can trust, be open with.'

I let Marika's words sink in. Could I be open with Ash or would I risk hurting him again?

Chapter 27

I found Ash in the kitchen, holding open the fridge, his head tipped back as he drank from a water bottle. He was dressed in running gear again. Was this his second run of the day? The sun had dipped low enough to signal our time in Cyprus was ending and I knew this was my last chance to talk with him. Marika had stayed long into the afternoon, and I was so emotionally exhausted after she left, I had drifted into a nap on my bed: my dream filled with images of the instructional videos I had watched the other day during my research. I had woken with a sense of calm and something else. Something I wanted to share with only one other person.

'Hey,' I said.

Ash flinched and wiped droplets from his chin. 'Hey.' He did a double take, clearing his throat as he clocked I was wearing only a white bikini. I had had it on under shorts and T-shirts all week, but this was the first time on its own in front of him. Self-consciously I tugged at the strings.

'How you feeling?' Ash said, not meeting my gaze but turning back to the fridge. 'I knocked on your door earlier.'

'Yeah, I was feeling a little wiped. But I feel refreshed now. I was going to try some yoga on the beach.'

'Nice.' He closed the fridge and walked towards the patio doors, looking everywhere except at me. 'I'm off for a run.'

'Ash. Wait.'

He stopped, his shoulders locked, before stepping outside and beginning his stretching routine.

I stood in front of him, forcing him to acknowledge my presence. 'What are you running away from? Is it me?'

He slowly stood up and looked at me intensely, his eyes boring into me. 'The truth?'

I nodded. 'Always.'

He steeled himself to find the words, biting his bottom lip. 'The truth is, Lina, I don't know how to be around you.'

'I've noticed. I'm sorry I've been such an inconvenience. I know this isn't how you thought things would be when I asked you to come to Cyprus.'

'It's not that.' He rubbed the back of his neck. 'I can't pretend any more that what I felt for you when we were twenty-one has just disappeared; that it's easy to only be your friend. And then you go and almost get yourself killed.' His nostrils flared. 'And I told myself that this was ridiculous, that friendship was better than not having you in my life forever. Only, being here with you, and you looking ... well ... look at you.' His eyes drank every inch of me, slowly, his mouth wide. 'You're the most beautiful girl in the world. I can't suppress my feelings for you any more, only—'

I leapt towards him, my lips crashing into his. The memory of that first kiss came to the forefront of my mind and I moaned as our mouths merged into each other's.

He pulled back suddenly, touching his lips – a look of surprise on his face. 'Lina, I can't. No matter how I feel about Nik, that I think he is *so* wrong for you—'

'Ash, please, listen to me. Nik and I aren't ... together ... intimately. I promise.'

'Really?'

'Yes.' I nodded to emphasise my answer. 'We're just friends, really good friends. But there's a lot I still have to tell you. Only, I'm scared. I'm scared of you rejecting me.'

'I would never do that.' He reached out to hold my hand, tenderly squeezing it.

I tugged him in the direction of the sand, picking up the picnic rug on the way. I shook it out, gesturing for him to sit down in front of me. He mirrored my cross-legged pose and I grabbed both his hands in mine.

'When we spent that day together in Cambridge, I felt so light and free. And I can be honest now and tell you that I began to realise I was having feelings for you. But when those girls – those friends of yours – told me you loved someone from back home, I assumed that going away with you would be so much more than a holiday with a friend. Everything suddenly felt complicated. You were giving up a huge opportunity to go travelling with me. And when we kissed and you told me you loved me, I panicked. Because ... being with someone intimately was something I had struggled with ever since the first time I had sex.'

'With Nik.' Ash's hands tensed within my grasp, and he tried to pull them away, but I held onto them.

'Yes, with Nik. Only, at the time, I thought it was perfectly normal. First time and all that. But when I came to see you in

Cambridge, I had been with Paul a few months – the only real relationship I had ever had, only it wasn't one. I was too embarrassed to tell him how much it hurt me whenever we ... had sex. I didn't have the courage to tell him why I hated every time we were together. I used to drink a lot, hoping it would numb the pain. I stopped believing I could be with anyone. On the day he dumped me, he told me I was a frigid bitch and that he couldn't be with someone who was ... damaged.'

Anger seeped into Ash's eyes. 'So why did you go back to him?'

I shook my head. 'I didn't.'

'But in that letter.' He lowered his gaze. 'The one you left me. You said he had messaged you and that you were going back to him.'

'A lie. I didn't know what else to say. Being with you would never have worked out – I convinced myself.'

'So, you left me that morning because you were scared I would reject you if we couldn't have sex?'

'OK, well ... when you put it like that, it seems pretty silly.' I pulled my hands away.

'No.' He reached for them again and linked his fingers through mine. 'Not silly at all. It was an intense time. I laid some heavy shit on you, declaring my undying love. You had just finished what sounds like a toxic relationship; you were vulnerable, needed a friend, and I let you down.'

'You didn't let me down.'

'We both let each other down.' He pulled my hands closer to his chest. 'And now?'

I gazed deeply into his eyes – those dark, inviting eyes. 'And now … I want to feel something with you, I want to try and find that connection … with you. I think it might help me understand if what I feel is because of what I have, the endometriosis, or something else.'

'I'll do anything. What did you have in mind?'

'Take your T-shirt off.'

His eyes twinkled in the orange glow of sunset. He yanked his running top off in one swift movement and my pulse quickened at the sight of his naked torso. I laid my left hand over his heart. It throbbed beneath my fingers, rhythmic and steady. With my other hand I took his left one and placed it on my chest.

He caught his breath sharply as I held my fingers over his, achingly close to the edge of my bikini top.

'Close your eyes,' I whispered, and he did.

I checked out his features in the fading light, wanting to kiss him but knowing that wasn't the objective. Not yet.

With my sense of sight shut off, everything else heightened. The waves crashing onto the shore seemed louder, as did the squawks of the occasional bird that flew overhead. Ash's smell invaded my nostrils – it was a heady tonic. Our heartbeats clashed against our fingertips out of sync.

'Breathe in and out, deeply. Try and match my breath,' I said, remembering one particular video I had seen during my research on the iPad.

His breathing grew heavier, more measured, until it matched mine and our heartbeats appeared suddenly to synchronise as if we had only one heart between us.

Without breaking contact, I shuffled forward. 'I'm going to sit closer to you now. Place your other hand anywhere on me, if that's OK. Remove it if at any time it's not comfortable or you want me to stop.'

I felt his fingers touch my shoulder. It was tentative at first before being a stronger hold. With my eyes still firmly closed, I moved myself into his lap, my legs wrapped around him. I leaned my body into his.

'I want to feel your skin over mine,' I said softly, and our hearts beat a little faster as my words floated into the air. I reached up to my neck and untied the knot of my bikini before loosening the strap at the back, letting it fall to the sand. My nipples immediately hardened in the breeze, and I leaned even closer until they met with Ash's warm, naked chest – a gentle graze against it, nothing more; our hands on each other's hearts restricting full contact.

A stirring in his shorts made me feel on fire down below but an anxious thought crept into my mind. This was what I wanted to banish.

'Stay with me,' Ash whispered close to my ear, his nose inadvertently brushing against my cheek – his three-day stubble tickling my skin. 'Stay here, in this moment.'

My head dipped. 'How did you know?'

'I could feel your shoulder tense. I can't apologise for how you make me feel, for how much I want you right now, but I am here for you, however you need me.'

I let my shoulder fall a little as his words brought me back to the sensations I was experiencing. 'I want to get closer.'

We dropped our hands from our hearts and Ash put his around my waist, drawing me in. He kept his other hand reassuringly on my shoulder as if he was going to continue to check in on me.

I pressed my chest even more into his and let my hands roam over his skin. They brushed against the muscles in his arm, up and down, the hairs on his forearms responding as I stroked him. My fingers traced over his back, luxuriating over the contours of his shoulders, dipping in and out of the ridges there. I then rested my hand on his cheek and brushed my lips over his. He responded softly – his tongue exploring as mine tasted his. I paused to catch my breath but left my lips touching his, not moving.

I didn't know where this was going but I tried to recall what I had found on the internet. *Become aware of the points of contact to continue to be present.* It was like my whole body was a sensor pad, but I tuned in to where the sensation of connection was strongest; his fingertips, my thighs pressed into his.

We stayed in this position, not moving, just feeling, our breath in tune for what felt like an eternity. I could sense darkness closing in as day was finally turning into night.

Then I rocked myself gently against him. No other thoughts came except that of desire, building and building.

'Move with me,' I said against his ear as I brought both my hands to rest around his neck. He obliged and I felt his hand move up into the ridge of my back where he applied a bit of pressure. We rocked against each other, slowly at first before increasing the speed but not by much. There was a crest of a wave in my mind, and I wanted to reach over it to the other side.

I tugged at the sides of my bikini bottoms and released the ties. 'I want you to be inside me, but I'm scared.'

'Don't be scared. You're here with me. I'm not going to hurt you,' Ash said.

I slid up his chest until I was no longer in his lap but on my knees. He moved his hand from my waist to the rug and raised himself so I could slide his shorts off and his boxers beneath them. Not once did he remove his gentle touch from my shoulder. It was a signal, a sign that this was OK as much for me as for him, I thought.

I opened my eyes then. It took a second to readjust to the moonlight. Ash's eyes fluttered open instinctively – his pupils dilating as he focused on me.

'You OK?' he asked.

I smiled and nodded. And this time, there were no other thoughts in my mind except the one that I knew with all of my heart: that I wanted him, wanted him *this* way.

As I lowered myself onto him, my mouth widened and my breath became more heated, more ragged, never once falling out of sync with his. I closed my eyes again and bright lights flashed behind my eyelids as a blaze of desire pulsed through me – feelings I had never experienced before. As I moved, the sensations heightened and I was able to control whenever the line between pleasure and pain blurred, became fuzzy around the edges, and I needed to go back to the better side.

Time stood still. The rush of waves grew louder; my heartbeat raced against every touch with Ash. The sand beneath the blanket was forgiving and soft against my knees as I moved and I didn't even notice at what point I was lying flat on top of him, his hand still holding my shoulder, gripping tighter and tighter until it trembled against me. And then he clung on as if he never wanted to let me go.

Our lips found each other then. His fingers caressed my cheek, my jaw, before reaching behind my neck and pulling me closer to him. He was no longer inside me and when he released his grip, I lay back down on the blanket; let him drink me in with his eyes. He didn't say anything but began stroking my arm, trailing his fingers down my side, along my leg. It was like he was painting me, his fingers the brush.

He propped up his head with his hand, a wide grin on his face. I didn't feel shy lying there naked, not after that experience. Sex before tonight had been under a veil – the embarrassment wound tightly in the sheets that I couldn't wait to cover myself in as soon as it was over, to mask the pain I had endured.

This time had been nothing but pleasurable. Would it always be like this? Or would it only ever be like this with Ash?

Chapter 28

The motion of the hammock lulled me towards sleep. Back and forth. But I fought against the soporific sensation, knowing this time with Ash was coming to an end. It was still night – the only illumination to make out his features was from the moon and the kitchen lamp glowing through the glass doors. At a guess we were a couple of hours away from dawn.

We were wrapped in the blanket, having needed to dry off from our moonlight swim. Though swimming was not what we had done in the end. We had made love again, the buoyancy of the water enabling Ash to hold me in his arms, giving me even more freedom to control the pace and position of our lovemaking. It was even sweeter than the first time.

'I don't want to leave here,' I murmured, not even sure if Ash was awake, our arms wound around each other, the sides of our heads pressed together.

'Me either,' Ash replied. He grasped me tighter. 'How you feeling?'

'A little sore.'

Ash shot his head up, panicked. 'I'm sorry.'

'Hey,' I said, stroking his cheek, brushing his lips with mine. 'It's a good sore.'

'Oh,' he said, a look of relief on his face. 'I don't want to hurt you, Lina. Ever.'

'I know you don't.'

He lowered his head, his mouth on my cheek, my neck, my sensitive sun-kissed skin tingling from his stubble. Moving down, he brushed his lips over my nipples which hardened at the briefest of licks.

'Could this position work?' he said cheekily.

'May ... be,' I said with a widening grin as I pushed the nearby bench with my foot, so we rocked again.

Side to side worked just as well, as it turned out. We had continued the practice of pressing our hearts together, to feel the rhythm again, to connect and to block out all other thoughts that were beginning to crowd my mind – thoughts of this time here, with him, ending.

'What do I do now, Ash?' I said, the hammock continuing to rock. 'I can't bear the idea of never seeing you again. I feel so lost. I thought being here would help me figure out everything. But you're right, I'm chasing a ghost. Even though it was incredible meeting Marika, all her stories about Mum made me feel like I didn't know her at all. It was as though she was talking about a stranger.'

'How were you meant to really know her? She died when you were so young. You were robbed of those years.'

'Hearing how adventurous she was makes me wonder if she was happy at all being in England. She was unhappy the night she died, that much I remember. What if it was because of me and Alex? We tied her down. England gave her nothing. She worked herself to the ground helping Dad run the business. Marika also said Dad had dreamed of having his own restaurant. That's hardly the deli, is it?'

Ash stroked my arm, up and down. 'We can't blame ourselves for the actions of our parents. They were grown-ups when they made these decisions. Responsibility lies with them. They are to blame if they make us feel that we ruined their lives.'

His inclusion of himself in that statement made me wonder if he was thinking of his own life. 'Now I can feel the tension in you. Here.' I reached to his shoulder – the same place I carried my worries before. 'While maybe we can't hold the blame, we can try and let go of the pain those decisions caused.'

'I can't.'

'But your dad's dying, Ash. Isn't it time to forgive and forget?'

I felt his hold on me slacken. I had hit a nerve.

'Have you forgiven me?' I asked.

'You didn't hurt me, Lina.'

'Yes, I did. I wasn't there for you when you really needed me.'

'You tried to get in touch. You told me.'

'But I didn't try hard enough. I should've been there. I should've found a way to be there ... for you.'

When I reached out to touch his face, his cheeks were wet. I kissed them as the tears flowed, softly at first, then harder, his shoulders shaking, trembling. He then buried himself in my chest and I clung onto him as tightly as I could. The hold that I wished I had been able to give him three weeks after I had left him in Cambridge with that pathetic note.

The day of his graduation. Divya hadn't arrived at Heathrow that morning. His parents had been frantic but hadn't wanted to worry Ash on his big day. But when a hospital in LA had got hold of him once the ceremony was over and he had relayed the news to his parents, his mother had fainted and needed to be carted off to Addenbrooke's.

A heart attack. Divya had had a heart attack. The heart that had been the cause of agonising concern since the day she was born because there was a defect had failed. Drugs, apparently. One wild, reckless night. But she had been doing the one thing she had always wanted to do before she died – DJing.

I had found out by chance. I was working in the deli, having fully taken over that summer after graduation while Dad recuperated, and an old school acquaintance had told me as though it was a piece of salacious gossip. She had come in for lunch, surprised that this was where I was spending my summer working, and was stunned that I hadn't heard the story. It was all over the local newspapers, apparently.

I had frantically called Ash, but the recorded message kept indicating that his number was no longer in use.

Several times I had made the journey round the corner to his parents' house but there never seemed to be anyone at home. When someone finally answered, it was his aunt. She had nodded repeatedly when I handed her a letter and asked her to give it to her nephew.

I felt Ash's sobs subside. 'I'm sorry,' he said as he leaned back and patted my chest with the edge of the blanket – drying away his tears.

'What for?'

He gave a slight shrug. 'I think I have bottled that up for many years. I didn't even cry at her funeral. I let anger prevail. It was easier that way. And easy then to push any sadness deeper as I threw myself into that internship and then my new job.'

'Did you ever get my letter?'

He shook his head. 'What letter?'

'I gave your aunt a letter from me to give to you. I tried calling you, but your number was not in use.'

'I dropped my phone in the Cam after my last exam, when we were celebrating, and I got a new one but didn't transfer the number. I wasn't thinking straight. I'm sorry. I didn't know you had tried to reach me. And my aunt was pretty shaken up; she probably forgot.'

All these years, I had assumed that Ash must have received that letter and chosen not to say anything in return, even if it was only to acknowledge it. Not that I deserved anything more.

'When I saw the For Sale sign on your old house,' I said, 'I didn't know if I would ever see you again. Even though the last place I wanted to go to was the ten-year reunion, I was secretly hoping you would be there.'

He put his arm behind his head. 'I hated going back there. Hated seeing everyone – the sad looks they gave me, the conciliatory slaps on the back as if they knew me or Divya.'

'Of course they knew you and her. You were both huge successes at school.'

'We were both desperately lonely.'

'You had me, didn't you?'

'Not really. I couldn't compete once Emily came on the scene.'

Her name made me tense and I knew Ash could feel it. He shifted his position, so he was holding me again.

'In the space of a few weeks,' he said, 'I had lost both my best friends. The last time I spoke to Divya, she begged me to come out to see her, see her in action. She sounded so happy on the phone. We were going to make plans while she was there in Cambridge. She had told me she was nervous about seeing Mum and Dad again. How can I ever forgive them for abandoning her, for cutting her off?'

'They were trying to protect her. They wanted her close to them, didn't they?'

He lowered his head. 'She knew her life would be cut short one day. She knew she was always going to be living life on the edge, but she had had enough of their suffocation. Better to not fear death and live life to the max, she once said.'

'She was an amazing person.'

Ash choked back his emotion. 'She was.'

'Have you spoken to your parents about her?'

He shook his head. 'No. I avoid it always. Their visits to Mumbai have always been short. I am always busy.'

'Are you, though?'

I felt his hold slacken a little. 'Not really. My work comes naturally, it's hardly challenging. I know how to deal with my clients. But I hate the silence in between. I constantly push myself harder, take on more and more work to fill any void. This is the first time I have stopped. What we did just now,' he said, looking deep into my eyes, 'out on the sand. It felt incredible.'

'Tantra.' I smiled.

He trailed his fingers down my arm, my skin igniting again at his touch. 'The ancient Hindu art of moving energy throughout the body for healing and enlightenment.'

'How do you know the definition of tantra?'

He pressed his lips together as if he had been caught cheating on a test. 'I'm sorry but I also use the iPad and there was a tab left open … so I was interested and perhaps I was wondering why you were suddenly researching it.'

I laid both my hands on his chest and stared into his eyes. 'This is why. I wanted to feel something with you, but I didn't quite know how to bring it up in conversation. You've been googling as much as I have?'

'Well … ever since you confided in me about your condition, I have been looking into a lot of things. I think now I finally understand what you've been going through all these years. I only wish I could've been there for you, that you could've trusted me back in Cambridge.'

How would our lives have played out differently if I had? Ash caressed my cheek tenderly and I stroked his wrist where he had once worn my friendship bracelet.

'I still have it,' he said, as if reading my mind. 'It's in my wallet.'

'I thought you might have ripped it off in a moment of anger,' I said, my head dipping.

He lifted my chin. 'Never. It's one of the most precious things to me in the world. I was afraid I would lose it. It had become threadbare.'

My heart swelled at the thought that he had kept it safe – our friendship, our love.

'Come to Mumbai,' he said suddenly.

My head jolted back. 'What?'

'Come and live with me. I know it's a big step, but ... I can't stand the thought of this being our last time together.'

I shivered and the energy flow between us began to lose its power. 'I can't leave Dad. Not after all this. If he knew that I had been in this accident, that he could have lost me, I'm not sure how he would continue. And I can't leave Nik, either.'

Yet again, at the mention of Nik's name, Ash stiffened. There were only inches between us, but it felt like a chasm. Ash sat up and swung himself over the hammock, reaching out to grab his running shorts and put them on. I lifted the blanket over me, the need to be covered up overwhelming. I steadied the hammock and climbed out, standing awkwardly.

'I can't explain why,' I said. 'But I need to be there.'

'Yes, it's a ridiculous idea,' Ash said, his whole body tensing.

'Would you come back to Birmingham?'

'No,' he said firmly. 'You know I can't. What would I do there anyway?'

'What you really feel passionate about?'

He scoffed. 'Are you talking about cooking? Please let that childish dream go. And what about you? Will you be a dancer?'

It was like a knife stabbing me in the chest. 'You know I'll never dance again.'

Ash squeezed his eyes shut for a moment. 'I'm sorry. I didn't mean that.' He rubbed his hands up and down my arms. Heat coated them, but it felt lukewarm. The spell between us, this magical night, was over.

'I guess we'd better get some sleep,' I said.

Ash nodded and picked up his boxers, balling them as if he was embarrassed. 'Night, Lina.'

Ash left and I slumped down onto the outdoor sofa. 'Goodnight, Ash,' I whispered.

What I really wanted was for him to stay, so we could talk through this impasse. Surely there was a middle ground somewhere. Was it really that black and white?

I guess it was.

Chapter 29

I stood outside the villa, my suitcase by my feet. Ash had ordered me a taxi but said he couldn't join me on the ride to the airport because he had a meeting. He had told me this by text. As I passed by his door, I heard voices coming over the speakers and knew he was in the middle of something but wasn't sure if he would come out and say farewell. Was last night's goodbye the only goodbye we would have?

In the distance, I could see a car approaching and my stomach flipped. I turned to look back at the house. The shutters were closed. No movement. As the car came to a stop, I was surprised when the passenger door was flung open and Marika stepped out.

She raised her hands to the sky. 'Thank God, I caught you. I thought I would have to race across town to the airport.'

'It's lovely to see you again, but you didn't have to come all this way to say goodbye.'

'I had to give you something.'

She reached into her handbag and thrust a plastic bag towards me. I unzipped it and pulled out two undeveloped photo films.

'What are these?'

'I found them. I can't believe they have been there for over thirty years. Remember yesterday when I told you what your mother said about that Shakespeare book being her favourite. Well ... I took it out of the bookcase this morning. It has stayed in the same position all these years ...' She continued to shake her head in disbelief. 'Lina, these films were behind the book. I think your mother put them there.'

'Why would she do that and not tell you?'

'I think she really was worried someone would come round to my house. I think she was trying to protect me. Perhaps she was waiting until things had quietened down and then she would contact me and tell me to develop them or send them to her.' She shrugged. 'I ... I don't know. But I want you to have them, in case they can solve the mystery.'

I flung my arms around her. She reciprocated the hug before gently pushing me back. 'Hey, hey. No. Don't you go saying goodbye the same way she did. We're going to see each other again. And you're going to text me as soon as you land. I want to hear about your life, how you're feeling, if there's any pain. OK?'

I nodded and saw over her shoulder another car coming up the road. It stopped in front of us, and Marika confirmed with the driver that it was my ride to the airport. This was it. This was my goodbye to Cyprus. A pain shot through me, but it wasn't like any of the pain I had suffered before – this was hollower, tinged with sadness; a feeling that I never wanted to leave here. I kissed Marika on both cheeks as the driver put my case in the boot and closed it with a thud.

As I slipped into the back of the cab, I heard my name being called from the villa. I turned to see Ash running towards the car. I asked the driver to wait a minute and stepped out.

Ash opened and closed his mouth as if he couldn't find the words he wanted to say, like a tortured soul.

'Thanks for everything, Ash. For taking care of me, for keeping me safe and for … yesterday.' I blushed as I looked back into his eyes which were darker and more intense than I had ever seen.

Then I was in his arms, and he was whispering something in Hindu into my hair. The heat from his hold radiated through me and warmed every part of me.

Why was it so hard for him to say anything to my face and in English, to tell me he still loved me as much as I loved him? *Tell me to stay, Ash. Tell me you'll think about moving back home.*

But none of those words passed over his lips.

'Safe flight,' he said, before turning back to the villa.

Marika raised her eyebrows in the direction of Ash and mimicked picking up a phone. It was as if she was saying, 'You'd better tell me everything that happened between you two.' But what was there to tell? Ash and I had made love, but the hurt left behind had nothing to do with the sex.

A strange smell greeted me in the flat when I arrived home, as if I had dropped some milk from my cereal bowl before I had left and not wiped it up. And without Dad, the place felt cold and empty. His flight from LA was due in tomorrow and

I was glad I had a day to collect my thoughts; to figure out what to say to him.

After a shower and a change into joggers and a T-shirt, my first thought was to retrieve the films Marika had given me. It was too late to take them down to the photo shop, but it was the first thing I wanted to do tomorrow. Reaching into my handbag, my fingers rooted around and didn't immediately find them. I emptied my bag onto my bed and searched through its contents. Nothing. Grabbing my jacket off the chair beside my desk, I emptied my pockets. Receipts and tissues. Where were they?

I texted Marika to tell her I had arrived safely but also to ask if by some miracle she had not handed over the films. Her reply was instantaneous. She had definitely given them to me but would take a cab over to the villa later on to see if she could find them and to enquire with the owner of the property if anyone had picked them up. She suggested I contact Ash, but I wasn't ready to do that ... yet.

As I returned to the living room, the cabinet caught my attention, where only a few weeks ago I had made the discovery of the journal. It felt like a lifetime ago.

The buzzer startled me. I padded down the stairs to open the door, and was greeted with the outstretched arm of Nik, his other hand clutching a white plastic bag. He leaned in and kissed me on the mouth and, for the first time, it made me take a step back.

'God, I've missed you,' he said, not even waiting for an invite inside.

'What are you doing here?'

He placed a hand on his hip and a mock-offended look covered his face. 'My best girl hasn't been in my life for almost three weeks, and you think I wanted to wait another second?' He shook his head. 'When I saw your text, I knew it was an SOS.'

'How could you possibly think "Hey, I'm back, pretty exhausted, so I'll catch up with you tomorrow" is a cry for help?'

He began to make his way upstairs to the flat. 'I knew you wouldn't get a chance to go grocery shopping, so I brought ...' he paused and placed the bag on the kitchen table, lifting out a foil dish '... your favourite chicken tikka masala from Mumbai Palace.' He lifted the lid and let the spices waft in front of my nose.

I inhaled the heady scent and was immediately transported to a time long ago, back when I was at university. It had been the summer of our second year, and I hadn't seen Ash in months. When his train from Cambridge came in, he hadn't gone home first to see his parents, he'd come straight here with a takeout from the same restaurant. I had lit up at the sight of him and laughed as he apologised that he hadn't cooked it himself. When he hugged me then, it had felt like being home, just like it had when he held me in Cyprus – wrapped in his arms for hours. The thought of never feeling that warmth again left me cold.

'You really are wiped, aren't you,' Nik said, and I realised I had not heard a word of what he was telling me. 'Come on, you,' he said, pulling out a chair and forcing me to sit. 'I have been desperate to hear all about your trip and I have some news to tell you too, which is why I also brought this.' He pulled out a bottle of champagne.

I held it and noticed it wasn't the cheap stuff. 'Tell me.'

'Nope.' He swiped it from my grip. 'We're saving it for later,' he said, tucking it in the fridge 'Anyway, I also got us a bottle of white. I am starving. I'll get the plates.'

I fished out the starters and sauces from the bag, secretly relieved that Nik had come over. Time alone would make me have to face up to the fact that I didn't have a clue what I was going to do now and, without the films to develop, the mystery of solving Mum's find would forever remain unresolved. And there was the tax issue to sort out too.

Nik listened to my tale about the dig and what I thought I had discovered. His eyes popped when I told him about the accident. I glossed over the details of the subsequent operation and what Marika had diagnosed I was suffering from, but it was when I finally confessed that I hadn't been alone that Nik appeared to choke on a spoonful of Bombay potatoes.

He sipped his wine with a slow, measured movement before clearing his throat. 'You've spent three weeks in Cyprus with Patel?'

'Yes,' I said, as if I had confessed to stealing the crown jewels.

'You told me you were going alone.'

'I was ... only, he got in touch right after we chatted and, well, I suggested he come, and he did,' I said, as if there was nothing more to say on the topic.

'He had three weeks' holiday?' Nik asked in disbelief.

'Well, no. We were only meant to stay a week but, after the accident, he wanted to take care of me. I was told not to travel until I felt better.'

'I wish I had known, Lina. I would've flown straight out. You told me you were having a great time, about all these amazing discoveries. How are you feeling now? Is there anything I can get you, do for you?'

Over the years I had relied on Nik to say these words to me. They were always a comfort. When I had my periods and the pain was unbearable, he would bring me a hot-water bottle, a steaming cup of tea, offer a foot or shoulder rub. And the mornings after my one-night stands – when I was staying at his because that's what we always did – he would bring me a morning coffee and pick up a breakfast combo from McDonald's. The perfect hangover cure.

But now? There had been no pain after making love to Ash and my period had begun this morning on the flight over with only a twinge here and there. Not a complete wipeout of pain. For the first time in fifteen years – the discomfort seemed manageable.

'This,' I swept my hand over the takeout, 'is more than enough. And besides, I don't need a knight in shining armour to rescue me. Ash was just there, it was convenient. And now he's back in Mumbai and that's that.'

Nik drained his wine glass and poured himself another drink.

'Any left for me?' I raised my eyebrows.

'Hmm?' Nik seemed lost in his thoughts.

'Is it time for the champagne?' I forced a smile.

'God yes, I forgot. Right.' He went to the fridge and pulled out the bottle, twisting the metal cord before popping the cork with a push of his thumb.

I held out my glass as the foam poured, giggling as it flowed to the top. Nik's lips twitched as if he was bracing himself to say something. He raised the bottle aloft and clinked it with my glass.

'Here's to the grand reopening of the deli in two days' time.'

My head jerked backwards. 'What?'

'It's all sorted.' He placed the bottle down and picked up his fork. 'You should have a letter about it amongst that pile on your doormat that you probably haven't had a chance to open.'

'But how?'

'Dad paid the fine. He's got an associate who is married to someone who works at the tax office. She's Greek.' He stabbed at his last piece of chicken jalfrezi. 'They owed a favour or something like that ...' He popped the cube of meat in his mouth and chewed.

'That sounds a bit backhanded.'

He touched my arm. 'Sorry, I didn't mean it to come out that way. There was still a fine, Dad just managed to get it lower, pleading that your dad wasn't of sound mind.'

'He hasn't lost his marbles,' I said, putting my glass on the table.

'I know, I know, but we had to come up with something. Aren't you happy?'

My mind churned with conflicting thoughts. Of course, Dad would be thrilled that the deli could be reopened but I wasn't sure how he would feel about his saviour being Nik's dad. He had rescued us once before with the *dolmádes* order – the regular income which I always knew was a lifeline for us.

'That's really very generous of your dad,' I said, my tone conciliatory. 'Please thank him for me.'

'You can thank him yourself this weekend. He wants to take us out for lunch on Sunday. You're coming over on Saturday night, right? It wasn't the same without you at the Fox.'

'I'm not sure. There's loads I still need to organise. I have to figure out what I'm going to do for a job.'

Nik leaned back in his chair with a smug expression on his face. 'I fixed that too.'

Curiosity seeped from my pores. 'What do you mean?'

He reached into the back pocket of his jeans and pulled out a sheet of paper. As I read the words on the page, the enormity of what Nik had done dawned on me. He was biting his bottom lip, a look of apprehension on his face.

'I've been accepted to do an MSci in archaeological studies at the University of Birmingham. How did this happen? I didn't even apply.'

'Don't you remember the run-up to your interview for that job at the museum? You said the only thing you could think of as to why you might not get it would be if someone more qualified applied. Well, once you've done this, there will be no one else more qualified and you'll have loads more

271

opportunities. I know I should've asked you, but I figured you would balk at the cost.'

'That was going to be my next question.'

'Dad thought—'

'Please tell me your dad isn't going to pay for the year's course?'

'It's only a loan. He knows you'll be good for the money once you're a rich and successful curator at the museum. And they will be falling over themselves to rehire you once you do this. Please, Lina.' He pulled me out of my seat and wrapped his arms around my waist. 'Things are going to be great. Your next year is fixed, and you won't have to worry about looking for a job – well, for now at least. More time for going to the Fox with me on a Saturday night.' His eyes twinkled.

My mind whirred. Everything was sorted. Life would get back to normal again in a blink of an eye, the last three weeks soon to be a distant memory. Only … I could never forget them or the profound effect they had had on me.

Nik drew me closer, and I nestled into his chest, inhaling his familiar scent. This was where I used to love to be. Here in his arms. That unconditional feeling of acceptance and belonging. It had been like this ever since that day.

Chapter 30

When we were twenty-one

I was on my hands and knees, sweeping the glass into the dustpan. There were shards everywhere. Why? Why did the thieves have to target the deli on the one day I was away in Cambridge?

A familiar tinkle from the bell above the door made me look up. Nik was bathed in sunlight like a Greek hero. My saviour. I dropped the brush and leapt into his arms.

'Hey,' he soothed. 'It's all right. I'm glad you texted me.'

There was a smell of cigarettes and sweat on the fabric of his shirt as if he had rolled straight out from an all-night bender. His eyes were bloodshot too. 'Did I wake you?'

'I needed an excuse to leave his bed.'

'Oh,' I said, a little taken aback by his admission.

He laughed. 'God, it felt good to say that out loud. Knowing you know is a godsend. How's your dad?'

My bottom lip wobbled, and I reached out to grab the back of a chair. 'Two cracked ribs, bruises all over his face, but it's his heart that I am worried about most. They are keeping him in hospital for a few days to monitor it.'

Nik lifted my chin with a delicate touch. 'He's gonna be OK, Lina.' He took in the scene around us, puffing out his cheeks. 'Jeez, this place is a mess.'

'It's like they knew when Dad would be locking up. It wasn't until I came from the hospital this morning that I saw the state they left it in. The table was turned on its side and a jug of water had been smashed to the floor. They took everything – the month's takings and even keepsakes from the flat upstairs.'

I sniffed, wiping my nose against my sleeve, and Nik put his arm around me. 'It'll be OK, I'll help you clear up. And the place is insured, right?'

I nodded, forcing a smile. 'Of course. We've got that special deal with Markos Insurance.'

'Then I'll help you file the claim. It's my job, after all.'

I nestled closer to him, my hands around his waist. 'You're the best.'

'I'm here for you, Lina. I'll always be here for you. And now that you've finished your degree and I'm back from Southampton, we can hang out more.'

'You mean you need your *beard* to hang out with you more?'

'Hey.' He bumped me with his hip. 'You know you mean much more than that to me, right? While I'm thrilled you called me, how come you didn't call that guy you're seeing?'

I extracted myself from his hold and went over to the counter. 'I need a coffee,' I said, grabbing the pot and filling it with water. 'Want one?'

'Did I hit a nerve?'

'We broke up.'

'Again?'

'For good this time.' I flipped the switch.

'He was an asshole anyway.'

'I thought you said he was cute.'

'Cute, but an asshole none the less. You deserve much better than him anyway.'

'I'm done with guys.'

'Would love to agree with you but ... you know.' His eyebrows did a merry dance.

I brought a couple of mugs to one of the tables and slumped into the nearest chair. The first sip burned my top lip. Of course it had. I hadn't added any milk and it had come straight from the boiled pot. Two sleepless nights were catching up on me. Nik sat down and reached out to hold my hand.

'Talk to me, Lina. You seem so troubled. Is it just your dad you're worried about?'

'I feel stuck. Like I am sitting in the corner of the deli, and I have no way out. I know I can't leave Dad now, ever.'

'Hmm, I guess so. It's your duty, right? The Greek way. And you are his only child here. But ...' He took a sip of his coffee. 'You don't work on a Sunday. You can let your hair down on a Saturday night after helping him lock up. He'd manage one night without you. You could then fulfil your familial duty and get to have some fun too.'

'I guess.'

'I'm thinking of buying one of those flats in town – you know, the ones close to the Bullring.'

'With what money?'

'Dad will be a guarantor for a mortgage and my income's steady because of my job.'

'Are you seriously going to work for your dad?'

'Are you seriously going to judge me on that?' He swept his arm around the deli.

'But you have choices. You could use your business administration degree anywhere.'

He cradled his mug, staring into the depths of the coffee. 'We're Greek, Lina. We don't have choices. We do what's expected of us. And Mum would be heartbroken if I moved out of Birmingham. It was bad enough being far away for university for three years. Maybe now I can avoid the daily phone calls and surprise visits. Besides, who else will do my laundry?'

I swatted his arm, drops spilling from his coffee which I wiped up with a paper napkin from the dispenser. 'I'm thinking of accepting the placement at the Birmingham Museum.'

'Good for you. So, we'll both be here. In Birmingham. It'll be a blast. And you can stay with me on a Saturday night.'

And that's how it began – our 'relationship'. We told each other everything. He was more than just my gay best friend. He became my chance to let my hair down for that one night a week. We would go wild, letting loose. I lost count of the number of times I told a guy I had had a one-night stand with that there was someone else and the reason why I didn't want to take it further. Some Saturday nights I would slump on Nik's sofa waiting for him to return after he had slept with a guy. It suited him that I was around, and no one

speculated about his private life – or, rather, his parents
didn't because we often had Sunday brunch together after I
had stayed over.

But then one Saturday night ... the line between friendship
and something more blurred.

Chapter 31

When we were twenty-four

I let myself into Nik's flat with the spare key – the one he had given me after our Saturday nights together had become sacred. It was the only way I could have some semblance of a life outside the demands of my museum work and the deli. It was also a way to avoid any judgement from Dad, as it had been painful enough having to always make curfew when I was at university. I was his precious little girl, he would often remind me. He didn't trust men. I often thought that his mindset had been solidified the night he caught Alex with Emily. A 22-year-old, who should have known better, taking advantage of a girl his sister's age, he had told me repeatedly.

I swayed into the flat, dropping my key twice. My eyes were rimmed with tears and my head was pounding.

'Good night?' Nik said, without looking up from the TV. He was sitting on his leather sofa, shirtless, his six-pack glowing in the light of the flatscreen – three empty beer bottles lying on the coffee table. His grey tracksuit bottoms hung low, showcasing the Calvin Klein waistband of his briefs. My heartbeat picked up speed. I still couldn't deny the effect he had on me. No one ever forgets their first crush.

I sniffed but turned my face to the TV, hoping he couldn't see my eyes glistening in the darkness as I sat down. 'It was OK. Why did you leave the club so early?'

'I'm so bored of seeing the same guys all the time. I wish we could go somewhere a little more ... lively.'

'We can, only you don't want to.'

'True. This guy you met tonight ... not the one, eh?' He turned and gave me a sympathetic smile, but his brow furrowed when he took in my face. 'Hey, what's the matter? Are those tears?' He reached to catch one as it escaped from my lower lid.

'I don't think there'll be a second date.' I forced a smile.

The truth was he was quite nice at the beginning. He was a friend of someone from the museum. A first-date drink had moved on to dinner and then I had agreed to meet Nik and some other friends at a club. It's what we always did. For me it was a safety measure and, for Nik, it was something to tell his parents if they asked what he was up to at the weekend.

My date and I had continued to drink a lot and, before I knew it, I was back at his. Things got heated fast, but the strangling anxiety soon kicked in. Was it better to get it over with – endure the painful sex and not see him again – than have to stop and say why this wasn't what I wanted? What was the point in taking it slow if it had the same result – I couldn't have a relationship because I couldn't have sex. In the end, I had asked him to stop, he'd called me a prick tease and I had fled his flat, hastily ordering an Uber which thank God was only a couple of minutes away. I wanted nothing more than to come back here, to my sanctuary, to Nik.

'His loss,' Nik said as he put his arm around me and pulled me tightly against his chest. I inhaled his warm skin. It was everywhere – his scent. I already knew it was The One by Dolce & Gabbana. I had seen the bottle in the main bathroom.

'These guys, Lina. They don't deserve you. The moment he opened his mouth, I didn't trust him. I'm not gonna lie. I was waiting up for you. I know the last thing you need is another dad in your life, especially when you've got one as over-protective as yours, but I feel this duty to you. I care about you. I hate seeing you hurt. This anger bubbles up inside me.'

Maybe it was the alcohol coursing through my veins or the ridiculous crush I had had on him since we were teenagers, but I found myself squeezing into him, stroking his chest, feeling safe, loving the feel of his tanned arms against my paler ones, the tattoo that snaked up over his shoulder so sexy, licking his hot, naked skin.

Up and down, my fingertips brushed him before they were replaced by my nails. I could hear him take a sharp intake of breath.

'That tickles,' he said a little huskily.

'Sorry,' I said and flattened my palm against him.

'No, don't stop. I like it,' he said, his voice now deep and ragged.

My hands dipped in and out of the contours of his muscles, feeling the hardness of his nipples as I grazed the tips of my fingers across his chest.

'How are you still single, Nikolas Markos?'

'Why do you ask?'

'Because … not only are you ridiculously good-looking, you're also kind, sensitive …'

'And?'

'Is that not enough?' I stopped stroking and raised an eyebrow. 'You fishing for compliments?'

His smile dropped. 'It's not like I have anyone in my life to pay me any. And why that's the case, I don't know. I haven't met the right person … for me.'

I held my hand firm against his chest. 'He's out there. You just have to have faith.'

He gripped my shoulder tighter. 'I don't even know if it will be a guy. Sometimes I think how much easier it would be to be with a woman, get married, have kids, lead a traditional life. Like my parents.'

'But then you'd be lying to yourself.'

'Would I?'

'Yes, you would. You're gay.'

'You know I hate labels, Lina. I'm fluid. I am me. I am at my best when I am with someone who gets me, who understands why this is so hard, why family matters, duty. Not every *guy* gets that.'

'Oh,' I said, slightly shocked by his admission.

It was then that I realised Nik's hand was gently caressing my bare arm. I closed my eyes and let the sensation soothe me; when I opened them, his head leaned into mine, nose brushing against my hair, breathing me in.

You could say what happened next was inevitable – the low lights, the alcohol, the neediness.

Nik shifted a little and searched my eyes, and I couldn't turn away. Then he pressed his lips to mine. At first it shocked me, and I pulled back. He was obviously feeling as vulnerable as I was. We had grown so used to each other, relying on one another emotionally, navigating our twenties together. But something had shifted tonight.

Without further thought, I kissed him with a sense of urgency, my mouth opening to his tongue. The kiss grew more intense, hands roaming freely until I found myself in his lap, his hands gripping my waist. He pulled me towards him, and I rocked gently, my head buried in his neck, eyes firmly closed, savouring the friction between my jeans and his hardness. He let me be in control. Perhaps it was the knowledge that this wouldn't go any further that allowed me to fully let myself go. I rocked and rocked until I felt the sweetest release.

I didn't think through my next actions because I was still on the high of my orgasm, the fact that there had been no pain. Obviously not – there had been no penetration. My hand inched down into his briefs and, for a second, I looked up to see whether this was what he really wanted. His eyes were closed, and he was moaning softly. I didn't stop even though I knew this was probably wrong. But was it, when it was what we both needed, what fitted?

Nik's moans continued, breathing growing more ragged, until a strangled cry came from his lips as he found his own release.

'Marry me,' he whispered.

'What?' I said in disbelief as I took in his face which had grown serious.

Always You

'If we're still single by thirty, marry me.' He held my head in his hands, stroking my cheeks. 'There's no other girl for me.'

The most ludicrous suggestion, borne by lust, but ... why not? I thought. Nik was kind, caring, sensitive and it would fulfil both of our needs.

'Sure, I'll marry you.'

283

Chapter 32

Now we are twenty-eight

I could see him in the distance. That familiar shock of black hair, with tufts of white sprouting out from his temples and moustache, like he was Omar Sharif. When he saw me, he smiled. It was only when he was within arm's reach that I noticed how much he had taken the sun.

'Dad,' I beamed, flinging myself into his arms.

'*Ángelé mou*,' he said, clutching me tightly before giving me a once-over. 'You're tanned.'

That familiar prickly feeling rose in my neck. 'So are you,' I said, wanting to deflect the attention, in the hope the flushes would abate. 'In fact, you look incredible. Have you lost weight?'

He patted his stomach. 'Everything is so healthy in California. They all eat kale.' He pulled a grimace and I laughed. Contentment filled his face, like the trip away had done him the world of good; and in that moment, I let another wall around me crumble a little, the one I had built since Alex left us, and I was grateful that Dad's time with him had had such a positive impact.

'Did I miss another heatwave in England while I was gone?'

'No, you didn't,' I said, taking control of his suitcase trolley. 'I went away for a bit. Felt like I needed a holiday. The pressure of looking for a job was getting to me. But everything's sorted now.'

He raised his eyebrows. 'It is?'

'Let's get home first and I will fill you in.'

Back at the flat, Dad's reaction to the deli reopening confirmed what I had originally thought. He mumbled something in Greek under his breath and, though my language ability was rusty, I could still pick out the word *ofeílo* which meant 'having an obligation to pay or repay'.

He told me Alex had offered to help, but he had turned him down. I didn't want to question why.

I let Dad freshen up while I fixed us both lunch – some of his favourite dishes that I had learned how to make from one of the many cookbooks stashed in a cupboard in the kitchen.

When, years ago, I had found *A Taste of Greece*, its spine cracked in places, I opened it up to reveal a wealth of dishes with little hearts in the margin. When I asked him what they were, his eyes misted over, and he said they were Mum's favourites. Those were the ones I made now. She hadn't been far from my thoughts since I had met Marika. I wanted to talk to Dad about her so desperately but didn't know how.

He came into the kitchen with a fresh shirt on, the top two buttons undone, his white vest visible underneath, as I pulled out a dish from the oven.

'You really are an angel. I missed your cooking.' He sat down and drank from his water glass before tucking into the bread and *spanakópita*, cheese and spinach oozing out from beneath the crispy filo layers.

'I guess we need to contact the suppliers if we're planning on reopening,' I said, after savouring a few mouthfuls.

He nodded. 'I will spend today organising everything. Now, I want to hear about what you have been doing.'

I didn't know where to begin. Should I tell him what I had found when looking through his paperwork?

I folded my napkin in half, then half again. 'I went on a dig.'

'How exciting. You always wanted to do that. I am so happy. Where was it?'

'In Cyprus.'

Dad's hand hovered in the air, grasping his fork tighter. 'Really?'

'Yes, I volunteered on a dig in Larnaca. The Kition one.'

The fork slipped out of his hand – a pained look on his face.

'It was Mum's dig,' I went on.

He wiped his mouth with his napkin. 'Yes, it was. But ... how did you know?'

'I'm sorry, I didn't mean to snoop, but when I was looking through your paperwork,' I said, tipping my chin towards the cupboard in the corner, 'I came across Mum's journal.'

He took a sip of water. 'Did you read it?'

I nodded. 'Are you mad?'

He reached out and tapped my hand. 'Mad? Of course I am not mad. Your mother would be so proud of you, my little archaeologist, finally pursuing this passion just like she did.'

'I wanted to try and find out what happened ... you know ... when she made that discovery of the tomb, and they didn't believe her.'

'And what did you find?'

'I think I did find something, only the son of the man Mum worked with didn't appreciate my questioning. I found the entrance to the tomb that she originally discovered, but ... I had a little accident when I unearthed it.'

'What?' Dad said, his tone harsh. 'Are you crazy? What kind of accident?'

'It's fine, Dad, I'm fine. And in fact, going to hospital was the best thing that could have happened to me because my doctor was Marika Lamos – you remember, Mum's best friend? She was—'

'Hospital?' Dad choked on the word. 'You were in the hospital?' His face turned bright red, and it soon became apparent that he was struggling to breathe. He held his hand to his chest and a wash of panic rose up my body.

I pushed back my chair, its legs scraping on the wooden floor. 'Dad? Are you OK?'

He gulped back his water before refilling his glass. 'A little indigestion,' he managed to say through gasps.

'I'll get the antacids,' I said hastily, before rushing to the bathroom to get the pills.

I helped him up from the table and let him rest on the couch.

After a while, his face turned back to its tanned state, and he was no longer finding it hard to breathe.

'Please, Lina,' he said, grasping my hand so tightly I thought he might crush it. 'Promise me, you will never put yourself in that kind of danger *ever* again.' He had a pained expression. 'I would never live with myself if something happened to you too.'

'I promise,' I whispered.

'Forgive me, but I need a moment.' He groaned as he stood, a little shaky on his legs. 'I will retire to my bed. Jet lag,' he stated firmly, as if it excused his desire to leave me. 'I will see you later.'

And with those words he walked out of the living room, leaving me confused, concerned and even further from uncovering anything more about my mother and her life in Cyprus.

I lay on my bed that night flicking through the course booklet that had come in the post while I had been away. I still couldn't get my head around the fact that Nik had organised all this without my knowledge and also why they had accepted my application. But I couldn't deny the sparks of excitement as I read the outline of the course. Maybe Nik was right. I might have got the job at the museum if I had this qualification. But then I wouldn't have gone to Cyprus, and I wouldn't have met Marika. And if I hadn't had the accident, would I have continued to live in pain?

Dad had been thrilled about the masters course when I mentioned it to him as I was getting ready for bed and saw him in the hallway. Life could return to some sense of normality, he had said. The deli would reopen, I would be studying during the day and going out with Nik on a Saturday; staying over and keeping up the pretence that we were a couple destined to be married one day. This was how it had always been.

Why, then, did my heart ache? An indescribable feeling coated the insides of my stomach – an emptiness.

Ash. Because I couldn't stop thinking of Ash.

My phone buzzed and I picked it up expectantly. Marika. It was a message to say no one had found the films. She was sorry but she had tried everything, including harassing the next tenants of the villa to let her unearth every stone around the flowerbeds where we had stood and said our goodbyes.

I stared at her message and rubbed my thumb over the ridges in my index finger, which were now smoother, before tapping out a few words to Ash. It would be well after midnight in Mumbai, so I was stunned when a minute later my phone vibrated with an incoming FaceTime from him. I held my breath and accepted the call. As his face filled the screen, I smiled.

'Hey,' I said lightly. 'How are you?'

He nodded. 'Good, good. Is this what you were talking about?' He raised something aloft and my hand went to my heart when I saw what he was clutching. It was the plastic bag containing the films.

'Yes, it is.' They were my last connection to Mum's life in Cyprus. 'Marika handed them over to me when she was saying goodbye. I must've dropped them.'

'I'm sorry, I was meaning to message you about them. I was going to hand them in to the property owner, but I had this feeling that I had to keep them with me. Want me to send them?'

'Would you? That'd be great.'

An awkward silence filled the space between us. Ash was sitting in darkness, as if I had interrupted him trying to get to sleep. I flicked on my bedside lamp and in return he did the same. His face glowed.

'I miss you,' I whispered.

His lips parted. 'I miss you too.'

'I almost wish you could bring me the films yourself.' I chewed my bottom lip.

My statement went unanswered, and I suddenly felt foolish for even suggesting it.

'Did you get home OK?' I asked.

'Yes. You?'

This was painful. I wanted him here in this room, now. I wanted him in my arms, in my bed; to feel him inside me again. He was like a drug. And right now, it was as though I was in rehab, already having to get over him when I hadn't even enjoyed the prolonged high.

'How are you feeling?' he asked.

'I'm good. I'm starting a masters course at Birmingham University in conservation. Nik applied on my behalf, and I got in.' I dared not look at the screen as I said everything. 'And the deli's reopening tomorrow. Nik's dad sorted it out with the tax office. In fact, I should probably be getting some sleep. Got to get used to waking up at five again.' My voice was shaking, and I had no idea how to rein in the emotion lacing every word.

'Is that what you want?' Ash said.

I clutched my mobile tighter. 'What?'

'Everything you've just told me.'

'Well, it's not like I can open up our mystery box and find out what I *really* wanted to do with my life, is it?' There was a hint of bitterness in my tone.

'No, but you can look inside your heart.'

I held my eyes steady with his. He leaned in a little and I brought my mobile closer to my face to somehow get that nearness again, to forget that there were four and a half thousand miles between us, fourteen hours in a plane, five and a half hours' time difference. If I could get that closeness again, maybe my heart could tell me what I wanted.

'I took your advice,' he said finally.

'About what?'

'I want to make peace with my parents.'

'That's great,' I said, my voice hopeful. Did this mean he was coming back to Birmingham? Or, hell, even London would be better than nothing.

'I called Mum. We talked. I told her I didn't want the distance between us any more. I tried to explain how much losing Divya had hurt me too, that I live with regret for not being there for her, for not ...' He let out a puff of air. 'I'm not sure what. But ... Mum said Dad's getting worse. And I know she wants us all to be together, so ... they're moving to Mumbai. Mum, Dad, Auntie and Gran; they will live close by. I'll get Dad the best doctors. I can arrange for him to have the best care. He'll be fine, I know he will. It'll be so much easier for me to care for them if they are here.'

'Wow. That's great.' I hoped my face didn't betray how I was really feeling. I also didn't want to question the fact that he had originally told me his dad's leukaemia could only be treated with chemotherapy. If that wasn't working here, then what treatment could he get in India that would be different?

'I owe you so much, Lina. And I'll never forget the time you and I had in Cyprus.'

A hard lump formed in my throat, and I couldn't swallow it away.

'I really hope it works out for your dad.'

I couldn't do it. I couldn't tell him what I really wanted to tell him. *Come here, for me, so I don't have to leave* my *dad.*

'Please send your family all my love. I miss your granny. Remember when I used to come over after school and pretend to be getting homework help from you, but secretly I would be in her bedroom watching Bollywood movies?'

'You were the worst student.' He chuckled.

'I did all right,' I said with a mock-offended tone.

'Sorry, I didn't mean it like that.'

'It's fine, Ash. We came from two different worlds. My parents didn't really care what I got up to. I understand you had different pressures.'

He yawned and quickly put his hand over his mouth.

'Sorry, I'm keeping you up.'

'No, it's fine.'

'It must be almost two a.m. Anyway, Nik's stopping by in a bit. We're having a drink at the Fox.'

His jaw did that clenching thing. He had turned his head, which made it even more visible. This time, I couldn't let my irritation pass.

'Why, Ash? Why is it that every time I mention Nik's name you get all tetchy? I've noticed it so many times. What has the guy ever done to you?'

'It's what he's done to *you*,' he said, his words clipped, turning back to face the screen.

'Nik has never done anything to me. He's been there for me for years.'

'What about when we were at school, huh? What about the time he scared us senseless with his notion that the world was going to end?'

'We were kids, Ash,' I said through a half laugh.

'And when he let you down for that dancing competition.'

The mere mention of that time sent my shackles up. 'He sprained his wrist. It wasn't his fault.'

'Then what about when he slept with you when he knew it was *me* that was in love with you? And then the fact that he hurt you.'

I couldn't even think about the second accusation because the first one had floored me. Nik knew that Ash loved me, back when we were eighteen?

'And despite all the things he's done, he's still very firmly in your life getting his fill of you or whatever relationship it is you two have.'

My hand increased its grip on the phone. I didn't know who it was I was most mad at – Ash for telling me this now, Nik for keeping the secret from me or *me* for getting myself tangled in such a mess.

'My relationship with Nik is none of your business,' I said.

He smiled, a slow thin-lipped smile but his eyes betrayed it – they were cold, unforgiving. 'You're right, Lina. What you do with your life is none of my business. But life isn't like a Bollywood movie, no matter what we believed when we were little. Maybe that box wasn't ever going to unlock our childhood wishes but I guess we'll never know. You know what?'

'No. What?' I said, still reeling from the revelation.

'I always believed Nik had taken our time capsule. Something he once said to me has bothered me for years and years. He made some quip about me wanting to be the next Gordon Ramsay at our leavers' assembly and only someone who had read my letter would have known that. He could have named any other chef. I had completely forgotten about it until I read those diary entries.'

'That's ridiculous, Ash. I knew how much you loved cooking; it was probably me he heard it from. And Ramsay is a household name – a mega celebrity chef.'

'Always defending him,' he said, his head dipped low.

'Well, he's been in my life longer than you have, so yes, I will defend him when he's not here to stick up for himself.'

Here we were again. The impasse.

'It's late,' Ash declared, as if time had suddenly pushed on a couple of hours. 'I have to go. Goodbye.'

And with those words the screen went black – the call disconnected. But it wasn't only the FaceTime connection that had been lost; it was ours too.

Chapter 33

The deli reopened with little fanfare the next day. When my alarm went at five, I groaned and rolled over in bed, not wanting to face the task ahead. Why? It had always been a part of my life and I had been so grateful to have it – it had always given me a sense of purpose, that I was doing something important: keeping my mother's memory alive, cooking her secret *dolmádes* recipe. And now that I hadn't been able to clear her name, it was all I had.

When I dropped off the order at Markos Insurance, I went in a little early – keen not to bump into Nik. But I made a point of telling Mr Markos how incredibly grateful I was for all he had done for me and for Dad. He was thrilled with the compliments.

Over the next few days, I helped Dad in the deli for the breakfast and lunchtime rush. It warmed my heart to see him engaging with his old customers. He seemed happy. At least I thought he was. We hadn't talked much about his trip to California. And I hadn't wanted to ask. The rest of my time was spent at the library. There was a lot of pre-course work I had to do, and it was seven years since I had been a student.

When I had told Greer about my plan to do a masters, she was thrilled. Students together. She said there were so many similarities between my course and the final year of hers that we could do regular study sessions – to brainstorm and support each other. She still hadn't heard anything back from the museum that was listed on the receipt I had given her, and the films hadn't arrived from Ash either. What did any of that matter, though, if I didn't have the two missing jewels? My only wish was that there would be a picture of Mum in the reels.

Saturday came. I swept up the deli floor after flipping the Open sign and could think of nothing more than taking a long soak in the bath. The door tinkled.

'We're closed,' I said without turning around.

'Not for me you're not,' Nik said.

I stopped sweeping and rested the broom against the wall before picking up a cloth. 'Even for you, Nikolas Markos,' I said as I sprayed Domestos over the counter.

'Are you avoiding me?'

'No,' I said, stabbing at a stubborn stain on the Formica surface.

He pulled out a stool and sat down in front of me, wiggling his mobile. 'Then what's behind this message? "Sorry, not up for tonight. Feeling tired. Gonna have a bath and an early night."' He repeated my words back at me with an irritated tone.

'I've been on my feet all day and I really want to crash so I can get some reading done tomorrow.' I noticed he was wearing his 'pulling' outfit: black jeans and blue silk shirt rolled at the sleeves, the bracelet I had got him for his eighteenth visible on his wrist.

'And did you not think you could do that at mine? I would've sulked initially that you didn't want to come to the Fox with me, but you know my bath is double the size of yours and I wouldn't have disturbed you if I happened to have a late one. I want you with me on Sunday. Pleeeaaaase, Lina. Dad's been asking questions.'

'About what?' I said, trying not to let him see how much his badgering was annoying me.

'You and I.'

I stiffened. 'There is no you and I, Nik. We're friends, that's all.'

'Hey.' He held his hands over my arms to stop me from wiping. 'Talk to me. Where's this little outburst come from?'

'It's not come from anywhere.' I shook his hold away and carried on wiping. 'It's how I feel.'

'Well, you didn't feel this way before you waltzed off to Cyprus. Something happened there and you're not telling me. In fact, you glossed over the whole trip the other day.'

'There's nothing to tell.'

'It's Ash, isn't it? He's messed with your mind again.'

'Agh.' I slapped the cloth down on the counter. 'You and Ash are insufferable. What is it between you two? Every time I bring up your name in front of him or his in front of you, I feel like we're back in the playground of Stockwell Primary.'

'Well, he started it.'

'See. You even sound like an eight-year-old. We were friends, all of us, good friends and—'

'No, we weren't. You and I were friends, and he stole you from me.'

I rubbed my temple, trying to think back to our school days but it was a blank. 'What are you talking about?'

'When we were in Year Three and Toby the Tank had his arm round my neck at the back of the bike sheds and you kneed him in the groin, we became best friends, right?'

'Yes,' I said hesitantly, not really recalling the exact day because it was over twenty years ago but clearly it was enough of a harrowing event for Nik to remember.

'We were inseparable after that. We kept getting into trouble and it didn't matter because we had each other's backs. And then Ash came along. The new boy. You always had a soft spot for waifs and misfits. You were a hero to so many others, but I thought he was just one of many, only he wasn't. And you started to spend less time with me and, when I needed you, you were always with him.'

'That was because you were mean to him, and I felt torn.' I scratched my head, not sure whether I was remembering a specific event or just a feeling and whether that was when we were a little older. 'I was friends with both of you, but I didn't think I favoured one of you over the other.'

'It felt that way to me. He came along and you weren't mine any more.'

'I'm not some prize, Nik. Is that what this is? You slept with me when we were eighteen because you knew Ash was in love with me?'

His face fell. 'What's Ash been telling you?'

'You're saying you didn't know back then that he had feelings for me, strong feelings? That when you and I slept together, you didn't know it would crush him to find out about us?'

His silence spoke volumes.

'Would it have mattered if you had known?' he said finally.

It was a question I hadn't dared to answer in my head since Ash had told me. I twisted the cloth in my hands. 'I don't know. My crush for you had been building for years. I think if I had known I would have felt even more confused. But then, I wouldn't have rushed things and ended up feeling so hurt that night. Then maybe I wouldn't have found my brother and best friend in bed together. I could've found out a different way and life might not be like this.'

I had no idea if that little outburst had made any sense or where it had come from.

Nik reached out to squeeze my hand. 'I promise I didn't deliberately hide that info about Ash from you. It wasn't really my place to say anything. To me it was like he was marking his territory and it irritated me. Still does. And when you came back from Cambridge that day when your dad was in the hospital, I knew something had happened between you both, that he'd gone and screwed up his friendship with you.'

'He didn't. I heard from another source that he was in love with me and ... well, it doesn't matter.'

Nik stroked the counter with his fingers, back and forth, lost in thought. 'That night of my eighteenth, I was really confused. Loads of things happened that night. Things I haven't told you.'

'Really?'

He nodded, picking up a crumb from the counter and flicking it away. I came around to the other side and pulled out the stool next to his and sat down bracing myself for what he was about to say – we had never talked about that night since it happened.

'I'm listening,' I said softly.

'That was the night Mateo – you remember, right, that Spanish guy you caught me jerking off the day after my party?'

'I remember.'

'He told me he really liked me. He said it was more than just a holiday romance for him. We were down the side of my house talking. I had told him that being with a guy wasn't for me, that I was just unsure of a lot of things. I remember he laughed at that. He was stroking my cheek, telling me to own who I was and be proud of it. The party was in full swing, I wasn't thinking straight. I knew it was risky doing anything in public, but I was tired of not being honest about something I think I had known for a very long time. Just as he was leaning in to kiss me, I heard him.' He paused and tensed as if the memory was too painful. 'Dad. It was like a strangled cry, quiet enough not to make anyone hear him, but loud enough for *me* to hear. He had come to check up on the party, to make sure it hadn't got out of control. He ordered Mateo to leave us alone and then ... he slapped me.'

I could see Nik's shoulders lock beneath his shirt, and I reached out to stroke his arm.

'That was it. A slap. No words. I didn't even try and defend myself, say nothing was going on. But he knew what he had seen, and he was disgusted. He lingered around after that. I couldn't handle the anger that was bottling up inside of me. I even felt disgusted with myself.'

'You should never have felt that way. You can't apologise for who you are.'

'And then there you were. Princess Lina. That's what Dad always called you.'

I sat back, surprised at this admission.

'Always his number-one girl. In fact ...' he laughed, but it was a little hollow '... he always cared for you more than me. He was nice to me when you were around, when you came over to study on all those history A-level projects we did together. But that night – the way he looked at me after he slapped me – I felt sick to the pit of my stomach. I so wanted to stand up to him – tell him I was gay and proud of it; I even went back into the party and was talking quite openly with Mateo on the sofa.'

'I remember now. You were sitting really close, before I sashayed over with my tits hanging out of my micro dress.' I grimaced at the memory.

A smile played on his lips. 'You looked gorgeous that night. And, God, those "I want to fuck you" signals you gave me.' He shook his head. 'No, the gentlemanly thing to do would have been to give you a large glass of water, not take advantage of you.'

'I don't think there was anything you could've done to stop me that night. I was a woman on a mission.'

'When you kissed me in front of everyone, I liked the attention I got and those losers from the football team gave me a few slaps on the back when I came out of my bedroom after we ... you know.'

'Ugh.'

'I know, toxic masculinity at its worst.' He shifted on the stool. 'Dad hadn't left the party that night; he was up in his room with Mum, waiting it out until midnight when he pulled the plug on the sound machine and told everyone to fuck off. He heard some of the guys talking about me losing my virginity; said they'd always thought I was a bender. I was so weak back then, I didn't correct them, didn't have the nerve to tell them that Mateo was my first. Dad gave me a knowing smile and ...' He held his head in his hands and shuddered. 'I'm so sorry but I felt validated again.'

I stroked his arm gently, seeing how painful these memories were to him.

He lifted his head up and shrugged off my hold. 'No, Lina. I don't deserve any sympathy from you. I used you.' He silenced my attempt at a response with his hand. 'It was wrong of me.'

I lowered my head, thinking back to the confused feelings I had felt that night myself and the pain. My first time. Little had I known back then that it would have hurt me, no matter who I had been with.

Nik tipped my chin upwards and stared deeply into my eyes. 'But, like I told you a few years back, I have always had strong feelings for you, still do.'

'But things change, Nik.' I removed his hand from my face.

'They don't have to, not if we don't want them to.'

'But you've obviously got some suppressed desire to please your dad at all costs.'

'I like who I am with you.'

'Because we're friends who know everything about each other. I guard your biggest secret, even though I still can't quite get my head around the fact that you've probably shagged half the gay guys in Birmingham, and I am amazed your parents have never found out.'

'I know how to pick 'em. They're always in town for a short while, visiting from other parts of the country or on holiday. It's a lot easier that way. No strings attached.'

'But no chance to have anything more long-lasting, more meaningful.'

'I'm sure that's overrated anyway.'

'No, it's not.' I picked at the ridges in my fingers. 'Nik ... something did happen in Cyprus ...'

He crossed his arms. 'What?'

'Ash and I ... we made love.'

'Oh.' The only word. A shift had occurred again.

'It was the first time ... it hadn't hurt.' I clenched my hands in my lap, before glancing up.

'I hurt you?' The look he wore was as if someone had punched him in the gut.

'Not intentionally, no. It's something that was wrong with me, something I hadn't known. The endometriosis made it always painful to have sex. Only, the more I ignored it, the more stressed I became every time I slept with someone new. It's a lot more complicated than that ... I'm still trying to get to grips with what the doctor who did the operation on me told me, but then … when it was me and Ash, it was good, really good. It didn't hurt. It was …' My mind drifted back to our time in Cyprus, and I got lost in a tidal wave of feelings – pleasure, desire and connection. 'It doesn't matter now.' I shook myself out of my reverie. 'There's nothing going to happen between us.'

'His loss.'

He said it with so much bitterness. I realised then that I was exhausted.

'You know what? I think I could really do with a drink right now.'

A broad grin spread across Nik's face. 'Now you're talking. I knew I could persuade you.' He leaned in for a hug, but it turned into an opportunity for him to tickle me.

'Stop it, you,' I said, trying to hold back my laughter. 'But I meant what I said, Nik. I don't want to marry you.'

He stopped the tickling and pretended he had been shot in the chest and collapsed to the floor.

'I'm serious, Nik,' I said, laughing. 'We can't keep pretending to your folks that this is going to happen someday.'

'I'll tell them.'

I raised my eyebrows suspiciously.

'What? I will. I promise.'

'Everything?'

His top lip curled upwards. 'Maybe. Now stop nagging, woman, and let's go out and get drunk.'

I finished clearing up and locked the deli like I had for years on end on a Saturday night. It was the way it had to be so I could always keep Dad safe. And now Nik and I had cleared the air, I felt better that we had shared some painful memories – it only served to make the bond between us deeper. I had chosen. It was simple. If Ash couldn't find a way to be in the life I had now, then there was no way that we could ever be together.

I ignored the pain that settled deep in my side at that decision. It was no doubt a delayed reaction to the operation – nothing more.

Chapter 34

A week later, a padded envelope landed on the doormat. The postmark showed it was from India and my heart leapt in my chest.

I took it upstairs while Dad was busy preparing the day's specials in the deli's kitchen downstairs and opened it.

Inside was a pack of photos – thirty-six of them with their negatives sitting in a see-through pocket. I shook the envelope and a handwritten note slipped out.

I thought it best to develop them in case the film got lost in transit. Hope they help solve your mystery. Ash.

My stomach twisted. No 'love Ash', not even a 'best wishes'. It read as cold as it must have been intended. I pushed those thoughts to one side as I took in each photo. One after the other – a slow and steady unearthing of the tomb with clear geographical markings. My heartbeat picked up pace as I studied them, waiting and waiting for that big reveal, when it would show what Mum had found, but as the last one came and I laid it down, I couldn't hide my disappointment. There was nothing. No big reveal. Not even a photo of Mum to prove it had been her. Why? Why would she hide these in Marika's house as if they were important?

I texted Marika to let her know it had been a dead end. She was sad but wanted me to look on the bright side. My discovery had led me to her, and she wasn't letting me go. She wanted me to come back and see her over Christmas and I told her that, without a job, my travelling days had to be put on hold, but I promised I would see if I could find a way to earn some extra cash that could maybe cover a plane ticket and pay for someone else to take over from my duties at the deli. I hadn't brought that idea up with Dad, but it had been on my mind. I had managed to pick up some bar work during the week and on the occasional Sunday, which thankfully meant that brunch with the Markoses became more infrequent although Nik still had to endure them. He once told me his dad had been displeased Nik had let me take on so much. I told Nik to tell his dad to butt out of my life and tell him in no uncertain terms that we weren't ever going to get married. He had promised me he would.

The first two terms of my course went by in a blur of lectures, essays, bar and deli work. The lack of a proper job weighed on my mind as well as how the hell I was going to pay Nik's dad back for the loan.

One day when classes had finished for the spring term, I found myself wandering around the corner of the flat. Something had drawn me to Ash's old house – something inexplicable. I closed my eyes and imagined the times I had come here under the pretence of studying. The smell of Indian spices, a house full of warmth, Divya's music pounding through the thin walls, and the Bollywood films that were always turned up too high because Ash's grandma was hard of hearing. I smiled at how his family had embraced me, pulled me through those dark times after Mum's death. And now they were gone – all of them.

I opened my eyes and studied the house a little more carefully. The side gate had been replaced by a door that appeared impenetrable; the stucco bricks a cold grey, having replaced the pebbledash. There was nothing that seemed familiar to me.

My phone buzzed and brought me back to the present. Greer's name flashed up on the screen and I immediately accepted the call.

'Hey, you, I haven't had a chance—'

'No time for small talk,' she barked, causing me to pull the phone away from my ear. There was chatter in the background, and I assumed she was in a coffee shop or restaurant. 'I heard back from the museum.'

My pulse picked up speed. 'What did they say?'

'They said that they delved into their records and dug up some info on who came in to sell that jewel. Seems the backstory was that it had been found on someone's property with no mention of an archaeological site. They had a written testimonial from the guy who sold it to them. I told them you had found this receipt in the office of the site, and I could tell they were beginning to get all suspicious. You know full well archaeologists don't get to keep anything they find, nor can they get any money for dug-up artefacts. If only you had the other two jewels, you could prove that they all belong to the same find and that the one the museum has was sold illegally.'

'But even if I had them, I still don't have the original receipt, nor do I have anything linking them to Mum – well, nothing except a diary, but that's not exactly hard evidence, is it?'

'Have you spoken to your dad about it? Maybe he has something hidden away that you don't know about – maybe he has some pictures of your mum from back then.'

'I never talk about Mum with Dad – he always looks so pained whenever I do. Maybe I should be brave and come straight out with what happened in Cyprus.'

'Yup, maybe you should. But I know it's not easy to talk about something that's so painful for both of you. But who knows, maybe it'll help you fill in some of the missing pieces and then you'll be able to move on with your life.'

'Thanks, Greer. You're a star for finding this out. God, I miss you.'

'Then come to California, baby.'

I took in the grey sky above, inhaling nothing but car fumes, and thought of sun and palm trees. 'One day.'

She tutted. A tut I knew all too well. Her usual response when I said 'One day'. My travel fund to go back to Cyprus was slowly building up but I couldn't deny I had thought a lot about going to LA. Something that Marika had said to me back in Cyprus had niggled me. She said it would've hurt Mum to know we weren't a family any more. So many years had passed, and Dad had found a way to move on and accept Alex and his wife into his life. Wasn't it about time I did the same?

Chapter 35

'God, I'm nervous,' Nik said, wiping his palms down the sides of his suit jacket.

'Don't be. It's going to be fine, though why you think coming out in a restaurant is a good idea is beyond me.'

'Less chance of him making a scene, I figured,' he said, pulling a grimace.

'Just remember, it's your life. You don't need his approval for who you are. Don't make any apologies. Own it. It'll be his loss if he doesn't embrace you with open arms.'

He leaned into me and rubbed his hand up and down my arm. 'I don't know what I'd do without you. You look sensational, by the way.'

I smiled and slipped my arm around his waist as we entered the restaurant. Adam's had been Mr Markos's choice – one of the top eating establishments in the whole of Birmingham. I had dressed up for the lunch in a simple mint wrap dress and heels and was wearing the bracelet Nik got me for my eighteenth, which I only ever wore for special occasions.

Dad had raised his eyebrows when I walked past him as he was serving a customer in the deli. I had kissed him on the cheek and told him I would love to talk to him later. Nik's coming out would be as good a time as any to talk to Dad about Mum and Cyprus. Maybe today would mark a turning point.

Nik's parents stood up from their padded seats to embrace us both and I noticed a bucket of ice was already positioned beside the table complete with a bottle of champagne. An uneasy feeling crept inside me, but it was too late to say anything to Nik.

After placing our order and having the waiter pour the bubbly, Mr Markos raised his glass and smiled broadly. 'To Nik and Lina.'

My hand hovered in the air as clinking sounded in my ear. They thought this was a proposal. Oh my God. I nudged Nik's leg under the table, but he merely stroked my knee affectionately. I leaned in to try and whisper in his ear, but the waiter appeared with a bottle of white for Mr Markos to sample.

Starters came and went with Mr Markos holding forth on how the business was going, asking me questions about my course. I had to correct him when he declared how proud he would be to know a 'doctor'. I explained I wasn't doing a PhD, but he brushed away my 'modesty', as he described it. Mrs Markos didn't utter a word, like always. Nik had said she had been under the weather recently, but with the absence of any physical signs of discomfort, I wasn't exactly sure what she was suffering from.

As I wiped my serviette over my mouth after devouring the most succulent lamb cutlets, I threw Nik a 'now's a good time' look, and he cleared his throat as his cheeks flushed.

'Shall we order another bottle of champagne?' Mr Markos said, raising his finger to attract the waiter's attention.

I stamped my foot on Nik's and a strangled cry came out of him. 'What was that for?' he mumbled, glaring at me.

'Come on, Nik. This is excruciating. You know your dad thinks we're announcing our engagement. Set him straight.'

'What are you two lovebirds whispering about?' Mr Markos chuckled. He turned to the waiter. 'Can we have—'

'No!' Nik said, finally finding his voice. His dad stared at him, alarmed. 'I mean, no thank you, we don't need another bottle of champagne.' The waiter nodded before retreating.

'But I thought we were celebrating.' Mr Markos glanced at his wife and smiled before beaming a little more broadly. 'I can hardly wait to bring you into our family officially, Angelina.'

Nik opened his mouth, but it seemed like he was choking on the words. I patted his back, perhaps a little too forcibly.

'We're not getting married, Mr and Mrs Markos,' I said. Their faces fell.

'I love your son very much but not in that way.'

'Then what are we celebrating?' Mr Markos said pushing his plate away, leaning forward.

'There never was a celebration, Dad. I just asked if you and Mum could come out for lunch with us. *You* assumed it was a celebration. I never said it was.'

'So … this is just another one of our Sunday meets. Why do it in a restaurant? Why lead us to believe it was something special, you stupid boy?'

I rested my hand on Nik's knee under the table to let him know I was there for support.

'The thing is, Dad ... Mum. This *is* something special. It's something important to me, something I have wanted to say for a very long time but haven't had the courage to. And Lina ...' he turned to me and smiled '... is here for moral support because she's my best friend.'

I returned his smile before looking back at the worried expressions on Nik's parents' faces.

Nik cleared his throat and twisted his champagne glass between his fingers. 'I'm gay.'

The table rattled as Mr Markos's hand came down onto it. 'No, you are not. This is nonsense,' he said, his tone measured.

'No, Dad. It's not nonsense. It's who I am, and if you can't accept that—'

'This is an embarrassment. You're in love with Lina.'

'As a friend, Dad.'

'But you slept together.' He said the word 'slept' as if we had committed a cardinal sin.

'That was ten years ago,' Nik said.

'No,' Mr Markos said firmly as he stood up from his chair. He reached into his back pocket and pulled out his wallet. 'This is not happening like this.' He threw a wad of notes onto the table before storming out.

A desperate look crossed Nik's face. 'I have to tell him that he's got to accept me for who I am.' He pushed back his chair, mumbling an apology to his mum for ruining everything before chasing after his dad.

Once Nik had left the restaurant, Mrs Markos smiled at me warmly. 'I knew,' she said. 'I always knew. I think I knew even before he did. He used to love curling up with me at the weekend, looking at the fashion supplements in the *Sunday Times*, always admiring the male models.' She pursed her lips, suddenly lost in thought. 'I'm so proud of my boy,' she said, folding her napkin and placing it on the table. 'Whoever he wants to be with doesn't really matter, as long as he is happy.'

My heart filled with joy. This is what Nik needed. Acceptance.

I stood up, grabbing my bag. 'Nik has to hear this. You have to tell him this, let me ...' I flicked my head to the exit. 'I'll be back in a minute.'

I spilled out of the restaurant only to see Nik and Mr Markos having a heated discussion. I wanted to reassure Nik it would be all right, that his mum understood and accepted him for who he was, but as I drew nearer, I caught the crux of the conversation they were having, and these next words made me stop dead.

'Just because you had an affair with her mum doesn't mean I have an obligation to marry her ...'

Nik didn't finish what he was saying because he had obviously been tipped off by his father's expression that I was behind him.

'You what?' I whispered the words through a lump in my throat.

Nik turned round and shifted awkwardly on the spot when he saw me standing there. 'Lina ...' He reached out to hold my arm. 'I didn't mean—'

I shrugged him away, anger bubbling up inside. 'What? You didn't mean for me to hear that?'

I brushed past him to look Mr Markos straight in the eyes. 'I don't believe you. You did not have an affair with my mother.' His face turned a dark shade of red and he averted his gaze from my piercing stare. 'Did you?'

Mr Markos dropped his shoulders and pressed a fist against his chest. 'We were in love. That much is true. We never wanted to hurt anyone, but yes, we had been together for a while before your mother ...' He paused, pulling out a handkerchief and dabbing his eyes. 'Before she ... died.'

His words hung heavy around me, suffocating me. I turned and through the glass I saw Mrs Markos looking at us hopefully. 'Does she know?'

'No, and I beg you please don't say anything,' he said.

I turned back to Nik. 'And you knew about this?'

Nik nodded.

Suddenly the nearness of both of them made my stomach twist in knots. Taking a step backwards, I clutched my arms tightly around myself. 'I have to go. I can't deal with this right now.'

Before I could push past Nik, he had grabbed my wrist – the jewel of the bracelet pressing into my skin. 'Please, Lina. Let's talk about this.'

'I have nothing to say to you,' I said through gritted teeth.

I clawed at his fingers that were still holding onto my wrist and inadvertently the chain of the bracelet snapped, the trinket dropping to the ground. It hit the tarmac before rolling away into the dip between the edge of the pavement and the restaurant wall. But I didn't stoop to pick it up. I didn't want it any more. Nik had lied to me. Our friendship had been built on falsehoods and secrecy but now it was all out in the open.

Clutching my bag close, I walked away in the direction of the bus to take me home, my quick pace breaking into a run, confusion and anger seeping through me. No. I refused to believe it could be true.

As I neared the deli, I prayed Dad wouldn't see me. I walked fast past the entrance and slipped down the side to the front door of the flat. I closed it quietly but before I could even make it up the stairs, Dad appeared in the doorway.

'*Ángelé mou,*' he said brightly before clocking my face. 'What is the matter?'

'It's fine, Dad. I'm just tired. I'm going to go upstairs and rest, but I'll be down to help you close up.'

'OK, if you're sure?'

I raced upstairs and slammed the door shut, rushing to my room before collapsing in a heap on the floor. Pulling out my phone, I thought of calling Greer. But she was at a conference this weekend. Who else could I turn to? My brother? After so many years of silence, could I really call him and say, 'Hey, did you know Mum was having an affair with Mr Markos?'

The thought of them together made me feel nauseous. How could she have cheated on Dad? My poor, sweet dad. He hadn't deserved that. I replayed the conversation with Nik and Mr Markos over and over again in my head but struggled to make sense of it all.

A while later, a knock on my door startled me. Dad must have been unconvinced by my 'I'm OK' declaration. I swung my legs over my bed, smoothing out my dress, ready to tell him I was fine. As I opened the door, I was shocked to see Nik, standing there with a rucksack slung on one shoulder.

'What are you doing here?' I asked.

'Your dad let me in. Wasn't sure if he would.' He shuffled his feet from side to side.

'You think I would run home and tell my father that the woman he was married to for seventeen years, who he then mourned for another fifteen, was in fact sleeping with someone else, and that they were in love?' I shook my head and began pacing the room. 'Wait, forget that last part. She's not here any more to defend her actions. I don't believe she was in love with him. She couldn't have been. She was happily married. I don't believe your dad, he's lying.'

'Lina, please, can you sit down? You're burning a hole in the carpet.' He chuckled.

My anger gauge began to rise. 'How is this funny to you?'

'It's not, but they were grown-ups when it happened – not two lovesick teens.'

He tugged my hand and forced me to sit down. I removed my fingers out of his grasp and grabbed a cushion and held it to my chest.

'Why aren't you madder?' I said, looking at his relaxed demeanour.

'I feel free. For the first time in my life, I can be who I am. I'm sorry.' He reached to clasp one of my hands. 'I didn't want for you to find out this way.'

'You thought it was a secret that could be buried along with my mother?'

He stood up, raking his hands through his hair.

'I wish I had known, Nik. Why didn't you ever tell me?'

'Because ... well, you know the relationship with my dad is rocky at the best of times. It's something that I found out when we were only thirteen, and when I threatened to tell Mum what I had seen, he begged me not to say anything. I had the upper hand.' He stopped pacing and gave his head a shake. 'For once. But then on the night of my eighteenth everything shifted again. He was disgusted with me and threatened to tell Mum about me and Mateo.' He dipped his head. 'And for some reason I was too ashamed for her to find out. If only I had known how she would have really reacted. Unconditional love.' He smiled to himself before letting his face fall again. 'A part of me wished I had told Mum about your mum and my dad. Maybe she could've found a way to leave Dad, move away from his domineering presence in our lives. But I was only thirteen and wanted to protect her instead.'

I absorbed Nik's words, trying to piece together what had happened. 'You say you caught your dad and my ... mum when we were thirteen. That's the year Mum died. How long had you known before?'

He scratched at a stain on his black trousers. 'Do you remember when I had to drop out of the dancing competition?'

I could feel the wave of the memory crashing to the forefront of my mind. 'Yeah.'

'I had caught them the day before. It was when your mum was dropping off the *dolmádes* order. No one else was in the office and I had gone there because I'd left some football kit. Agh.'

'What?'

'It's all coming back to me. I had only joined that stupid team to please Dad. I hated playing.'

'But you were really good.'

'I preferred dancing, but I was being teased horribly for doing it back then. I felt like I was torn in two. When Toby the Tank tackled me during that practice game, it was completely my fault. I wasn't thinking straight, and a part of me wanted to get hurt so I would have a reason to pull out of *Strictly*. But then I couldn't play football either. So, it was a lose–lose situation.'

'That must've been hard. I'm sorry I didn't know about the teasing. I wouldn't have forced you to be my partner if I had known.'

We sat in silence for a while as I tried to absorb everything. Could I really be mad at Nik for not telling me? I was mad at Mum, no question. She felt even more of a stranger to me now. She wasn't the woman I thought she was at all. Certainly not a devoted wife. It made me want to protect Dad even more. It was simple. I would never tell him any of this. Mum was nothing but a cheat. Maybe she had even lied about making the discovery of the jewels. Maybe it had been her plan to sell the other two.

'Umm.' Nik shifted awkwardly on the spot. 'Seeing as this is confession time, there's something else I need to tell you.' He reached into his pocket and pulled out the bracelet that had snapped off my wrist. 'You need this.'

'Thanks,' I whispered, holding it in my palm and stroking the jewel with my thumb. The fall onto the pavement had thankfully not dented it.

'I didn't buy that for you,' he said, before biting his bottom lip.

'Huh?' I looked at him, confused.

'Well, I did get it made into a bracelet, but I didn't buy the gemstone. I stole it, from you.'

My heart began to thunder in my chest, the realisation dawning on me that what Ash had suspected might be true. I tried to focus on Nik's mouth, his lips, praying that he wouldn't utter any more words to confirm my suspicions.

But there were no more words. He reached into his rucksack and pulled out a metal box with a lock. *The* box: containing the time capsule.

'It was me,' he continued. 'I took it. I . . . I know what you're going to say. My stupid jealousy again. Heck, I was eight. I only meant to scare you and Ash with all that apocalypse stuff and the-world-ending-in-twenty-years nonsense. I just did it to be an ass, I know that, but when I found out what you two were going to do together, I followed you. Dug it up straight away. Picked the lock. Saw everything that was in there, including those jewels. Ever since you told me about your mum's discovery, I have been trying to figure out how to tell you about it.'

My weight sank further into my mattress. All this time I had been wearing one of the jewels and the third wasn't far away.

'Here.' He handed it over. 'This belongs to you.'

My fingers trembled as I took it in my grasp. This box also contained the hopes and dreams of me and Ash and how we thought our lives would be right now.

'I want you to go.' I swallowed back my emotion. 'I want you to go,' I repeated. 'Now!'

'I want to stay,' Nik said. 'I want to be there for you, for when you open it. Cos now you have a way to clear your mum's name. That's good, right? I'm sorry it took me so long to tell you. Really, I am. I hadn't meant to do it. But I told you I was only eight.'

I held onto the box tighter, a steely determination washing over me. '*Go*,' I barked. 'I don't want to hear any more of your excuses or your apologies.'

Nik got up, mumbled sorry again and left.

I stared at the bracelet in my hand and the tin container. I now had the two missing jewels from the find. But there was only one person I wanted to open the box with. And he never wanted to talk to me again.

Chapter 36

I flipped the sign to Closed and picked up the broom to sweep the floor. It had been a busy day. Lots of families had stopped by to pick up salads and wraps for picnics in the park. A humid June Saturday had driven people in for a brief respite from the stifling heat. It was rare we had the air con on because it pushed up our electricity bills, but today I was glad for it.

Once I had cleaned up and restocked the fridge, I was planning on crashing upstairs with my books. Exams were in two weeks and then I would be free. Free to do *what* was another matter. I hadn't yet spoken to the museum about any possible openings, but Greer had heard on the grapevine that my German replacement would be moving on.

'*Ángelé mou*,' Dad sang out as he came through from the back. 'My wonder. You work so hard. I hope tonight you will rest.'

'Just have to finish up first, Baba.'

'Is Nikolas wining and dining you tonight?'

I shook my head. 'No, not tonight.' Or any night. Nik had tried many times over the last two weeks to say sorry again. Texts, missed calls, voicemails littered my phone.

'Is something the matter between you two?' Dad asked, concerned.

'No,' I said a little too sharply. 'I just need to do a lot of studying. There's no time for a social life at the moment.'

I turned my back to him, conscious of the fact that he would know instantly that I was hiding my true feelings because he knew all too well about my blotchy affliction.

'Angelina,' Dad said softly. 'Can you turn and look at me?'

Busted. Instead of putting my hands over my neck, I was suddenly overwhelmed with the need to be honest. He stepped in front of me and stroked my arms.

'You can tell me anything – you know that, my sweet girl?'

I wrapped my fingers around the handle of the broom. 'Not this time, Dad.'

'Come and sit down,' he said, ushering me to the nearest table. 'You must be exhausted. You get up at four every day and I see your light still on when I go to bed.'

For the last two weeks, I had deliberately made the Markos order earlier than usual and dropped it off an hour before I needed to be at university – only so I didn't have to bump into Nik or Mr Markos. The night porter was always there so it had become an easy thing to stick to, but the early starts and late finishes had begun to take their toll. I had already fallen asleep in two lectures.

'I'll be fine once my exams are over.'

'You need a break after them. I know we have never discussed this before but perhaps you should go away somewhere.'

'I can't leave you, Baba. I will never leave you.'

Dad tapped his chin, lost in thought. 'You are so young, my sweet girl. I worry that I have held you back.'

'You haven't at all. I love my life here with you.' He gazed out of the window. 'Don't you?'

'Recently, I have been feeling so tired.' He shuffled back to the counter to grab a cloth and brought it over to the nearest table.

'Is it your heart?'

He shook his head, wiping the surface down. 'I'm just getting older. That's all.'

'Maybe you should cut back on your hours. I'll be finished with my course in a couple of weeks and then I can take over more.'

'You should be figuring out your future, Angelina.'

A knot of tension formed in my shoulder, and I tried to rub it away. 'I've been looking at the job ads, but nothing has come up.'

'Where have you been looking?'

'Around here. I was going to contact the museum and see if there was any volunteer work I could do. I'm sure the pub could use an extra pair of hands, too, once it's reopened – they're adding a whole new restaurant at the back. That could fit in with the deli hours.'

'And what does Nik think?'

I swept with long, measured movements. 'Nik doesn't control what I do with my life.'

'But his father seems to think otherwise.'

I pinched my lips tight at the idea of Mr Markos's financial hold over me.

'Why are you so sensitive when I mention the name of Nikolas or his father? He is our best customer; he has done so—'

'Much for the family,' I finished for him. 'I know,' I said, propping the broom back in the corner of the deli and brushing the debris into a dustpan. 'They have always done so much.'

'But I would never force you to be with someone you didn't want to be with.' He shook his head. 'The youth of today. I don't understand your relationship with Nikolas. You used to be happy with him – you stay over at his place, which I have always accepted even though you know how old-fashioned I am when it comes to romance. Something happened between you, didn't it?'

'There's so much to tell you but I don't know where to start.'

He went to the coffee pot and poured out two cups before bringing them over to the table. 'How about at the beginning?'

Awash with the need for honesty, I sat down with Dad and accepted the mug he pushed towards me.

Dad didn't say a word as I told him about finding the hidden jewels – one that had been on my wrist for years, the other in the box Nik had stolen; Nik's 'coming out' lunch with his parents and the pact we had made to marry by thirty. I told him about the endometriosis, how Dr Lamos had diagnosed me and performed the operation. A pause punctuated every revelation. Dad didn't once touch his coffee. I sipped mine until a few marks remained around the edges. I remembered Mum used to love looking into her cup to see if there was a hidden symbol left on the rim. A form of tea-leaf reading – popular in Greece and Cyprus – she had told me. One of the few memories I had of her.

My fingers twisted in my lap as I braced myself to tell him the rest.

'After Nik came out to his parents, his dad got angry and stormed off. I followed them outside and heard them talking about something – something I wasn't ever supposed to find out, I think. Mr Markos claims that he and Mum ...' My heart pounded in my chest and a cool chill spread across my face.

'That they were having an affair,' Dad finished for me.

I drew my head back. 'Yes,' I whispered. 'You ... knew?'

He lifted his cup and drained it in one long sip. 'Yes, I knew. I found out a week before she died. It was my fault.'

'It was not your fault, Dad. She slept with someone else. What an evil thing to do.'

'Silence,' Dad said in a tone I had not heard him use before. I could tell he immediately regretted it. He squeezed his eyes shut, as if he was trying to block out the pain. 'Your mother was not evil. She was loving, passionate, kind. And I failed to give her the life I had promised when we first came to these shores. We were meant to come to Britain for a bright future. Instead, we got this.' He swept his hand around the deli.

Suddenly all its faults stared back at me – the chipped floor, the rusty cooker that kept needing new parts, the refrigerator that was no doubt pumping out noxious gases into the air.

'We ended up failing each other. We never took a break just the two of us. We stopped caring for one another. Nik's dad was everything I could not offer her.'

'But she still cheated on you.'

Dad held up his hand wearily. 'Your mother is not here to defend herself. She simply fell in love with someone else – someone who appeared to give her more than I could.'

'You mean money.' I grabbed the holder of sugar sachets and began to rearrange them.

He gave a half smile. 'You are cynical, Angelina.'

'But it's true, isn't it?'

'He is very charming, I know that. He wanted to take her back to Cyprus, so she could clear her name. He wouldn't have let her run in the first place, she told me once. But I was only trying to protect her – I told her that. I told her that things would change. I wasn't angry at their affair. It was a wake-up call to how we had let the rot set into our marriage.'

'Because of us. Because of me and Alex.'

He reached out and grabbed both my hands to stop me from fidgeting.

'We never regretted having you or your brother.'

'But we trapped Mum. She wanted to be someone, I read it in her diary. Her passion for archaeology was evident in every single word, every sentence she wrote.'

'Yes, she was indeed very passionate. Life was passing her by, and her dream was drifting further away. The day she died ... she had promised we would sort through our problems – she wasn't going to leave me for him. For the sake of the family, she wanted to try again. She had given me one more chance, but I never got to show her how much I cared for her. I had told her I needed time, that I knew I would forgive her eventually for her affair but that we needed to talk. We were going to talk that night – the night of the accident.'

My eyes misted over. 'It was my fault,' I said, pulling my hands away from his hold.

'What was your fault?'

'The accident. She was speeding, trying to get to Alex's play. I was a burden, the cause of her death. She wouldn't have been speeding if I hadn't waited to pick up my trophy. She would've known the roads were icy, would've taken more care. It was my fault ... it was ...' I couldn't speak any longer, the sobs choking my breath, my arms shaking.

Dad's chair scraped as he pulled it close to me before encircling me in his arms. I buried my head into him, almost sixteen years of guilt flooding out from every pore. Dad stroked my back, up and down. It was rhythmic and he didn't stop until I caught my breath and the last of the tears fell.

Minutes passed. Shadows from the trees outside moved across the room.

I grabbed a handful of serviettes from the small dispenser on the table and wiped my eyes and nose.

'Angelina, I wish we had spoken about this before. The accident was not your fault. We can't ever know what your mother was thinking or why she was speeding. I blamed myself too. I should never have let her take you to the dance competition with the car. *I* should have taken you or I should have told her that it wasn't necessary for us all to be at your brother's play.'

'Is that why you called her that night? You were wondering where she was?'

'I didn't call her that night. There was no reception in the theatre. It wasn't until the play was over and I was in the lobby that my phone came to life with the call from the hospital.'

Who called her, then? Was it Nik's dad? She had been so irritated – that much I remembered. But I had always assumed it was me she was irritated with.

'All these years, you have blamed yourself?'

I nodded.

'And all these years, you have lived with so much pain with your condition, and you felt you could never turn to me. That fills my heart with so much sadness.'

'Women's problems aren't really what you want to talk about with your dad.'

He nodded in agreement. 'I understand. It is something to share with a mother or even a best friend. Someone like Emily. And since she was taken out of your life, you have only had Nik. And now he is no longer in your life either.'

'It's OK now. The pain is less. Dr Lamos is a wonderful person. If it wasn't for her, I don't know where I would be now. The aching had begun to affect my day-to-day life. I knew it wasn't normal, but I had seen several GPs and the last one told me it was IBS. Reduce your stress, he said, keep a diary of what you eat. I never told Nik how bad it really was. But yes, he was always there for me, hot-water bottle at the ready.'

'My brave daughter. My warrior. I am pleased you got the treatment you needed. And Ash. You love him.'

I shredded a serviette in my fingers. 'What makes you say that?'

'I see it in your eyes. When you described what happened in Cyprus. Your face lit up when you talked about him; a different way to how I hear you talk about Nik. I was sad Ash moved to India. When he returned last summer I hoped maybe something might happen between the two of you. And then when you told me you had gone to Cyprus with him, I wondered if it meant something more. But you didn't speak of him after that.'

'We got close in Cyprus. But his life is in Mumbai. He would never consider coming back to England. And we got into a fight because his jealousy over my relationship with Nik is insufferable.'

'Does he know that Nik is gay?'

'No, he doesn't. It was always a secret I kept between Nik and myself.'

'What a wonderful friend you have been to him.'

'Shame the same thing couldn't be said of him.'

Dad tutted. 'That's not true. You told me yourself, he has always stood by you, looked out for you when you were in pain. He obviously cares deeply for you.'

'So why hide the box from me?'

'Maybe he was merely trying to protect you.'

'From what?'

He shrugged. 'Maybe you should ask him that. My opinion is you have two young men who care deeply for you, one to keep you safe and happy here in Birmingham because that is what you always said you wanted, and one who wants you to fly – to be the kind of person perhaps you could have been if you hadn't lost your mother so young. You took on her duties. You took care of me and your brother for so many years before Alex betrayed you and took the only other special female you had in your life, and then you continued to care for me, always sacrificing yourself. Perhaps that box represents the life you had hoped to lead, and Nik was scared he would lose you if you opened it. I have no idea what you wrote, but we shouldn't ignore the dreams, the hopes of a child. That child was not burdened with death, grief, pain. That child was free. I know I would love to find out what you wrote.'

He rubbed his thumb over my knuckles. I stared at the wrinkles in his hand, the moles punctured with dark hairs.

'Like Ash, I want you to fly. Be free. I don't need you to look after me any more.'

I pulled my hands away and tucked my hair behind my ears. 'I've told you, Baba; I'm not leaving you. I'm happy here in Birmingham. Ash and I are two very different people. We might have had a chance together years ago, but life changes. And besides, why should I leave Birmingham and follow whatever my dream was if he isn't willing to do the one thing he really is passionate about?'

'I'm not sure. He has responsibilities and—'

'So do I.'

'But if you didn't have to care for me, how would you feel then? What would you do?'

I'd get on the first flight out to Mumbai to tell Ash how much I love him.

I remained tight-lipped and shoved those thoughts to the back of my mind.

'Open the box. Read where your heart was when you were a little girl.'

'I can't. I don't remember where I put the key. And Ash has the only other one. And before you even suggest it, jumping on a plane is not an option. I don't have that kind of money.'

'You will. Maybe.'

'How?'

'I am transferring ownership of the deli to you and then you can sell it if you want. I want to move to the US to be close to my first grandchild.'

'What?' My fingers clutched the edge of the table.

Dad nodded. 'When I went to see your brother, we had so many bridges to build. I know you think he was being selfish in not helping us out with the taxes, but the truth was he couldn't. He hasn't had the success as an actor that he hoped. He does the odd commercial here and there, but they have been trying for a baby for a while and were told IVF was the only option. It is expensive in America. They used all their savings for three rounds. When I visited, they had lost hope, but Alex seemed so happy when I was there and Emily was thrilled that we had become father and son again. They were planning on trying one more time. Today I got the news that it was successful.' Tears welled in his eyes.

'Why didn't you tell me?'

'I didn't think you wanted to know. You haven't yet forgiven your brother or Emily for what happened.'

'Marika Lamos said Mum would've been sad to know Alex and I weren't speaking.'

He laughed. 'God, that woman was strong-willed. She was in love with your mother, you know?'

I leaned back in my chair. 'She was?'

'Not that she would ever admit to it. But she guarded her like a hawk. She once took me to one side and said she would break my neck if I ever hurt your mother. But now it seems I owe her my life for helping my little girl. And yes, she is right, your mother would be sad. But you have your reasons. I can't tell you what to do or whether you should go and make up. That has to be your decision like it was mine. But I feel so good about it now.'

'But if you have thought about going back to the US, why haven't you told me this before?'

'When I returned, you were so pleased about the deli reopening.'

'I was trying to be happy for *you*.'

'Oh.' He smiled. 'Perhaps we should have told each other the truth before now. The deli has been a hard slog for so many years. When I was in LA, the mother of a friend of Emily's introduced me to the cooking scene out there. It was exciting. I might even think about starting my own restaurant.'

'Then you will need the money. I don't want you to sign the deli over to me. Sell it. Take the proceeds and set up the place you have always dreamed of.'

He shuffled his feet under the table. 'The mother ... the one belonging to Emily's friend, she wants to invest in a business. She is a widow too and came into some money and has a real passion for Greek food. The truth is, Angelina ... This mother … Clara is her name. We became friends while I was there, close friends …' Dad's cheeks pinkened and it was the most adorable thing.

'You're in love.'

'I am too old for such things.'

'No, you're not. Why didn't you tell me, Dad?'

'Again, I didn't know how.'

'I never expected you to remain a widower forever. But you seemed so devoted to the business here and you only ever spent your day off with your bridge friends.'

'I think I was too afraid of how you would react. I figured if I remained single then you would still have me. You had lost a mother and a brother; I didn't want you to feel abandoned by me too.'

I smiled and laughed a little. 'That's exactly how I felt.'

'I know I haven't been a good father to you—'

'That's not true,' I protested.

'Please.' He held his palm up. 'Hear me out. You were thirteen, only just a teenager. I was grieving and didn't know how to look after two young children, but I didn't have to because you sacrificed the rest of your childhood to care for the men in your family. You never truly lived.'

My phone buzzed on the table, and I gasped. An incoming call. From Mumbai.

Dad noticed Ash's name on the screen. 'I think you need to take this. Tell him how you feel.'

I tapped my fingers on the table, Dad's words swimming around my brain.

Tell him how you feel.

In time to the rhythm of my heart, I picked the phone up, hit Accept and placed it to my ear.

'I miss you.' The words tumbled out before I even said hello. 'I mean, hi.' I swallowed a laugh. 'What a lovely surprise.'

'I know it's been a while,' he said, with no response to my declaration.

'Too long,' I murmured.

'Listen, this is just a quick call.'

'Oh.' It was hard to mask my disappointment and my boldness was slowly evaporating. His tone was crisp, to the point, as if this was a business meeting.

'Something rather interesting has happened and I had to speak to you straight away.'

'What is it?' I asked, pushing away all thoughts of telling him that I wanted to be with him wherever he wanted to be.

'You know you gave me those two films and I developed them and sent them to you?'

'Yes,' I said, my interest piqued.

'Well, I had a call this morning from the photo shop. They were horribly apologetic; said what they had given me were only the photos from one of the reels. They discovered they hadn't given me the other pack. By way of an apology, they sent me them digitally. Lina, these ones have your mum in them, showing exactly how she made the discovery, with date stamps, proof that it was her that found the jewels.'

I couldn't speak.

'It's a shame we didn't find that box,' he said.

'I did. I mean, it's been found.'

'Really? How? Where?'

'It's a long story.' And not one I wanted to get into now. I would tell Ash one day that he had been right all along, but not today.

Now I had everything. The missing piece of the puzzle. I could now clear Mum's name.

'Trouble is you're the only one with the key,' I said.

'You've got one too.'

'But I can't remember for the life of me where I hid it. I've turned the flat upside down looking for it, but I can't find it.'

'I remember where it is.'

'You do?'

Dad raised his eyebrows, palms facing up. He was probably struggling to follow the conversation with only one side to hear.

'You told me that when you were scared there was only one place you would go ... your parents' wardrobe. You stuck it at the back. I wrote it in that diary of mine.'

My chest was expanding, filled with relief that I could now open the box, but a pang of sadness was swirling around inside me – now I didn't have a reason to get on that plane to Mumbai.

The truth? Fussing about the lock had merely been a pretence. I could have broken it or picked it like Nik had done if I had really wanted to.

Now nothing bound me to Ash any more. Nothing.

Chapter 37

Now we are twenty-nine

The sun beat down on my head and arms, having left the air-conditioned comfort of the airport. My eyes were heavy, the three a.m. alarm, to make my flight at six, catching up with me. Fourteen hours later, here I was. California.

A squeal floated along the sizzling tarmac. I turned to see Greer waving frantically in the distance before giving me a crushing hug and lifting me in the air.

'It's good to see you too,' I laughed.

'You made it!'

I grinned broadly. 'Here I am.'

Yes, here I was. It had been a crazy few weeks. While studying for my finals, I had managed to help Dad pack up the deli and the flat. It had been a lot more straightforward than we thought. One of Dad's oldest friends had decided to buy the business and our home as a gift for his son who had been directionless for a while but was a great cook. We had paid Mr Markos back the tax money and the new owner had funds set aside to renovate and said I could stay on in the flat when I returned for as long as I needed until I had figured out what I was planning to do.

'Where do you want to go first?' Greer asked.

'I barely slept on the plane. My nerves are frazzled.'

'You worried about seeing your family?'

'Not Dad, obviously. But yes, I am about seeing my brother and ... Emily.' It felt good to say her name out loud.

Dad had been desperate to pick me up with Alex, but I had said no. I didn't want our first meet in over ten years to be like this with me having rolled off the plane: in desperate need of a shower and some sleep.

'I told Dad I would go round for dinner tonight. I'm meeting his fiancée.'

'He didn't waste any time.'

'He said he doesn't feel he has any time to waste. They've been Skyping daily for hours every evening since he told me about her. I'm so happy for him.'

'Does that mean you'll come back for the wedding?' She linked arms and leaned into me.

'Hope so.'

The proceeds of the deli and the flat after expenses were definitely enough for a flight back to LA but I was conscious that I needed to be careful with the money that was now sitting in my account. I still had to find a job and somewhere to live. But there was one thing I was desperate to do and that was travel. I'd unearthed the itinerary I had created when I was eighteen – it was buried in a box in my wardrobe. India, Cyprus and California were on it – I couldn't believe I was clocking up another country from the list.

'So ... this is LA?' I said, looking around at the four-lane highway in front of me and the five-storey concrete parking lot.

'No.' She elbowed me in the ribs. 'This is an airport, duh. I'm going to show you the real LA. But first, let's go to mine and get you showered. Mum's cooked up a storm and then we can go explore.'

'When's the meeting at the museum?'

'Tomorrow. Got the goods?'

I patted my waist where a discreet bum bag was sitting between my jeans and knickers. It contained the two jewels – the ones the museum said they were very interested in seeing. The digital photographs had already been sent. The box was tucked safely in my suitcase. I hadn't wanted to leave it back home.

We drove away from the airport in Greer's jeep and once we turned onto Palisades Avenue, it was possible to see glimmers of palm-lined promenades and the sea at every junction. Greer lowered our windows and let out a yelp as the breeze lifted her frizzy hair and mine battered my cheeks. Her smile was infectious. As she turned up her stereo to a hip-sounding beat, I laughed and shut my eyes, letting the music soothe me.

The apartment block we turned into was a stone's throw from Santa Monica Beach. A cool marble foyer greeted us, and the concierge nodded as we sauntered in. Greer's parents went overboard in the reception they gave me. I had a room to myself with a hint of the ocean from the balcony and in full view of the communal pool. A feast was laid out for lunch, and we chatted about our time together at the Birmingham Museum and whether Greer had been difficult to supervise. I told her parents nothing but exemplary tales of how she was a hard-worker and Greer gave me a cheeky wink and mouthed 'thank you' when they weren't looking.

After I had a mid-afternoon nap, we rented bikes and Greer gave me a whistle-stop tour of the surrounding area. We sipped iced coffees once we had cycled one long stretch of the beach and later had shaved ice as we watched skaters cruise down the cycle lane. She had plans to show me her university tomorrow and take me to the Natural History Museum of Los Angeles County where her love for archaeology had begun.

The day slipped by in a haze of heat, laughter and exploration. Greer pulled into a flower shop in downtown LA early evening, and I selected a stunning bouquet of orange wildflowers. She then drove me to a place I had searched for online. It was a dilapidated building with graffiti scrawled everywhere. We pulled up behind a car with its tyres blown and Greer turned to me once she put the gear stick into park.

'Are you sure this is the place?'

I nodded. 'I'm sure.'

Greer peered over her shoulder and gripped the steering wheel. 'I'm giving you five minutes and I'm keeping the engine running.'

'It's not that bad round here, is it?'

'Oh, you sweet naive tourist.' She leaned across to open my door. 'Hurry up.'

I slammed it shut and walked over to the entrance of the nightclub. A poster showcasing the next few gigs was slashed across the wall. It was peeling at the corners and beneath the edges I could see glimpses of previous show announcements.

I wondered if she would've had her name here. Divya. *A rising star on the club circuit,* the article I had unearthed from the web had said. *A tragedy. A life lost too soon.* The coroner's report had cited misadventure. Alcohol and drugs had been found in her system. Her boyfriend had said it was impossible, that she had been clean for months. Ash had said his parents hadn't believed this man who they could never imagine their daughter would have been in a relationship with because he wasn't Indian. Divya was many things, but she was not someone who would have so blatantly defied her parents, they thought. They wanted to remember their daughter as the sweet, kind girl who left them when she was only twenty.

I laid the flowers down and closed my eyes. Her warm smile came to my mind; the way she treated me like a little sister, how she taught me and Ash to dance. A sob caught at the back of my throat, and I swallowed it away.

Ash. I would do anything for him to be here. What would have happened if he and I had travelled that summer? Would she still be alive? Had she been battling demons for too long? Would the thought of her brother coming to see her have changed the course of her life?

A car horn hooted. Greer was ushering me back with a flick of her head to indicate we were no longer alone. A group of youths were approaching in the distance.

'Goodbye, Divya,' I said. 'I'll never forget you.' I blew a kiss into the hot air and left.

As we sped off, I fished out a tissue from my bag and blotted my eyes.

'You OK?' Greer said, fixing her gaze on the freeway ahead.

'Yeah, I am. I only wish I could've shared that moment with someone else.'

'Ash?'

I nodded. 'Yes.'

'What's the deal with you two, anyway?'

'There is no deal. I'm not sure if we're even friends any more.'

'Have you forgiven Nik?'

'I'm still avoiding him.'

Greer didn't respond. I think she could sense the tension radiating off my shoulders and my inflamed neck would be visible too. Dealing with Ash and Nik would have to wait until I returned home. For now, it was the prospect of dinner with my whole family that had me fidgeting in my seat.

As we pulled up outside a single-storey house in the Hollywood Hills, Greer switched off the engine. 'Call me anytime. I can come and get you if it all becomes overwhelming.'

I leaned in and hugged her. 'You're the best. But I am going to have to be grown up about this and face up to everything that's happened.'

Greer peered out of the window at the whitewashed building and its hanging baskets bursting with colourful flowers. A manicured garden sat either side of the path leading to the front door. Ground sprinklers were spraying the lawns – a rainbow forming in the mist as the dipping sun caught the droplets.

'Your dad's fiancée is a retired actress, huh?'

'Apparently. She had a few roles on daytime soaps in the mid-nineties.' I stared at the building, imagining Dad living here permanently. It was a world away from the deli's flat.

I kissed Greer goodbye, smoothed down my floaty blue skirt and tugged the hem of my white T-shirt. A grand ring sounded from the doorbell as I pressed it, and I took a hesitant step backwards.

The door swung open and there was Dad, his arms outstretched.

'*Ángelé mou*,' he bellowed as he pulled me into his arms. 'My lovely girl, you made it. Come, come, Clara is excited to see you.'

He held my shoulder as he directed me into the living room – framed movie posters lining the pastel walls – and out through the glass doors at the back. The view took my breath away. We were so high that you could see all of Los Angeles sprawling down below like a still from the movie *La La Land*. The pool was no more than ten feet long – a lap pool, I guess you would call it.

'Lina, my dear,' a voice said from behind and I turned.

Clara was attractive, with bobbed white hair framing a sun-kissed face with deep crow's feet lining the corners of her eyes. She grinned broadly. A lilac floral dress floated around her as she moved towards me. A kiss on both cheeks before she held my arms and gave me a once-over.

'Wow,' she drawled. 'You're even more stunning than the photo your dad has in his wallet. His eyes definitely, but your mother's beauty.' She winked with a nod towards Dad. He laughed at this. It was a laugh like one I had never heard him utter before. And in that moment, I was grateful for this woman I had only just been introduced to, for bringing that happiness to his life.

She linked arms with me and pulled me towards the outdoor table which had every drink imaginable laid out. 'I want to hear everything about you, my dear. I hear you're some incredible Lara Croft, solving a long-buried mystery.'

'Hardly,' I said.

Her shoulders danced. 'Such modesty. You're *so* British. Tell me, what can I fix you?' She swept her free arm over the table. Not only were there drinks but there was an amazing spread of canapés.

'A glass of rosé would be lovely.'

'Your gorgeous father has been busy in the kitchen too.' She patted her stomach. 'I'm going to have to buy some more spandex.' She laughed theatrically as if she was on the stage. She took a pair of silver tongs and fished out several cubes from an ice bucket and placed them in a glass before pouring the pink wine and handing it to me.

'You must come and see how the restaurant is shaping up. I've been taste-testing all the main-course dishes and know it's going to be a huge success. But don't you worry, I'm gonna be taking good care of your father – no spending hours on end slaving away in the kitchen. We're supporting a local outreach programme to find some undiscovered talent – kids who couldn't afford culinary school but want to train with the best. And your dad is certainly the best.' She noticed him waving through the window from the kitchen and simpered. She really seemed smitten with him.

'Today, however, I haven't been able to drag him away from the stove – think he's quite nervous and wants tonight to be perfect. It's the first time you've all been together in some time, right?'

I nodded and pulled my glass close to my chest.

She took her own cocktail glass, which had a stick spearing an olive floating in it, and raised it to make a toast. 'Here's to family – new and old.'

The sound of the doorbell made me spill a bit of my drink but thankfully it didn't splash on my T-shirt. A tightness gripped my insides – a dizzy feeling engulfing me. I reached out to grab the edge of the table, which was a long distance down, but thankfully I was met with a reassuring hold.

'It's OK, sweetie, I got you,' Clara said. 'Breathe.' She elongated the word as if she was getting me ready to go on stage. 'They're as nervous about seeing you as you are about meeting them. It's going to be fine.'

My eyeline moved from the flowers on her dress up to her eyes – sympathy etched into their coral-blue colour.

'Angelina,' I heard my dad sing out from behind. 'Look who's here.'

I turned around and there they were.

Chapter 38

My brother seemed taller than I remembered, his hair longer on top, more styled. His hand was firmly clasping Emily's shoulder. A tentative smile was playing on her lips.

Clara linked arms with me and pulled me forward, my legs taking a moment to stop feeling wobbly.

'Hey,' I managed.

'Hey,' they said in unison, before letting a laugh puncture the awkwardness as they turned and looked at each other.

Where should we even begin? It had been almost eleven years.

Then a breeze caused Emily's floaty pink dress to lift. She held onto it to stop it rising any further and that's when I noticed the bump.

'Wow,' I gasped.

She stroked her stomach. 'Yeah, it's getting bigger by the day.' Her voice was as sweet and as soft as I remembered but with a thick Californian twang. 'Five months now.'

Alex patted the bump affectionately. 'It's a miracle.'

She caught his smile and beamed back at him.

Those looks. The one he gave her and the one she returned. They were frameable. There was so much love in their expressions. And suddenly eleven years of hurt dissolved.

'You look amazing, Emily. Really good. It's ... umm ...' I swallowed, gripping my glass of wine tighter, conscious of Clara's arm still entwined with mine, giving me extended comfort. 'It's lovely to see you ... both,' I added with a little nod towards Alex.

A collective exhaling of breath filtered around me and any earlier tension from Dad seemed to evaporate as he stepped forward and patted me and Alex on the back, bringing us close together.

There were tears rimming Dad's lower lids. 'My children,' he whispered with a sniff.

'Oh Filip,' Clara chided. 'Tears in the first five minutes. Pace yourself, pace yourself.'

Everyone laughed and the atmosphere lightened even more.

'Drinks!' Clara announced. 'And please come and eat some of this gorgeous food before I hoover the lot.'

She rubbed my arm affectionately before letting go and heading to the drinks table.

Clara fixed a couple of cocktails – handing over the virgin one to Emily and the whisky-based one to my brother. She held forth, telling us all about the plans for the new restaurant, joking about the inept builders she'd had to scold this morning for putting the bar area in the wrong place.

Dad announced dinner with a flourish, and as we settled down for one of his signature dishes, which he had given an LA twist to, focus turned to my discovery.

'Mum would've been dead proud of you, Lina,' Alex said as he sliced into his baked aubergine.

'Thanks,' I said.

'More than proud,' Dad beamed.

'Stop, you two, it was no big deal,' I said, reaching for my tumbler of sparkling water.

'I heard it was a risky move, though,' Emily said. 'You were almost killed.'

'Dad! What did you tell them?'

'More wine,' he said, dodging the question.

'I won't find out until tomorrow what's going to happen. I'm going to show the curator of the museum the other two jewels and hopefully he can follow up on everything.'

After going into more detail about my time as a volunteer in Cyprus, the conversation moved on to Alex's new TV role as a forty-something widow with two kids making his way in the world of online dating. He described the premise of the show as he touched the greyish streaks in his hair which the make-up department had put in yesterday and which would stay while he filmed the pilot.

Dinner went by in a flash and, before I could offer my assistance in clearing up, Dad and Clara had stood and told me not to move a muscle, but suggested I stroll over to the bench at the bottom of the garden as it was close to sunset and the view from there was apparently stunning. Dad said pudding would take a while to get ready.

I pushed back my chair and grabbed my glass. Alex leaned in and whispered in Emily's ear before laying a gentle kiss on her cheek. 'I'm going to help the olds. I'll join you in a bit.' He smiled at me hesitantly as if he wasn't sure whether he should leave us alone. He stroked her belly before kissing her on the lips. His adoration was endearing.

Emily and I made our way over to the terrace. The scent of honeysuckle and roses diffused the air, and the view was indeed spectacular I noted before sitting down.

Emily drew in breath sharply and held her belly.

'Is everything OK?' I said.

'Oh, I'm fine, it just catches me off guard every time I feel her move. It's like butterfly wings floating inside me.'

'Her?'

She nodded. 'We found out last week. We're going to name her Elina, after your mum. And it's part of her aunt's name too – someone I hope will be a big part of her life.' There was hesitation in her expression.

Emotion choked me at the thought of Mum's real name being passed down to her granddaughter and the second reason left a lump in my throat.

'That's a lovely sentiment,' I said finally.

'It was your brother's idea, but I love it. When your dad told us the full story, I couldn't believe what your mum went through, having to escape like that and the fact she felt the need to change her name.'

It took me a moment to digest her words. I had been so preoccupied with Mum's affair with Mr Markos that I had almost forgotten about the earlier years of her life and what drove her to the UK in the first place.

Laughter drifted over and I turned to see Clara through the window of the kitchen with her arms around Dad and Alex.

'She's a lot of fun,' I said.

Emily glanced over and saw the unfolding scene. Dad was obviously saying something funny, and it was a lovely sight. 'She's a real livewire. Her daughter is the complete opposite.'

'Your best friend?' I said, before realising my tone had probably come out a little accusatory.

'My *California* best friend.' She clasped her hands under her chin.

'Listen, Emily, I'm sorry—'

'No, no, no.' She shook her head rapidly. 'I'm the one who should be saying sorry.'

'But you tried to talk to me, and I didn't listen.'

'A letter?' She rolled her eyes. 'That was the coward's way out.'

I thought back to the day I found it in my locker all those years ago. The hurt and confusion I had felt.

Emily stared at the panorama of the LA hills with a faraway expression. 'It was all very *Romeo and Juliet*. Disapproval from both sides of the family. The overwhelming urge to run away.'

'Why didn't you tell me?'

She shrugged. 'I was scared. Scared of you telling me I was making a huge mistake.'

'Was it a mistake?'

She twisted her lips, and I knew she was chewing the inside of her mouth – a nervous habit she'd had at school. 'I think it was a mistake to leave the way we did, but Alex was going to come here regardless. And I was swept up in the romance of it all. The truth was a little less glamorous. I ended up waiting tables for a very long time until his first pay cheque came through. But Alex encouraged me to continue my studies. I signed up for a management and finance course at a local college, got some good qualifications and I work at a local accountancy firm.' She paused for breath, smoothing her dress over her legs. 'I know we hurt a lot of people with our actions: your dad, my parents, you. Especially you. You were my best friend and I hurt you a lot. Once we arrived here, we got so caught up in trying to make a life for ourselves that we began seeing it as us against the world.'

'What happened to the dancing career?'

She wrinkled her nose. 'I was a background dancer in one pop video that tanked. Nothing came of it after that. Except that's how I met Clara's daughter – she was one of the technicians at the recording studio. I soon realised it was a fantasy trying to make it in this town, so I turned to college and waitressing. But Clara said that after the baby's born, maybe I could think of helping out with the restaurant, make it into a family enterprise.'

Family. All this time, I had wanted to deny that Emily was family. All the years after Mum's death she had been my family. She was more than my best friend, but I hadn't been able to see what she'd done as anything other than a betrayal. It wasn't as if she had set out to do that from the start. She'd just fallen in love.

I let her words sink in and a pang of regret filled my heart that it had taken us so long to have this conversation. 'I've missed you.'

Emily beamed. 'I've missed you too. Are you free at all in the next couple of days? I could get some time off work, we could go out to lunch, or a drink. Anything, really.' Her smile was bright, her tone excitable, the dimples in her cheeks deepening. It transported me back to happier times.

I nodded. 'I'd like that.'

Alex appeared by her side and leaned in for a kiss on her cheek.

'Everything OK?' he asked as he laid a protective hand on her shoulder.

'Yeah, everything's great.' She stroked his hand and gave him that look again. The one that reminded me how in love they still were.

'Clara wanted to show you ... umm ... some plates she picked up at the thrift store.'

Emily looked confused until Alex rolled his eyes towards the house. 'Oh, OK,' she said as she stood up and let him sit in her spot.

It was an Oscar-worthy performance – a not-so-subtle attempt to give me and Alex some time alone.

'Hey, little sis,' he said as he leaned his arm on the back of the bench and slouched. It reminded me of how he used to sit on the sofa at home in Birmingham. That thought reminded me pointedly that I had no home to return to after this trip. It was finally time to move on with my life.

'How've you been?' he said.

'Hmm. I'm pretty much homeless, jobless and my relationship status is ... non-existent.'

'Ouch.'

I smiled. 'I'm not complaining. It's been a rollercoaster year and I'm looking forward to seeing where life will take me next.'

'Ca-li-for-ni-a per-haps?' he said tentatively.

Inside the kitchen, I noticed Dad, Clara and Emily were peering out but pretended to be busy the second they caught me staring at them.

'I'm not sure … but I'd like to come back. Specially to meet little Elina.'

'She told you, huh?'

'I think it's a lovely name.'

'Don't think we would've found out about Mum's real name unless you'd found her diary and gone on that archaeology adventure. Dad was prepared to take her secret to his grave. You really are a hero.'

'Let's see what the museum says first. The jewels might be fakes, for all we know, and I have no idea what will happen if they're not. The police seem to be doing a good job of covering things up in Cyprus and …' I stole a brief glance over my shoulder again. Dad was proudly removing something from the oven. 'Listen, Alex, before they come and call us for dessert, I just wanted to say …' I twisted my hands in my lap '… sorry.'

'You've got no reason to be sorry. I screwed up. I knew what I was getting myself into with Emily, but I couldn't stop myself. I knew you'd be upset but I let my heart rule my brain. We should've been open about things. Maybe we could've saved everyone a whole lot of pain.'

'We were both young and impetuous back then. Poor Dad. How he ever managed to raise us, I'll never know.'

'I never thanked you, though.'

'For what?'

'For effectively stepping into Mum's shoes when she died. Cooking for me and Dad every night after school, doing the laundry, housework, helping in the deli. I was selfish. All I ever thought about was my acting. And I know you've put your life on hold for Dad – all those years when you could've left Birmingham, but you didn't.'

'It wasn't a hardship, Alex. I love Dad. I wanted to be with him, to protect him.'

'Because you felt guilty about the accident?'

I squeezed my eyes shut at the mention of it.

'Dad confided in me. He's worried about you. He feels responsible for letting you take care of him when you had imagined a different life for yourself.'

'You don't understand, Alex.' I sat further forward on the bench, 'Neither of you get it. If I hadn't waited to pick up that stupid trophy, none of this would've happened.'

'That's not true, Lina.' He held onto my arm. 'It was an accident.'

Tears began to build; a tidal wave of emotion threatening to engulf me every time I thought about the night she died.

'Is this why you've never danced again? Because you blame yourself for what happened?'

I nodded. A simple nod. 'I've never opened up about what went on in the car that night.' I tried to swallow away the pain as Alex moved his hold to my shoulder where he patted me gently.

'I'm here, Lina, if you want to unburden yourself.'

I pulled away – the need to fold in on myself overwhelming me. Looking out to the hills in the distance, I could see it – that evening in sharp focus.

'I got my first period that night,' I said, my jaw tightening at the memory. 'Mum and Dad were shouting at each other; you were cross because you were worried about being late for your play and I was too embarrassed to ask Mum where she kept her sanitary products. After the show I began cramping,' I said, subconsciously clutching my stomach. 'And I needed to change the pad I had bought at school. I kept nagging Mum to take me home, though I didn't tell her why, but she got really impatient with me. And then I got angry with her, started accusing her of favouritism. My last words to her were ...' I choked on a sob, beginning to rock forwards and backwards '... so horrible. That stupid dance competition. Maybe if I hadn't been so obsessed with *Strictly Come Dancing* or so desperate to become Emily's friend, none of this would've happened. We would've gone to your play all together and Mum would still be alive.' I shook my head defiantly, unable to hold back the emotion much longer. 'I won't *ever* dance again.'

As the tears rolled down my cheeks, my eyes blurred and, in a heartbeat, I was enveloped into the warm embrace of my brother, the shaking snuffed out in his strong arms.

'You poor kid, Lina,' he said, stroking my back. 'That's so much misplaced guilt to carry around. Mum loved watching you dance.'

'How do you know that?' I sniffed, leaning back and brushing the tears away, accepting the tissue he had magically produced from his pocket.

'I distinctly remember. I was running lines in my room, and she came and asked to borrow my camcorder. She wanted to sneak up and record you and that boy ... what was his name, that Greek kid that used to hang around?'

'Nik.'

'Yeah, him. She stood in my doorway and filmed you, muttering to herself in Greek, saying what a graceful beauty you were.'

'But she said lessons were wasted on me.'

Alex's face fell. 'That was my fault. Mum and Dad ploughed so much money into my acting lessons. I know they got into huge debt doing it. They wouldn't have had a penny to spend on you. In fact, that's what drives me. Every time I get a rejection after an audition, it's knowing what they did for me that spurs me on; to never give up. I'm sorry you were never given the chance to fulfil your dream.'

'Who knows if it was my dream?' I said, scrunching up the wet tissue.

'It's not too late.' He raised his eyebrows.

I let the fragrant air seep through my nose as I pondered his words. A calm feeling began to wash over me – a feeling of relief, that the pain of what happened with the accident was finally beginning to lift.

'What are you going to do now, Lina? We'll support you, no matter what.'

'I appreciate that. For now, I want to enjoy this.' I flicked my finger back and forth between me and him. 'Reconnecting, being with my family, getting to know my future mum-in-law and hopefully finding out the truth about what happened to Mum in Cyprus.'

The rest of my life would remain on pause. For how long? Who knew?

Chapter 39

I sat on the edge of the chair as the museum's curator examined the jewels under the microscope. Greer reached over to grab my hand and grinned nervously.

'Exquisite,' he said, putting his spectacles back on. 'Absolutely breathtaking. It almost makes my heart break to say it.'

'Say what?'

'Seeing this –' he pointed to a glass display which held the jewel the museum had been holding for over thirty years '– being reunited with the other stones.' He shook his head. 'We know now we can no longer keep hold of what we have. It has to be reunited with the ones you have brought to us. They need to be displayed together but they can't be shown in this museum because the first one was sold to us illegally.'

'You know for sure?' I said, allowing a small smile to break freely on my face.

'Those pictures you sent. Very incriminating. In the back of one of them was the gentleman who sold us that jewel.' He nodded to the glass case. 'We will arrange for it to be sent back. We've called the authorities in Cyprus to tell them.

There's not a lot we can do here. We can press charges, but we don't even know where this guy is now. You say you found the receipt in the office on the site. We can tell them what we know but the rest will be up to them. I really hope it all works out. The truth needs to come out and we'll do all we can to make sure it happens.'

I floated out of the museum with Greer, both of us squealing periodically as we stood outside the entrance. She insisted my name was officially Lara Croft.

'We've got to celebrate,' Greer said, hopping on the spot.

'I feel light. Like a great big burden has been lifted.'

'I hope they track down the loser and lock him up and then blow up the whole operation. That would be justice.'

'Hmm.'

'Why so pensive?'

I puffed out my cheeks. 'I was thinking back to the trip to Cyprus: the dig, the accident, the week after that ...'

'With Ash?'

I pinched my lips together. 'I miss him. Badly. I screwed up our friendship, our chance at being together. And look at me now, I'm as free as a bird,' I said, stretching out my arms, looking up to the deep blue sky.

Greer poked me in the ribs, and I giggled, linking my arm through hers as we began to walk back to the car, down the steps to the pavement. 'The things holding me back from being with him were my obligation to Dad and the deli, my life in Birmingham. Now I have none of those things.'

Greer stopped walking. 'Then go to him,' she said, unlinking her arm and clutching mine, giving me a slight shake.

'The last time I spoke to him, I told him I missed him, and he said nothing. I'm too scared to even call again.' Greer rubbed her hand up and down my arm, the movement comforting. 'And I am so desperate to open the box with him. It feels like the right thing to do.'

'Then surprise him. What have you got to lose?'

My phone buzzed and I clocked Nik's name next to the message. I had seen the opening words of every text he had sent me every few days since our last meeting. They all went along the lines of *Sorry. Please forgive me. I never meant to hurt you* but I hadn't opened any of them.

'Who's the message from?'

'Nik.'

'Still can't believe he never told you about hiding the box.'

'I think he either figured I would forget about it or that maybe his prediction of the apocalypse would come true. Ash appearing the night of the school reunion brought it all back out into the open.'

I sucked in air through my teeth.

'What?' Greer said. 'What's on your mind?'

I sat down on the steps and Greer joined me. I held my knees close to my chest. 'I miss Nik too.'

She nudged me. 'God, your life is complicated.'

'Nik has been by my side for so long. I really considered marrying him for a while – which would have been wrong on *so* many levels, but I couldn't imagine him never being in my life again.' I held my head in my hands. 'Could I really be in love with both of them?'

'Sure you can. There are many aspects of love. I did a minor in psychology in my first year. Sternberg's Triangle of Love.' She made the shape using her fingers. 'Passion, intimacy and commitment. Love relationships vary depending on the presence of one, two or all three of these components. What you have with Nik and Ash could be aspects of all of these. But it's commitment that you've got to decide on. Who is it you want in your life forever?'

Was it selfish of me to say both? Ash and Nik had been best friends of mine for significant parts of my life but was it possible to have all three aspects of love with only one of them? That was the question. I closed my eyes and flashbacks popped in my mind. Good times, great moments, laughter, dancing. I nodded.

'Yes. I think I know now. Deep down, I think I've *always* known.'

Chapter 40

Another day, another airport. Having spent the first twenty-nine years of my life not travelling anywhere, I had clocked up over twenty thousand air miles in the last eleven months. My destination now?

Mumbai.

It had been relatively straightforward changing my return flight and adding another itinerary. Clara and Emily had thought it wonderfully romantic; I was less sure. I couldn't shake the feeling that our last call had left me with – the businesslike efficiency of the exchange – but then I had been so caught up in the discovery of the missing photographs that I hadn't thought to check in with Ash about what was going on in his life. Maybe his dad had taken a turn for the worse. It had been almost a year since our eventful trip to Cyprus. Surely he had moved on.

Touching down in Heathrow only to board another flight six hours later had seemed bizarre but the time was made bearable as I was on the phone to Nik for most of it. When I landed, I called him, and we talked through everything that had happened. He reckoned my plan was fabulous. I feigned shock at the thought that he approved of me declaring my undying love to Ash, but he had merely said, 'I want you to be happy, Lina. And if Ash makes you happy, then go get him.' When I asked him where that left us, he said he would always be there for me in whatever way I wanted him to be.

Nik's life had changed for the better too. He had quit his job, sold his flat and paid back the deposit money to his dad. His mum had bravely turfed Mr Markos out of the house and was filing for a divorce – the loveless marriage she had been trapped in for years was coming to an end, and her mental health had improved as a result of the separation. Nik was crashing in his childhood home until his sale went through before beginning his own travelling – first stop Spain where a certain hot Spanish guy was waiting for him, so he said. I couldn't be happier for him being out and proud.

My nerves had cranked up a notch as we soared further away from England. Should I have called Ash? Told him I was desperate to see him so we could open the box together?

As my senses adjusted to the heat and polluted air outside Chhatrapati Shivaji Maharaj International Airport, I waited in line for a taxi to take me to Ash's apartment building. He had written the address on the back of the envelope that contained the first collection of photos. Thankfully I had stored it in my phone.

A panic gripped my chest as the driver sped away. I clutched the handrail tightly as the vehicle weaved in and out of different lanes. My stomach was already feeling queasy after not having eaten much of the aeroplane offering and my last full meal having been a greasy fry-up at Heathrow.

The taxi arrived at an apartment complex, and I paid the fare before collecting my suitcase that the driver had recovered from the boot. I wheeled it into the reception where a jovial man behind the desk stood up and bowed his head, asking if he could be of any assistance. I explained that I had come to visit Ashok Patel. Bizarrely, he asked if I was Rina. I thought it was his accent and nodded, saying that yes, my name was Lina.

He slapped his forehead and said that Ash wasn't home but at the hotel and that he would arrange for a car to take me there. I was bemused. How could Ash be expecting me? Had someone from my family tipped him off that I was coming? Or perhaps Nik had finally got in touch to make amends and mentioned my plan.

I asked if there was somewhere I could freshen up first. My linen shirt was engulfed with sweat patches and my jeans were sticking to my legs despite the aggressive air con in the foyer of the airport and the taxi.

Locked inside the bathroom, I unearthed the blue-and-white-striped summer dress that Emily had helped me pick out only a few days ago. She had said Ash would find me irresistible in it and I had giggled. It had thin straps and a rope belt at the front with beads holding the ends. I smiled as I slipped it on and clipped up my hair. Going shopping with Emily had been a blast – and in those precious few days together we had managed to fill in all the gaps of the last eleven years apart. Our broken friendship had been mended.

Ten minutes later the taxi arrived at a five-star hotel on Juhu Beach. I had stored my suitcase back at Ash's apartment at the insistence of the concierge, but I had placed our box safely in my handbag which I was clutching close to my side.

I was invited to go to the deck and was told that Ash was completing a business meeting and would join me outside for drinks.

This all seemed too good to be true, but I didn't want to question how it had come to be.

As I stepped outside, I caught my breath at the view ahead. Something drew me to the sand; something far, far into the distance had caught my eye. I slipped off my sandals and stepped down towards the sea, thankful that the sun had sunk low enough that the sand didn't burn my feet.

'I've been here before,' I whispered.

But that was impossible.

Then why did this beach seem so familiar?

A burst of colour drew me closer. An arch bathed in roses became more noticeable the closer I got. Then there was music; a sweet melody floating along the shore in time to the waves lapping against the sand. The sky was awash with hues of orange and red. So much colour. So much vibrancy.

And then it hit me.

'Hello?' A voice made me turn and I immediately snapped out of my reverie to see Ash in a dark grey suit, a look of bewilderment on his face. 'Lina? Wh-wh-what are you doing here?'

My heart crashed several floors in my chest. 'You weren't expecting me?'

'I was expecting a lady called Rina.'

'Oh. Then, umm ... surprise,' I said tentatively, my shoulders hunching, teeth on display.

'Are you a mirage?'

'That's the pollution, I guess.' The horizon was murky – no sharpness to the incoming sunset. 'It's pretty bad.'

'I can't believe you're here.'

'Me either. But I had to come. I needed to come. I wanted to open this ...' I reached into my shoulder bag and pulled out the box. 'I wanted to open this with you.'

A smile slowly crept across his face. 'But didn't you open it already, to get the jewel out?'

'I closed my eyes when I did. I couldn't look at everything else. I was too scared.'

'But now?'

'Now I don't feel scared any more. I feel ready.' I pulled out my cardigan from the bottom of my bag and laid it on the sand. With a dramatic flourish of my hand I signalled that I wanted Ash to sit.

He tapped his watch and bit his bottom lip.

'Oh God, sorry, I forgot you're meant to be meeting someone.'

'It's OK, we've got a little time.' He took off his jacket and sat down, leaving me enough room to sit beside him – his shoulder pressing reassuringly into mine, his head turned towards me, eyes taking in every part of my face, the disbelief still showing on his.

'So where had it been all these years?' he said.

'Nik dug it up the night we buried it. He let his jealousy get the better of him. Snuck out like we did and followed us to the park.'

'The noise we heard; it must have been him.'

I looked into his eyes before instinctively focusing on his mouth, those lips that I ached to touch again.

Ash cleared his throat.

'Hmm? Oh yes, the box. Here we go.'

I flipped open the latch and peered inside. A small pack of photos lay on top. 'Oh my God, look how young I was.'

It was a picture of me on my eighth birthday. My hair in braids, school uniform on. An iced cake lay in front of me, the figure 8 spelled out in Smarties. A cheesy grin was on my face, a hint of wrapping paper in the foreground but no clue as to what gifts I had received. I flicked to the next one and it was of Ash with his family. I handed it to him, and he seemed lost in his thoughts. He brushed his finger over the image of Divya.

'I'd do anything to see her again,' he said finally. 'I miss her so much. She was my world.'

Even from the side view I had of his face; I could see the tears in his eyes. 'I'm sorry, I didn't mean to bring you sadness.'

'It's OK. It's good to see her like this, looking happy.'

The next one was of my parents. Dad's arm was on Mum's shoulder, but her smile lacked warmth and her arms were hanging straight down. Had she been unhappy even then?

The rest were of me and Ash at various stages of the first eight years of our lives.

I peered back into the box and took out the first Ziploc bag. Inside was an envelope with my name on it. The letters were big capitals – each one a different colour. I held it tightly in my grip, my hands shaking. I suddenly felt the warmth of Ash's leg against mine and I instantly calmed down.

'Want me to read it?' Ash said.

'No, it's OK. I can do this.'

I gently picked the seal and pulled out the coloured piece of lined paper.

Dear Me, 28 me (that is sooooo old)

I hope you are OK. Nik said we would all be dead now. I think he is a liar. He is my best frend but I like Ash more. He is my new frend. He is very smart but kind. He helps me with my maths.

Our eyes met as I paused, his smile overtaking the earlier sadness.

Ash likes to cook and will be on the tv soon. He will be famous when he is 28 and I will visit all his restarants.

I dared not look up to see his reaction but smoothed my finger over the paper as it wrinkled in the breeze.

Mum said I could be anyone. I want to be an arkiologist when I am 28. Like Lara Croft. I want to have lots of money so I can explore the world and live in a bigger flat. I want my brother to be nice to me and Mum to be happy and I want Emily to be my new new frend. Secretly I want to dance not go to Greek school. Maybe if I dance, Emily will be my frend.

I hope Dad has a nice big restarant because the deli is small.
Mum said I cant have a cat. I want a cat when I am 28.
I hope all my dreams come true.
Love Lina

I tried to swallow away the lump that was growing larger in my throat and placed the letter back in its plastic bag and tucked it in the box.

A dancer, an archaeologist, an explorer.

Ash's hand rubbed my back in a slow, measured movement. I leaned into him and rested my head on his shoulder. I closed my eyes and was aware of the waves crashing, his scent and the need for all aspects of his love.

When I opened my eyes, a movement to my right caught my attention. There were large film cameras and an ensemble of people in traditional Indian dress.

'What's going on over there?' I asked Ash.

He dropped his arm and peered over to where I was pointing. 'Probably another Bollywood film.'

I narrowed my eyes and was awash with a déjà vu feeling. 'I think I've dreamed about this beach before. It feels so familiar.'

'Well, many films have been made here; I am sure you would have seen one when you were watching them with Gran.'

'I never stopped,' I admitted.

He turned to me with those dark eyes – the ones I had wanted to see again ever since Cyprus.

'I find them comforting,' I said for clarification. A memory suddenly popped into my mind. 'Wait. I think I know this beach from one of those old movies. There's a man on a horse playing a pipe and he's in love with a girl who is walking on *this* beach, I think, and then she's on a camel.' I shook my head as I thought how bizarre it sounded. 'It was hilarious, I seem to remember. Your gran was translating it for me.'

'I think that's *Seeta Aur Geeta*. It's one of her favourites.'

'When I used to be in serious discomfort, I got referred to this pain management team who suggested these mindfulness techniques. They told me to try and go back to something, a memory, a time I was happy.' I leaned my shoulder more into his. 'I was happy when I was at your house. The energy. Divya playing her music, the scent of spices from something you were making, the leftovers you packed me home with sometimes so I wouldn't have to cook for Dad and Alex, your gran and auntie always arguing about who the hottest Bollywood star was.' I smiled. 'It was like home – how I always thought a real happy home should be.'

'It's interesting how you saw it like that. I saw that I had to cook otherwise I would get a ticking-off from Dad for not doing my chores; the tension in the evening once you'd left. Restrictions, expectations. Dad allowed me to cook as an obligation, not because I was passionate about it.'

A faint tune carried across the waves – it was coming from the film set. 'I want to go and see,' I said, feeling buoyant, the urge to do something I hadn't done in years overwhelming me. 'I want to . . .' The words caught in my throat as I stood up.

He looked at me bewildered as I bobbed up and down, scrunching the sand between my toes.

'I want to dance,' I said, finally finding my voice.

'Really?' Ash said in disbelief.

I turned and ran. My hair broke free from its clasp until it was spilling out over my shoulders. I ran and ran until I reached the raised stage with garlands of flowers encasing every inch of the arched structure.

The sun was setting further into the horizon; the water now a burnt orange.

'You don't have to do this,' Ash said from behind.

I faced him. His jacket was slung over his shoulder, his white shirt unbuttoned at the neck, tie loosened. He was holding the box that I had so casually left in my haste to be here and placed it along with his jacket on the sand.

A guitar strummed and a chorus of women appeared in brightly coloured saris. This had been my dream, the night of the school reunion. But this was no Bollywood movie – this was real.

'I want to. Dance with me? Once before you go?' I asked.

He pursed his lips as he stared into my eyes. Finally, he nodded and stepped towards me, placing one hand on my hip, the other outstretched to clasp mine.

The guitarist plucked the strings; his voice melancholic. I rested the side of my face on Ash's chest and closed my eyes as all the memories of us dancing when we were thirteen washed over me. I could feel Ash's grip on my waist tighten, his cheek lying on top of my head.

I didn't want this moment to end. Because nothing ever mattered when we were dancing. 'I love you, Ash,' I whispered by his neck, my lips caressing his skin ever so slightly. 'It was always you.'

'Sir,' a voice interrupted us.

We broke apart and I could see Ash's cheeks were wet.

'I am sorry to disturb you, sir, but the photographer is here to see you.'

'Right, yes, of course.' Ash wiped his face with his hands. 'I'm sorry, Lina … I … have to go.'

'Yes, I forgot, you have a meeting.' I smoothed my hands over my dress, painfully aware that my declaration of love had gone uncommented on. 'Are you getting some headshots?'

'No.' He stared at the ground unable to meet my eyes. 'Rina is a special-events photographer.' His arms hung like dead weights by his sides. 'My parents hired her for this evening. I am asking my girlfriend to marry me tonight. Our families are old friends and it's my dad's dying wish to see me married.' That's when his gaze met my thunderstruck expression. 'I'm sorry, Lina.'

His words echoed around me, and I willed them to stop repeating themselves. The backdrop began to blur, my heartbeat was racing. This was the stupidest thing I had ever done. Ash was going to propose. He was in love with someone else. My Ash could never be *my* Ash.

There was nothing else for me to say except …

'I'm happy for you.' I stepped forward and held his hands in mine, squeezing them tightly. 'I'm happy for … my best friend. You'll always be my best friend, Ash, no matter the distance between us.' I struggled to suppress the ache that was encasing my heart. 'You and me. Forever.'

'And for always,' he whispered. 'I wish I could stay, but we're heading off to see relatives out of town the next few days. Will you still be here when I get back? We still have the rest of the box to go through.'

'Actually,' I dropped his hands, hugging myself, 'this was only going to be a short trip. I'd love to stay longer but I have to get back to Birmingham.'

'Of course,' he said, a note of resignation in his voice.

'Not to live, though.'

'Really?' The tone in his voice was one of surprise.

I smiled brightly, praying the anguish inside me didn't show on my face but overcome with a new life-changing realisation. 'This letter, the one written by me when I was eight, has reinforced everything. I'm going to travel ... find myself.' I gave a brief laugh, though it was tinged with sadness. 'Sounds like such a cliché.' But what was the point in telling him the reason why Birmingham wouldn't be my home even after my travels? How could I tell him now that I had believed home was wherever he was?

I reached for the box and handed him all the things he had put inside, including the statue of Vishna that was meant to look after us twenty years later.

'Thanks,' he said, holding everything close to his chest. 'And thanks for coming to see me.'

'My pleasure. Goodbye, Ash.'

As he walked away into the distance, I couldn't watch him. I turned in time to see the actor and actress embrace on set.

And there it was.

The only happy endings were in Bollywood.

I stroked my arm in time to the waves washing ashore. I had taken a risk and I was proud of myself. I had danced away my demons and there was no guilt left in my heart. I felt loved by more people than I ever had in my life. I would always love Ash but loving him meant letting him go. I understood how much his family meant to him and that he had made the right choice for him. But now it was time to begin my next adventure.

The question was, in which country would it begin?

Chapter 41

Nine months later

The kettle whistled on the two-ring burner, and I dragged my weary body over to it. Steam rose from the mug as the water soaked the Lipton teabag. A splash of milk rippled across the surface, and I stirred it before disposing of the bag in the compost pot.

Birds chattered outside the open window and the occasional moped sped by. The March day had brought warm afternoon temperatures which climbed the higher up the hill you lived. The cooler evenings meant the fan wasn't yet needed. This place was perfect, and I was lucky to live here permanently.

A flyer caught my attention by the back door and I scooped it off the mat. There was an opening – a new restaurant in town.

A perfect fusion of Mediterranean and Indian cuisines, it read.

The photos of the dishes were sumptuous-looking. My motivation to cook tonight was non-existent but I didn't have the energy to go out again – a takeout would suffice. This place seemed too fancy for such an offering, so I tossed the leaflet aside.

I sat down at the kitchen table and stretched out my back, lifting my arms high into the air. Hunched over for hours on end at work without a break had meant two things: one, I was starving; and two, I needed to visit the local masseuse soon before I got curvature of the spine. The grooves on my fingertips had smoothed out from years of *dolmádes* prep, but my fingernails bore traces of earth that would take days to scrub away.

I took in the leaflet again as I sipped my tea. A highlighted box at the bottom made me sit up.

One free Bollywood dance lesson with every three-course meal.

The words were in neon red against a yellow background. My throat suddenly felt tight, and that familiar flush crept up into my neck. I couldn't let my mind go back to that night or to him. I had let him go. This was my new life, I thought, as I looked around and out the kitchen window into the garden and the sea beyond. The Mediterranean Sea, flowing out from Larnaca Bay. My home. Cyprus. It had been my home for five months now after a long spell of travelling the world by myself. I was still alone but not lonely. Doing what I loved, but not with Ash.

A knock at the door startled me. I hadn't been expecting anyone.

'Lina,' a voice chirruped.

'I'm in the kitchen, Greer.'

She bounded in, her mud-stained overalls swapped for a cropped green top and denim skirt.

'What are you doing here?' I asked. 'Thought I said goodbye to you already.' I raised an eyebrow.

'I'm on a mission,' she said, stretching her hand to me. 'Let's go out. Let's paint the town.'

'I'm exhausted, Greer.' I swatted her arm away and propped my head on the kitchen table. 'All I've managed to do since I got home is make a cup of tea. I'm still in my work clothes.' I pointed at my paint-splattered dungaree shorts. My hair was still scraped back in a messy bun – a paintbrush holding it in place.

I watched as she danced around, her hips swaying to a beat she was humming.

'Why are you so perky?'

She threw her hands in the air, her gold bangles rattling up and down her arms. 'I only have three more nights here and I want to party. And I want *you* to come with me.'

'Not tonight, please. I told you I was coming home for a shower and to slob on the sofa.'

'No, you are not,' she said, poking me in the ribs until I couldn't bear her prodding any longer and sat up straight. 'You are coming out with me. It *has* to be tonight.'

'Why?'

She pinched her lips and shrugged her shoulders. 'No reason.' She continued to sway around the room – one hand in the air like she was screwing in a light bulb and the other patting a dog.

'Are you doing Bollywood dancing?' I asked.

She didn't answer but spun around, her beaded braids fanning out. 'I'm in the mood for a fusion of Mediterranean and Indian food.'

'Are you, now?' I eyed her suspiciously. I thrust the flyer towards her. 'How about this place?'

'Well, what do you know? Looks perfect.'

'Greer, if this is where you wanted to go tonight, you could've just come out and said it.'

She smiled, a hint of cheekiness creeping into the corner of her mouth. 'OK, you got me. I have been watching this place being built for weeks and the smell coming from the open door on my way here made me drool.' She flopped dramatically into the chair beside me, her tongue lolling out.

'OK. I'll have a quick shower, then.' I pushed myself from the table and headed up the narrow stairs to the single bedroom in the eaves.

'And wear your best dress,' Greer called from downstairs.

'Why?' I shouted back.

'It's their grand opening. And trust me, I think you'll want to be wearing something nice. We get a free dance lesson with the food.'

My heart thundered in my chest like the beat of a bhangra drum. Closing the bedroom door behind me, I slithered down onto the floor and closed my eyes.

'No,' I whispered. 'I could never Bollywood dance again, the way I danced with you.'

Chapter 42

In the distance I could see it: a yellow awning stretching over a veranda – the sea a deep blue on the other side. Candles flickered on every table. And Greer was right, the smell wafting over from the restaurant was intoxicating.

We were led to a spot closest to the pavement and Greer insisted I sit with my back to the open-plan kitchen. A set menu was placed in front of us, and we ordered a bottle of red to go with the array of dishes we chose.

The *aloo chana chaat* tartlets were spicy but my tongue cooled with a heaping of *tzatzíki*. I noticed Greer kept looking over my shoulder repeatedly but every chance I had to turn around she would suddenly burst into laughter and point to something she had noticed out over towards the sea. My suspicions began to grow during our main course until I couldn't stand it any longer.

'Spill, Greer. You're hiding something from me.'

She waved at her full mouth and kept on chewing, leaving my statement unanswered. I took a sip of my sparkling water and scanned the restaurant. It was the perfect location; set back from the beach by a quiet courtyard and a little bit off the beaten track so that it wouldn't entice raucous revellers spilling out from the bars further down the sand. Strings of lights hung in two low-lying apricot trees and the moon shone bright over the water – waves gently lapping against the shore.

What struck me as odd, though, was the absence of other diners. We had the whole restaurant to ourselves. If this was their grand opening, I was glad we had decided to come after all – otherwise, it would be empty.

As I took a bite of chicken in a creamy masala sauce, my fork dropped dramatically onto my plate, sending a splash of red liquid over my pale blue dress. I dampened my serviette and tried to wash out the stain, all the time looking at the couple walking towards us. They were entwined – holding each other like their life depended on it. Step for step, they matched each other. They came closer and the realisation hit me that the vision was real.

'Nik?' I squealed, before pushing back my chair and running over to him.

He dropped his hold on Mateo and opened his arms towards me. Before I knew it, I was spinning round and round as he lifted me off the ground, delirious that my best friend, who I hadn't seen in almost a year, was in Cyprus.

When he put me back down, I grinned inanely and gave him a once-over: shirt flapping open revealing an even more taut physique. Mateo shuffled back into him, placing his arms tightly around his waist. Nik gazed adoringly at him before planting a kiss on his lips. It was a truly wonderful sight.

'You're here?' I said.

'You think I would miss the start of your new enterprise?'

'But how did you—'

'A little birdy told me,' he said, winking at Greer.

She did her best impression of feigning shock, as if she had nothing to do with it.

'Come and sit with us. I want to hear all about your travels,' I said, directing them to our table.

I asked the waitress to join another one to ours and, before I could catch my breath, beer, more wine and an assortment of dishes had been brought out, as if the restaurant had been expecting these surprise guests.

We chatted for a while about Nik and Mateo's foreign adventures and the opening of the museum in two days. Yes. My museum. The Elina Sallas Museum of Archaeology. The old site where I had volunteered had been raided on the orders of the new head of police in the region, and it was unearthed that it was a front for many illegal activities including the sale of Mum's jewel. With the support of the local mayor, it was agreed the site be closed and allowed to be reopened under my stewardship with a plaque on the front recognising the true discoverer – my mother, Elina Sallas.

Nik sat next to me and held my hand, leaning across the table to clasp Mateo's as well. 'I couldn't be happier for you, Lina. We're so excited to come to the opening.'

I slumped in my chair. 'You won't be if I don't get it ready in time. I've still got loads of carpentry and painting to do.'

'That's why we came two days early.' Nik grinned broadly.

I squeezed his hand. 'You mean it?'

'Of course.'

I mirrored Nik's smile and looked back at Greer who also had her pearly whites on display but was cocking her head in a strange manner.

'We'll help too.'

No, it couldn't be. I spun round in my chair to see my brother standing behind me. My jaw dropped and I flung myself into his arms. 'Alex!' I screamed, hugging him tightly.

'Wait, we?' I said, pulling back.

'Surprise!' came a chorus of voices through the restaurant.

Dad and Clara appeared from behind Alex and in their wake was Emily wheeling in the pushchair containing my gorgeous niece.

I held my hands to my open mouth before dropping them and looking back briefly over my shoulder to Greer. 'Thank you,' I mouthed. She blew me a kiss.

What had begun as a tête-à-tête now turned into a massive reunion. Greer had orchestrated for the opening night of the restaurant to be a family affair. We talked and ate the finest food and drank the best wine. As the evening went on, I realised my face ached from laughing so much. Everyone was staying at a local hotel not far from the restaurant, so we enjoyed our celebrations late into the night. It was a comfort knowing that I had many pairs of hands to ensure the museum was ready for its first visitors in a couple of days.

Marika had sent her apologies as she had been caught on a late shift at the hospital but had the day off tomorrow to greet everyone and she was looking forward to meeting Dad again after all these years.

As the waitress began clearing our plates, I took her to one side and asked her to send compliments to the chef.

'You can tell them yourself if you want. I will bring them out.' She scuttled away laden with empty dishes as I sipped the sweetest dessert wine, my cheeks glowing in the warm evening breeze.

I pulled my shawl over my shoulders and took in the scene around the table. There was so much to be grateful for. My family, my best friends. There was only one person absent from this scene. I hoped Ash was happy with his new life. I had told myself that once I was settled, I would send him my new address and maybe find a way to stay in contact, no matter how hard that would be for me.

'You enjoyed the food?'

I turned to see a lady with silvery hair tied neatly back in a bun, an immaculate white chef's jacket adorning her frame.

'Yes.' I beamed. 'It was amazing. Such an unusual concept.'

She folded her arms across her chest. 'Niche, I guess you would call it.'

'Have you always had a passion for Indian food?'

'No, not really. I grew up all over the world, an armed-forces child, and always loved the idea of cuisines fusing together to produce something original. It was during my time teaching here in Cyprus that I had the good fortune to meet someone with a similar passion who became my investor. Their love is Indian food. I was having a hard time finding the resources for something like this and they were looking for a venture to support. With the finances in place, we can begin to help the local community, offering jobs to refugees who are looking to make a new start in life here in Cyprus. We also plan to offer cooking classes to the local children.' She swept her arm behind her. 'And the decor is all thanks to local designers who have struggled during these difficult economic times.'

I took in the brick walls and colourful artwork which adorned them.

'It's all beautiful,' I murmured.

'Thank you. It was a pleasure to host you and your family the night before our grand opening.'

'Oh, so tonight wasn't the big night?'

'No, thank goodness. Our Bollywood teacher got delayed and won't be here until later – flight issues – so I apologise that there won't be a free lesson with your meal. But please do pass by tomorrow if you are in the neighbourhood.'

'Well, we are all honoured to be your first guests.' Everyone chatted around me – laughter punctuating the warm air. It was another frameable moment.

The chef nodded before turning back to her kitchen. As she left, a bhangra beat filtered out from the nearby speakers, upbeat and melodic.

'Now we're talking,' Nik said, wiping his mouth and pushing out his chair.

I rested my hand on his arm. 'The chef said there wouldn't be a free Bollywood class with the meal,' I said, assuming he knew about the offering.

'I don't need it,' he said proudly. 'Mateo and I did a course out in Goa. We're experts now.' He shot his boyfriend a smirk and in return Mateo blew him a kiss. It was adorable watching them. They acted like newlyweds, which they soon would be as a summer wedding was on the cards after Nik had proposed at the Iguazú Falls in Argentina during their South America travels. I couldn't be happier for them.

Nik held out his hand. 'Will you dance with me?'

I drank in the joyful scene around me and nodded. And this time, I was sure. I didn't have guilty feelings any more. Although I could never dance the way I danced with Ash, it no longer meant I couldn't *ever* dance in that style.

Taking a large sip of my wine for courage, I grasped Nik's hand as he led me out to the courtyard. As the music increased in tempo, Nik thrust some daring moves before Mateo came onto the dance floor. Before long, my whole family got up and moved from side to side in time to the beat.

As the music floated into the night sky, other passers-by joined in. The atmosphere was convivial, inviting.

I closed my eyes and let the music engulf me, soothe me, wash away those memories that had been buried in my heart for so long. It wasn't my fault Mum had died. I knew that now. I held my hands aloft and swayed, caught up in the emotion of the crooner's words which I didn't understand.

'You need to thrust your hips a little more.'

I froze. That voice. It couldn't be.

I turned and gasped. Ash was standing there, dressed casually, out of breath, a huge smile on his face.

'Wha-what are you doing here?'

'I got delayed. I'm the entertainment.' He raised his arms with a brief shoulder shrug. 'Or rather ... I was meant to be giving someone special to me a free Bollywood lesson.'

'But ... how ... when ... why?'

Ash reached up and grabbed my hands which were still held aloft and brought them towards him.

I was vaguely aware of Greer ushering everyone back to the table and winking cheekily at Ash before she left. It was like she had been winking conspiratorially all night.

'Did Greer have something to do with you being here?'

He wound his fingers tightly in mine and his warmth seeped through me. 'Yes, she told me where you were. I was out in LA a few months ago ... with my parents. We wanted to find out about the life Divya had out there. It made us feel closer to her. It was an emotional time.'

'I can imagine.'

'I got in contact with Greer, and she told me all about your plans to move here, how you'd discovered that the jewel had been sold illegally.' He shook his head. 'I'm sorry.'

'What for?'

'For not having faith in you during that first week we spent in Cyprus.'

'It's fine.'

'No, Lina. It's not fine. Ever since you came back into my life, I had this overwhelming desire to keep you safe because ... that night, when we danced in the *Strictly Stockland* competition, I blamed myself for the accident.'

I stepped a little closer. 'Why would you blame yourself?'

He dipped his head. 'All that Bollywood dancing. If we hadn't done that dance, then we probably wouldn't have won, and you would have left that night not in a rush. I ... I strongly believed that it was my fault and that it was my duty to protect you after that. But then I lost your friendship, and the moment you were back in my life you almost got killed. Again. My fault.'

I stroked my thumbs over his knuckles, tilting my head, forcing him to look up at me. 'None of that was your fault, Ash. You know how strong-willed I can be.'

He nodded, a smile touching his lips. 'But then I let my stupid jealousy get in the way of having you remain in my life, and it was torture for me. But now I realise ...' he glanced over his shoulder at Nik who was canoodling with Mateo '... that you have always been nothing but a good friend to me *and* to Nik. We crossed paths in Birmingham.'

'When were you in Birmingham?'

'I came to find you, but you were still travelling. It was our stopover before going to LA. Nik and I ... we talked.'

I peered over at Nik and he pretended not to have seen me and began talking wildly to everyone else around the table. I chuckled. It was obvious they were all training their ears to our conversation.

'Nik made me realise that being jealous of your relationship with him is ridiculous. We've reconciled our differences now and he graciously gave me Greer's details so we could touch base in LA. Lina ... when you came all that way to see me in Mumbai ...' he sighed and closed his eyes for a second before gazing deeply into mine '... you had never looked more beautiful, so alive, so radiant. Dancing with you on that stage with the movie set behind us, it transported me back to that time we danced as teenagers. The emotion choked me.'

'That's why you were crying?'

He nodded. 'Seeing those photos, hearing your words, seeing your bravery in fighting your demons … It made me realise how much I had been running away from all of my problems. I was terrified. Terrified to open my letter and see into my heart.' He took another tentative step closer to me.

'What did you write?' I said, increasingly unable to deny the effect his nearness was having on me, even though I had put that chapter of my life to bed – the one where I thought we would be together. 'What was in your letter?'

'Apart from saying I thought you would be a dancer and I the next Gordon Ramsay, I said, "When I am twenty-eight, I don't care what I am, as long as Lina is with me."' He pulled my hand to his cheek.

'But … you're … married?' I asked cautiously.

He shook his head slowly and brought both my hands to his chest. 'When I met the photographer that day you came to Mumbai, I realised that I would be making a huge mistake. I thought of running back to you, to find you and tell you this, but I stopped myself. I had this feeling, deep inside of me, that I didn't really deserve you – not until I had figured out my life – and that I should be respectful of your desire to figure out yours without me complicating things. I then convinced my parents to come travelling with me, see all the places they wished they could have travelled to but couldn't because they spent their whole life working hard for me and Divya. But first it was important for me to tell them that who they wanted me to marry wasn't the one for me.'

My heart beat more wildly, the more Ash opened up.

He laughed. 'God, it sounds so presumptuous of me, that so many months later you would still want me in your life ... after you told me you loved me, and I said nothing.'

An ache settled in my chest at the thought of Ash finally realising that I had a place in his life in Mumbai. I steeled myself to say the next few words and pulled my hands from his grasp.

'You're right. I think what happened was for the best. It was better that I figured out my life on my own. I needed to find out what I really wanted to do, what I felt passionate about, and I found it ... here.' I swept a hand around my surroundings.

He pinched his lips, lost in thought, staring deeper into my eyes, as if he could look into my soul.

'I do want you in my life, Ash. But my life is here now. And yours is—'

'Right here too.'

I froze in disbelief. Had he *really* uttered those three words?

'As soon as my parents and I returned from our travels, I realised that what I did with my life didn't make me happy, had never made me happy. The only times over the years that there has been joy was when I was cooking and being with you. Always you. So ... you are standing right where my new life is. Here.' He pointed behind him. 'This restaurant, my investment, my chance to give back to those less fortunate than myself, and hopefully ...' he let his shoulders rise '... with you in my life too.'

I couldn't believe it. Ash was the investor the chef had spoken of.

'But what about your family?' I asked.

'Dad is in remission. He is being well cared for in Mumbai and they all want me to be happy, to fulfil my dreams in the same way Divya tried to do, but with their support this time.'

'I don't know what to say.' I could hardly believe this night and the words to express my surprise and joy weren't forming coherent sentences in my mind.

'You don't have to say anything,' Ash said. 'There's only one thing I want.'

'What's that?'

'Dance with me?' he said, stretching his arms out.

The music turned up a notch, soft and melodic, and I brought Ash's hands up to my chest, close to my heart. 'Yes. I will dance with you.'

Ash leaned in and kissed me on the lips before drawing me in with his arms.

We danced the night away and pretended that we never had to go home because home was right here with our hearts beating as one.

Acknowledgements

I am very lucky to have an incredible team working on my books with me. Huge thanks to my editor Katie Loughnane, whose love for this novel and its characters has had the most profound effect on my writing. I am beyond grateful for your editing nous, warmth and compassion. I wouldn't be here without the support of my incredible agent Kate Burke, who always has my back and is there for a morale-boosting coffee when needed; and to Sian Ellis-Martin and the rest of the team at Blake Friedmann, I have so much appreciation for all the behind-the-scenes work you do on my novels. A special mention to Jennie Rothwell, who worked on the synopsis with me before moving on – I hope you love it! Thanks for being such a good friend and confidante.

It's an honour to be published by Century. My heartfelt thanks to everyone at PRH that has worked on *Always You*: Joanna Taylor (managing editor); Natalia Cacciatore (marketing); Laura O'Donnell (publicity); Amy Musgrave (cover design); Mathew Watterson, Claire Simmonds, Olivia Allen, Evie Kettlewell (UK sales); Richard Rowlands and Erica Conway (international sales); and Tara Hodgson (production). Immense gratitude to Sarah-Jane Forder for her expert copy-edit, which pushed my writing to new depths, and to my friend Dimitris for his help with all the Greek words. I'm glad my terrible accent amused you so much!

Ideas for my novels are born from obsession. For *Always You*, it was a fascination with Bollywood that sparked something in me. A massive thank you to Aruna Boucher and Minal Choksey for your insights into Indian culture and sharing some childhood memories with me, and to Hugh Nianias for inspiring the character of Nik and Lina's career. My muse for Ash was the hugely talented actor Sidharth Malhotra, whose movies I pored over. Lina's family was inspired by my old school friend Elena Phyrillas, whose parents I remember so fondly from my childhood.

I wrote and edited this book during some difficult times in my personal life and my bestie Dee Spence was a rock throughout. Our Friday coffee meets propped me up on many occasions. I love you so much. The rest of my circle of girlfriends have also been a huge support to me over the last year, so a special mention to: Hannah Tigg, Sarah Brett, Katrina Stamas, Felicity Hall, Sarah Banham and Fiona Schneider. And to my family friends who have been there for me too: Farida Ali Khan, Jan Jones, Pamela & David Warren and Peter & Rachael Nichols, I appreciate you all in so many ways.

My writing pals – you saw me through the craziness of being a debut author and are still all there for moral support: Lucy Keeling, Emma Lloyd-Cowell, Lia Middleton, Meera Shah and Emma Hughes.

The reception *It Must Be Love* received from readers and #bookstagrammers was beyond my wildest dreams. As the early reviews trickled in, it was a massive confidence boost as I was wrestling with the first draft of *Always You*. To every person that wrote a review, sent me a message and took a photo and posted it on Instagram: I smother you with kisses and hugs – you are all heroes and the reason why I continue to write. Nothing fuels me more than my stories connecting with someone. I love the #bookstagram community and have become friends with so many wonderful women with whom I share my love of reading romance. I also appreciate my Bake-Off book club girls, who are always there to offer words of encouragement on our group chat.

To my mother, who I am beyond lucky to still have in my life: sharing my writing journey with you fills me with so much joy. Thank you for all your unconditional love. And to my brother Piers who has been a tower of strength this year and the rest of my Pressdee family – Sally, Charly, Georgina, Ellie and Alex: I am proud to be your sister-in-law and aunt. This book is dedicated to my two daughters – Miranda and Rose. Mummy did it again! You continue to amaze me every day and I appreciate you humouring me when I talk about my characters as if they are all real!

If you follow my Instagram, you'll know that I spend an inordinate amount of time writing and editing at my favourite coffee shop – 63 High Street – and that is because of the friendliness of the baristas – Ans, Hannah and David – who greet me every morning with a warm smile and of course a great cup of coffee. My pets are also all over my feed so I should really offer up a lot of treats to Biscuit, Eloise and Flair – my demanding trio of fluff who I adore.

In *Always You*, Lina suffers from a condition that shockingly affects one in ten women and can take on average eight years to get diagnosed. I salute all you warriors out there and hope Lina's journey resonates in some way and encourages more women to seek out answers to their suffering. Also, let's talk about periods more!

And finally, thank you to you! For buying this book and reading it. Please do get in touch on social media and let me know what you think – I'm @carolinekauthor on Instagram and Twitter.